Trouble Undone

In Ashwood, Volume 5

Kinney Scott

Published by Kinney Scott, 2019.

TROUBLE UNDONE

First edition. August 12, 2019.

Copyright © 2019 Kinney Scott.

ISBN: 978-1950800063

Written by Kinney Scott.

Also by Kinney Scott

Watch for more at https://kinneyscott.com.

Now I see the secret of the making of the best persons. It is to grow in the open air and to see eat and sleep with the earth.

-Walt Whitman

ONE

Kelsey dug into her pocket, found her phone, and held the button down. The device vibrated, switching off. Stress bled away on a wisp of air escaping from her lips. When a single cumulus cloud blocked the sun, she pushed her sunglasses to the top of her head and freed her senses.

Arms stretched overhead, she gulped salt-flavored oxygen. The move drained tension from her neck, shoulders, and spine—tightness that had accumulated during her four-hour drive to the coast. One by one, each vertebra settled, grounding her to Driftwood Shores.

Kels circled to open the rear gate of her Nissan Xterra. She lifted her surfboard, dug through her gear, and slung her backpack over her shoulder. A papery swish turned Kelsey's head. She smiled as her friend, the owner of this tiny home community, pushed through hip-high coastal grass.

Followed by her orange cat, Faye leaned a hip against the Nissan's fender. Kelsey grinned at the woman who never changed. Long braid, tanned skin, and barefoot, Faye welcomed her to this almost-mystical place. "Glad to see you're back where you belong."

"Good to be back. Have you got room for me?" Kelsey shifted the backpack to her other shoulder.

Faye painted the air with a brush of her hand. "Take your pick, honey—it's here for you." A determined gust of offshore wind caught Faye's heavy denim skirt and snapped the material around her legs like a ship's sail.

With a tilt of her eyes to the west, Kelsey signaled her intent. "I'll set up camp in my usual spot."

"Groovy. I'll come find you later." Turning away, Faye shot a backward wave over her head and hollered, "Stop by and see me. I'll pop a bottle of wine, fry some oysters, and we'll catch up." The

1

woman disappeared the way she came, followed by her cat on a meandering path through papery grass.

Kelsey wandered to her hiding spot at Driftwood Shores, bare foot, flip-flops dangling from her long fingers. As her toes sank through the crusty surface sand into the cool grit below, she wondered if pitching her tent was necessary. When Mark met her at the coast, she usually spent the night with him in his tiny house, their legs tangled together in his bed. But there was no telling when the surfer would arrive.

Unable to decide, she ditched her pack against a clump of saw grass, slid her too-warm flannel from her shoulders, and secured the sleeves with a knot around her waist. Drawn by the pounding surf, she walked toward the waves until she could taste salty mist on her lips.

The tide pushed in, sea splashing her shins. White foam clung to her toes and her feet melted into wet sand. In ankle-deep water, she studied the break. Like elongated ripples of corduroy, the waves peeled left, pushed across the Pacific by a distant Alaskan storm. Mark's surfing app—as always—had accurately forecast these enhanced swells. She considered returning to her car for her board, but the water wouldn't let her go.

Stripping away outer layers, Kelsey abandoned her clothes on a sun-bleached log and jogged into the water wearing her coral bikini top and black board shorts. Her hair hung in a sleek line down the center of her back, pale as straw, long ends dipping in as she pushed hip-high into the water.

The Pacific reflected the denim sky, but the water was clear enough to see her long legs, distorted by the beveled sunlight. Surrounded by the sea, the frigid cold numbed the tips of her fingers and toes. Sucking in three deep breaths, she relaxed her mind before committing to the plunge. Eyes open beneath the waves, Kels let the sting ease while flecks of organic matter danced around her like green fireflies.

Her toned arms cut through the surf and she ducked under the frothy waves, popping up again in the smoother water beyond the break. Buoyant and free, Kelsey swam parallel to the coastline until her sluggish limbs forced her back toward land. Riding the swell to shore, she stood again in waist-high foam, feeling tired, wobbly, and satisfied. She collapsed on the sun-warmed beach to lay on the sand as her limbs quaked and her stomach rumbled. Even though she was hungry, she remained in place until the yellow sun dipped below the purple horizon.

Near dark, Kelsey made herself a quick, familiar meal. Perched near her campfire on a smooth log, she slurped Top Ramen from a paper cup. The grass nearby rustled, and Bramble pushed through ahead of Faye. "A few of us are hanging at the clubhouse," she said. "There's plenty of wine if you want to join."

"Rain check?" Kelsey shrugged, needing quiet more than company.

"Anytime, honey." Faye scooped the cat that circled her feet and Bramble purred low and loud, transmitting the rumble through the air.

"Tell everyone hey for me." Kels watched Faye walk away into the dark, and a soft pang of envy mixed with the noodles in her gut. She wondered about Faye's kind of freedom—no television, no computers, no phone. Could she ditch her cell for more than a day? Or would she miss that vibration when an alert signaled a message against her thigh.

Restless, Kelsey pulled on her running shoes. The moon rose, giving her just enough silvery light for an evening run. Dark cold muddy dots spattered her bare legs as her feet thumped the sand and her mind emptied, replaced by a hit of euphoria. When she returned, she took a quick shower and hurried back to her sparse camp.

With her hair wrapped in a white terry towel, she dove inside her tent and huddled in her sleeping bag, cold and wide-awake. Shivering in the low light, her fingers hesitated over the buttons on her phone before she turned it on. She squinted as the screen flooded her tent with blue artificial light. "Shit, what a mistake."

A flurry of inconsequential messages from Venture Sister would annoy her until morning. Mark hadn't called or sent a text. Nothing tied the surfer down—he swept in with the wind and left again just as quickly.

He'd show at some point . . . unless he didn't. Either way, this trip to the coast satisfied her need for peace.

***

A soft zip at the tent's door woke her. "Just me, Kels." Mark's familiar voice nudged her senses. She eased her sleeping bag open, pulled an extra blanket from her knapsack and made room. The tent filled with Mark's scent as he slid out of his clothes and settled in.

"God, you feel good," he said when his cool body made contact with her sleep-warmed skin. "You tired, Mermaid?" he asked with a hint of need.

"Yeah. I swam today." The waves had absorbed her stress, leaving her body slack. He spooned her back, thighs, and butt against his muscled torso, caging her with his arm. She felt his erection nestled against her ass but was too tired to respond.

Before returning to sleep, Kels coiled her fingers into his, and eased Mark's hand from her hip. She slid his calloused touch under her cotton tank top to cup her breast. Mark stroked the velvet skin with his thumb and slowly inhaled the ginger scent from her damp hair.

***

Bitter coffee woke her in the pale morning light. Outside her tent, Mark hummed, as he often did when a tune planted deep in his head. Even off-key, the melody sounded familiar. Kelsey grinned, loving the sound, but she couldn't recall the words.

With a swift whirr, the tent flap zipped open, and he ducked his head inside. "Pure glass this morning, Mermaid. Want to catch a sunrise session?"

A breathtaking grin wrinkled the corners of his eyes, dazzling her with raw masculine beauty. When he rolled in late, she'd felt his warmth and inhaled his salty scent, but until now, she hadn't completed the sensory intake of everything that was Mark.

"Give me five," she said already moving. Kelsey slipped into her bikini top and board shorts, then grabbed her toothbrush and jogged off to use the shared facilities.

Scrambled eggs and bacon waited for her when she returned. "You cooked!" She laughed, surprised.

"I can make more than Pop Tarts." He halved the pile of eggs and added four slices of bacon to each plate. She could tell from his monstrous portions he'd been surfing consistently and needed mega fuel.

Kels left her bacon for later, scooped a third of her eggs to Mark's plate, and sank onto the log to eat. Her bare skin stole heat from his thigh. The pair ate in silence, listening to the distant cadence of the surf.

Mark finished, pulled apart the small fire with a stick, and scattered sand over the dying flames. Up early, he'd already applied a topcoat of wax to their boards—a routine he always enjoyed.

They paddled the channel wearing black wetsuits that cut the cold. Beyond the break, Kels perched atop her barely submerged board, squinting into the sunrise. She watched nature shift the atmosphere, her face warming as gold rays burned the clouds from the distant coastal range.

Stomach flat against his board, Mark took a quick glance over his shoulder, and propelled forward to catch his first wave of the day. Popping with effortless precision, he rode the ridge crouched like a predator.

Kelsey followed on the next swell, her board hissing between her feet and the sea. Her wave broke too soon, and she pushed with her back foot to gain momentum. Weightless for a moment, she pitched over the lip of frothy water, laughing. Nothing gave her the same sense of freedom—a loose connection to a watery world secured only by three inches of poly and fiberglass.

With the waves to themselves they repeated the route—riding, paddling, riding—until the tide shifted and the surf died out.

Surfboards tucked under their arms, they wandered back to Driftwood Shores as the tiny home community had begun to stir. A few residents on morning dog-walks waved at the familiar pair. Mark paused to say hello and tossed a frisbee for an energetic German shepherd.

Desperate for fuel, Kelsey's arms trembled as they made it back to her tent. "I could already eat again," she said.

"You won't get an argument from me." Mark located the makings for BLTs, and they assembled sandwiches on top of her cooler. From another box, she pulled out a Ziploc bag and shared her favorite dessert—thick wedges of Rice Krispy Treats.

"Damn, why are these so good?" Mark asked past a mouth full of sticky goodness.

She licked marshmallow off her thumb. "I make 'em extra goopy."

With a gleam in his eye, he grabbed her hand and sucked her index finger clean. A bold hit of sugar and lust left Kelsey feeling lightheaded, and she leaned into his torso.

"Give me some sugar," he said before meeting her lips. His kiss tasted like salty bacon and sweet marshmallow. *Delicious.* She leaned in for more, ready to feast.

"Damn. You're tempting, but if we don't get moving, we'll miss the tide. The swells will be killer a few miles south." Groaning with regret, he deepened the kiss again and pressed their hips together until she moaned into his mouth. A squeeze of her butt finished the intimate tangle, yet left her frustrated, it had been too damn long.

They left her camp intact but took the food and surfboards. Ready to move when the waves called, Mark had blankets and a tent in the back of his Subaru. As they drove away from Driftwood Shores in search of perfect surf conditions, Kelsey glanced back. She didn't spot his tiny home anywhere in the community. "Where's your place?" she asked.

"Left it in San Diego." Mark fiddled with the radio and found a clear station. "Settle in, Mermaid, we'll be on the road a while."

Ten minutes down the highway, a familiar tune vibrated from the speakers. Mark grinned, increased the volume, and drummed the steering wheel. Singing along, he massacred the words of the song he'd been humming all morning.

TWO

Commercials droning on and on annoyed him, and Mark flicked off the radio. "How's Venture?" he asked, hoping Kelsey was ready to talk. Something—most likely work—consumed her thoughts.

"We're so busy. I'm booked solid for the entire guiding season. When Sig asked me to take on more hiking tours, I had to give up most of my rafting trips." Kels shrugged off her irritation, but her beautiful, kissable mouth held a slight pout. Mark looked again as she kneaded her lip, then forced his eyes back to the road.

"So, more of the same?" he asked.

"Yeah. Corporate trips for city escapees. At least they pay well."

He longed to invite Kels to join his upcoming trip to the Maldives, and he could easily cover her costs. But Mark knew she wouldn't take a break from Venture—the rapidly growing guide service she shared with Sig.

Kels pretzeled her leg, tucked her ankle under her thigh, and pivoted to face Mark. Her aquamarine eyes mirrored her giddy smile. "The summer won't be a total loss. I have a Whitewater Kayak Festival slotted for Memorial Day weekend on The Little White Salmon. Amanda's shooting a film with Parker Knight, and they've contracted Venture to run safety on that class-five river." She bounced in her seat, excited about the high-profile whitewater event.

Mark suppressed a grimace when he heard the familiar name. He'd lost respect for the famous adventure photographer long ago, but he kept that to himself—if only to bask in the glow of Kelsey's buoyant mood. "Parker Knight. Damn. How did your friend land that gig?"

"Amanda meeting Parker? That was good luck or bad, depending on how you look at it. There was this big blow-up with Kent at a party last Halloween. Amanda caught Kent doin' the deed with his old girlfriend, and she got super-pissed—angry enough to leave Ashwood for Hood River, and that's where she met Parker."

"Crazy."

"I know, right? And it was a random thing. Parker was filming on Mount Hood. I guess she needed an extra set of hands for a snowboard shoot. Amanda got a call and—"

"One thing led to another?"

"You got it."

Mark linked the dots. Life could be so random. He'd always felt the best things arrived unexpectedly, and Kelsey was one of those best things. They'd met over a year ago by chance, when her friend Natalie came to the coast.

Natalie was hot—but taken, and she never possessed Kelsey's magnetic pull. Since that autumn, he'd found more reasons to surf the Northwest coast, but the churning waves weren't as enticing as the woman from Ashwood. Everything about Kels fascinated him, her outlook, her determination, even the way she loved her small town. She still hadn't invited him to her place, but Mark hadn't given up hope.

When a lumbering motorhome slowed their progress, Kelsey opened her window. Wind whipped her ponytail into a white-blonde fray, pale as the wheat that surrounded his home in Kansas. He didn't miss home much. Kelsey had replaced that longing. Always drawing him back, the flexible tether they shared seem to fit. She hadn't asked for more, yet each time they met on the coast, this woman nestled farther under his skin.

***

Mark took the beach access road, drove south on hard-packed sand until the crowds thinned, then he wheeled his car around to face the waves. They wrestled into wetsuits and grabbed their boards, preparing to take on the spring tide sets. A light offshore breeze groomed the break to clean perfection. Kels lasted on those swells until the lineup filled with aggressive surfers snaking waves.

She left the mounting breakers to Mark and a few other experienced surfers. On her way back to set up camp, she hummed his tune. *Damn*, now that song was stuck in her head. The conditions held, and Mark outlasted a mob of kooks to catch decaying rollers. The crowds thinned until he surfed alone.

From shore, Kelsey watched the dance of the man on his board, amazed by his effortless grace. She'd missed him more than ever during their last separation and the next would be even longer. Their open arrangement suited their circumstances, but it wasn't always fun.

She returned to their camp, knowing Mark wouldn't be too long. As sunset approached, the buzz of dune buggies faded, and campfires lit up like constellations along the shore.

Mark appeared, his hair dripping, his board tucked under his arm. "You found provisions," he said accepting a cold beer, gulping it down in one long draw.

"Chili dogs okay?" she asked, stirring the bubbling contents of the pot.

"Perfect. Thanks for setting up camp." After changing into a worn sweatshirt, he took a seat next to her on a weather-smoothed log. The chili bubbled while Mark held four hotdogs on metal skewers over the flames.

He pulled two more beers from the cooler, one-handed, and passed a cold bottle to Kels. They ate chili dogs topped with cheese while he shared the details and dates for his next excursion—several months abroad with his first stop in the Maldives. For a moment, Kelsey couldn't breathe. She blamed the smoke but dreaded the moment when they would part.

Mark stopped talking and stared into the flames.

"What is it?" she asked. Rare unease rippled from Mark—his worried silence as loud as a scream.

He cleared his throat with a cough. "I know it's last minute, but is there any way you can carve out time and come with me to—"

"Don't say it. Damn, it's so tempting." Kelsey covered her panic with a rigid smile. "I almost wish you'd never asked. You know I can't go anywhere right now. Winter maybe, but during summer? Not a chance."

"Winter then." Mark kissed her, and his warm lips stamped a promise on their plans. "I'm holding you to it, Mermaid." He nodded, and his gaze inked the date with permanent marker onto a mental calendar. They'd never planned this far ahead. Kelsey waited for that commitment to scare her, but it didn't. Not this time.

Mark relaxed again. He reclined on the old blanket and pulled her to him. The night air swirled and the fire snapped, dying to a heap of red coals. Their hands intertwined and explored as the heat between them climbed. His calloused fingers slipped beneath her shirt, drawing lazy ribbons of desire against her skin.

He kissed her and eased a few inches away. "I'm gonna miss those eyes, Mermaid. The color changes with your mood, just like the sea." Their lips met again, and she needed to feel his touch everywhere. Kelsey rose from the ground and gave him that look. He stood, ready to follow.

Laughter from a crowd partying around a nearby bonfire echoed over the crashing surf. "I wonder how long they plan to live it up?" Kelsey asked as Mark climbed in and zipped the tent flap closed.

"Until their beer runs out, I guess. And I plan to take advantage of their noise." He pulled off his shirt, tipped his head, searing her with his gaze. "Turn off the light."

Kelsey hesitated. "I don't know if I should. The view is spectacular." The light cast mouthwatering shadows over his lean chiseled abs. If she doused the lantern, she'd end the stunning show.

***

With a short chuckle, Mark flicked the switch, killing the compact light source. If he'd left it on, Kels might notice he was blushing. Damn, it had been way too long.

He stilled, waiting for his eyes to adjust. Rough fingers drew away the thin blanket that covered her lean athletic body. In the near dark, her naked skin shimmered with an ethereal glow.

"Mermaid, you're so beautiful I can't breathe," he said, prowling over the gorgeous prone offering. His hair hung in shaggy waves, the damp ends tickling her breasts. A bright giggle shook her body beneath his lips, skin warm and sweet. One long kiss planted below her belly button brought a full laugh from Kelsey, and she reached down, tangling her fingers in his hair. "Stop. That tickles. And I've gone soft, taking too many easy trails."

"Not possible." Strong and lean, she was only soft in a few places and Mark planned to sink deep into one slick space soon. But not yet, not until he heightened her longing. Tonight, Mark wanted enough memories of Kelsey to last the next few months.

He and Kels weren't exclusive, not officially. Yet, since they met, other women hadn't tempted, and his random one-nighters had nearly disappeared.

On all fours again, Mark pondered where to begin. Careful fingers caressed her breasts. Already tight, the tender peaks begged for his attention. Sucking the responsive flesh, he flicked his tongue until Kelsey's legs dug into the slippery sleeping bag. To quiet her moaning cries, he moved to her sweet mouth and feasted on her lips.

As he tasted, her touch skated from his hair and raked over his shoulders, before grasping his biceps. With lifted hips, she encouraged him to nestle tight against her heat. Their bodies aligned, his cock skated against her soft mound, teasing, but not entering.

With his arms planted on either side of her head, he took his weight with his forearms. Kelsey squirmed, using his length to grind against her slick bud. Then her legs parted, providing a welcoming space.

"Condom," he whispered as the crown dipped a fraction inside. He'd never fully entered a woman unsheathed. As desperately as he wanted all of her, without a commitment, he wouldn't cross that line. Digging inside his backpack, he located a sleeve of condoms and tore into one with his teeth.

"Let me." She touched and teased, rolling the latex down his considerable length. Weight over her again, his lazy kisses brought them quickly to the desperate point they'd just left. Still, he made her wait, peppering her neck with light nibbles. He felt her tense and smiled against her throat, chuckling when her moan took on an edge.

"Impatient, Kels?"

"It's been months." Her desperate words revealed a clue—she'd only been with him.

That confession spurred his action, and he claimed her with one strong plunge. Acute pleasure shot optical stars and Mark swallowed hard, trying to salvage control. Moving with slow purpose, he savored the exquisite slide.

"Oh, God. Please, harder." Kelsey's need for tender and rough challenged him. Reading this complex woman was as exciting as riding a fully developed wave.

Plunging deep, he sensed her surrender and cherished that rare event. Angled to increase the connection, he slid past every point of contact and her body began to quake. Her breath caught in her throat. Trembling, their bodies slicked with sweat and hovered near release.

Clenched tight around him, her arms and long supple legs encased his torso. His thighs shook, but he ignored the tremors and pulled almost entirely out to deliver frantic, untamed thrusts.

The wild penetration shattered the woman beneath him, and she cried out. He swallowed her sensual moans with his lips, taking pleasure from her reckless need. Mark lost himself in Kelsey's embrace. Eyes closed, head tilted back, he let go. The exquisite pleasure ebbed and peaked, taking everything from him. Spent, he collapsed over her body and she pulled him close, receiving his weight.

As his heartbeat slowed, the pounding in his ears subsided. With a long inhale, he let the cadence of their breathing sync. She struggled for breath against their thin mattress on the ground and under his weight. Mark pulled away, took care of the condom, then spun to his side, caging Kelsey's spine against his chest.

His left hand settled over her soft breast and she hummed, satisfied. Her heartbeat slowed first, then her breathing. Gradually, her shoulders went slack next to him as she found sleep.

In the distance, alcohol-slurred laughter echoed from a nearby bonfire. Dark amplified their voices, and Mark picked out bits of drunken conversation between surfers planning a trip to remote beaches in Canada. He envied their freedom—a choice to follow those waves, or not. A grin spread when they brought up his blog. As nice as it was, he realized his success had become a trap. This dream job kept him from Kelsey, a woman he needed more time to appreciate.

THREE

Kelsey glanced at the clock on the wall above Sig's bald head. The hands had only moved a fraction from the last time she checked. She gnawed on her thumbnail while her business partner brought up their shared work calendar on his computer, but she couldn't seem to focus. Today that damn clock was the most important thing in the room.

Mark's two-day flight would touch down in the Maldives within the hour. She'd never missed him like this. Shit, did she *even like* missing him this way? Twisting in her chair, Kels squashed the mental distraction and tapped the screen to re-awaken her tablet.

Sig rattled off questions, and she confirmed dates for guiding trips spanning over the next six months. Grayed out areas on her calendar—those reserved to do as she pleased—sparsely dotted the tiny white squares.

When Sig tried to snare another string of precious days off, she clenched her jaw and prepared for a fight. He leaned in, thin lips quirked with a familiar sly grin, and their friendly battle of wills was on. *Bring it, old man.*

Sig opened with his usual point. "These are high profile customers, kiddo."

"When has *that* ever mattered?"

"And they want to include a day of rock climbing."

"Tempting, but no."

"Shit, Kels, they've specifically requested you."

"I can't imagine why. I push the women so far past their comfort zone—they must think I'm an epic bitch."

His bushy, white-blond eyebrows lifted as he grinned. "Surviving Kelsey Fisher comes with bragging rights."

"I can't give up that weekend in August. That's the annual family barbeque. If I miss it, rumors will fly that I've left Ashwood for good.

15

And I'm not ready to do that, just yet." Ashwood's remote location was inconvenient but calling anywhere else home seemed wrong.

Sig's weathered hand smoothed over his scalp. "Fine. I'll offer a different guide. Girl, I wish you had a clone."

"Yeah, right. More of me to piss you off." Their eyes met with understanding. He loved her like family, and she loved him right back. The business they shared tangled their lives deeper than genetics ever could.

Now that she'd won that round, Sig drummed his meaty fingers against the desk, ready to move to the next item on their agenda. And she could see from the furrow on his forehead it had the big man nervous. "Have you contacted Parker Knight about the Little White trip?" he asked. Extra publicity surrounded the renowned adventure photographer, and it promised to increase Venture's global reach.

"Got it handled." Kels nodded too quickly, earning Sig's close inspection.

"Humor the old man, and give Amanda Michaels a call, just to be sure."

"Fine, but I'll send a text." He nodded, impatient, and she listened to his concerns while her fingers flew.

"At this level, athletes are picky as hell when it comes to their gear. How many of the paddlers need kayaks?"

"Just a couple coming from Australia and Europe. And I'll bring extra throw bags and rescue harnesses when I pack the first aid kits."

Sig leaned back in his chair with his hands laced behind his head, king of his small domain. The chair groaned as he taunted gravity. When Kelsey lifted her eyebrows, he laughed off her warning. A text rattled her phone, and he tipped forward again to listen. "Amanda and Parker have the cameras, drones, and Go-Pros covered," she said.

"Good. Purchase new gear if we need it, I don't want to look like a noob."

A noob. Kelsey swallowed a chuckle, but knew if she didn't carve out time for a run on the Little White, she'd be counted among the green ones. That river, practically in her backyard, was more than familiar. Still, she had to get in a couple of solid runs to sharpen her reaction time, or she'd spend the weekend driving shuttle vans and babysitting gear.

At least her week spent surfing had improved her strength. Aching muscles weren't the only benefit—her body still hummed with the memory of Mark's touch. Kels lost herself for a moment, dreaming of the Maldives.

Sig's cough interrupted her faraway thoughts. "Guess we're done here, kiddo."

"Sorry. I was thinking about the river. I need to give Kent a call." Pulling something together on short notice would be a challenge.

His broad hands planted on the desk, then Sig pushed off and stood to pace the room. "Do that today. I want you prepared. And Kels, thanks for taking the lead on this, I know how busy you are."

"No problem." Kels stuffed her tablet in her pack and headed for the door. She had scarcely enough time to run home, wash clothes, and catch up with friends before returning to Hood River to take on her next scheduled hiking trip.

***

The uneven boards at Northside Grill creaked beneath Kelsey's feet. She shifted on the familiar worn surface, leaning to line up her next shot.

"Daring choice," Kent mocked.

Bent at the waist, she slid the smooth stick in the crook between her fingers and thumb. "Save it, asshole. You can't rattle me." A swift crack snapped, and with blurred speed, the ball disappeared into the pocket. She whooped and laughed after sinking the shot.

"Damn it, Kels, you're a fuckin' pool shark."

Slight guilt—very slight—pushed her to reveal the truth to her best friend. "There's a reason. Sig's wife wanted him to get rid of the pool table. Instead of selling it, he and a bunch of the guys from Venture hauled the beast to work."

Kent shook his head in disgust. "Jealous."

She circled and chose her next move. "At first, I thought the table might waste time, but it brought our team together. Now, instead of waiting for meetings with our faces buried in screens, we talk, work, and shoot a game."

"I wonder if Seth would go for that?" Kent asked. She saw his mind working, already imagining a pool table at Whitewater Homes.

"Don't be greedy. You've got Mosquito's taproom right next door."

"Yeah, but Wade won't add tables. He's already snaked enough clients from Northside Grill, not that Iris cares anymore." Kent raised his eyebrows, snaring her attention with the promise of small-town gossip.

Kelsey glanced around her favorite bar. "Have you noticed? It's too quiet in here tonight."

Crouched over the pool table, he kept his voice down. "Rumors are spinning that this place is going on the market. Hey Kels, do you want to buy a bar?"

"Shit, are you kidding? Then where the hell is Iris?" Even though she was shocked, Kelsey sank another shot.

Kent huffed. "Last I heard, she took a vacation."

"Do you think Iris will be ready for the Whitewater Kick-off Event? It's less than a month off."

"Chill. So long as everyone gets a meal and a beer, they'll be fine. It's the river they're after."

Kelsey nodded. Rumors didn't mean shit, but she made a mental note to give Iris a call to put her concerns to rest. After stalking the table, she sank another blistering shot, then bent to finish him off. "Eight ball, corner pocket," she said, pointing with her cue, ready to annihilate.

Kent leaned on his stick and shrugged. "Damn, I never had a chance."

***

On a cliff overlooking The Little White, Kent scouted their line while he waited for Kelsey to make her decision. She knew he'd already spotted the best route, but this moment was for her, and he gave her time to sharpen her eye.

She swallowed hard. This was not going to be easy. "Damn, the strainer is new."

"Yeah, that tangle of logs came down river this winter."

"If I stay to the right, I should be able to boof the drop before we take on those rapids."

"Just watch the lead in, that hydraulic's a bitch."

Twenty minutes later the pair put in at an eddy and paddled in. The powerful current immediately pushed them left. Kelsey pulled a few draw strokes and recovered prime position. The water rushed so fast she didn't have time to think. If Kent hadn't taken over the lead, she would have ended up swimming the frothing water at Chaos—something she never wanted to do.

As the run progressed, the river exploited her weaknesses. To recover, she needed to roll a few more times than planned. Her mistakes exposed her flaws, but did not beat her, yet she knew she wasn't prepared, not yet. After they popped free of their spray skirts and climbed from their kayaks at the takeout, Kels mentally carved out another day on this river before the big event. She didn't have any other choice.

FOUR

A month later the throngs crowding the Whitewater Festival's kick-off night surprised everyone, except maybe Parker Knight. Kelsey leaned against the far wall assessing the athletes. Each one had *that look*—cocky grins masking glassy-eyed intensity. Even though she shared that common drive, Kels felt like a twelve-year-old mingling among them. Home turf advantage relaxed her a bit, and no place felt as comfortable as Northside Grill.

Across the room, Iris pulled a tap of the local IPA, clearly pleased by the hungry crowd of whitewater worshippers. In a glance, Kelsey could see there wasn't a chance Iris would ever let her bar go. She flashed a grin and passed a foaming pitcher over the bar, all while taking an order from the next person in line.

The sound system crackled, then a lean man with gray hair at his temples tapped the mic. "Can everyone hear me in the back?" he asked and got a few thumbs up. "Great. The sooner we get started, the sooner we can eat."

Cheers rode the energy in the room, pulsing from eager paddlers hungry for food and white water. After going over the three-day schedule he moved onto safety procedures. They'd all heard the spiel before, but the paddlers paid attention. Heads nodded like marionettes on connected strings when he stressed the need for rescue vests and throw bags. He signaled to Kelsey as she snaked a path between tables carrying her stack of clipboards. She felt eyes on her when the guy announced that everyone needed to claim one volunteer slot during the event.

A large sign-up sheet on the back wall listed the various shuttle departures, the earliest leaving before dawn. Vans moving to and from the fairgrounds would ease congestion at the kayak put-in near Underwood Bridge and at the takeout point on Drano Lake.

Chatter increased after he answered a few questions, then his booming voice lifted over the din. "We've covered the essentials. Burgers are just coming off the grill, and Iris assures me pizzas will be out of the oven in about ten. Find a pitcher and have a drink, but don't overindulge. If you show up at the put-in with a hangover, I'll pull your foolish ass. This river challenges the best, and everyone knows *water always wins.*"

Kelsey left the stack of clipboards on a front-and-center table, encouraging stragglers to claim empty volunteer slots. She caught the owner's attention and pointed toward the kitchen. Iris gave a nod, letting Kelsey know it was fine to wander into the depths of Northside Grill.

Through the kitchen doors, she found the person she was looking for and draped an arm across Amanda's shoulder. "I guess I shouldn't be surprised to find you in here," she said as they both stared into the distorted heat rolling from the massive pizza oven.

"Hey, I put in plenty of hours at the deli before my photography gig. I like it here. A kitchen always feels like home."

Home. Kelsey was glad to have Amanda back in Ashwood, even for a few days. She missed this girl, her energy, her easy laughter, even her drama. A timer rang and Amanda spun a long wooden paddle into the oven's gaping mouth. She peeled out the pizza, slid the pie onto a steel table and sliced.

"Anything I can do to help?" Kelsey asked, while watching the food-driven-dance.

"Actually, yes." Amanda's voice lowered to a whisper as she scanned the kitchen. "Could you keep Kent busy?" They both searched now—as if Kent would spring around the corner like a ninja. "He's been hovering, and it's making me nervous."

Kelsey shrugged. "Kent? I hardly noticed he was here." Still, she had to wonder what her best friend was up to *now.* "You know, that turd might be avoiding me. Shit, I think he's trying to weasel out of admin."

"Sounds about right, but he's here somewhere. All I have to do is make eye contact with a hot foreign guy, and like an apparition, Kent materializes from thin air."

"Crap." The stupid spat between Amanda and Kent had become exhausting, and Kelsey wondered how much longer the awkward standoff had to last. "Don't you think he's groveled long enough?"

"When has Kent ever groveled? Not that I care—he just needs to back off." Amanda jabbed the end of the pizza paddle against the floor, like Neptune's trident. Even though her eyes flashed with fury, she still looked ridiculous.

Kelsey bit the inside of her cheek to keep from laughing. "You don't even live here anymore. He can't bother you *that* much."

When Amanda's lips tightened over her teeth, Kels wondered if too much attention was actually the problem. Maybe Kent hadn't bothered Amanda *enough*.

Amanda's hand relaxed and slid down the pizza paddle. "Whatever, it doesn't matter," she said, averting her watery gaze. "I've moved past *Halloween night*. Hell, I'm smarter because of it. But this possessive crap he's pulling has to stop."

"I'll deal with Kent, it's the least I can do. I needed his help for this whitewater event, because I can't run The Little White without him." The admission humbled Kelsey, an uncomfortable feeling she didn't have to endure often.

Another timer rang and Amanda spun to slice the next sizzling pie. "No worries. Focus on the river. I'll just ignore the jerk."

Kelsey sighed and left the kitchen to deal with this poorly timed distraction. Back in the dining room, conversations melted into an indiscernible buzz. Kayak teams sat together, hunched over plates, downing pints of beer. Accents swirled from Europe, Mexico, Canada, and Australia. They'd come to run her river—five miles of pristine slot rapids, packed with stunning vertical drops, moss-covered canyons, and treacherous boulders.

After the meal, the kick-off meeting fell under Parker's control. The room quieted, awed by the famed adventure photographer. As if she could control the rotation of the Earth, Parker Knight sketched her elaborate plan to capture this weekend's event from the river, shore, and sky.

"We need signatures from paddlers who agree to share their footage. You'll be compensated and listed in the film's credits." Grins spread, clearly hoping to have a shot included in her film.

"If you didn't bring your own camera, see my intern, Amanda." Her shy hand lifted and gave a wave. "She'll help you mount Go Pros directly to the kayaks. We want to capture the boiling water from the boat's point of view."

Parker released everyone and, as predicted, Kent moved Amanda's direction the moment an Australian slid into the chair next to her. Kelsey gritted her teeth, eyes on her jealous friend, wondering how long he would hover. *Shit, Kent's making a damn fool of himself.*

The lean, muscular Aussie scooted his chair closer to Amanda, a move motivated by the din in the room. He turned his head, and Kelsey spotted the black and blue marks of a recently broken nose. Was he a brawling asshole or a high-risk athlete? Didn't matter much—those fading bruises didn't detract from his easy grin.

Kent invaded the Aussie's peripheral vision and got a sharp glance. "Only be a minute, mate." A tinge of annoyance tightened the relaxed accent.

"Take all the time you need—*mate*—I'll wait for Amanda." Kent stressed her name with a hint of ownership, and Amanda bristled.

She narrowed her eyes and silently mouthed, "Back off."

Her demand had the opposite effect. Kent only stepped closer.

Challenge accepted, Amanda lifted her brows and lit her smile, directing flirtatious heat toward the Australian. She leaned in, he let his gaze wander, and their body language went from friendly to interested in a flash.

Feet planted, Kent folded his arms over his chest with a caveman's grunt.

Good God, what a dick. Kelsey rolled her eyes, grabbed her arsenal of clipboards, and moved in. "Hey, Kent, I could use your help." She shoved the stack of clipboards into his hands.

He pushed the pile back. "Maybe later, Kels. I'm waiting for Amanda."

"Take the clipboards and follow me. Amanda will find you when she's finished." Kelsey's sharp tone launched a shiver through Kent, and she grinned. Apparently, nothing had changed since first grade.

"Okay. Fine. Let's get this sorted." He marched away but didn't move far enough to miss Amanda's exasperated exhale.

Kelsey caught snippets of the Aussie's words, laden with a sexy accent. "Don't worry. He's just sending a message. I'd be tempted to do the same if you were *mine*."

Amanda huffed, "Oh no. I'm not his. He lost that chance a long time ago."

Puppy-eyed disappointment shifted Kent's expression. But what did he expect? Irritated, Kelsey had hit her limit. "Can we *please* finish this?" She punctuated her question with the toe of her shoe on his leg.

"Jesus, Kels. Lighten up."

Leaning in, she whispered, "I'm saving you from yourself."

His eyes narrowed, but he accepted her warning. "You're right. I'm sorry. I know this event's important." Kent turned his chair toward her and ignored the flirty giggles radiating from the table a few feet away. "Spread out the map, let's take a look at our safety plan."

The pair studied each challenging section of the river and decided to place two spotters at Boulder Sluice and another pair at the hidden cave below Sacriledge. The fourteen-foot drop at S-Turn would also need a minder, as would Bowey Hotel. Kent traced the line of the big drop at Wishbone, and she worried a bit about the dangerously deceptive hydraulic at Horseshoe. No one would portage Stovepipe—not in this crowd—but fortunately, the flows were plenty high.

***

The prep-party at Northside Grill ended early and everyone scattered. The time was meant for sleep, but Kelsey was too anxious to take advantage of the extra hours. At least she had a real bed and her own space. Some kayakers camped near the river, and the lucky ones had secured cabins near town. When Amanda had asked, Kelsey carved out room at her snug little cottage for Parker's entire team. Most of the crew would crash on her living room floor, but no one complained because a roof was a rare luxury for that lot.

Kelsey watched, hip propped on the counter in her kitchen, while Parker reigned over a team meeting in the living room. After reviewing specific locations where they'd already taken test shots, Parker unleashed her inner-bitch to make sure nobody made any bone-headed mistakes. Technical jargon began to sound like a foreign language, and Kelsey wandered outside with a beer in her hand. The lawn chair creaked as she sat and listened to the wind in the trees. Lifting the bottle to her lips, she downed another gulp, and waited for that two-beer-tired feeling to set in.

It didn't. At 2:00 AM, Kels pounded her pillow and flipped it for the fiftieth time. Laying on her back, she stared at the red light on her smoke detector and wondered why it seemed to be moving. If she didn't get some sleep, she'd be useless on the river in the morning. The bodies lining her living room floor didn't help. If her space was her own, she'd wander into her kitchen and grab a snack, or even better, dash out for a mind-clearing run. She blinked at that little red light. Trapped.

Reaching out, her hand fished over her bedside table, landing on her phone. When she touched it the screen lit, staining her room light green. She stared at the screen and whispered, "What time is it in the Maldives? Mark, are you a half-day ahead, or a half-day behind?"

Her first text was short, tentative, just to see if he would respond.

Hi. How are the waves in the southern hemisphere? Awkward, she hated the wait. Maybe he didn't have service. Maybe he had better things to do. Maybe he didn't give two-shits. Her screen lit, and the phone jumped in her hand.

Thinking about you today. Knew you'd be taking on that whitewater. I'm jealous. Waves have been flat. Should have stayed in the States.

Kelsey read his words. He'd been thinking about her. It shouldn't matter, but it did.

Can't be that bad. All that warm water.

His reply filled her screen. *True. Board shorts and a rash guard beat wetsuits every day. How are conditions on the river?*

Her fingers flew. *Awesome. High flow.*

Mark answered quickly. *You going to run it?*

With a smile, she typed. *Ready to take it on.*

Will you help me tackle The Little White someday?

Count on it. She couldn't think of anything else to say, then added, *Gotta catch some zzz.*

He didn't make her wait for his reply. *Night Mermaid.*

Night Mermaid. She could hear his warm voice in those two words. Missing him, Kelsey stared at the phone until her screen faded to black.

FIVE

Bleary-eyed and humming with caffeine, Kelsey hit dawn patrol. Neoprene-clad athletes met at the fairgrounds to load orange, blue, and turquoise river runners into trailers before they claimed seats in crowded vans. Kelsey passed the nose of Kent's vehicle and waved.

He rolled down the window, leaned out and yelled, "Nothing stinks quite like dank neoprene."

She laughed and circled the van to open the passenger side door. Her best friend grinned until Kelsey offered that front-seat spot to the Australian. She shot Kent a warning glare—*play nice*—before she climbed into a vacant seat in the second row. The Australian glanced over his shoulder and thanked her as she scrambled in.

Kent kept his eyes forward when the Aussie asked, "What's the flow?"

"Just under four."

"Bloody hell, I can't wait to kick off." Spinning around, he introduced himself, "I'm Brayden, by the way." Electric anticipation rolled off the guy, and the vibration transferred when her hand squeezed a hello onto his shoulder.

"I'm Kelsey, good to meet you."

"You a local?" he asked as the van pulled onto the highway.

"We both are." Kelsey nodded.

Kent picked up her thought. "Born and raised." His glance in the rear-view mirror checked the trailer, making sure everything was secure.

"So, you run The Little White often?" Brayden asked, sizing up the strength of Kent's experience.

Kelsey grinned when her best friend's knuckles gripped the wheel a little tighter. "I try to put in about once a week," Kent said without even a glance to the side.

Brayden nodded and settled back in his seat. "Ah, you're lucky to live here."

"Made the best of it."

Leaning forward, Kels asked, "Where are you from?"

"Melbourne."

Melbourne. When Kent pressed the accelerator to climb a steep hill, the engine noise made conversation difficult. Kelsey sat back, shoulders curled, suddenly feeling small. Brayden could have said he was from the moon. Raised in Ashwood, she didn't know anything about Australia but felt too foolish to ask. Pulling out her phone, she was pleased to find one bar and pulled up her map. Her fingers brushed the screen moving the satellite image away from the last thing she'd searched for—Maldives.

Her fingers swept across blue ocean until she hit Australia. For the next few minutes, names like Werribee and Korumburra caught her attention, and magnified her insignificance. She'd rarely traveled outside the Northwest, and never the States. Her footprint on the Earth was shallow. Like a hiker in the wilderness, she left no trace behind.

Kent angled the van and trailer onto a tight spot along the graveled shoulder. A hand-held radio crackled from its position on the dash, and Amanda's voice filled the van. "Knight group two is set."

She'd called from mid-river. Kelsey blew out a breath as she pictured where those photographers had hiked in with heavy gear, navigating steep scree slopes of jagged rock.

After unloading, Kent gave the keys to one of Kelsey's Venture employees. The van would wait at the takeout on Drano Lake, loaded with coolers stocked with beer and soda, until thirsty paddlers arrived.

Kent and Kelsey put in first, needing time to move to their minding locations downstream. Each intended to spend the day in separate pools, waiting, equipped with throw bags and first aid, in case a kayaker tangled with a rough spot.

In her green kayak, Kelsey floated in a calm pool, yet she trembled with adrenalin. Breathing deep, the earthy air centered her. *Nothing to worry about.* With this contingent of world-class paddlers, boredom was her biggest enemy.

***

Brayden nodded to his team before they took off. Class-three water warmed up his skills before he descended into churning rapids. Dodging logjams, he chose a route through Boulder Sluice with confident strokes.

A wide grin took over his face when Brayden spotted Kelsey tucked into an eddy before he dropped into turquoise pools of frothing water. The white-blond braid dangling from her helmet was impossible to miss. His paddle dug deep as he curled right to avoid a tricky hydraulic. Exuberant whoops and hollers from his team echoed over the roar of the river in the narrow canyon.

At Wishbone Falls, he caught a glimpse of the photographers perched behind long camera lenses—ready to catch his descent through the fern-lined gulley. Lifting his knees, Brayden maneuvered his boat and plunged into the deep emerald pool.

From there, The Little White poured into three channels. Brayden chose the right side to avoid a dangerous undercut against a rocky wall. Holding up, he gathered with his mates before taking on the thirty-three-foot drop at Spirit Falls. Another group of paddlers nearly caught up and their shouts urged his team's charging plunge.

Lost in joy and adrenaline, Brayden paddled past Kent, charging downstream to take on Chaos and its deceptively challenging ledges.

The run sped by in a euphoric blur. He'd have caught a ride back to the bridge for another run if he could, but Brayden settled for a couple beers, a sandwich, and hanging with his mates on Drano lake's rocky shore.

***

At least he wasn't too bored, and Kent didn't mind getting wet. He helped two swimmers, both avoided injury and scrambled back into their boats to finish solid runs. As the sun peeled from one side of the canyon to the other, Kent knew the last kayaks would soon rush by. His joyous laughter boomed when he spotted Kelsey following the final group. Tucking behind, he trailed her through Master Blaster to the takeout.

Bright kayaks, rowdy boaters, and coolers filled with sandwiches, soda, and beer crowded the wide spot on the shore. When the party disbanded, the celebration only took a short break to reconvene later at Mosquito Creek Taproom.

***

After escaping the mildew odor in the vans, Kelsey rushed to the car she'd parked at the fairgrounds. Her foot mashed the accelerator in a hurry to beat everyone home. She smelled like a swamp, and every time she turned her steering wheel, her shoulders ached like a son of a bitch. The rationed five-minute shower would fix the foul smell, and a couple of Ibuprofen should numb her body's pain. If only there was a pill to make people disappear. Just walking through her front door tested her patience. Kels wasn't the first to arrive, and the shower was already running. *Shit*.

"You're back," Parker said, on a quick glimpse from her laptop. "I caught some shots of you hucking Spirit Falls today. Take a look at the footage my drones captured—I can't wait to begin the edits."

Parker tilted the laptop, clearly craving admiration for the shoot. The glance Kels took was only for the photographer's benefit. She'd never liked examining pictures of herself and videos were even worse. Not that she didn't like the way she looked—crap like that just made her too self-aware.

The hiss of the shower cut off and Kels moved, eagerly anticipating an escape, but no one came out of the bathroom right away. Pacing, she turned back to Parker. "Do you still plan to interview paddlers tonight at Mosquito Creek Taproom?" she asked, hoping the answer was no. If the cameras weren't around, she'd be able to relax with a beer, maybe two.

Parker nodded. "Absolutely. The personalities and backstories—that's where the gold is." Her eyes gleamed with more than the reflection from her computer screen. Without looking away, she went on, "All I need now is a bit of drama, an injury or two, then my film will be perfect."

Kelsey cringed. *Was tragedy Parker's idea of a big payoff? Fuck that.*

Amanda emerged from the bathroom, already dressed, her hair wrapped in a towel. "I'm done. Who wants to clean up next?" she hollered, then her eyes hit Kels. "Wow, beautiful day on the river. I would kill to have your skills. Damn, that drop over Spirit Falls had to feel amazing."

Kelsey had been satisfied with her run and grinned. "I forgot how much I love that river. Wish I could take it on every day, but there's not much I can do about it. It's nearly impossible to find clients with that skill set."

Amanda peered over Parker's shoulder to study the footage. "Maybe in a few years I'll be ready for that whitewater."

Kelsey nodded. "Let me know. I'm ready when you are."

Parker tore her attention from the screen and glanced between the two women from Ashwood. "Wait. Are you the chick who guides expeditions for women?"

Chick. Why did that sound so condescending coming from Parker? Kelsey took a few steps toward the bathroom before someone beat her to the next shower as she answered, "Yeah, that's me."

Head tilted, eyes narrowed, Parker scrutinized Kelsey. "Hmm, there might be a story there."

"I'm sure it's already been told." Her casual shrug was meant to put the photographer off, but the slight move only sparked a challenge. Kelsey wondered if anyone ever told this woman *no.*

Parker lifted her shoulders and squared her body. "Not the way I'd tell it. I'll have Amanda contact you in a month or so. I've got a project that's beginning to gel."

Irritation propelled Kelsey toward the bathroom, but she wanted the last word. "My summer's booked solid."

"We're looking at October or November in Patagonia," Parker said quickly, eyebrows elevated, luring Kelsey in.

Kels blew out a breath and succumbed to temptation. "Now that sounds interesting . . ." *Patagonia.* Only a fool would pass that up, and she wanted to know more, but just outside, gravel crunched as a car pulled up. Doors slammed, and booming laughter bled through from her front yard. "I gotta grab the next shower."

By the time her five minutes were up, the mass in her living room had quadrupled. Wrapped in her robe, Kelsey hurried from the bathroom to the only solitude available in her little cottage. She dashed to her bedroom and was wriggling into snug jeans when her phone rattled on her dresser. Mark's name appeared with an incoming text. Eyes locked on his words, his voice echoed in her head.

Thinking about you. How was the first day on the river?

Kelsey smiled - **Perfect. High flows, only two swimmers. Kent took care of both.**

How about you?

I finished with a good run.

Nice. His single word hung there, and Kelsey waited, questioning if she should add more. When she couldn't think of anything to say, she typed three different versions of goodbye then hit delete after each one. God, she hated this awkward crap, and remembered again why she didn't do relationships. It was too much work.

The moment she gave up, a picture came through. The pearl-white sand and turquoise water didn't look real. There wasn't a single person on the stretch of palm-lined beach.

Kelsey gasped and typed, *Beautiful.*

I want you here with me, Mermaid.

When she read his simple reply, she couldn't breathe and hated herself for overthinking. Mark managed to share whatever popped into his mind. Would she ever be that free?

A moment later the door to her bedroom creaked open, and Amanda slipped in. A pink sticky mess covered her entire chest.

"What the hell happened to you?" Kels asked, shoving her phone in her pocket as she surveyed the goopy damage.

"Strawberry smoothie disaster. Unfortunately, I packed light. Can I borrow a shirt?"

"Sure. Grab anything."

Amanda peeled off her wet sloppy shirt and tossed it on Kelsey's damp towel. Both girls stood in front of the open closet wearing jeans and bras. Kelsey found a tank top and pulled it on, then she picked up Amanda's ruined shirt by one corner and snorted a laugh. "Do you want me to toss that in a load?"

"Nah . . . I'll just rinse it out and take it over to Mom and Dad's on Sunday. Is this okay?" Amanda asked as she pulled a flowy top from a hanger.

"Sure, wear anything you want. So, you're visiting your parents this weekend?"

"I promised Mom I'd stop by for dinner on Sunday. Hey, thanks for letting our crew crash here. It's a tight squeeze, but everyone feels comfortable with you. My parents would have hovered for sure."

"I get it. My parents are the same. Still, I wouldn't trade the way they hover for anything." Kelsey hesitated, bit her fingernail, and hoped to get the timing right.

Amanda picked up on the cautious vibe hovering in the room and sliced a glance her way. "Yeah, I guess . . ."

Even though Kelsey was bad at this stuff, she took a breath and a chance, because the standoff between her friends had gone on far too long. "There's a heavy price for unlimited freedom . . . just ask Kent."

Amanda propped her hands on her hips. "What's this really about?"

"He's trying to change. And I was hoping you'd cut the guy some slack while you're in town."

"Slack? If I give him too much rope, he'll strangle me with it. Or maybe he'd use it to tie up Jasmine again?" Amanda sneered. "But now that I think about it, *that kink* sounds kind of fun. Maybe I'll take whatever I *need* from Kent then leave Ashwood without looking back."

"Jesus," Kelsey pressed her fingernails into her palms and blinked hard, wishing she'd kept her meddling mouth shut. She stood and watched as Amanda blazed into the swarm of people buzzing through the living room. The entire house pulsed with energy—a hungry drive Kelsey understood, maybe even shared, but wasn't sure she admired anymore.

***

A delicious aroma surrounded Mosquito Creek taproom and erased the memory of the throngs at her house. Her stomach rumbled as Kelsey inhaled the thick cloud of onion, pork, and teriyaki sauce, but a greater thirst drove her inside. She heard snippets of exaggerated stories as she passed hungry athletes who leaned over picnic tables and relaxed in Adirondack chairs. The place was packed, and it took a minute to find her friends in a knot behind the bar.

"Look at you, scoring points and helping out Linnea." She teased Kent as he hefted a tray of steaming pint glasses from the dishwasher. After a day on the river, he still had energy to spare.

"I'm just lifting the heavy shit—no big deal." He kept moving as Kels eased her hip onto a tall stool.

Pregnant and glowing, Linnea put an arm around him. "And I appreciate it, even if you have ulterior motives." She gave him a squeeze. "Kent, are you just using me to lure unsuspecting women into your clutches?"

He kissed her cheek, and she smiled. "Yes, damn it. Just play along."

Linnea poked him in the gut, and he laughed, but something across the room had him distracted. Kelsey turned to find the team of photographers coming in through the wide bay doors. The hometown girl in that crowd hurried across the room and Kent blushed. Kelsey couldn't remember the last time anyone had that power over her best friend. Amanda ignored him and trapped her cousin, Linnea, in a hug.

"Lord, I've missed you. Girl, you and this baby bump look amazing. I can't believe how much has changed this year. And to think we once worried that Rick might never make a move."

"Rick obviously has that covered," Kent teased then ducked quickly to dodge Linnea's playful slap. He left without a word to Amanda and gave the girls plenty of space.

Kelsey followed him outside. The smells billowing from Island Time's food truck broke her will. "Should we grab something before it gets too busy?" she asked.

"You read my mind." After checking all the specials written in chalk, Kent chose guava chicken, Kels the mango Mahi. Starving, they sat across from each other, both hunched over paper plates.

Amanda appeared at the end of their table and asked, "Mind if I join you?" Kent scooted down and grinned, making room for her on his bench. Under a canopy of evergreens, the three sat together, spearing their food with flimsy plastic forks while awkward silence expanded.

Kelsey rolled her eyes before filling the silent void. "Any snags with the shoot so far?"

"Only one." Amanda leaned in and whispered, "One of our drones is hung up in a massive cedar tree."

With one long blink, Kent recovered from his awkward daze. "Shit. How are you going to get that down?"

To make sure Parker wasn't around, Amanda swiveled her head, then leaned in. "It's over the river. A couple of guys are using a second drone to knock it down before Parker figures it out. Glad this isn't on me, though."

"So, the rumors are true?" Kelsey chuckled and took a bite of her food before it cooled.

"Mm-hmm. That drone is replaceable, but in *the world according to Parker*—replacing people is even easier." Amanda shrank into herself and stared at her plate. "Living the dream."

The din inside the taproom suddenly silenced. The abrupt change turned their heads toward the open bay doors. "They must be showing today's footage . . . I guess I better go." Amanda licked her lips and glanced at her plate but abandoned her food and rushed inside.

Kelsey had never seen Amanda so tense. This gig had gone beyond important and was now an obvious burden. After snarfing their food, Kent and Kelsey tossed their garbage in the right coded bins—compost, recycle, landfill—then followed Amanda inside.

Near the back of the dimmed room, the three locals stood together and watched the crowd's reaction to Parker's work. Raw video footage and action shots sprung from the big screen, fetching cheers and loud applause from the paddlers who crammed the taproom.

Kent watched Amanda instead of the film, and Kelsey worried. She didn't want him to get hurt, even if he probably deserved it.

The short film faded, the lights came up, and Parker moved to the front ready to take questions. Her eyes dashed around the room like a searchlight to locate each member of her team. Impatient, she waved them forward. After a few questions from the crowd, an impromptu meeting began, and Amanda melted into her Hood River team.

Kent returned to picking up messes scattered around Mosquito's taproom. Linnea smiled his direction and thanked him with a wave. Eventually, Kelsey followed him outside, dragging a bag of garbage behind her.

"Thanks, Kels," he said as she lifted a bag into the dumpster.

"No problem. Garbage duty is not a big deal."

"Not what I meant. I was talking about Amanda. Thanks for smoothing things over."

"Glad it helped."

"I miss her."

"She'll be back—her roots are in Ashwood." Kelsey knew she was lying the moment the words left her mouth. Once people escaped, few came back to their little town.

Kent pulled his keys from his pocket. "Hey, Kels, I think I'll take off for a while."

"Going home?" she asked, willing to follow.

"Nah. I thought I'd head over to the river. Maybe I can help the crew get that drone out of the trees." He spun around and walked backward, giving her a smile that melted most girl's hearts. She was immune to the charm, but not the love. The bond they'd shared since grade school was unbreakable, unconditional, unwavering.

When he climbed into his pickup, Kelsey wandered back inside the taproom. Foundry was working their way through an upbeat set—the music thumped, swaying the bodies on the floor in a pulsing hypnotic wave. Amanda's eyes met Kelsey's from a tangle of women on the dance floor. Lunging forward, she yanked Kelsey into the throng.

Exhausted, it wasn't where Kels wanted to be. She shook her head, took a step back, and landed in a pair of large hands. She spun, ready to jump down the throat of the man with the big mitts but found the glinting eyes of the Australian looking back. *Brayden.* Kelsey relaxed and smiled. Never missing a beat, he gripped her waist when she tried to move from the floor. "Dancing really isn't my thing . . ."

"Follow me, just for one tune." Brayden's accent did her in and Kelsey nodded. By the third song a slower beat took over, and his grasp felt comfortable. Not the arms she missed, but it was nice to feel someone's touch.

SIX

Kels woke before her alarm to an amethyst dawn bleeding through her windows. It shed just enough light to navigate her steps over sleeping bodies on the way to her kitchen. Bitter coffee grounds loaded, and brew light on, she left to brush her teeth while her elixir brewed. Face washed and blond hair in a snug ponytail, she dodged a few zombies on her way back into the kitchen to find an empty carafe.

The batch she'd put on ten minutes ago was gone, and the asshole who drained the last cup hadn't bothered to make another pot. Muttering, she repeated the process. The coffee maker sputtered and hissed on her second attempt to brew desperately needed caffeine. Kelsey leaned against the counter, determined to get the first cup.

"Have you seen Amanda?" Parker asked, sipping from a full, steaming mug.

"Not yet. I just got up."

"Her car isn't here, and the trunk's loaded with equipment we need for today's shoot." Kels glanced outside, finding some of their team already loading gear.

"Give me a sec, I'll see if I can track her down." Kelsey dashed to her room, located her phone, and hit the contact. Crap, straight to voicemail. Now what? If she called Amanda's parents, she'd set off a shitstorm that would likely end with a search party—*that* was not an option. Kent was Kelsey's next best choice.

"Fuck," she mumbled before placing the call.

On the third ring, he answered. "Hey, Kels, I'm busy here. What's up?"

"Uh. I hate to ask, but have you seen Amanda?"

The pause on the other end stretched *way* too long. "Maybe . . . Why?"

Her eyes hit the ceiling. "Parker's trying to track her down. There's equipment in Amanda's car."

Kent hissed, "Shit. That could take a while. Amanda's car is still at the taproom."

"What the hell happened last night?" she whispered into the phone.

"Nothing. We'll meet you as soon as we can."

***

Dust kicked up behind Kent's lifted truck when he pulled into the fairgrounds, followed by Amanda. Parker dogged her employee, unleashing fury on a wire of barbed expletives. Damage done, Amanda's apology didn't matter, and the smirky side-glances from her colleagues didn't need an explanation—her days were numbered. Under a fresh burden, her shoulders slumped as she worked quickly loading gear into vans, because the river wouldn't wait.

The situation wasn't tragic, Amanda hadn't actually been late. She merely wasn't available when her queen called. Later, when Kelsey paddled by on the river, she spotted Amanda all set in her usual place. Waving her paddle as she passed, Kels sped farther downstream and found her safety position at the edge of a churning pool.

Half the day trickled by without incident. Bobbing in the water, almost complacent, Kelsey jumped when a lone paddle floated into view. Her adrenaline spiked when she spotted a dry bag. Gathering both, she waited, wondering if a kayak or a swimmer would follow, but neither appeared. It wasn't until the end of the day that she heard the entire story.

After hitting a rock, the paddler had turned sideways, leaned upstream, and capsized. When he found himself wedged in a hole, he popped his spray skirt, and escaped, swimming. Even though he kept his feet up, he'd found a spot near a logjam to snag his foot. The river's current won and fractured his leg before the team pulled him free.

Kent had jumped in, clipped a rope to the injured kayaker's rescue harness, and with another minder on the dry end, hauled the swimmer to a rocky ledge. Two members of the local rescue team immobilized the leg in an inflatable cast and hiked him out. Feeling great after pain meds, the guy appeared at Mosquito Creek Taproom that evening, instantly becoming the center of attention.

Amanda got lucky. Parker forgot about the early morning mess as she filmed the story from every direction. The only person who interested Parker more than the victim, was the charismatic rescuer.

Keeping a safe distance from Parker, Kelsey watched Kent handle the interrogation with ease. "He's a natural," Amanda leaned in and murmured as Kent answer question after question in front of Parker's cameras.

Kelsey tilted her head and whispered, "Why am I not surprised?" When she couldn't bear the suspense any longer, she asked, "What happened between you two last night?"

"Nothing."

"Just spill. You know I'll hear it from Kent, eventually."

"Yeah, so why should I even bother?" Amanda tried to escape, but Kelsey followed—not caring if she was as annoying as sharp gravel in Amanda's shoe.

"Fine, I'll tell you," she huffed. "After they found the drone, Kent came back to the taproom, totally wired. We went over to his place, had some ice-cream, then fell asleep while watching a movie." Though Amanda shrugged it off, it didn't stop the blush from scorching her face.

Kelsey grinned at the sight. An innocent movie night? Kent had definitely lost his edge.

***

When a meeting snared Amanda, the noise inside the taproom pushed Kelsey outside. She sank onto the farthest picnic table, wondering when she could leave. If she ditched the party, maybe she'd get an hour of peace at her house, or even better, the luxury of a ten-minute shower. Tempting.

Warm and sweet, a gust of summer wind blew needles from a towering fir and a few landed in her beer. Her fingers fished out the debris before she took another drink of the hoppy IPA. The crackle of the sound system turned her attention back to the taproom as Parker's voice echoed through the open bay doors. Applause and cheers for the latest film clip tightened the muscles in her shoulders and neck. The woman might be a celebrity, but glorifying an injury pissed Kelsey off. At Venture, there simply wasn't a bigger fail than an injured client.

She'd endured her fill, and Sunday couldn't come soon enough. Once her house emptied, she'd scrape together a few hours and locate her lost equilibrium on a lonely trail. Kelsey closed her eyes, listened to the breeze, and counted down the minutes until she could be alone.

Brayden's accented voice floated over her shoulder. "Kelsey, may I?"

Her eyes popped open, and she turned toward his smiling face, but his grin had a certain tightness, maybe pain.

"Grab a seat. Have you had enough tall tales?" she asked.

"Yeah. Close calls don't intrigue me. Conjures too many ghosts."

"Sorry to hear that," she said, but Brayden waved off her sympathy. He clearly didn't want to rehash a painful memory.

A quick cough cleared his throat, and he recovered his easy smile. "And you? What's your excuse for hanging outside?"

"Parker's crew is staying at my house. It's more challenging than I'd anticipated. It might be pathetic, but I'm hiding."

"Nothing wrong with that, and you'll have your place back soon." He took another drink from his half-finished beer.

"True, but not for long. I'll be gone again by Tuesday."

"Work?" he asked.

"Mm-hmm, back to guiding, climbing, and rafting." A strand of her corn silk hair escaped the tie at the nape of her neck and caught in the breeze. Without hesitation, Brayden hooked it behind her ear, and a shiver danced from the heat of his touch.

"Perfect," Brayden murmured.

Kelsey didn't know if he meant her appearance or her job, but it didn't matter. Either way, Brayden's attention made her blush. "Where are you headed after Ashwood?" she asked.

"To the coast. I'm splitting this vacation between my kayak and my surfboard."

A blooming smile gave Kelsey away.

"Ah, you must be a surfer," Brayden said with a crooked grin.

"I try," she admitted. "But I've only been at it for a little over a year."

"Any trips planned?" Brayden leaned in, revealing his keen interest in her as plainly as his interest in surfing.

"No trips to the beach for me," she said with a shrug. "For the next few months I'll be in the mountains guiding."

"My loss. Maybe you can let me in on the secret surf spots?" Brayden asked while the glimmer of hope in his eyes faded. She missed that hot look immediately.

"Happy to share my faves . . . the few that I know. Give me your info, and I'll send them over."

"Thanks, Kels." After they exchanged numbers, he stood, holding his empty pint. "Hey, can I buy you another?"

The way his accent stretched the question made her smile. "Sure, thanks. I'm having Sweet Venom."

Kelsey pulled out her phone. Using Mark's app, she confirmed the places she'd surfed and sent Brayden a text. The line inside the taproom was long. When the man and her beer didn't come back right away, she checked out a few of Mark's recent posts. Today's first picture showed Mark on a beach, perfect sets of even waves in the distance. She scowled. In the second shot he was sandwiched between two women, both beautifully tanned and wearing miniscule bikinis. Her fingers shook as she moved to the next shot in the series. He was laughing while those girls had their lips planted on his cheeks.

Jealousy knotted her stomach. *Shit.* At least the bitches weren't topless. She pictured Mark riding those head high waves nonstop. *He could be riding those women just as hard.* One flick of her finger closed the app, but her thoughts lingered, and her anger simmered. She was so fucking tired of being alone.

Gravel crunched as Brayden approached, and it gave her time to paste on a smile. "Thought I'd never make it back," he said and handed over her beer.

"No worries, two's my limit when I'm working." Kelsey took a long draw, letting the ice-cold liquid seep past her smoldering anger.

"The party inside is really ripping. Looks like some of my mates will be too pissed to paddle tomorrow."

"Too pissed to paddle? I like it." Kelsey shared his infectious laughter. He was so easy on the eyes. "Are you doing the tourist thing before heading back to the southern hemisphere?" she asked.

"Yeah, I reckon I'll follow the coast and see where the waves take me. I've got two weeks yet."

"Lucky. I haven't had a summer vacation since I was fifteen."

"What? Your job isn't a constant holiday?"

"Not always. About half of the trips are more like babysitting."

"Is winter your slack season?" he asked, seeming disappointed that she had so little time.

"Yeah. But I'm not a big fan of snow."

His brows lifted and his voice enticed, "I've got a solution. It's warm in Australia that time of year. Could I tempt you, Kels? I'd love to show you the Great Ocean Road." Brayden's accent was as hypnotic as the renewed hope in his eyes.

Something shifted. She'd enjoyed the easy flirtation, but now it meant more. Biting her lip, she recalled Mark with his arms hooked on the hips of those beach bitches. *Fuck it.* Her life had always been her own. And Brayden, with his dark hair and deep tan, was right here and smoking hot.

"Would I get to see kangaroos?"

"I can do better than roos." His wide grin revealed a crooked tooth, a slight flaw that only increased his charm. "Once you visit Melbourne, I reckon you'll never want to leave."

"That could be inconvenient . . . for you."

"Not from where I'm sitting." Brayden stretched his hand across the table, knitting their fingers together, tempting her with the slightest touch.

Thundering drums shook the taproom and cheers rose over the band. Kelsey groaned. She wanted no part of that tonight. Maybe her escape didn't have to be a solo run.

When she spotted Kent and Amanda on a quick escape, Kels retracted her hand from Brayden's, yet her skin tingled from the contact. It surprised the hell out of her when Kent took the time to drag Amanda over to their table. "Shit. That was a nightmare," he said grabbing Kelsey's shoulder. "Thank God, I finally got away from those damn cameras."

"So, you've had enough?"

"Enough of the party? Yeah. But the river? No." Kent sank to the spot beside her at the picnic table. "I have an idea. We should put in on the river at the end of the day tomorrow and take a run. I'm tired of being a spectator."

"And a fisherman."

Kent's eyes gleamed and he laughed. "You got that right."

A nod tipped her head. "Okay. I'm in. Let's finish the weekend with a final run."

Roped with muscle, Kent's arm slung around her shoulder holding her in place as he planted a kiss on her cheek. Brayden winced and Kelsey huffed—she'd found another guy who read too much into her connection with her best bud.

Still standing, Amanda bent in half at the waist to sling both arms around the pair. "Mind if I capture that moment on film? I'll see if I can line up the drones to get some aerial shots."

Kelsey shook her head. "Don't bother. I just want to put in and paddle."

The arm slung around her squeezed, but Amanda didn't answer—her friend would put a drone in the air whether she liked it or not.

Kent sprung from his spot at the table, pulling her ponytail as he stood. "I'll see you tomorrow on the river, Kels."

Her eyes followed the pair as they dashed off together, until a mosquito buzzed near her ear. She brushed the insect away, knowing if she stayed outside much longer, she'd be a pincushion. It was a good enough excuse to make an escape. "Want to take a drive?" she asked.

Brayden's eyes met hers with a surprised blink and a quick nod. "Lead the way."

"Are you willing to leave your car here?" Kelsey asked as they crossed the gravel lot. The word *overnight* wasn't said, but the message was sent and received.

"No worries. I got a ride over here with my mates."

Kelsey grinned when his hand landed at the small of her back. Before she circled to the driver's side of her car, his index finger stopped her by one belt loop. Lassoed by a muscled arm, she found her body trapped against his chest. "If there wasn't such a mob in my cabin, I'd—" He finished his thought with a bold, thorough kiss.

His lips were warm, the kiss intoxicating, and Kelsey ignored the pit of guilt coiling in her stomach. She pulled away and caught his eyes dancing in the dim light.

"Damn, you're hot as hell. I'll follow you anywhere you care to lead. To your place, then?" he asked.

She shook her head. "No way, not with Parker's camera equipment scattered all over my living room floor."

Brayden whispered against her mouth, "Ah, now you're just heaping temptation." He tasted her lips again.

The heat that pulsed between them erased her hesitation. "Let's get out of here," she blurted before she changed her mind. "There's a definite advantage to hooking up with a local."

Kelsey quickened her steps, running away from her thoughts of Mark. They had separate lives in separate hemispheres. After seeing those pictures, she knew he wasn't pining for her, and she was tired of spending every night alone.

The half-hour drive to Osprey Lake passed too quickly. Comfortable conversation simmered between them, talking of jobs, surfing, and rivers they'd paddled.

Following the lake road, she slowed near her parents' place for a moment but drove past the cluster of guest cabins—moving on to a more secluded spot.

Kelsey continued along the shore, finally turning into a narrow lane that led to Seth and Natalie's tiny home at the east end of Lake Osprey. The tiny home sat empty, especially since Natalie's older brother, Ben, was working in North Carolina this summer. Borrowing the place wasn't a problem, Natalie would understand, if she ever found out.

"What is this?" Brayden asked as the headlights swept across the modern, sleek home.

"A tiny home. My friend owns it. She ran a coffee shop out of the place before she married the guy who built it for her."

Kelsey climbed from her SUV and used her phone as a flashlight to locate the hidden compartment where Natalie kept a spare key. Eager, it took about two seconds to open the door. While she turned the knob, Brayden's lips landed on her neck and she sighed. Warm and teasing, the sweep of his tongue began whisper soft. Her body pivoted, and his hands explored, pulling her close to taste the contours of her barely opened mouth with kisses as hot as his accent.

Her feet shuffled over the threshold and the door clicked shut behind her. In a smooth move, Kelsey found her body trapped against the sturdy vertical plane. His hands traveled over her clothes, and she accepted his touch while reaching around his muscle-hardened torso to tease his shirt from his jeans.

"Not yet," he said as her fingers found his belt. Those two commanding words unfurled regret. Her senses sharpened enough to inspect her surroundings, and everywhere she looked, she saw Mark.

He'd followed her into this tiny home—parked at the beach—the first time they'd met. Then her eyes landed on the couch, where they'd hung out eating cinnamon rolls and ham and cheese croissants. Kelsey blinked hard but couldn't shake the memory of Mark slumped on the cushions, his hair messed by her fingers, with a cup of coffee wrapped in his hand.

She took three steps back and rounded the kitchen counter to put the solid surface between herself and temptation. "Um." The words wouldn't come. Short-term flings were easy but letting a guy down *before sex* was new territory for her.

Brayden's grin faded. "Am I missing something?"

"God, I'm sorry . . . you have to know, I didn't bring you up here to—"

Recognizing her change of heart, his eyes widened, and his hands shot up, stopping her apology. "Hey, no worries. Not a problem putting on the brakes. I'll admit, I'm disappointed, but if we're not on the same page, I understand." Brayden adjusted his jeans and chuckled.

Kelsey spun away, blushing for one hundred different reasons while she tried to gather her senses. "Do you want to go back to Mosquito Creek Brewery?" she asked, still hiding her flushed face.

He circled toward her, tipped her chin with his finger, and melted her heart with a soft grin. "Not if I can convince you to let me cook dinner. This place looks like a chef's dream."

"Dinner?" Bubbled laughter relieved her layered tension. "If you like to cook, I love to eat. Or I could make some Top Ramen and Rice Krispy Treats."

"Tempting, but why don't you let me take a look around," he said, giving her shoulder a squeeze.

Kelsey spun and opened the refrigerator, knowing Natalie kept the place stocked. At the same moment, Brayden popped open the cupboards and pulled out pasta.

The rest of her tension faded when he plugged his phone into the sound system and put on an eclectic playlist. Following his instructions, Kelsey found cooking wasn't *that* bad when someone else took charge. She chopped Roma tomatoes while he minced garlic and onion. Soon, Italian aromas filled the space and she was talking easily again. Occasionally, Brayden brushed her body with a casual touch and awareness sparked between them, but he didn't push for more.

Over dinner, he convinced her to consider a trip to Australia this winter. She nodded, secretly hoping she wouldn't be able to accept. But she and Mark hadn't made any firm promises about the future, so she kept her options with Brayden open, for now.

After dinner, Brayden pushed her out of the kitchen while he cleaned up. The couch was soft, the blanket was cozy, and the wine eased the tight muscles in her neck.

Kelsey wasn't aware that she'd fallen asleep until she woke at dawn to the smell of coffee and the sight of a shirtless man standing in front of an open refrigerator.

"Oh crap, what time is it?" she asked, sitting up so fast her head spun.

"Don't worry, I set an alarm before I crashed with you in my arms."

Kelsey blushed and pulled the thin blanket over her tired body. "I'm sorry . . ."

Brayden shook his head. "Don't be, I'm not. And waking next to you will go down as my best night in the States so far, maybe ever."

When she opened her mouth to protest, he raised his eyebrows and grinned. She didn't believe him but was too sleepy to put up a fight.

"If you take a quick shower, I'll have eggs ready by the time you finish," he offered. Her stomach rumbled, and she obeyed the gorgeous bare-chested guy in the kitchen. A man who loved to cook could become addictive.

Before they locked the tiny home, Kels found a pad of paper and a pen. Her message to Natalie was short and vague, and she intentionally left the number of house guests a mystery.

SEVEN

As expected, the numbers on the river dropped drastically on Sunday. Those with hangovers didn't even bother to show up. This river deserved their respect, and only a fool would take a chance on these rapids with half their senses intact.

At the close of the day, a loud holler caught Kelsey's attention just as the last group paddled by. Even in full gear, Kelsey recognized Kent on his comfortable descent over S-turn. Early afternoon light sparkled through the trees as he wheeled into the eddy where Kelsey had spent her morning.

He yelled over the din of the turbulent water, sharing his excitement. "I've got my truck parked at a wide spot on the road just above us. Do you want to portage out and drive back to the bridge?"

"Absolutely. I hadn't thought that far ahead." Kelsey was surprised he'd remembered their last-minute plans. He seemed too focused on Amanda last night at Mosquito Creek taproom to have noticed anything or anyone else.

They paddled to the rocky shore, yanked their neoprene spray skirts from their boats, and scaled the steep path to the road with the cumbersome kayaks slung across their shoulders for the rugged climb.

Once they were secure in the quiet cab of his truck she asked, "So what's going on between you and Amanda?"

Kent's easy grin didn't mask the worry in his eyes. "Nothing's changed . . . at least not yet." She didn't have to ask—Kent was keeping a respectful distance from Amanda—a woman he'd always worshipped from afar. "Probably a good thing she's headed back to Hood River," he added as he pulled onto the road.

"Hood River's only thirty minutes away. You know where to find her." Kels encouraged him to take a chance because something about Amanda and Kent felt right.

"And she knows where to find me. I'll wait and let her make the first move, but she probably won't. She knows I'm not relationship material."

"You can change."

Kent shrugged off her suggestion. "Change? Like that's going to happen. Enough talk about relationship shit—we've got class-five rapids in our sights." He pounded the top of this steering wheel to the beat of his anticipation. Kelsey's legs bounced. A run on the Little White with Kent was the perfect way to end the weekend. Still excited, he came around the blind corner near Underwood Bridge a little too fast, then slammed the brakes and jerked the wheel to avoid two rusted out cars pulled alongside the road. "Fuck. That was close."

"Looks like word got out," Kelsey groaned.

Kent squeezed his rig between the others. "Damn."

"Always happens. Stupid kids show up trying to blend in." Kels shook her head, expecting an afternoon of fishing out inexperienced rafters and cleaning up a yard-sale of shitty gear tossed into the river from random capsized boats.

She was pleasantly surprised by the quiet at the put-in and shrugged. "Maybe I was wrong. I guess those trucks could belong to anyone...hikers or maybe skinny dippers," she said with a grin.

"Been there." Kent laughed and they shared a look, remembering too many parties with too much beer.

The hum of the river washed that pleasant memory away. Taking up her paddle, she settled into her kayak and her heart rate accelerated.

Kent took the lead through Getting Busy, and slalomed a line through Boulder Sluice, completely at ease. It wasn't until the fourteen–foot drop above S-turn that Kelsey noticed the signs—a skinny kid wearing baggy gear clung to a rock along the bank. Frozen in place, he dangled above the churning foam. If he slithered a few feet to the right, he'd be able to climb out, but without direction, he may never spot the nearly invisible escape route.

Kent paddled against the current, attempting to communicate with the stranded kid. Over the roar of the rapids, he yelled toward the fear-frozen teen. Recognition dawned. The boy nodded and then leaned out far enough on the ledge to spot the narrow trail hidden beneath the ferns. After a quick thumbs-up, the boy began his climb.

Kelsey scanned the river, trying to spot the teen's empty kayak or his buddies downstream. Seeing nothing, she signaled to Kent before she paddled on.

A cluster of four boats around the next bend, one kayak missing a person, accounted for his friends. With no room to pull up, she slid past into the drop at Wishbone, hoping the group would follow her well-chosen line. If they were experienced and paid attention, this group might have a chance. After the next two drops, the river widened into a pool with a steep but serviceable trek back to the road. Once the group caught up, she'd encourage them to climb out.

After landing her plunge, Kelsey spun and paused in the wide pool at the base of the falls to watch their attempt—and be there if the situation got hairy. A paddler appeared. Caught up in the adrenaline rush, he boofed into an easy aerated landing. He pulled alongside, his grin wide, waiting for his remaining friends before they took on the rapids in the skinny, fern-lined gorge.

Her curl of tension eased. These guys might be young, but they seemed to have their shit together. At the top, an orange kayak hung back, his hesitation exposed raw panic. The boy came over the drop, penciled into a hole and instantly disappeared. Hydraulic foam sucked him under, burying his boat behind a curtain of turbulent white.

"Fuck." Kelsey grimaced as the boy's paddle popped to the surface. Digging in, she sped toward the base of the falls, while praying he had the strength to hand-roll or pop the skirt and swim.

The foaming water gave her paddle nothing to grasp, and Kelsey's boat floundered in the aeration, but she still managed to find his orange hull pinned to the wall by a boil of raging water. He was trying to push off the rock face but needed more space to maneuver. Taking hold of the grab loop on his boat, she pulled with everything she had. The effort gained the teen enough space to punch out and escape the cockpit.

Now a swimmer, he worked toward shore, lucky to see two friends, one in a kayak the other following the trail along the rocks on the bank. His buddy waded in after him, up to his knees.

Waist-deep in water, the skinny kid stared at Kelsey, his eyes wide with fear. Caught in the current, she dug her blade, but the froth gave her nothing to grab. While Kelsey's boat floundered, time slowed, and her eyes locked on that kid. His mouth gaped open in a silent scream. Then suddenly, everything stopped.

***

The kid at the top of the falls had heard tales about this epic run, but if a girl could do it, then so could he. Just like he'd seen on YouTube, he lifted his knees and pushed off, whooping and smiling with the weightless sensation—until the boat he'd borrowed from his brother hit something solid.

Fuck. Was that a log?

His cheap-as-shit paddle flopped around and there wasn't any resistance in the churning foam. He looked toward shore and found his buddy pushing toward him in knee-deep water, screaming, scrambling, reaching.

Something popped to the surface a few feet in front of him. Bobbing like a toy, a green kayak hull bounced against a rock. *That girl.* Limp and upside down, she disappeared down the fern-lined canyon into a boil of white. Beneath the churning surface, he could barely discern her dangling arms and blonde hair hanging like a curtain in the water below the hull of her overturned kayak.

***

Kent couldn't decipher the chaos. From his spot above the drop, people seemed to be scrambling every direction. He chose his route and made his way to help Kelsey rescue this pack of idiots.

But when he landed in the pool below Wishbone, Kels wasn't anywhere in sight. A kid standing and struggling against the current yelled wildly, flailing his arms down river. Kent prepared for the worst, but never imagined the slow-motion horror of the next few minutes.

He paddled past the first turn into the canyon and found Kelsey's boat jammed sideways against a moss-covered rock. A young guy had maneuvered his kayak below her and was desperately trying to keep her head above water. By jamming himself in place, he used one arm to keep her aloft. The kid's flimsy boat bowed between the current and a boulder, ready to collapse.

Kent knew he had one shot to release her from the cockpit. Working in silent unison, they slung her limp body across the nose of his kayak, ripped away her spray skirt, and hauled her to a narrow ledge on shore.

Before Kent could think, he was out of his boat, leaning over her body, and surveying the damage. Her helmet had cracked—split in opposite directions—and a trickle of blood spread beneath her nose. He left the helmet in place as he checked her airway and began rescue respirations. She gurgled and coughed up some water and, thank God, began to breathe on her own.

"Kels! Kels! Can you hear me?" he yelled, willing her to move. When she didn't respond, he clasped her body against his. Her warm breath puffing steadily on his cheek gave him a sliver of hope. Frantic shouts to call 9-1-1 echoed around him as his fingers caressed her cold skin and he breathed with her. *Inhale, exhale, inhale, exhale.*

When Kelsey hacked another bubbling cough, Kent stroked her blood-soaked hair away from her pale cheek. "It's okay, Kels. I've got you." He held her cold hand, while matching his breathing with hers. How long this went on, he didn't know. A burst of activity jolted him from a mental fog, then from above, a rescuer arrived with a metal basket.

"Let go. You need to give us room to work." The medic eased Kent's arms away from Kelsey's rag-doll body. They fit a collar on her neck, strapped her into the basket, and before Kent could process what was happening, hoisted her away on ropes. Kelsey disappeared into the evergreen branches above him, a clump of her wet, blood-stained hair dangled like seaweed through the gaps of the metal cage.

A hand squeezed his shoulder. "Kent, buddy, we got to move. Kels needs you at the hospital." He knew the voice but couldn't respond.

"Why are you here?" Kent blinked at Rick, not noticing the rescue gear Rick wore.

"I got here as quick as I could. Kelsey's on a helicopter bound for Portland. Come on, let me help you climb out."

Kent nodded and mechanically put on the harness. He stood still, then lifted his arms like a child as Rick checked the straps. They scrambled, dangled, and scrambled again before the team of rescuers hauled them to the road above the river.

Hands touched him. Someone took his pulse and asked a few questions. Kent stumbled as Rick led him to the passenger side of a waiting SUV. The engine growled, and rapid acceleration pushed his body against the seat. He stared out the window and watched evergreen trees whiz by on a silent descent from the foothills of the cascades.

EIGHT

With beer running low, the masses at the takeout on Drano Lake began to pack up their gear. Brayden helped, distracted by his plans for tonight. He wouldn't be joining his friends at Mosquito Creek taproom. Instead, Braydon had agreed to meet Kelsey at Northside Grill with a mob of locals. Even after she put the brakes on last night, he wanted to stay on for a few days in Ashwood. The option appealed to him more than leaving right away for the coast.

He'd never met a girl who was this captivating. With eyes that flashed from green to blue when her mood shifted, and the way she cared deeply about her friends, Kelsey Fisher was someone he wanted to know better. He didn't intend to leave the States without nailing down future plans with this woman.

The roar of rotors cut through the air and Brayden tipped his head skyward. Everyone on the shore tracked the path of a life flight helicopter swooping low. When it banked hard and turned north to follow the path of The Little White, he felt the concussion of the blades in his chest. The helicopter raced toward the horizon, hung like a dragonfly, then disappeared into the towering evergreens.

Brayden scanned the crowd, took a headcount, and wondered who was missing. The locals—Kent, Amanda, Kelsey. *Shit. They'd planned that final run.* His mouth went dry. Frantic, he found Kelsey's number.

The call went unanswered—not unusual—and Brayden swallowed panic. Her phone was probably stowed in her dry bag or hidden in her car. Still, he couldn't shake uneasy nausea. He rushed to a woman who was carrying a handheld radio. "Hey, do you know what's going on?" he blurted.

Eyes wide, she took too long to answer. "One of the safety team. Oh my God, I can't believe it, a drone must have caught the whole thing, because our drone pilot is totally freaking out."

Brayden didn't give a flying fuck about the person running the drone. "Damn it, who was injured?"

"A local, and I totally know who it is. We've been staying at her house this weekend. I think her name is Kelly."

She had the name wrong, yet he knew instantly—that helicopter was picking up Kelsey. Brayden grabbed her shoulders, wondering why this stupid girl had been trusted with a fucking radio. "Do you have a car?"

She winced and yanked her arm away. "A van. Why?"

"I need to see how she is."

The girl nodded but didn't move. He yanked her forward, pulling her to the line of waiting vans. "Which one?"

Staggering toward the closest van, she fished her keys from her pocket. She glanced into the empty van then back at Brayden. "I can't leave everyone here."

"Just take me to Ashwood. You can come back."

"I guess I could do that." With a nod and a nervous sigh, she opened the driver's side door and climbed inside. She turned the key, backed out slowly, and moved toward the main highway. Brayden considered pushing her out as she waited for oncoming traffic to pass.

The van shook as the helicopter flew directly overhead and disappeared into the western sky. "Forget Ashwood. Take me to Portland!"

"I can't do that! This van doesn't belong to me. And you don't even know where they're taking her."

"Give me your radio." He snatched the device from her hand and turned up the volume. He didn't have to speak, the frantic chatter on the channel told him everything he needed to know. Brayden lost a short shouting match and eventually agreed to go back to Ashwood. Catching a ride to Portland from there wasn't difficult—he wasn't the only one making the frantic run.

***

Kent sat shoulder to shoulder with Rick in the ICU waiting room. The crowded room was hot, and a snore rumbled from his friend. With a baby at home and another on the way, the poor guy probably never slept. Every few minutes Kent looked up as another person tried to find a spot in the stuffy space. Finally, he couldn't take it anymore, and escaped to pace the hallway.

The hall was quiet, except for a mechanized hum that resonated throughout this wing of the hospital. The annoying noise was as pervasive as the sterile odor. While he paced, Kent spotted a man in scrubs walking toward the waiting room. The surgeon stepped inside to share the first shred of news with Mary and Dale Fisher. Hidden from their line of sight, he listened from the doorway.

Kelsey, his best friend, the only person who had always stuck by him, was alive but in a medically induced coma. This coma was part of the treatment to give her body and brain time to heal. She would be on life support while a cocktail of drugs circulated through her system. Her parents sobbed through terrifying questions—what are her chances . . . how bad is her brain injury . . . will she ever wake up?

The jumbled answers tumbled loud in Kent's head—observe her progress, young and healthy, quickly recover from her abrasions, broken ribs, shoulder dislocation. Still numb, he heard but couldn't comprehend how this could have happened. They were just taking a final run down the river to finish the weekend right.

Kent turned and moved quickly down the hall. With little warning, he bent in half and threw up into a garbage can. After a final gut-wrenching heave, he couldn't straighten and stand. Elbows on his knees, he spit, swiped his mouth with the back of his hand, and saw stars. *Fuck. Just don't pass out.* A small hand met the center of his back.

"I'm sorry," he groaned, embarrassed, and left his head down.

"Don't worry about it." The cool fingers squeezed his shoulder. "Can I get you anything?"

"No. I'll be okay." He escaped to the bathroom, rinsed his mouth, and used a few paper towels to wash his face. Staring at his reflection, he was surprised he didn't look physically different, because nothing felt the same. When he pushed open the bathroom door, the same woman in scrubs met him with a can of Sprite in her hand.

"I thought you might need this, to settle your stomach. I'm sorry, you must have had difficult news."

Kent accepted the cold aluminum can from her outstretched hand. "My friend's in the ICU."

"I know she'll get the best care possible." Her soothing fingers touched his forearm and squeezed. "I've got to finish my rounds."

Kent popped the top. The hiss swiveled her eyes back to his. "Thanks," he said.

She held his gaze for a moment and smiled. After a quick nod, she padded silently down the hall in blue rubber shoes that looked too big on her small feet.

A second lemon-lime gulp gave him a hit of sugar that woke his senses. Unfortunately, the hit also brought everything back. Kent sank his butt onto the floor and folded himself to contain the overwhelming pain. He'd only wanted time with Kelsey. She'd been so busy lately, with Venture, he could practically feel her slipping away. While trying to steal a few moments with her on the river, he'd nearly killed his best friend. Fuck. She had to wake up.

With his legs bent in an A-shape he tipped his head down and gazed at the floor between his shoes. Numb, he stared at the aqua-blue flecks embedded in the beige tiles. Each speck glittered, the same color as Kelsey's eyes.

NINE

"Thanks, Amanda." With a pained smile, Kent took the white paper bag from her hand. She'd brought him a Tillamook cheeseburger and fries. Amanda passed the strawberry milkshake, no whipped cream, just the way he liked it.

Amanda tried not to cry. "I wish I could do more." She'd never felt so guilty or so useless. Eyes hot, she studied the broken version of Kent. He looked terrible—dark circles ringed his eyes and his beard grew in patchy. He seemed fragile and Amanda's empty hands twitched, longing to hold him, but Kent wouldn't let anyone close.

The hospital limited the numbers in the ICU, and this fact kept everyone except Kent and the Fishers at a distance. But that turned out to be a blessing. The moment Parker Knight posted the video Amanda captured with the drone, the calls from the media had been relentless.

Amanda shuffled foot-to-foot, waiting, and hoping that Kent would ask for something more than his favorite fast food. She'd do anything to lessen his pain.

"This is great. Really." He looked at the floor then down the long hallway behind her, anywhere but her eyes. Clearly, Kent didn't want her around. "I better get back," he mumbled.

She started to reach for him, to give him a quick hug, but he turned and walked away. Amanda watched the elevator doors close behind him and stepped in a wide circle, with no particular place to go. The numbers standing vigil in the ICU waiting room had dwindled once Kelsey was stable. Even her sister, Elizabeth, had gone home to take care of her active little boys.

Part of Amanda wanted to drive back to Ashwood and hide at home. Her mom and dad would welcome it, yet, every day she spent away from Hood River added another layer of stress to her already hectic schedule. She needed to get back to school and to the captivity of her internship with Parker Knight.

Amanda took a wrong turn in the hospital. *Great.* On top of everything, she'd turned herself around in the confusing labyrinth of identical corridors. While she searched for signs that would lead her to the main lobby, her phone buzzed. An email from Parker Knight held her in place. Gulping, she read the words twice.

Amanda - Your footage has gone viral. Get to Portland. Line up an interview with Kent. I want his candid reaction to the rescue. Use your time at the hospital to talk to the family. Don't worry about perfection. Just use your phone to get some footage. Even a glimpse of Kelsey would be great. Awesome work with the drone - keep it up - Parker.

Her stomach threatened to bring up her breakfast. *What the hell? Viral. More footage of Kelsey? Not doing it.* Recalling the way he looked, Amanda knew a candid reaction from Kent would be nothing but a visual document of a broken man. She didn't even consider the possibility. Light-headed, Amanda turned off her phone and buried her device in her pocket. Maybe she could delete the message or say she never got it. Maybe she could toss her phone in the Willamette River. But her grade and internship were on the line.

Amanda knew that with every passing second, the viral video brought Parker greater recognition, and the whole thing was entirely her responsibility. Kelsey had asked her not to film that final run, but she had made the call to put the drone in the air.

Sprinting toward the nearest exit, she had to leave. If she wasn't in Portland, she couldn't do Parker's bidding. One elevator ride and a few turns put her in sight of the main parking lot. On a sprint for the door, a familiar face caught her eye. Hunkered near the exit, a haggard version of Brayden stared at nothing.

"Brayden?"

***

He couldn't pull her face into focus. Brayden blinked but his eyes felt like sandpaper. "Oh, Amanda, it's you."

"How long have you been here?" she asked.

"Since the accident."

"For three days?"

The high pitch of her voice hurt his head. He nodded slowly. "I just need to know . . . is she . . . did she?"

"Oh, no, Brayden, she didn't." Amanda's unspoken words hung in the air.

Thank God, Kelsey hadn't died.

Amanda planted herself in the seat next to his and grabbed his hand. "But it's not good. The doctors have her on a ventilator while she's in a medically induced coma. Something about giving her brain time to recover."

A padlocked memory broke free of its chains. Brayden pulled his hand from hers and broke out in an instant sweat. Everything flooded back in this too familiar setting. His buddy capsizing. Trapped in his boat. Water. Fighting the suck of a vicious hydraulic. Frantic resuscitations on a muddy riverbank. Waiting. Praying. Weeks of false hope. Death.

He had to get out. Brayden stood. His knees wobbled then held. "Bloody hell, I have to go. I'm sorry." He bent and gathered the duffle he'd shoved beneath his seat. Without looking back, he shuffled toward the door.

"Wait." Her voice turned him around, but his feet landed near the front entrance and the wide glass door swished open behind him—he was steps away from escape.

"Where are you going?" Amanda caught up as he backed into the warm sunlight.

"To the airport." He stared at the parking lot and remembered he didn't have a car. "Could you give me a ride?"

"Sure. Wherever you want to go."

His hand scraped over several days' growth on his chin. Looking down, he'd worn the same rumpled shorts for days. "Damn. I reckon I stink."

Amanda touched his shoulder. "It's okay." On the way, she convinced him to stay at a hotel near the airport, just for one night. She dropped him off. He ate, showered, slept for twelve hours, then caught a flight, but not toward home. He flew to Hawaii to escape the memory of a woman he barely knew.

TEN

At first, Kent figured moving one floor below the ICU was a good sign. Kelsey's parents thought so, too. There were fewer tubes, machines, and monitors, and Kels could have more visitors, even her sister and her two rambunctious nephews. But in the back of his mind, Kent wondered if the staff was giving up on her, because so little had changed.

Her doctor said the brain swelling had responded well to the medication. The drug cocktail was gradually being tapered, and they all waited for Kelsey to give a sign of real hope.

From his perch in the doorway, Kent watched Mary stroke Kelsey's hand. Blue veins showed through her pale skin, lean fingers unmoving in her mother's grasp. Her pale blonde hair, tangled wildly across her pillow, took on a greenish cast under the harsh hospital lights. This wasn't Kelsey. She'd hated sitting still.

"Please, sweetheart, wake up," her mother begged, squeezing her hand, but the touch got no response. Mary looked so tired, and she wouldn't take a break. Kent worried about Mary, a woman he owed everything. Kelsey's mom had been there for him since kindergarten—from the day his own sorry excuse for a mother had taken off.

His hand found Mary's shoulder. "Let me take a turn."

"Thank you, Kent." She stretched as she stood. "I think I'll wander down to the cafeteria and get something to eat. I won't be long."

"Take all the time you need. Oh, and don't forget to take the elevators in the old wing."

Mary grimaced. "Got it." Everyone connected with Kelsey was hiding from Parker.

Yesterday, Kelsey's dad had spotted one of her minions taking pictures of their lakeside home from a motorboat floating a few feet offshore on Osprey Lake. There wasn't a thing they could do to stop them—the lake and the boat launch were open to the public.

Still worried about Mary, Kent sank onto the warm chair. This small room wasn't his entire life. He'd trimmed his hours at Whitewater Homes, leaving enough time to drive into Portland nearly every day. But Mary hadn't returned to Ashwood since the day of the accident. Her husband, older daughter, and Kent insisted that she needed to take a break. She smiled and explained that as long as Kelsey was in Portland, this was where she intended to stay.

Kelsey twitched slightly when Kent lowered the rail on the bed. At first, he hoped she was responding to him, but her arms jerked and then settled again, all on their own. These sudden movements—new and out of control—bothered him more than her once peaceful stillness.

After she quieted, he scooted the uncomfortable plastic seat closer, found the bed's remote, and lowered her a few inches so he could reach his arm across her waist and feel her breathe.

"You feel like watching TV today? I could order pizza, deluxe extra cheese. I'll even leave on the onions."

Her breathing changed slightly, and Kent paused, unable to move, afraid that if he chose to do something, it would be wrong. When she resumed the normal pattern, a steady inhale, exhale, inhale, he kept talking.

"You won't believe it. My dad's on his way to see you. He's bringing a load to Boise and coming here the day after tomorrow." Kent shifted and pulled his arm from around her waist to hold her hand, hoping to feel a returning squeeze.

"I don't think Dad ever cut a trip short for me when I got hurt. Not even that time I broke my arm when I fell out of that big cedar by the lake." He laughed aloud. "Shit, your dad was pissed that day. But, hey, I didn't force you to follow me up that tree. You know, we never did build that fort."

That summer, between third and fourth grade, had started rocky. The treehouse plan was off, and with a cast, he'd lost swimming and climbing privileges, at least at the Fishers' place. Eventually, he and Kels figured out a way to duct tape a garbage bag to his arm so he could swim. And he learned to climb trees just fine with one good hand.

Kelsey was close to her sister, but Kent knew the bond he shared with his best friend was tighter. Kels had to love her family, but she chose to love him. He lay his head across her stomach and breathed her in. The hospital smell tried to mask it, but when he was close, he could smell her favorite lotion. Each time the nurses gave Kelsey her bath, Mary smoothed it on her daughter's arms.

Kent sniffed and closed his eyes. A tear dripped from the corner, leaving a warm trail toward his temple. "Damn it, I'm so sorry, I know how much you hate crying. Shit, if only I'd gone down the river first. Or if we left earlier. No. We shouldn't have gone at all. God, Kels, I'd change places with you if I could."

He lifted his head enough to wipe the tears from his cheek with the back of his hand. "You gotta wake up. I need your advice. I think I'm falling in love with Amanda, and you know this is new territory for me. I need your help to convince her I've changed." Kent sighed, long and slow when she didn't move.

Damn it, he listened to the chirp of the monitor and her heart rate didn't even change. If *that* revelation didn't reach Kelsey, nothing would. The room seemed to shrink around him when a stark realization hit. There was a real chance Kelsey might never wake up. The IV pole beeped with another alarm, ending his bedside confession.

In a few moments, a nurse appeared to change out the bag of medication, smiling as she came in. He'd grown used to the frequent routine, and without being asked, he stood and yanked the sheets to help reposition Kelsey's limp body in her bed.

Before she left, the nurse asked if he needed anything. He said no—the staff here worked hard enough and didn't need an extra burden. The nurse turned toward him before she left. "Have you thought about bringing her favorite music or maybe food?"

"Food. Why? Kels can't eat." The idea seemed cruel to him.

"Sounds, smell, touch—all these things fire different parts of your girlfriend's brain."

Kent nodded but didn't bother to correct her misconception. "I'll see what I can pull together, thanks."

All the staff assumed Kels was his. Not true. Even while perfectly still, Kelsey Fisher belonged only to herself, everything about her was much too free to be contained.

***

Mark stared at swaying palm trees and listened to the crashing surf. He chased away his worry with another gulp of local beer. At least a dozen text messages he'd sent to Kelsey went unanswered. At first, he figured she was somewhere on a mountain trail, probably happy to be far away from towers, completely unplugged. He got that about her—disappearing off-grid was a secret pleasure they shared.

But she'd never gone this long without at least a picture or a hello. The next swallow of beer didn't go down as smooth. He didn't think she would move on with another guy without at least saying goodbye. Still, he couldn't shake the feeling that something was off. Heading to the States early was an option, but if he went, he'd drag Kelsey back to this spot.

She'd love this hide-away. They could burrow in, eat regional food, and drink local beer. They'd lose track of time, just the two of them carrying their boards on a secret path to a private, local surf spot. He took another sip of beer, knowing this perfect gem wouldn't go on his blog—revealing it, and worse, profiting from it, just felt wrong.

As Mark inhaled the tropical breeze, he convinced himself that everything was fine. Kelsey might be unreachable in the Cascade Range for days or even weeks, and when she emerged, she'd laugh at the ridiculous number of messages he'd sent. Shit, he was gone for that woman.

God, he wished she was here.

***

Armed with the instructions from Kelsey's nurse, Kent was on a mission. Within days, he'd crowded her sterile hospital room with vivid reminders of home.

He'd already brought chocolate cookies from Goldfinch Bakery, the cozy afghan her grandma crocheted, and her favorite gray sweatshirt—the one with holes in the cuffs. It smelled like she'd just pulled it off after a hike, leaving it infused with the scent of her lotion and campfire smoke. When he'd found it under a pile of blankets at her house, he put it to his nose, inhaled, and sunk onto her unmade bed and cried.

Jogging past the nurses' station, he waved and smiled, ignoring the flirtatious glances from the now familiar faces behind the desk. Kent pulled Kelsey's fully charged phone from his pocket. He was ready to put the device in her hand and give it a call. He hoped that a vibration and familiar ringtone might nudge her back to the present.

Kent stopped cold as he entered Kelsey's room. She was sitting up, hands covered, arms tethered. "What's going on?"

Mary's smile mingled with the ever-present exhaustion lining her face. "I think your efforts paid off." A sob broke through her words. "You did it, Kent."

"Thank God." Crossing the room, he covered Kelsey's sock covered hand with his. Her aquamarine eyes weren't quite as bright, but at least she tracked his movements with broken jerks.

"What's all this?" he asked wanting to rip the restraints away.

"She's trying to tear out her IV's. The doctor said it's normal."

Dale appeared in the doorway, bringing his wife a meal. "Are you sure you want to eat in here?" Dale seemed worried about both his wife's exhaustion and his daughter's recovery.

"I want to stay. She perks up when she smells food. Do you want an apple or half of my sandwich?" Mary asked, offering Kent the bland cafeteria fare.

He'd learned to eat before he walked into the hospital. "No, thanks. I already grabbed something on the road."

When she gave up the seat closest to Kelsey, Kent spun the chair to focus on beautiful, stormy eyes he hadn't seen in weeks. The azure color hit him, and emotion swelled in his chest, making it difficult to breathe. To keep from crying, Kent half-listened while Kelsey's parents discussed alternatives they'd been given for their daughter's long-term care. It wouldn't be long before she had to move from the hospital to rehab. All the best options were in Portland, far from Ashwood. Shit, she wasn't coming home.

An optimistic voice called through the door. "Knock, knock, it's just me." Natalie stepped inside, her arms loaded with things for Kelsey. Her husband, Seth, hung back in the hall with his brother-in-law, Ben. Suddenly, the room was bursting with more people than the rules allowed.

"Oh, Kelsey, you're sitting up!" Natalie put her bundles on the foot of the bed and rushed to hug Kelsey. The heart monitor sped, and her breathing changed, but other than that, she didn't respond.

"We'll give you all some room," Mary and Dale said in unison, thankful for the unwavering support. Mary took the rest of her lunch down the hall, to eat in a quiet alcove near the elevators.

Ben squeezed past Kent. Natalie's brother greeted Kelsey with a tender kiss on her forehead. Kent grinned, he didn't mind moving out of Ben's way—everyone knew the guy had a thing for Kelsey.

"What's with the bandages?" Ben asked, stroking Kelsey's blonde hair.

"She tried to take the needles out. That's good, don't you think?" Kent glanced hopefully from Natalie to Ben.

"I think that's very positive," Seth answered from his spot by the door.

"I've got a stack of cards from friends and snickerdoodles from Aunt Elsa." Natalie took a seat by Kelsey, ready to read the cards aloud. As she opened each get-well message, she commented on the images and held the sentiments in front of Kelsey's unaware gaze.

After laying the cards at the end of the bed, Natalie popped the plastic lid from a container of fresh cookies. With a quick jerk that shook the bed, Kelsey's arms snapped against the restraints.

Natalie smiled hopefully and waved the cookies under Kelsey's nose. "These do smell delicious. Here, take a whiff, Elsa made them just for you."

A low moan charged the atmosphere in the room. Kelsey blinked and licked her lips. Kent held his breath and stared. For the first time in three weeks, her movements seemed intentional.

***

Kelsey pulled her arms through soothing tropical water... so clear, so warm. No matter how far she swam, her sluggish muscles barely made any progress and she couldn't find the surface. Yet, she didn't want to go to shore—her buoyant watery world was so peaceful. She'd never held her breath this long. Maybe something had changed, and she'd turned into a mermaid.

Her stomach growled. No wonder her arms wouldn't bring her to the surface. She'd skipped breakfast. Kelsey swallowed. Starving, thirsty. No, she'd gone beyond thirsty—her lips were dry, and her mouth was parched. But how was that possible under all this water? It had to be a dream.

Kelsey broke the surface. It was glaringly bright, but the sunlight didn't warm her face. Something, maybe seaweed, was tangled around her arms and she struggled against the bindings. *Somebody help. I need to get free or I'll drown. Stop struggling. Just float and let the water support you. Don't panic and you'll be fine.*

***

"Pure glass."

"Glass? Are you thirsty, Kels?" Natalie swiveled, looking for water. Kent stood wide-eyed, not knowing what he should do.

"Sunrise session. Pure glass," Kelsey rasped.

Seth moved first, rushing to the nurses' station. "She's talking. What should we do?" he asked as a guy looked up from his computer. The nurse stood and moved calmly into Kelsey's room, followed closely by her parents.

The nurse spoke with a firm, yet friendly voice. "Hey, Kelsey, nice to meet you. I'm Chris." Her eyes squinted at him. "Why don't we have a few of you wait in the hall while Kelsey adjusts," Chris said.

No one moved too far, deciding to stay huddled in a clump near the door.

"What did she say?" Mary asked, "I can't believe I missed her first words."

Natalie took hold of Mary's hand. "Sounded like '*Pure glass.*' I offered her water and then Kels said, '*Sunrise session. Pure glass.*' Do you know what that means?"

Seth put his arm around his wife. "It means she's back."

***

The end of visiting hours pushed Kent from the hospital. He grinned, his steps as weightless as a rock skipping across the surface of Osprey Lake. Distracted by joy, he didn't hear the slapping foot falls trailing close behind.

"Hold up," the voice called from over his right shoulder.

Almost every night he had to avoid these fucking piranhas. "What do you want?" he barked on a turn.

"Aren't you Kent Thomas—the hero who rescued Kelsey Fisher?" Kent stared into eager eyes. This guy was new—neatly trimmed beard, crisp flannel shirt, and pristine hiking boots. He probably bought his Northwest costume in the airport. What a fucking poser.

"Who wants to know?"

"I'm with Parker Knight. We want to get an accurate update from you about Kelsey's condition." Kent was impressed, this guy had the balls to aim a very expensive video camera right at his face. "We heard she's awake. Do you think she'd be willing to talk with us?"

The speed of the facts was *too damn good*—someone in the hospital was feeding Parker Knight information. Kent cupped his palm over the end of the lens. "I'm only saying this once. If you don't get the fuck out of here, I'm going to shove this camera up your ass."

The fool wouldn't back off. "Hey, I'm just doing my job. You and Kelsey Fisher are famous. Dude, that rescue footage, it was epic man, totally viral."

Kent's neck heated. Growling past clenched teeth, his lips barely moved. "Tell me you didn't just say *viral.*" The guy shrugged and huffed a laugh. Swift as a striking snake, Kent snatched the camera from the douchebag's scrambling fingers.

"Wait. You can't take that, it's private property."

Camera in hand, Kent turned and walked toward his truck. "Don't worry, dipshit, I'll make sure Parker gets it back," he yelled without turning around.

The guy ran after him, Kent spun and held the camera away from his body at shoulder-height. "One more step and I'm smashing this piece of expensive shit to the ground."

"Fine, but if we don't get it back, I'm calling the cops."

"You do that."

The ninety-minute drive barely diminished his fury. Kent walked through his front door and set the camera on a table. After a couple of whisky shots, he recorded his own footage, telling Parker Knight what would happen if her people got too close to Kelsey again.

The next morning, he stared at the camera. Deleting his impromptu video felt weak, so he left the rant intact. It would have been easy to drive thirty miles to Hood River and personally deliver the equipment to Parker's favorite intern. But he couldn't face Amanda—he simply didn't have the strength to keep his feelings for her in check. Especially now that she'd moved on. Not long after the accident she stopped coming to the hospital, too busy for him and everyone else from Ashwood. No, sending the camera Fed-Ex was better, less personal. Amanda was gone.

She didn't bother to call or text when she got it, but Kent knew the camera had arrived. By the week's end, he caught snippets of his footage, artfully edited, on Parker's blog.

ELEVEN

"I can't fucking do it!" Flung by her fury, a walker whizzed across her hospital room and crashed against the wall. One lone tennis ball escaped the walker's aluminum leg, hopped through the door, and wobbled down the hospital corridor. From his hiding place around the corner, Kent watched the yellow ball escape and prepared for what he knew was coming next. He could scarcely breathe as Kelsey's first sob echoed the depth of her frustration.

Natalie grasped Kent's shoulder and pulled him away from the doorway. "She won't be like this forever," she whispered barely loud enough for him to hear. He didn't know how Natalie did it. Solid and patient, she remained optimistic even though Kelsey hadn't been able to recognize her or remember their friendship.

Kent nodded, took a deep breath, then slipped into Kelsey's room, standing back when the therapist righted the walker and left it within Kelsey's reach. "We'll try again tomorrow," her therapist said as he grabbed a clipboard and left for the day. Once her therapist crossed the threshold Kelsey used the tip of her foot to nudge the walker away.

Grasping the walker, Kent leaned his weight over the handles and met his best friend's eyes. "If you walk down the hall and back with me..." He glanced at the tiled floor, struggling to come up with something Kelsey couldn't resist. "...I'll make you Rice Krispy Treats."

Kelsey's eyes narrowed, staring him down. He didn't care if she knew she was being manipulated—so long as she wanted what he offered.

"Extra goopy?" Kelsey asked.

He gave her a nod. "Yup. Just the way you like them. "

"Fine. Where are they?"

Damn, she wanted the reward now. "Give me a sec." Kent dashed into the hall and found Natalie waiting.

"I got this," she said. "Ben's place isn't far. I'll be back in no time."

"I'm so glad your brother lives in Portland." Kent leaned in, carried by optimistic joy, and kissed her cheek. "Thanks for this, Nate."

He moved cautiously and suppressed a smile when Kelsey agreed to start walking. He'd chosen her reward wisely—she'd always been addicted to anything marshmallow. Sweat left a dark line down the back of her shirt on her second lap around the hospital floor. Rounding the corner of the hallway, Kent glanced ahead and found Natalie emerging from the elevator carrying a pan brimming with marshmallow goodness.

"Have you had enough?" he asked.

Kelsey stared at the floor and set her jaw. "One more lap." In one ecstatic glance, Kent and Natalie celebrated while Kelsey took another determined step.

When she finished, they huddled in her room over the goopy marshmallow and cereal square reward.

"Thanks, Nate, you've always made the best Rice Krispy Treats." Kelsey mumbled around another bite.

"You remember me?" Natalie asked, her eyes brimming with tears.

A nod confirmed it and Kelsey took another bite. She hadn't made much of either achievement, but an incredible hurdle had been crossed. Momentum carried Kelsey forward. Her exercises expanded, the walker disappeared, and her physical therapists added Thera bands and weights. Each morning PT stressed her body, and every afternoon she played games to strengthen her mind. Kent, Natalie, and Ben traded off days, shared every step, and stayed to hang out, always armed with sweet rewards.

***

Kelsey could have kissed her sister when Elizabeth asked Mom to take the boys out to get their favorite treats. She giggled when an argument broke out over which flavor of donut was better. One little guy insisted that the Fruit Loop topped donuts were the bomb, while his younger brother claimed that the Captain Crunch were the *very, very best*. Her nephews' voices disappeared when the elevator doors shut, and Kelsey burst out laughing.

Her sister joined in and flopped onto the hospital bed, then they both ended the belly laugh with a sigh.

"I bet my boys smuggle you a chocolate donut, one topped with sprinkles," Elizabeth said.

"I don't know. They'd have to get it past Mom." Kelsey shook her head. "She's worse than the nurses."

"Oh, is Mom driving you crazy?"

"Crazy doesn't begin to cover it. She hovers every time I move, quizzes me like a gameshow host, and just yesterday I had to kick her out of the bathroom while I was taking a shower. I swear, she was afraid I'd fall and hit my head."

"I know, but she was so worried. Sis, we all were." The silence between them said more than words ever could. If Kent hadn't pulled her from the water, she'd be gone.

"I brought you something." Elizabeth grinned as she pulled a bag filled with a pink manicure set and three colors of polish from her oversized purse. "I know this isn't really *you*, but it's been so long." Elizabeth giggled just like when they were little girls, sneaking into Mom's room to steal her bright red lipstick.

"A manicure! What a great idea." Kelsey crisscrossed her legs on the hospital bed, directly across from her sister. She actually missed being able to indulge in this simple pleasure. Rock climbing had kept her nails super short and the paddles she handled gave her wicked callouses. Now, when she glanced down at her hands, she saw long healthy nails and smooth skin.

Her sister pulled out a new file for each of them and they went to work. "You know, when we used to do this, we talked about boys." Elizabeth leaned back on the bed to peek down the hall. "Are there any hot doctors making rounds today?"

"Doctors? Yeah, but not as smokin' as the new physical therapist. I swear, he went into that line of work just to have twenty-four-hour access to a gym."

"Is he as good looking as your surfer?" Elizabeth asked with a teasing grin.

"Surfer?" Kelsey glanced out the window trying to place someone who floated beyond the edge of her recollection. "I'm not sure who you're talking about."

"Oh, you kept that guy to yourself for over a year. You'd sneak off to the coast and meet Mark whenever he was around." Elizabeth didn't push, not like her mother would have.

"Mark." Kels bit her lip, waited, and shook her head when she got nothing.

"Don't worry about it, Sis, you'll remember him when you're ready."

A shrug dismissed the thought. "I guess." While she tried to recall even the faintest echoes of the surfer, Kelsey went through the motions of her manicure—soaking her hands and applying lotion. Feeling like a twelve-year-old again, she carefully mimicked each step of the ritual to get everything just right.

She relaxed into each step and joked about how hyper her nephews would be filled with all that sugar. Elizabeth groaned, and Kelsey snorted at her sister's expense, but her laughter stopped when her sister twisted open the cap from the bottle of polish.

The potent smell overwhelmed Kelsey's senses and bright light suddenly crowded her vision. Her arms tightened as vicious tremors took hold. Pulled by a wave she couldn't control, Kelsey's speech slurred. Elizabeth moved quickly from the bed, and all their supplies crashed to the floor. A swishing sound filled her ears, then nurses surrounded her, grasping while struggling to keep her on the bed.

As her senses returned, Kelsey closed her eyes to try and shut out the feel of the hands invading her personal space. Her senses sharpened, voices loud and frantic, and her nostrils burned, assaulted by the scent of the fingernail polish.

"Leave me alone!" she yelled, in words that came out garbled and raw.

Kelsey curled into a ball. Holding her legs, she tried to hide the warm pee that had soaked her yoga pants, blankets, and mattress. She lay there, exhausted, wanting only sleep, listening while her sister cried.

***

The seizure was only a minor set-back and didn't alter moving day. Kelsey fought nausea during the entire ride to The Center for Brain Injury. While clutching a little blue puke bag, she told herself this was normal but wondered if her equilibrium was entirely to blame.

"Mom, could you roll down your window."

"Sure, sweetheart. Do you want Dad to pull off the freeway?"

"No, I just need air."

Sixty mile-per-hour wind churned around her, and the turbulence seemed to help. When a gag clogged her throat, she blew a circle of air from her lips to ease it away. The strangled sensation increased again as her dad stopped the car in front of The Center. Then it hit her—she wasn't sick, she was afraid.

The Center was deceptively beautiful—lush lawns hemmed in by perfectly pruned trees. The landscaping surrounded a one-story building painted with welcoming colors, but the cheerful pastels couldn't fool her. By moving to rehab she was merely exchanging Alcatraz for San Quentin. An improvement, but not by much.

Her shuffled steps followed her parents to her room. Mom and Dad turned when her duffle hit the linoleum floor with a solid thud. She kicked it toward the boxes her parents had placed neatly in the corner and abruptly told her parents to get out.

Wide-eyed shock shifted her mother's features as if she'd been slapped. It took Kelsey an extra moment to realize she'd been too blunt. "Mom, I'm sorry."

Her mom plastered on her patient smile. "That's okay, sweetheart. I've planned to stay in Portland. I found one of those extended-stay hotels. It's only a mile from here."

"Please, Mom. I'll be fine. If you leave me on my own in Portland, I'll work even harder to get home."

"But I've already made reservations . . ." she argued.

"Mom, please. Could you at least give me a couple of days to get my bearings?"

"She's right, hon," her dad encouraged. "And her friends will be here."

Her mom's eyes brimmed with rejection tainted tears. "Okay. Fine. But only for tonight. Tomorrow, I'll bring fried chicken and apple pie. Homemade. They have a terrific picnic area where we can enjoy some family time outside."

Kelsey shook her head. "That's too soon. Ben's stopping by today, after he gets off work, and Kent's coming tomorrow. Give me three days, Mom. Please . . . just three days."

Her mother didn't answer, but her chest heaved as she pulled her daughter into a tight squeeze. Once the threat of waterworks was gone, she whispered, "Only if you *promise* to call me if you need *anything.*"

"I've got my cell. I'll call." She nodded against her mom's cheek, barely suppressing her tears. "Go, go, go . . . before I change my mind."

***

Ben left work early to see her. The guy at The Center's front desk seemed to expect him and pointed the way to Kelsey's room. Ben found it, propped his shoulder against the door jamb, and watched Kelsey unpack. She was so beautiful, he could scarcely breathe. With her blonde hair trapped in a ponytail, she looked so eager, even happy—like a college freshman moving into her first dorm. If only this place was that rite of passage.

"Knock, knock." Ben stepped over the threshold.

"Hey!" Kelsey's aqua eyes danced. That honest smile—as it always had—weakened his knees.

"What do you think of my new home?" She laced her fingers in his and pulled him inside.

"It's nice. You've got your own room." Ben led her to the window and slid the curtain open. "And a million-dollar view." He laughed when she growled at him.

"Of the parking lot, smartass." Without releasing his hand, she shoved him sideways with her shoulder. The move didn't shift his sturdy stance. Her thinner body felt different—fragile, almost temporary. Kelsey unlaced her fingers from his, and Ben closed his fist, savoring the lingering warmth.

He settled his hip on the windowsill while she unpacked. Kels didn't have much, but she paid careful attention to the placement of each individual item. "Where is everybody?" he asked. "I thought Kent wanted to help you move in."

Kelsey bit her lip. "Um, I sorta lied to them. Everyone else thinks I'm moving in tomorrow."

Ben snorted a chuckle, but she only shrugged and kept unpacking.

"I didn't want a big fuss. Do you think they'll be mad?"

"Mad? Nah, they'll get it." Ben couldn't help but wonder, *why me*?

Kelsey glanced his way, seeming to hear his thought. "I'm glad you're here," she said. "You're the only one who treats me the same. Everyone else acts like I'm breakable."

Ben nodded but knew his unaltered behavior came from a selfish place. He'd *always* wanted Kelsey and still did. Even after the accident, what he felt for Kelsey had never changed.

"Once I'm finished unpacking, we can take a walk outside and escape this awful hospital smell." Kelsey kicked a cardboard box in his direction, and something rattled inside. "Can you crush that for the recycle bin?" she asked.

"Sure, but where do you want this?" He bent and grabbed her cell phone still attached to the end of its charger.

She met his request with a shrug, and her hand swept the air. "Plug it in...wherever."

He found an outlet behind her bedside table and plugged in the charger. The screen filled with the last image she'd viewed—a tropical paradise.

"Planning to escape?" he asked. With a twist of his wrist, he turned the phone toward Kels so she could take a look.

"Oh, that. Some guy keeps sending pics from his surfing trips. I was checking out his messages and trying my best to remember him." Kels tapped her head. "But so far, no luck."

Ben's jealousy flared, but it also mixed with a selfish dose of relief. *Mark*. She didn't remember him. Carefully, Ben smoothed his reaction. "Is this guy coming to see you?" he asked.

"I don't think so. I haven't even replied to any of his messages."

"Does he know about your accident?"

"Probably. Who doesn't? Haven't you heard? That bitch, Parker Knight, made me famous." Anger and pain laced Kelsey's forced laugh.

Ben put the phone down, closed the distance between them, and reached forward to caress her face. "I'm sorry," he whispered.

"Don't." Kelsey shook her head and stepped away.

Ben accepted her rebuff with a hard swallow. He'd learned to tolerate her rejection over the past couple of years. But now it was different. Even though she might not admit it, she needed him.

The moment he heard about the accident on The Little White, he dropped everything in North Carolina and rushed back to his Portland home. When he realized how much Kelsey needed him, he rearranged his work schedule to help in any way he could.

He'd do anything for Kels, even protect her from Parker Knight. Everyone hated the way that photographer profited from Kelsey's misery. Like vultures, her team descended to peck a few more scraps of tasty information. Without telling Kels, he and all her friends had agreed to keep her new home at The Center a secret—anything to protect her from Parker's relentless hunt.

***

After Ben left The Center, Kelsey went through her usual routine. She stretched for a half-hour to keep her muscles limber, washed her face, smoothed on lotion, then arranged everything carefully on her bedside table before going to sleep.

In the middle of the night her eyes shot open, and her heart thundered in her chest. She couldn't remember where she was or how she'd landed in this unfamiliar place. Reaching to the side, she felt around her bed for a lamp or light then found a familiar lifeline—a hospital call remote on a long cord. The illuminated face seemed a little different, but she located the red button with a white cross on it and held that button down.

She stopped shaking when a soft knock tapped against her door. A compact man with dark hair walked in. The light from the hall spilled around him, making it impossible to see his face.

"Where am I?" Fear frayed her words, and sweat dampened her palms, leaving a wet blotch on the sheets where she clutched it in her fists.

"Can I come in?" he asked.

His calm demeanor let Kelsey release her fingers by a degree. "Just tell me where the hell I am."

He settled into a chair and turned on the lamp. It illuminated the room, but the bare walls didn't give her any clues. She sat up in her slick shorts and tank top to get a better look at the guy.

"Kelsey, my name is Travis. Why don't we start with what you remember, and I'll fill in the gaps?" The way he settled back into the institutional furniture looked like he meant to stay. Her eyes darted around the room, and the mystery seemed more like a game.

"Did you move me to a different wing?"

"No, but we will be continuing your rehab here"

"My parents were here earlier. And Ben. Am I still in Portland?"

"Yes. Mary and Dale will be back to visit in a few days." Travis paused, giving her time to assemble the pieces.

"Okay, now I remember," she blurted, sitting up straight. "The coma—it left me with shit for brains. I'm still in rehab."

Travis chuckled. "That's one way to look at it." He leaned forward onto his elbows and his hands knitted together.

Kelsey swung her legs from under the blankets, sat on the edge of her bed, but didn't try to stand. "How long will I be here?"

"Let's wait a few days before I tackle that question." Travis stood, looking ready to catch her if she decided to make any sudden moves. Kelsey hated that nervous posture and rolled her head back and forth to deal with it.

"Where are my things?"

"In the closet and the dresser," he said.

"Do I have to stay in bed?" she asked, as she recalled the annoying bed alarms in the hospital.

"No. But for tonight, why don't you stay in your room. Are you hungry? We've got popcorn, fruit, and pudding on this wing." His smile was genuine. She nearly took him up on his offer, but she was only craving Rice Krispy Treats.

"No. That's okay."

Kelsey planted her bare feet on the floor, stood slowly, and waited for the sloshy feeling in her head to pass.

"Good, you remembered to take things slow." Travis seemed satisfied, and took a step toward her door, ready to leave her on her own. "See you tomorrow."

"Good night," she said, before the door clicked shut.

Kelsey searched her closet for her tablet, plugged it into the outlet by the bed, and plumped her pillows. She settled in, took a swig from a bottled water, and turned the tablet on.

A slow breath prepared her. She had tried to look twice before, but fear obliterated her curiosity. Typing the photographer's name in the search engine brought Parker's blog to the top of her screen. She selected the site and scrolled down the page. It looked like an Ashwood travel blog—featuring the taproom, Northside Grill, and even her house with its red front door. *Fuck.* Parker Knight had completely invaded her life.

A stock photo of a life flight helicopter looked so harmless, but it was the link she couldn't force her fingers to touch. She held her breath and stabbed it. The video clip began peacefully—dark evergreens towering over a fern-edged river. Two kayaks, one green and the other blue, danced across the rapids, then a precise guitar lick echoed, humming like adrenaline. Kelsey's heart pounded and climbed up her throat. The thin tablet shook in her hands as she shoved it under her blankets, yet the pulsing electric guitar wouldn't stop. Kelsey covered her ears and squeezed her tear-filled eyes to block out the video and terrifying noise.

**

"Get out." Kelsey's anger obliterated Kent's smile, but he didn't turn away. If anything, his steps sped across her room. She locked her eyes straight ahead and ignored him. Crammed at the head of her bed, she hugged her knees to her chest, limbs lost in baggy clothes that used to fit her toned body like a glove. Her jaw clenched, warning him off, daring him to turn around and leave. But her best friend didn't flinch. He stopped a few inches from her and took a deep breath.

"What happened?" he asked, his voice even and smooth.

Kelsey's gritted teeth barely permitted her answer. "You tell me. I thought you were on my team. Turns out you were giving information to the enemy. Do you like playing superhero? Does it help you get laid?"

He flinched when she struck a raw nerve, and Kelsey felt guilty. Almost.

Kent spoke carefully. "You've been on Parker's website. Shit Kels. How much did you see?"

"Enough to know you've got a warped God complex." Her fingers posted air quotes. "*Kent won't let the River Win.* I loved that tagline. Did you *really* single-handedly wake me from a coma? Parker Knight's exclusive says you did."

Her best friend seemed to shrink in size as his solid, athletic body folded to her bed. He bent forward, elbows resting on his knees, hiding his agonized features in his hands. "Did you see it?" He muttered past his fingers. "I mean the accident on the river. Fuck, I haven't had the balls to watch that footage."

His breath hitched on a long inhale, evaporating her anger, leaving pity and fear. She might not like it, but Parker's story wasn't far from the truth. This man, her rock, her best friend, *had* brought her back twice—from the river and from a coma. Yet, Kent wasn't superhuman, and she'd found his kryptonite. One reminder of that moment on The Little White made him weak.

He dropped his hands from his face. A sheen of sweat bloomed over his upper lip and his body trembled. Jesus, he was just as terrified by that viral video footage as she was, possibly more, but for opposite reasons. She would never remember the details of that day, and he couldn't forget each terrifying moment no matter how hard he tried.

"That footage was bullshit, Kels. The day you woke up, some random asshole from Parker's team caught me in the hospital parking lot. I stole his camera, took it home, downed a few shots, then filmed my own interview. They edited every second and manipulated the message."

Kelsey nodded, understanding his predicament. She unfolded from her spot at the head of her bed and let her legs dangle parallel to his.

His gaze tracked to the side, finding her eyes. "I'm sorry. I should've just busted that asshole's camera. Thought if I threatened Parker, she'd leave you alone. It backfired, I guess."

Her hand covered his. "What did you say in that video?"

"I told Parker to back off, or I'd become her worst fucking internet troll—dog her blogs, expose her bullshit, destroy her if I could. Might have worked if I hadn't mailed the camera to Amanda."

"Amanda?" Kelsey held her breath as memories filled empty gaps like a tsunami—a tall girl with dark hair, bubbly, smiling, and way too trusting. Damn it, why hadn't she recalled her friend from Ashwood until now? Her chest tightened and she blinked back tears, but she stored the personal crisis for later when she could deal with the painful lapse on her own.

Lost in his thoughts, Kent stood and staggered toward the window. Looking over the horizon, he blew out a long, slow breath. "Yeah. I bet Amanda cleaned it up. Or used the video to keep Parker happy. A few days later, about ten seconds of my recording appeared on Parker's blog. They'd spliced it with footage from an interview I did in Ashwood."

"An interview, why?"

"I pulled a guy out of the river who busted his leg."

Damn. He was an even bigger hero than she'd imagined. Kelsey stood and paced the room. "I'm sorry. When I saw the video, I overreacted. It was easier to blame you than a woman I don't remember at all. Parker Knight could walk right up to me in the hall and I'd have no clue."

A burst of laughter drained away the remnants of her irritation, but Kent growled, still dealing with his anger. "Shit, she better not try or I'll—"

Kelsey spun. "Don't worry about it. I can't get out and they can't get in. But today I've got a pass, and I'm starving. Didn't you promise me ribs and beer?" She remembered liking both.

"Food, yes. Alcohol no. It'll mess with your meds."

"Fine. Get me out of here." Hungry and impatient, Kelsey grabbed her phone, stuffed it into her pocket, and turned toward the door.

Kent lifted an eyebrow, inspecting her while he smiled. "Maybe you should grab a hat."

Confusion pulled her brows together as she wandered to the mirror above her dresser. "Damn, give me a sec."

She'd forgotten her appearance again. Crap, she'd even gone to the cafeteria this morning with bed head. Not that anyone cared. So long as she showed up dressed, the staff left her on her own for meals. Her needs weren't as demanding as most of the other residents, men and women who'd already spent months at The Center. Her timeline had a foreseeable end—yet getting out frightened her. She wanted independence, but wasn't sure what freedom meant anymore.

***

A week later, Kelsey sank into her seat across from Natalie and Seth. Nate spread out sandwiches on a courtyard picnic table, and Seth looked away, trying unsuccessfully to hide his concern.

Spotting her reflection in the window, Kels couldn't ignore her distorted image. The dark blue sweats she'd pulled on this morning hung from her body like a limp laundry bag. She'd skipped a shower and tied her tangled hair at the back of her head. Her T-shirt wasn't fit for public, but it hid the fact that she hadn't bothered to put on a bra.

Why should she give a shit? It didn't take long for the bright-and-shiny to wear off this place. She saw The Center for what it really was—an expensive nursing home.

Kelsey ignored Natalie's annoying voice, chirping away, carrying on a one-sided conversation...something about Seth building food trucks for restaurants in Portland...blah, blah, blah. Her turkey sandwich tasted like sawdust. She popped the top on her can of soda and washed a dry bite down her throat with a forced gulp. If she opened her mouth to talk, only an angry scream would come out, that and foul-smelling breath, because she hadn't bothered to brush her teeth. Kelsey took another bite of sawdust sandwich, closed her eyes, and chewed.

Seth ignored her silent tantrum and asked if Natalie wanted to visit a local showroom. He told his wife that he needed to check out some new flooring for a tiny home.

Tiny home.

That single detail burrowed. It wiggled in and loosened a lost memory. Natalie's tiny home. Images flashed and jumbled, clicking into place like rusted gears. There was a guy she couldn't quite place. Was it Mark? Maybe.

"I want to go to the beach," Kelsey blurted, surprised when the words jumped from her lips.

"The beach?" Seth repeated.

"That sounds great." Natalie latched onto the idea before Kels had a chance to retract it. "We'll put something together for next week."

Natalie sketched out details while Kelsey listened, stunned silent by the reckless plans. Fear tightened her stomach, but she refused to admit it. Could she endure an escape to something that beckoned, yet also didn't seem real? She wrapped her half-eaten sandwich in the paper and tossed it into the trash. The beach. If there wasn't anything for her there, why did she want it so desperately?

That night, she stared again at the long list of text messages. *Mark.* Who was he really? He'd consistently sent pictures, but the frequency was slowing. His most recent shot was taken on a rugged beach in Australia. He wore a slick wetsuit preparing to take on waves that had the power to separate his limbs from his torso. Damn, that man, whoever he might be, was sexy as hell. A wave of need flashed over her body and faded away just as quickly.

A thin string tethered Kelsey to her past. Where was the woman who craved adrenaline more than air or even sex? Neither interested her much anymore. Yet, a wispy filament remained, attached to all her yesterdays.

Flicking off her bedside lamp, she lay in the dark and tried to recall Mark's details—his voice, his scent, his touch. But all she got was a sense of the ocean. Damn it, she had to find yesterday-Kelsey before she saw this surfer again.

TWELVE

Mark craved this untamed place and the challenge of surfing large swells off Australia's Victoria coast. Wild, rugged, and fierce, the rip was nothing to mess with, and the cold kept beginners away. Clad in a wetsuit, with a hood and boots, he felt like he was back in Washington. While he hummed a slow tune, he searched the rocky shore and found a spot on the horizon. He lifted his gaze and imagined her there—his Mermaid, white-blonde hair blowing in the breeze.

Her silence hadn't bothered him at first. They'd taken breaks from communicating before—he'd be off the grid on a beach, or she'd be too far from a tower in the mountains. Not a big deal. But the silence never stretched this long.

The anxious phase—checking his messages daily—had come and gone weeks ago. To keep from going crazy, he'd mentally let her go but still sent an occasional photo, one that he thought she'd like.

Somewhere along the way, he'd lost Kelsey. A woman that fine wasn't going to wait for a man like him forever. A part of him knew their paths would cross again, someday. And he'd endure the pain when he discovered why Kelsey had moved on.

***

Ben stood in her doorway and winced. Kelsey lay on her unmade bed, eyes focused on the TV attached high on her wall. A heap of clothes lay piled in the corner and shoes littered the floor. A neglected plant drooped in the pot on the windowsill. She ignored him, pressed the remote, and went from *The Price is Right* to *Dr. Phil*.

He'd seen enough. Ben forced himself to take a step into the stale smelling room. "Take a shower, Kels. We're breaking you out of here, at least for today." Glancing around, Ben wondered if she even had clean clothes.

"I don't feel like it." Her eyes cut his way, only for a moment, before they slashed back to the screen.

"I took a day off work to take you to the beach. Get your ass moving. It's close to eighty on the coast, and I'm leaving in twenty minutes with or without you."

"Eighty . . . at the beach?"

Ben nodded and stood between her and the TV screen, blocking her view. Defiant, her eyes flashed aquamarine before she flung the remote at his head. Ready for her outburst, Ben caught the remote mid-air, lifted his eyebrows in victory, and smothered his laugh when she moved.

While she showered, he ducked into Travis's office. "Anything I should know?"

Travis pinched his lips as he considered the question, then answered, "She may get carsick, and she'll probably sleep a lot on the way home. We got her to dangle her feet in the pool yesterday, but Kelsey couldn't go in. Water is still a real issue, so I'm not sure how she'll react to the waves."

Ben took a moment to absorb every detail. "Kent said she wouldn't go near the Columbia when he took her to the park last week. She just walked on the paved paths through the lawn."

"Even though she can't remember the details of the accident, it still grips a piece of her," Travis said with a nod. "Do you have my number?"

"Yeah. And the front desk."

"Just enjoy the day, and don't try to do too much." Her therapist studied Ben for a long moment. "I wish Mary and Dale didn't live so far away. This environment's beginning to hold her back." Travis scrubbed his hand across his face before turning back to his computer.

***

After leaving Portland, Ben drove west, skirting the wide Columbia River on narrow roads that angled toward the coast. Her silence gave his fantasies room to wander, and he questioned his decision to take this trip alone with Kelsey. Even absolutely still, she was so damn tempting.

The sunlight streaming in the windshield heated her perfume, or maybe it was her shampoo. Whatever the scent was, it was warm and spicy, and made his mouth water. Softer and paler than she was last summer, her legs stretched in a slender line from beneath her baggy shorts. Flipping through stations, she listened to music, and wiggled her toes in her flip-flops. Ben wished she would just say something.

"Would you mind if I roll down my window?" Kelsey asked as the trees thinned, and dunes began to hug the highway.

"Go ahead." With the wind whipping, her just-washed platinum hair swirled, and he turned off the music that had filled the gap in their conversation for miles.

Kelsey stuck her hand out the window, flattened her fingers to make a wing, and let the turbulent wind take her palm on a wavy flight. Ben admired the sleek muscle definition that was returning to her arms. Her entire body was reclaiming the gazelle-like energy that once defined her physique. Eyes back on the road, Ben slowed as the ocean came into view.

Kelsey leaned forward and stared. "I didn't know how much I missed it," she murmured for her ears more than his. Her smile danced with familiar joy, then she took in a shaky breath but closed her mouth again.

"What's on your mind?" he asked.

"I'm not sure you want to know."

"I think I can handle it."

Kelsey sat up straighter and gave him a look. "Okay. Well, did we ever . . . you know . . . hit the sheets?"

Swerving a bit, he overcorrected, then coughed. "You surprised me with that."

She laughed. "I'm sorry if I've forgotten a hot one-nighter. I know I've had more than a few."

He fought the jealous fire that expanded against his ribcage. "No. We didn't have a one-nighter." Ben shook his head, regretting that fact for the thousandth time.

"Huh. Why?" She'd always been blunt, but now her filters were even thinner.

He blew out a breath before he answered, "I guess it was a combo of bad timing and the fact that I wanted something sort of permanent."

"Really? Crap." Kels seemed a little embarrassed. "I hit on you, didn't I?"

"There was a lot of flirting back and forth. I was an idiot not to make a move."

Kels settled back in her seat and grinned. He recognized the return of her playful confidence, but needed to set some boundaries, if only for himself. "I'm not going to lie, I'm tempted to pull this car over right now and explore everything I know I've been missing. But it's a timing thing, again."

Kelsey's flirtatious grin vanished, and her eyes flashed with instant fiery anger. "I get it. I'm damaged goods now."

Pissed, Ben hit the brakes and turned into a long drive that disappeared between dense windblown pines. He pulled the emergency brake and spun to face her. "Don't put words in my mouth. That's not what I was thinking. God damnit, of course I want you. You're as vibrant as ever. But, if I acted on that now, Kent, Seth, and even my sister would line up to kill me."

Propped snug against her door, she studied him for a long moment. Her expression softened and a sigh slipped from her lips. "I'm sorry. I didn't mean to make today complicated." Clearly nervous, she trapped both hands under her thighs, and her eyes misted. "It's been so long since anyone touched me."

Her words coaxed a move. Ben wanted to hold her, needed it, but Kelsey shook her head, stopping his momentum. "That's not true," she said with a huff. "The nurses poke, and my physical therapists yank and prod. I guess I'm just tired of being broken."

The need to wrap her in his arms tingled his fingertips, but the car seemed to have barriers built in everywhere. He turned off the engine, opened his door, and flew to her side of the vehicle. Before she was able to speak, he hauled her from her seat and into his arms.

Smashed against him, Kelsey's fingers gripped his shirt. Warmth, longing, and comfort seeped from his body to hers. She slid her arms around his neck and plastered her chest against his. When their eyes met, he couldn't resist the pull. Ben bent his head and claimed a tentative kiss. As he stroked the heat expanded, and he gave her as much as she would absorb. Her arms clutched, and her mouth tasted, drinking him in like a dry sponge. His hips moved forward as his hands slid in two directions. One trapped her hair at her neck and the other fell to her ass, urging her slim hips against his groin.

"Do you feel how much I want you?" Ben whispered against her lips. She wriggled in his arms and pressed into his mounting desire. Easing away a fraction, her bright aqua eyes studied his face, while Ben stared back with steeled control.

Kelsey moved her lips over his again, exploring. He let her take from this moment what she needed, responding, but never demanding more. Up on tiptoe, she tasted him, then her kisses softened and slowly diminished. Eventually, her body eased away.

"You're right, I'm not ready for this." She closed her eyes and tipped her head against his chest. Ben stroked her hair, fighting the desire to plunge ahead, to sear her body with two years of bottled-up lust.

In a few minutes, she backed away. He held the passenger door open as she slid inside. After circling to the driver's side, he adjusted his pants, climbed in, and turned the car around to speed back onto the highway.

They didn't speak, but when Kelsey moved to turn on the radio, she let her fingers come to rest on his thigh.

A few miles south, a sign directed him to a beach access road. Choosing a careful route over the sand, he avoided the loose ruts near the dunes. After the engine stopped, she sat perfectly still for a moment, watching the waves from the safety of the Audi. Ben waited, willing to leave if this was too soon for her to endure.

Abandoning her flip-flops, Kelsey pushed her door open. She circled to his side of the car and extended her hand. Their fingers knitted, and she led him away from families with barking dogs and kids building sandcastles. After walking for a silent half-hour, she stopped at a log, sat, and asked him to take off his shoes. He kicked them off, peeled away his socks, and tucked both behind a log.

They walked toward the waves with fingers entwined, and Ben followed her into an inch of water. Her hand trembled in his when the waves pushed over their feet ankle-deep. Without a word, she claimed three steps forward. A larger wave surrounded them, but she didn't budge, and Ben found himself laughing with Kelsey in knee-high surf. She turned to him, wrapped her arms around his waist and thanked him with words first, and then with a kiss.

In damp shorts, they stayed on their private section of the beach, far away from cars and people. Kelsey let her head drift to his shoulder, and they watched as clouds swallowed the coastline. There wouldn't be a view of the sunset today.

***

Kelsey jolted awake when the engine cut off. "We're back." Ben's voice soothed her senses and helped her remember where she was—in the parking lot at The Center. He waited for her to move before opening his door.

The short walk to the entrance tingled her senses. She wanted more than a short goodbye, but the *chaperone* seated at the front desk made her as tense as a freshman at prom. Kelsey kissed his cheek to end the awkward suspense and thanked Ben for the trip.

She hurried to her room and watched from her window as he drove away.

Later that night, Kelsey realized the thank you she gave him wasn't nearly enough. Ben probably didn't recognize this trip as a crucial tipping point, but Kelsey felt it, and accepted the plunge.

After a dreamless sleep, she woke early, ready to push herself, and her muscles and mind made an instant rebound. Over the next two weeks, the visits from her family and friends revived detailed memories—some good, some bad, but all useful.

Surfing with Mark starred in her best recollections, but his text messages had stopped. She let those visions remain in her past—along with the person she once was. The future could be good again, but it would be different, and she needed to accept that fact if she ever wanted to leave the safety of The Center.

THIRTEEN

Shoulder to shoulder, Natalie lay next to her on the blanket. They gazed at fuzzy white contrails the planes had left like giant hashtags on the sky. Moving as little as possible, Nate tore a big chocolate cookie from Goldfinch Bakery in two and handed over half.

"The chocolate's so warm from the sun, it tastes like Maggie just pulled this from the oven," Nate said while chewing her first bite.

Kels mumbled past the decadent sweetness, "Don't tell Aunt Elsa, but I think Maggie's cookies have her snickerdoodles beat."

Sitting up, Natalie shook her head. "You really think so? I'd have to do a side-by-side taste test to be sure."

"We could do that. Elsa brought me a batch when she visited yesterday."

"I didn't know she'd been here. Too bad I missed her."

"Every Thursday, rain or shine. Sometimes she brings a friend along to help with the drive from Seattle, but I wish she wouldn't make that trip on her own."

"I miss your great-aunt. We should plan a mini-vacation and maybe spend the night."

Natalie's road trip suggestion constricted Kelsey's throat. She closed her eyes and fought unexpected panic. The Center's orderly routine used to seem like a prison, but now it felt safe. She'd come to depend on the predictable routine.

"Maybe in a few weeks? I'm not ready to endure Seattle traffic," Kelsey said when she'd calmed herself enough to speak.

"Let me know."

"Could I ask a favor?" she asked, sitting up, while Natalie finished her cookie.

"Anything, Kels."

"If you see my mom around Ashwood, do you think you could drop a hint about Aunt Elsa? I worry about her making that drive."

"Sure. But why don't you tell your mom yourself?"

Kelsey picked at a tall clump of grass and tore it up by the roots. "I sort of asked my parents to give me a little extra space—and I'm afraid I wasn't nice." She winced remembering the shocked look on their faces. When she'd forgotten to measure her words, the blatant truth had slayed her parents like a sharp sword. "Mom means well, but she's obsessing about getting me home." Kels tapped her head with her fingertips. "I can't control *this*."

"Everyone wants you home—Kent, your family, Seth and I—we'd all be happy to take turns to bring you back to Portland for therapy. Don't you *want* to get out of here?"

"Shit. Not you, too." Kelsey bit the tip of her tongue, stopping her angry words until her thoughts caught up. "It's safe here," she whispered. "And if I went home, I'd be trapped at the lake. You know I haven't been cleared to drive."

"Because of the seizure? But it's been more than a month."

"The seizure, and I'm just not ready." She hadn't told her friends, but the halls at The Center sometimes confused her enough to get lost.

Natalie reached for her hand, but Kels pulled away before she made contact. "Don't you dare feel sorry for me. It's not that bad. I jump on the Max Train and go to the park anytime I like." Kelsey knew this was an exaggeration. She'd done it twice, but the freedom had been absolutely exhilarating.

"Sorry. I just miss you. But I guess if you came back to Ashwood, you wouldn't get to see Ben as often. Is he coming today?" Natalie asked, digging for information.

Kels blushed and shook her head. "He's away on business."

"When does my big brother get back?" Nate's eyebrows lifted.

"Three days." Biting the inside of her cheeks, Kels fought her grin and refused to give Natalie the dirt she really wanted.

Ben's sister looked ready to burst. "Ah, come on, spill it. What's happening between you two?"

Flopping back on the blanket, Kelsey tossed her arm over her face and masked her eyes beneath the bend of her elbow. "Not as much as I'd like. Ben has the patience of a saint."

"Isn't that a good thing?"

"Not good. Not good at all. You've seen him."

"Yeah, and?"

"He's hot. It's obvious, even to you." Lifting her arm, she peeked at Natalie from the edge of her vision.

Natalie chuckled, reached out again, and this time Kels accepted the touch. "You and Ben have always had *a thing*. Still, it seems like more this time."

"You're right, there's more. But I don't want to tangle how needy I am right now with love." The 'L-word' slipped out and hung there, neon bright.

"What? You're falling *in love* with Ben. Oh, my God. This is epic." Natalie's whispered intensity scared Kelsey.

Fighting panic, she pleaded, "Please, please, please . . . don't say anything."

"I would *never*. Still, you can't imagine how thrilled I am. Before—" Natalie stopped the words that were about to tumble from her mouth.

"It's okay to say it. Before the accident, before I drowned, hell, before I nearly died. I've come to terms with it. I've changed, and who I was before may never match who I am now. Everyone has to accept that."

"I know. I loved you then, and I love you now."

"Thanks, Nate. Love you, too."

Kelsey still wasn't sure if she loved Ben or just needed him way too much. Needing him meant giving up something of herself—a part she might want back.

***

Kelsey gripped the paperback Travis loaned her from The Center's library. With a long blink, she tried to rest her vision before she read the last line again. Her eyes hurt. Her brain hurt. And reading tested her patience. She didn't remember ever liking fiction very much. Outdoor guidebooks were fine, useful, and losing herself on a trail was better than losing herself in the pages of a book.

She tossed the paperback aside, wondering when Ben would call.

While waiting she grabbed her phone, let curiosity win, and Googled her name. Tiny squares loaded with *the video*, tempting her fingers. Her hands sheened with sweat, and in the same moment a call vibrated the device. The sudden movement startled her, sending the ringing phone clattering to the floor. As it hit the linoleum, her phone went silent. "Shit."

After her heart stopped thundering, she picked it up and carefully touched the shattered screen. The once smooth surface rasped against her fingertips. The screen lit again but didn't respond to her touch. Damn it, she couldn't even answer Ben's call.

Irritation threatened to bloom into rage, something she was learning to control. She paced the room, focused on her breathing, and brought the hot emotion back to a warm simmer. Out in the hall she searched for a familiar face at the main desk, but no one was at the helm.

While wandering through The Center, she passed a guy making his way with the help of a walker. One leg refused to cooperate. He lifted it with a shift of his hips and forced his step forward. "Great job, Alex," she said patting his back before she moved along.

"Thanks, Kels," he answered on a labored breath.

It occurred to her that her once staggered gate was nearly limp free. The nurses' station at the rear of the complex was always a center of activity. Travis greeted her with a smile. The sight of her phone was all it took for him to offer the cordless, and her problem was almost solved.

"I can't remember any contact numbers." She shrugged, not caring if the entire staff knew. The admission put a familiar look on Travis's face as he mentally added a new task to her list of things to work on.

"Who are you trying to call?"

"Ben." In seconds, Travis produced the info and Kelsey punched in the numbers. She found a quiet alcove and sank onto an orange plastic chair.

Ben picked up before she even heard it ring on her end. "Kels, is everything okay? Why are you calling from this number?"

"I'm fine. I dropped my phone and shattered the screen. When you called, I couldn't answer."

He huffed, "Oh, that's good. I was about to call Natalie back to see if she knew where you were."

"You talked to your sister?" A stab of worry slashed through Kelsey. *Had Natalie spilled everything?*

"Yeah, she said she had a great time with you yesterday."

"It was great." *Mostly.* "But she's siding with my parents—I guess everyone wants me to move back to Ashwood. Maybe they're right, maybe I should go home."

"I've been thinking about that and have an idea . . ." When Ben stalled, she wriggled her butt impatiently, and the chair beneath her squeaked. The shrill, irritating sound only enhanced the silence. He cleared his throat and pressed on. "Ashwood's too far from The Center, but my place isn't."

Kelsey sucked a shocked breath, and the sound echoed in the tiny alcove. "I can't move in with you. You'd hate me within a week."

"Just think about it," he pleaded softly. "I've given this a lot of thought and I'm not going into this with any expectations."

Kelsey trembled. His expectations could mean so many different things, all of them scary.

"What about my crazy sleep schedule?" she argued.

"You'd have your own room."

"And my mood swings."

"Swing away . . . I'll be at work most of the day."

"I don't want to beg rides from you."

"You love taking the Max train."

That stopped her. "I do love the train."

"And maybe if you weren't so bored, you wouldn't feel so...edgy."

Edgy? Ben put her on edge quicker than anything. Just hearing his voice over the phone made her warm. Living with him would take their smoldering attraction to scorching.

Even with that complication, she was tempted. It was too soon to live alone, and her parents' place was too far away. "Give me a few days to think about it," she finally blurted.

"Great! That's all I ask. It will work, I promise. Hey, I'm still at the office and have an early meeting to prep for. So, I gotta go."

"Already?" She couldn't mask her disappointment.

His voice softened. "I miss you."

"Miss you too," she said, not caring if he knew how much.

FOURTEEN

Kent carried Kelsey's small duffle to his truck. She grinned, noting it was easier to keep up with his long, loose limbed gate. "Thanks for letting me stay overnight at your place. I gotta see if I can handle life away from The Center before deciding if I want to move in with Ben."

He tossed her bag in his truck. "No problem. I can't wait to hang out. But are you sure about this? Living with Ben? That's big."

"I want a normal life again, but I won't do it if I can't handle waking up in a regular house. This overnighter at your place is a perfect test run." She opened the passenger door and they both climbed in from either side.

He leveled a stare before starting the engine. "Not what I'm talking about, and you know it. This won't be an accurate test, unless you and I plan to break with tradition and hit the sheets."

"Shut up. Ben and I haven't slept together," Kelsey huffed and buckled in.

Kent smirked. "Not yet. But he's waiting to pounce."

"Maybe he's waited long enough," she mumbled under her breath.

Kent started the truck, pressed the accelerator, and the engine growled. "I like Ben. Damn, I couldn't hand pick a better guy for you. At least I know he's solid."

"Can we talk about something else?" Flicking on the radio, Kels killed the conversation, tuned him out, and used the thumping bass to measure her breathing. But her anxiety climbed as each mile brought her closer to Ashwood and the river that skirted its western edge. She'd gone home once since *the accident*, but today's visit wasn't numbed by prescription meds. Kelsey needed to get through this overnighter without chemical help.

Miles passed, and her breathing picked up. Kelsey closed her eyes and turned away from Kent. When the road made its narrow climb toward Mount Adams, she gripped the armrest to still her trembling hands. "Pull over," she blurted, fighting a wave of panic.

He stopped barely off the shoulder, and Kelsey bolted a few steps away from his truck. Killing the engine, he opened his door, and slammed it shut. She staggered toward the ditch, bent in half at the waist, and gripped her head between widespread fingers. Kent sprinted to her, halting his steps a few inches from her feet.

His strong hands spread warmth between her shoulder blades. "You gonna be sick?" he whispered.

"No."

"Scared?"

"Yeah."

"Come here."

Kelsey crashed into his solid embrace, inhaling the scent of his laundry detergent, his soap, and a bit of his exhaled air. Trapped against his chest, threads of panic slithered away, and her taut muscles relaxed.

"You okay?" he asked, already knowing the answer.

"Give me one more second," she whispered, soaking in his strength. A shuddered breath cleansed her lungs and she shivered in the eighty-five-degree July heat.

"Sorry about that," she said, ready to pull away. Kelsey moved but Kent tightened his arms.

"Never apologize for needing me," he insisted. He kissed her temple then relaxed his arms, giving her space to move. Those three extra inches revealed where they were. A stand of fir and cottonwood on the other side of the road hid musical water tumbling over rocks.

His eyes held her panicked gaze. "Have you been back?" Kelsey asked.

"Yeah. A few days after, I got in a kayak . . . I had to prove to myself that I could." Kent inhaled a slow breath and tilted his head, studying her shifting mood. His eyes brimmed and shimmered as he recalled a day she would probably never remember.

Kelsey broke away. "I need to see it," she called as she ran.

He jogged to catch up. "We'll need to cut through the Albright place if you want to reach the river," he warned, knowing precisely where that route would lead.

"I know where I'm going, Kent. I've got to see it," she yelled, sprinting a few steps ahead.

He shut up and followed. She stumbled, snaking her way down the narrow deer trail that switched back and forth on a descent to a deep pool below the falls. When Kent's feet paused behind her, she was left with the sound of The Little White.

Filtered light seeped through the evergreen canopy, dancing over the water and moss-covered rocks. Summer had dropped the river to a peaceful tumble. She didn't know how this turquoise river could ever look menacing. It was simply beautiful.

Kelsey edged her feet to the spot where wide flat stones met lapping water. She filled her lungs with the rich aroma of the forest—piney, damp, alive. She'd never ride this river again, never harness its energy with the stroke of her paddle. Mourning all she'd lost, she crumpled at the edge of her river, wrapped her arms around her legs, and wept.

***

After dinner at Northside Grill Kent sank next to Kelsey on his threadbare couch. "Do you regret this visit?" he asked.

"No. It's okay. I just wish everyone would stop treating me like a circus freak."

"You're a celebrity, not a freak," he argued. Their night at The Northside had hit a few rough spots, but Kent led her to the dance floor when the attention got to be too much. Once the newness of her presence in the room wore off, they joined Maggie, Grant, and Dillon at the pool table to hang out with the remnants of her old crowd.

"Are Maggie and Dillon seeing each other?" Kelsey asked, trying to fill in the gossip gaps.

"I don't think so." Kent shrugged. "But you know I never pay attention to that shit."

He fell silent for a while and she recognized that far-away stare. "When are you going to give her a call?"

"Never. She's gone. Amanda's got better things in her future than a guy who's never getting out of Ashwood."

Kelsey leaned over until their shoulders touched. "You can change that. You don't have to stay here."

"I know. But the thought of four years of school makes me cringe. It's not for me."

"I never said you needed a degree. And I've been thinking. At some point I've got to talk to Sig about my half of the guiding business. I don't know if I'll ever have the stamina to take on Venture Sister full time again. You could help."

"Kels, I'm not the right fit for Venture Sister. If you haven't noticed, I've got balls."

She smacked him on the arm. "I know, you ass, but Sig will still need a partner. One who can keep up with our clients. You can hire women for the Venture Sister trips."

Suddenly protective, he clenched his teeth and asked, "Is Sig pressuring you to sell out?"

Kelsey chuckled. "Not at all—he's struggling to handle the increased demand. Parker's film only heightened Venture's popularity. Sig's swamped and will take me back no matter what I'm able to do."

"Then why pass this jackpot off on me?" he asked while taking another draw from his half-full beer.

She frowned. "I won't go back as a mascot."

"Don't say shit like that." Kent was irritated, but Kelsey didn't care. He needed to hear the truth.

"Fine, I'll lie if it makes you feel better. I'll jump right in when I'm *one hundred percent.*"

Her sarcasm pissed Kent off, and he grabbed her air quote fingers in one hand.

"You'll get there." He promised and wrapped her in reassuring arms.

Kelsey took the bear hug and the encouragement, but it didn't change a thing. She sighed and wondered what one hundred percent would look like.

***

The following morning her alarm went off in an unfamiliar place. Kelsey blinked at the bedside table—it held her careful arrangement of her new phone, bottled water, and hair tie. It took a moment to absorb the strange surroundings, until the aroma of coffee mingled with that musty old house smell. Kent must be up.

When they were young, the fact that a high schooler lived on his own seemed grown-up and kind of cool. His house was exactly the same, but now the place needed help. Hollow and dingy, cobwebs floated in the corners of the room, some stretching in long dusty tendrils to limp faded curtains—something his mom had probably hung before she took off. Kels did the math in her head. Had it really been twenty years?

She pulled on a sweatshirt and realized that the overnighter had worked. The unfamiliar place didn't faze her at all. Kelsey pivoted back to her phone and swept the screen. Her fingers trembled—every molecule seemed anxious to give Ben the good news.

FIFTEEN

"Is this the last box?" Seth asked Kelsey as he took another load from her room at The Center to his truck.

"I think so." Kels nodded. "I have to do a final check before we all meet at Ben's place."

Ben's touch on her shoulder turned her head. "Our place," he said with a grin. The thought stopped her. Except for that summer when she rented a room to Natalie, she'd always lived alone.

Travis met her for the final inspection. "I get the feeling you won't miss me at all." He laughed aloud.

"I'll miss our late-night games of rummy and blackjack." Her voice caught a little as she chuckled.

"I won't. You're a card shark." With the way his eyes danced, she knew he was lying.

Kelsey gave him a quick hug. "I'll be back for Pain and Torture in a few days."

"I'm proud of you," he said with a squeeze. "You got my cell?"

"Yes. Ben does, too." She promised to call her therapist if anything, big or small, came up.

***

Natalie, Ben, and Seth waited for Kelsey to settle upstairs on her own. She'd asked them to give her a little space while she unpacked. Ben turned to his sister and shrugged when they heard the shower upstairs rattle the pipes. He realized their plans to go out for a celebration dinner needed to shift.

Natalie ordered Thai and had it delivered. Seth found something to keep busy and repaired the leaky kitchen faucet while Ben exchanged family gossip with his sister. They shared good stuff about Mom and their stepbrothers in Arizona, and crap about Dad and his latest gold-digging arm candy. Ben figured Dad was grooming this one to be wife number four.

The scent of food lured Kelsey downstairs. "Sorry, I lost track of time," she said as Seth and Natalie popped open paper containers of Thai food then spread the feast across the kitchen counter. Clearly nervous, Kelsey stood back and watched.

She jumped when Ben eased in behind her and wrapped his arms around her waist. "God, you smell delicious," he said, against her still damp hair. He took it as a good sign when she didn't inch away.

"I had to take a shower and get that hospital stench off my skin." A slow breath shifted her body in his arms. "Sorry if I messed up our plans."

"Hey, no worries. This is better."

Kelsey leaned into him and whispered, "Thanks for understanding."

***

"Did you have fun tonight?" Ben asked after Natalie and Seth left. He looked way too tempting on his end of the couch.

"Had a great time. Sorry again about the disappearing act."

"No apologies. Set a pace you're comfortable with." Her frown moved him closer, and he reached out to pull her calves over his thighs. "I mean it," he insisted.

"Okay." Kels shivered as he smoothed his hands over her bare skin. She'd have to remember to wear sweats instead of shorts, but not because she was cold. Even when he only touched her ankles, what she wanted from Ben scared her.

Needing distance, Kelsey pulled her legs from his lap and planted her feet on the floor. "I know it's early, but do you mind if I disappear?"

Ben nodded. Disappointment flickered across his features before he put his easy smile back in place. "No problem. I've got work to catch up on. If I finish it tonight, we can escape the city tomorrow."

"Actually, I'd like to explore the neighborhood on foot, if that's okay. I need to learn the lay of the land." It was first on her list of tasks that would help her settle in.

"I'd like that." Ben invited himself along and Kelsey smiled, genuinely happy. She knew he had a life that didn't include her, and probably dated. But she doubted he had a girlfriend, or he wouldn't have asked her to move in. Still, she didn't want to assume they'd spend weekends together.

***

After breakfast, Ben let her take the lead. She led him a few blocks past an elementary school to a cluster of local shops. "Thanks for bringing me along," he said as he slung an arm around her shoulder, the touch friendly rather than possessive. "Looks like my neighborhood has so much more than the pub."

Kelsey loved taking the role of trail guide again, even if the path was just in Ben's neighborhood. He seemed surprised by the shops only four blocks from his front door. As they explored, his intoxicating grin tempted her. He hadn't shaved this morning and looked extra sexy.

They bought three books at a tiny bookstore, before she led him to a coffee shop. Huddled over pages detailing Portland's historic neighborhoods, they sipped iced tea and devoured oatmeal cookies. Kels found a yoga studio and wandered in to grab a schedule. As she came out, a line of yoga pant-clad women walked into class. Kelsey envied their fit bodies, but Ben never checked them out. She smiled at him when she realized he might be falling for her, too.

Ben didn't want to take a break, but he had to take a call from a client in Japan. She told him to head home and promised to follow soon.

"Are you sure?" he asked, his eyebrows scrunched with worry.

"You have to trust me. I'll be on my own most days—what are you going to do, quit your job?" He hesitated, and she wondered if he was actually considering it.

She gave him a playful shove. "Ben. Please go, or I'll call Travis and ask him to move me back into The Center." That teasing threat seemed to do it, and he nodded, accepting that she could get home on her own.

"Are we still on for dinner?" he asked before he left.

"Yeah, I won't be long, but I'd like to shower and change before we go out."

"Take your time, but not too much." He kissed her forehead before heading off.

The seven-thirty reservations gave her plenty of time to visit a few more shops. Kelsey waited and watched while Ben rounded the corner and disappeared on his way home.

She spun back toward the yoga studio and memorized the neighborhood. At the last moment, Kelsey took out her phone and snapped a picture of the names on the street corner, unwilling to leave anything to chance.

The clothes she tried on at a little boutique didn't fit quite right. She'd have to learn to dress differently now that her body had softened. It wasn't bad, she just wasn't used to having curves. While passing the counter on her way out, Kels stopped to admire a display. A pair of green and blue beaded earrings caught her eye. A tiny mermaid dangling from the jewelry brought tears to her eyes as vivid memories flooded her mind.

"Can I help you?" the girl behind the register asked.

Kelsey nodded and handed her the delicate earrings without a word. After paying, she left the shop with a small bag in her hand. The warm breeze tickled her hair across her neck, and a voice kept repeating. *I'm gonna miss those eyes, Mermaid. The color changes with your mood, just like the sea.*

She circled the neighborhood as small, vivid details about Mark fell into place like drops of rain. They'd been so much more than friends. He'd understood her drive, accepted her need for space, and coaxed her into his heart. But his messages had stopped, maybe because he'd seen Parker's footage. With such an active life, he probably couldn't picture himself with damaged goods. She'd probably never see him or hear his voice again.

Overwhelming sorrow sucked the air from her lungs. Pain coiled her stomach and her body curled around the ache. The sticky heat tightened her throat, and she had to sit down. Cool shade under a canopy of maple trees drew her toward a park. She found a quiet bench and watched kids climb the playground equipment and careen down a slide. Watching them play, Kelsey let their joy and laughter strip away her dark thoughts.

It was better this way. A man like Mark shouldn't have to settle for a woman who couldn't keep up. Maybe she'd reach out and say hello if she ever got back in the water. If.

She still had time. Time to locate the woman she'd lost to The Little White.

***

Ben paced the living room, sick with worry until he spotted Kelsey walking down their street. He'd asked where she'd gone, and she said she'd explored a park, but he suspected that she'd taken a wrong turn on her way home.

Running late, she dashed upstairs to get ready for their dinner out.

From his perch in front of the baseball game, he heard the hot water creak in the old pipes. Her shower gave him time to check the app on her phone. Her map revealed the truth, she'd aimlessly wandered in circles, clearly lost, before heading home.

Ben closed his eyes and considered his options—he could bring it up and piss her off, or he could add a tracking app to her phone and link it to his. Damn it, he knew he wouldn't be able to concentrate at work if he was worried about losing her on the streets of Portland. He had no choice, and it wasn't difficult. In moments, her phone synced with his, and he could track her with a single click.

When her soft steps creaked the old wooden floors upstairs, Ben put her phone back in her pack and shook away the guilt.

"Hey, Ben?" she hollered from the top of the stairs. He wandered to the landing and was about to climb the treads when he spotted her long sleek legs peeking from beneath a white cotton towel. His hand gripped the rail as his world shifted.

Unaware of the mouth-watering angle the staircase created, Kelsey asked, "Do you mind if I dress up? I haven't had a reason to wear a skirt in forever."

"Yeah. That would be . . . perfect." Ben willed the towel to untangle from the place she'd tucked it, next to the swell of her ivory breast.

"Cool." Kelsey spun quickly.

"Oh, God," he mumbled when he caught a glimpse of her gorgeous naked ass.

Kelsey turned. "What was that?" She peeked over her shoulder and the towel eased up a fraction higher.

"Nothing," Ben croaked. Her steps bounced down the hall, and the door shut quickly. A happy tune filled the upstairs as Kelsey sang to herself, completely unaware of his exquisite torture. His mind wandered, imagining her standing in front of her closet, considering her clothing options without a single stitch on.

The baseball game lost its pull. To keep from climbing the stairs, Ben went outside to clear his head. After a few laps around his yard, he turned toward the scrape of a rake next door and wandered out his back gate to say hello to Nancy.

"Hey, Ben, how are you?" His neighbor pushed a bit of sweaty hair away from her suntanned face.

"I'm good. Your garden looks amazing."

"Thanks. I'll bring over some beans tomorrow. I've got more than I can eat and don't feel like canning in this heat." Her two kids were grown and hadn't come home from college this summer—one was in Nevada, the other Wyoming. "Did I see a new roommate move in last weekend?"

He nodded. "You remember my sister?"

"Of course. Natalie."

"Her friend, Kelsey, will be spending some time in Portland. She's staying with me for a while." Ben wondered if it was too soon to ask Nancy to watch out for Kelsey, just in case she needed anything while he was at work.

"Great! You two can eat more beans." She shook her head and laughed aloud. Nancy glanced over his shoulder, and her eyebrows raised. "Looks like she's wandering this way."

The last time Ben saw Kelsey she was wrapped in a towel. That distraction had nothing on the snug sundress she wore now. The shimmering blue-green fabric matched her ever-changing eyes.

"I spotted you from my upstairs window." Kelsey pointed over her shoulder.

Ben cleared his throat before he could speak, "Kels, this is Nancy."

When she stopped a few inches from his shoulder, he could feel the warmth radiating from her just showered skin. "You must have grown those delicious tomatoes we had this morning. Thanks for sending them over."

A warm breeze caught Kelsey's clean scent and delivered it to Ben. He went a little drunk on the pleasure with just one inhale.

"Grew them right here," Nancy said with a sweep of her arm. The backyard didn't have an inch of grass. When she lacked square footage, she forced her garden up, with trellised beans, kiwi, and squash climbing high on bamboo structures.

"It's nice to meet you," Kelsey said, as she squinted in the bright sun. "I'll be staying here for a month or two. Let me know if you need a hand in your garden. I'd love to learn your secrets."

Ben wondered about Kelsey's secrets, too. This interest in gardening surprised him, perhaps the accident had settled her some.

"I would love an extra hand, anytime. Your dress is lovely, Kelsey. Are you and Ben marking a special occasion?"

"We're celebrating my escape from a brain trauma center," Kelsey said without censor. "I was in a kayaking accident this spring." When Nancy winced Kels quickly added, "Oh, don't worry—I don't remember it. Home's too far from the therapy I need. When Ben offered to let me stay here for the rest of my rehab, I leapt at the chance." She leaned to the side and gave him a shoulder bump. "I hope he doesn't regret it."

Ben shifted, put an arm around her, and spread his hand across the base of her back. "We should have moved you here sooner."

Nancy glanced between them and her smile widened. "Come by anytime, Kelsey. I need all the help I can get with this jungle. And if my music is loud, pound on the door, I'll hear you eventually."

"We'd better go, we've got that reservation." He flexed his fingers on the sway of her back and Kels turned. "See you soon, Nancy."

"Bye for now, these weeds wait for no one." The scrape of the hoe resumed as Kelsey walked ahead of him. They cut through the house, locking doors, and picking up keys on the way.

"I like her. You know, she reminds me of Seth's mom," Kelsey said as she skipped down the front porch steps.

"Exactly what I thought." Ben caught up and held open the Audi's passenger door. He lifted his hand to her face before she took a seat. "These earrings are pretty," he said, "but this one's caught." Kelsey held her breath as he carefully untangled her white-gold hair from the mermaid dangling against her neck.

SIXTEEN

The late morning Max train filled, and Kelsey gave up her seat to a young pregnant woman. She thanked Kelsey and pulled a parenting book from her backpack. While watching the girl turn from page to page, Kels wondered what it would be like to plan her life around a baby. Maybe that's what Ben had meant when he said he was looking for permanent.

Trying not to stare, Kelsey glanced above the girl's head and watched Portland zip past the windows. She hadn't anticipated the satisfaction that came from navigating a city. Leading hikes deep into the wilderness was always a rewarding challenge, but this was good too. The city had a living quality—a heartbeat all its own.

At the next stop, a few people left, and a guy sprinted to make the train. As he boarded, he tossed his long dark hair from his face and revealed a fading green and purple bruise around his eyes. It must have been one hell of a fight. The train jolted, and her eyes wandered back.

The hairs on the nape of her neck prickled, and Kelsey felt like she knew him. *Brayden*. But it wasn't him. Brayden was leaner and more athletic, but those bruises were the same. Kelsey stared at the train's grimy floor, and a sly grin bloomed as she recalled his handsome face. It was just as if they had parted ways yesterday. She'd never forget the way her name sounded on his lips, especially when he asked her to visit Melbourne this winter.

It all came flooding back, mingled with the knowledge that this vivid memory was only a day prior to her accident. Remembering Brayden was such a relief, his name, lingering on her phone, had bugged her for weeks. She dug into her pocket to scroll through those messages again. Brayden's frantic texts had ceased the same day as her accident. *He knew*. Of course, he knew. Everyone did.

119

As she stared at the screen, the morning of *that day* puzzled back into place—waking up with Brayden on the couch in the tiny home, having breakfast, then leaving a note for Natalie. Kelsey shook her head and couldn't figure out why Natalie had never brought it up.

For a moment, Kelsey's fingers hovered over Brayden's message, and she was tempted to say hi. No, that time had passed. She swept the screen and filed Brayden next to Mark in a strong box with a heavy lock, secured safely in her past.

***

Travis handed her a towel. "Great workout today."

"I enjoyed it, too." Her therapist clearly liked the challenge of working with her. With a demanding physical career ahead, her goals were different than most of the patients he worked with. "Are you ready to take another stab at the pool?"

"Could we wait until first thing tomorrow?" Kelsey asked. She hated finishing with a fail, and she still hadn't conquered her issues with water.

"Fair enough. Want to grab a snack in the cafeteria?" he offered.

"Sure, thanks. I'll meet you."

When other staff joined them, Kelsey felt, for the first time, like a friend rather than a patient. She didn't say much, but listened in while they talked about their kids, their weekend, and their hobbies. Something had shifted when she moved away from The Center. Her life was gaining momentum, moving forward with noticeable speed. Maybe it had never really stopped. Yet now she could spot a finish line and moving on to the next challenge didn't scare her. Like everything in her life, this crossroads with these people was temporary.

***

The house was too quiet when she got home, but music spilled from next door and drew her to Nancy's garden—a perfect place to lose herself while Ben was at work. She changed into shorts and a tank top and showed up wearing some gloves she'd found in a storage shed in Ben's backyard.

Her neighbor's genuine smile greeted her. "I see you've come ready to work."

"If you'll have me."

"You may regret it. Would you rather weed or harvest?" Nancy asked.

"Weeding. I want to get my hands dirty." Kelsey held up her gloved hands and laughed.

"Dirty it is. And after the weeds, I've got some Yukon Golds ready to dig."

"Perfect."

Kelsey worked under a small patch of waist-high corn, laying down a layer of mulch after she yanked out the stubborn weeds. Later, she took off her gloves to enjoy the loamy texture of the moist earth as she sifted through the dirt to find the pale potatoes. In no time, she'd filled the woven basket with a pile of tubers.

"Time for a break." Nancy's voice turned her head from her task. "You strike me as a person who doesn't know when to stop,"

Crouched close to the ground, Kels glanced up. "You can tell that much just by watching me weed?"

"Gardening reveals a lot about a person." Nancy reached to give Kels a hand up from the ground. She led the way to a bench in a shaded corner where a small cafe table held a tray of berries, tiny tomatoes, and two tall glasses of raspberry iced tea.

When they sat, Kelsey took in the wall of green that surrounded them on all sides. She gulped the tea and asked, "Have you always done all this?"

"Not until I got married. I met my husband in a botany class. He grew up on a farm in Iowa and got me hooked. Now, with so much time on my hands, I think I'm getting obsessed. But it helps me avoid worse addictions."

Kelsey recognized a connection. "I get it. After the accident, I had trouble sleeping. Some of the meds worked almost too well, and I used them as an escape. Ben showed up and pulled me back from the edge."

"I did that for a while after my husband died. But pills weren't my vice. I drank while my kids were at school," Nancy admitted. "A part-time job and this garden helped me get out of that rut. Then, after both kids left for college, I started the same cycle. As soon as I realized what was happening, I ripped the last patch of the grass from the backyard and replaced it with tomatoes. Hell, at some point, the front lawn may have to go." Nancy laughed aloud and popped a cherry tomato into her mouth.

Kelsey immediately loved this honest woman. "How long have you lived here?"

"About sixteen years, nine of those with Carl. Pancreatic cancer took him fast. I don't know if fast is better or worse. God, I miss him." She smiled, remembering something that brightened her expression.

"I guess I'm the one who gave my family a scare," Kelsey admitted. "There's this river, The Little White, it's famous for world-class rapids. I don't remember any of the details, but my friends told me I paddled in to rescue a less experienced kayaker out of a jam. Another boater came over a waterfall and hit me from above. The impact and drowning both did damage, and now I'm working to get myself back together."

"Your family must have been so worried."

"Yeah, and Mom still is. She'd love to have me home, resting under a blanket, recuperating with her homemade chicken soup."

"That'd be pure punishment for someone as active as you."

"It would definitely lead to day-drinking." They shared a laugh and a victory over life's obstacles.

"How did you and Ben meet?" Nancy asked while brushing a wasp away from the food.

"Ben's sister, Natalie, rented a room at my house two summers ago. She was staying in Ashwood while her tiny home was being built. Natalie and I got along right away, hung out, and Ben showed up later for a visit. He made a move to Portland to stay closer to his sister."

Nancy nodded. "Are you and Natalie still close friends?"

"She's the best, stuck by me through all the brain injury stuff. Natalie married the guy who built that tiny home. When she met Seth, it was only a matter of time."

Nancy hummed. "Ah, yes. Seth and Natalie. I met them when Ben first moved in. You're right, that girl didn't stand a chance."

"Hearts broke all over town when she snagged him. But they're perfect together."

Nancy rattled the ice in her glass, fished out a cold raspberry, and popped it in her mouth. "Ben told me he didn't grow up with his sister."

Kelsey plucked a stray dandelion from a small patch of forgotten weeds next to her chair. She spun the flower between her fingers and watched the milky white liquid pool at the base of the stem. "Yeah, it was a bad divorce. His dad's a complete ass, but I think Ben feels like he should have tried harder to see Natalie. Like it was his duty or something. That's too much for a kid to take on."

Nancy nodded. "My oldest is like that. He'd right all the world's wrongs if he could."

"Ah, well, I'm the youngest, and I only look out for myself." Kelsey tried to laugh but the truth in her words stung.

***

Ben couldn't reach her by phone. And Kelsey hadn't sent a text like she promised she would. He hadn't planned to use that tracking app so soon, but he had no choice. There wasn't another way to see if she'd arrived safely at home.

One click relieved a suffocating layer of fear. The little red dot confirmed that Kelsey had made it back to their place. Damn it, now more than anything, he wanted to ditch work to be with her. When he tried to leave early, a new hire assigned to his department asked for extra help. He sent Kelsey a quick text letting her know he'd be late, but she didn't respond.

He tried not to obsess while he drove, but as each mile passed without a reply, he became *that guy*—a weaving aggressive asshole snaking through Portland traffic. Bursting through his front door, he couldn't find her. Her small backpack sat in the hall with her phone stuffed uselessly in the side-pocket. Ben dashed upstairs but she wasn't there. He fought the desire to search the neighborhood long enough to change into shorts and felt slightly better, finding relief from his sticky-hot tailored pants.

Maybe she'd gone to yoga or to that coffee shop down the street. Knowing how much independence meant to her, he grabbed a beer and paced the backyard. The grass looked ragged. At least mowing the lawn burned off a layer of energy.

***

Kels left Nancy's when the mower's engine revved, but she let Ben finish cutting the lawn. It gave her time to admire the way his shirt clung to the sweat on his back. When he disappeared behind the shed to put away the mower, she wandered into the kitchen and grabbed two beers, then found a spot on the bottom step of the deck and waited.

"There you are," he said, grabbing the cold bottle from her extended hand. He watched her carefully, waiting for an explanation about where she'd been. Kelsey's independence flared, and she sipped a drink of her beer instead of answering his insistent gaze. Ben glanced at his bottle, dripping with moisture, and thirst took over. His throat moved in slow waves as he pulled long swallows. Sighing, he folded onto the step next to her. His bare left knee rested against her right. The hint of human contact relaxed her immediately.

"Today was perfect." Her hand slid to his sun-warmed leg. He smelled like cut grass, fuel, and man.

"Why perfect?" Ben mirrored her touch, then took it further when he caressed the inside of her thigh, flicking his thumb as she talked.

"For the first time since the accident I felt like me . . . like I have a real life. I rode the train, gave up my seat to another passenger, and spent the afternoon working in Nancy's garden. I've got potatoes, beans, and tomatoes to show for it, too."

When her stomach growled, she pulled him inside to help her make dinner. They ate fresh vegetables and steaks that Ben cooked on the grill. While they cleaned up, Kels took advantage of the small kitchen and lingered into his casual contact—hips, shoulders, hands—every glancing touch tightened the tension between them. After dinner, Ben sank to the couch and pulled Kelsey against his torso before she was able to settle on the opposite end.

He flicked on the TV, but the game wasn't important to either of them. His hand followed a strand of hair that had escaped its tie on a path to her clavicle. Easing closer, she gave him room to drop those expert fingers to the swell of her breast. She inhaled when his touch found her pebbled nipple, covered only by the thin fabric of her tank top.

Each sensation felt new, like teen-aged sexploration—a game to figure out what felt good. She savored the press of his fingertips into her pliant skin and the puff of his breath against her neck. His kisses tasted like sin and home mixed into one—a dangerous place with a safety net to land in. Somehow, he knew to move carefully, letting Kelsey pull away when she'd had enough. A part of her still wasn't ready for more.

Kelsey stood, needing space. Their hands were still connected, and Ben held onto her fingers for as long as possible as she backed slowly away.

"I guess I need to take a shower," he said. "I smell like the lawn."

She liked the way he smelled, considered joining him in the shower, but wasn't ready and didn't want to mix hot messages with cold. A tilt of her head let him know where she was headed. "I'll go upstairs, read a book, and leave you to it."

***

Chilled water poured down his back, cooling his desire. As badly as Ben craved Kelsey, he understood she needed time and space—space they both knew was shrinking. A knock on the door startled him and his cock jumped to attention again. His anatomy hoped she had changed her mind.

"Can you stay in there while I brush my teeth and . . ." Kelsey laughed, nervous.

"No problem. I won't peek." The one-bathroom duplex hadn't posed a problem until this moment because their schedules were so different. Tonight, from dinner prep to the couch, and now in the bathroom, they seemed destined to stumble over each other.

Her toothbrush tapped against the edge of the sink, but she left the water running. A few moments later the toilet flushed.

"All done." Another nervous giggle—a uniquely sweet sound coming from Kelsey—trailed away as she pulled the bathroom door closed behind her.

The water hit him in the face, cold and bracing. Yet the punishment did nothing to his throbbing groin. If he planned to sleep at all, taking care of this wasn't optional. Determined to speed the process, he adjusted the temperature up a few dozen degrees, turned away from the spray, and let the pulsing jets trail over his shoulders and down his spine. One hand leaned on the far wall the other pulled long heavy strokes. Patient at first, he closed his eyes, remembering the way Kelsey's nipples pebbled when he caressed the responsive tips. He imagined his fingers and tongue finding another bundle of nerves that he intended to explore. Pulling harder on his cock, his grip paired with his fantasy. Hips thrusting, his hand tightened in a violent pursuit of his release. Hotter than the water streaming over his butt, he watched as cum shot from the purple tip. He groaned, almost satisfied, not caring if Kelsey heard. She'd done this to him, taken hold of his mind and body—and transformed him into a mass of desperate need.

The hot water was fading. Ben stumbled a little as he exited the shower and found a mirror dripping with condensation. After drying off, he pulled on jeans but not a shirt, then wandered downstairs. He poured a glass of whisky and escaped outside to his deck.

The liquor burned, but he didn't feel centered until he lit a cigar. The rare indulgence reminded him of who he was and where he'd come from. Both good and bad, his father had influenced him. The work ethic he'd embraced, an occasional cigar wasn't too damaging, but the way Dad treated women disgusted Ben. Working on wife number four, his dad was careful, and wouldn't let them slip on an engagement ring unless they signed a prenup. They'd become a single blur, slender bits of arm candy who all looked and acted the same. The woman in his home couldn't be more different.

When he wandered upstairs, Kelsey's light was still on. Ben spotted her through the gap in her door enduring a book—an activity she didn't enjoy. His arms tingled, longing to tuck her soft curves against him all night. It would happen, eventually. The barrier she'd put between them seemed fragile, nearly ready to collapse.

Ben's knock nudged the unlatched door open. "I just wanted to say goodnight."

She looked up from her book and reached out her hand welcoming him with a smile. As Ben sat on the edge of her bed, she wrapped her hand around his neck and pulled him to her lips, giving him a tender kiss.

"Mmm, you taste yummy," she sighed.

"Shit, sorry about the cigar."

"Don't be, I like it."

The way she accepted his vices tempted him even more. He closed his eyes, found what was left of his patience, then kissed her forehead before he left her room.

SEVENTEEN

"Can I buy the next beer?"

Brayden bound from his seat and gave Mark a pounding man-hug, "Shit, good to see you, mate"

"Are you coming or going?" Mark asked when he spotted the duffle near Brayden's foot on the floor.

"I left Hawaii yesterday. Been avoiding reality for way too long, and I gotta get back home. You?" Brayden asked and flagged down the server.

"Damn. We just missed each other. I left Melbourne this morning. Got a ticket for the Big Island. I stopped by your place, but your flat mates didn't know when you'd be back. How long were you in Hawaii?"

"Longer than I should. I extended my holiday twice. Started out in Tofino, worked my way south to Washington state. I'd planned to follow the coast to California, but . . . plans changed."

"Hey. You were in my backyard. Did you find some of those surf spots I recommended in Oregon?" Mark asked as his beer arrived.

"I wanted to . . . even had a girl in mind to join me, but then everything went to shit." Brayden raked his hand through his hair. His eyes blanked and he stared across the stream of people moving like a swarm of insects in the busy airport.

"Did she leave you stranded on the sand?" Mark teased before he noticed the naked pain on his friend's face.

"Nah. We never made it to the beach. We spent an amazing night together by a lake, a night that left me wanting more . . . and then . . . I never saw her again. It was fucked."

When the server passed, Brayden asked for two shots of Jack Daniels. Mark leaned his elbows on the table, giving Brayden time. Clearly shaken up, his friend was lost in his thoughts, and watched while the bartender poured the golden liquor. He waited until both shots were in front of him before he continued. "There was this kayak festival in Washington. High profile. That famous photographer, Parker Knight, had a hand in filming the event."

"Not on The Little White?" Mark interrupted.

"Yeah, do you know the river?" Brayden asked, before he downed the first shot. Mark couldn't speak. He nodded, his fear simmering.

"Started out great, then on the final day, some kids took to the river that had no business being on those class-five rapids. They got into trouble, and this girl, Kelsey, she dropped in to save them."

Kelsey. Mark could barely hear Brayden's voice over the roar of blood that rushed to his ears.

"She pulled one of these kids out of a hydraulic. Another smashed in over the drop, knocked her out, and she drifted down river. Her friend, another local, pulled her out. I reckon they hauled her out of the canyon by rope before the heli took her to Portland. It was a mess."

Mark couldn't ask. He didn't want to know.

"So, I sat around the hospital for days, hoping she'd wake up. Damn, I only spent a little time with the girl—but I can't seem to shake it—something about her still has a hold on me." Mark stared at Brayden, his eyes glazed with fear. "Last I heard, she was still in a coma." Brayden groaned, knocked back his second shot, and clunked the glass on the table.

"That's it? You left?" Mark fought a boil of anger, jealousy, and fear. "God damnit, don't you even know if Kelsey is alive?"

Shock and confusion shifted Brayden's features. "Shit, do you know this girl?"

Mark stood, realized he had nowhere to go, then sat again. Every eye in the bar sliced his direction. "Yes. Jesus. I've spent weeks with her. I was working my way back to Washington . . . to Kelsey."

His thin description didn't begin to capture how much he cared about that fascinating woman. How every day he longed to close the miles separating them and see if there was a chance that she still wanted him in her life. The silence he took for rejection wasn't rejection at all. And like a fool, he'd stopped his messages to Kelsey weeks ago. Yet nothing had changed on his end. This girl, with eyes like a storm and corn silk hair, still haunted his thoughts.

With shaking hands, Mark fished the phone from his pocket and scanned the long line of unanswered texts, wondering who he should call to learn the truth. Her *last* message was more than two months ago—the night before her final run. Shaking and frantic, he placed a desperate call.

***

She woke in the dark to a buzzing sound. Half asleep, Kelsey fumbled with the phone as it went silent. The display showed Mark's name under *missed calls*.

Kelsey dropped the phone on her blanket. Why had he called? Was Mark back in Washington? The last time she checked his blog, he'd said he was going from Australia to The Big Island. She had at least another month before she had to face him. Another month to find what was left of the Kelsey he remembered.

An overwhelming swell of dread clawed at her throat and she couldn't breathe. Fear crowded her mind and her vision blurred. Rounding her lips, she inhaled measured breaths and wondered if panic could trigger another seizure. As soon as the phone's screen went to black, Kelsey exhaled.

A few seconds later, a new wave of panic crested when a tone chimed. She spun the phone to read the text.

I just heard about the accident. Are you okay? Please, say something. I need to know.

He must have spotted the video, but that didn't make sense. Nothing on the internet left anyone guessing. Parker's latest follow up story told the world—in glorified, exaggerated detail—the joyous tale of her miraculous recovery.

The desperation in his words forced her reply. Choosing her words with care, Kelsey typed and retyped, praying a small lie would buy her time.

I'm getting better. Still in Portland. I'm not allowed to talk right now. I need to go.

The fact that he knew about the accident didn't change a thing—she *still* couldn't face him. And the words she'd typed weren't really a lie—she *was* in Portland. But just to be safe, she held down the button and turned off her phone.

***

"Thank God." Mark gulped down sick dread, gripped the table, and pressed his spine against the chair.

Brayden tore his hands through his long, shaggy hair. "She's alive." He exhaled as if he'd dropped a two-ton weight. "What did she say?"

"Not nearly enough. She's in Portland, somewhere, still recovering. Shit, that was almost two months ago."

"It had to be bad, she was in a coma. Mark, she might not ever be the same," Brayden warned.

"The same? Do you really think that changes anything?"

"Sorry, mate." A shake of his head mirrored Brayden's shame.

Mark needed more, anything that would give him a clue. "Maybe she's still in the hospital. Do you remember which one?"

The Aussie shrugged.

"Never mind. I'll call in the morning their time and find out what's going on." Mark clenched his hands and tried to stop shaking. "I can't believe I almost lost her."

Brayden cleared his throat. "I'm sorry. And you have to know, she . . . I . . . we didn't ever. Damn it, I didn't know she was yours."

Mark stared at his friend again, seeing Brayden through different eyes. For some reason, he didn't feel jealous. "Mine? I'll never own her. But when I get back, I won't make the mistake of taking her for granted again."

***

She couldn't sleep. Kelsey pulled on jeans and a sweatshirt, brushed her hair and teeth, and left before Ben's alarm. This early in the morning, the Max train was teaming with commuters wearing everything from suits to Carhartts—all different costumes for different work. She missed her hiking gear and wondered if it was still heaped in the corner of her closet.

At The Center, she hurried to the locker room, changed into her swimsuit, and was determined to take on her shadowy demons—the water that still haunted her dreams. She flicked on the lights and approached the pool cautiously, but she couldn't go in.

Cool air whooshed across the warmth of the pool and pushed toward her when Travis opened the men's locker room door. Kelsey didn't turn, but she knew he was studying the frightened blonde-haired girl with her legs dangling in the shallow end of the pool. The water was still as glass—it had stopped rippling a long time ago.

"Ben called me, he was trying to find you," Travis' words echoed on his approach. His weight squeaked the wooden bench as he took a seat a few feet behind her.

Kelsey stared into the pool and considered the way the water distorted her toes. "I'll call him back later."

"Did something happen between you and Ben? Do you need to move back to The Center?"

"No. I was just hoping I'd be ready for the water today. But I'm not."

The bench squeaked as Travis moved. His bare feet slapped the tile softly as he sat next to her, and the water rippled when his feet slipped in. "Kelsey, your success is not defined by getting into this pool. If you want to—great. If not—no problem. What you're doing here isn't a sprint. It's not a marathon either. It's your life, yours to do with as you please."

She turned to him and nodded. "I want to swim. Someday."

"Okay." His grin spread as he stood. Travis extended an open hand to help her to her feet. "I've got a few hours before my first appointment. Want to play some rummy?"

"Sure." She pulled her feet from the water and glanced back at the pool. In the ripples, she could barely make out her reflection. Distorted by the tiles and bright lights, she looked like a ghostly version of herself. She stayed for a moment, waiting while the water smoothed. As soon as her reflection focused, Kelsey turned and walked away.

***

Ben took the day off, wanting to be home when Kelsey showed. He called his sister, worried that he'd crossed some invisible line. Natalie listened, then she offered to come with Seth to Portland right away. Around noon, when Kelsey walked in the front door, she met him with a kiss and apologized for leaving before he woke. Ben told her about tonight's impromptu plans and quickly offered to call his sister back to cancel.

Kelsey wrapped Ben in her arms. "No, it's okay. I'd like to see Nate and Seth. It'll be warm tonight. We can all go out and have a beer."

Everyone was starved when Seth and Natalie pulled up. Since they all craved something different, they decided to walk a few blocks to the food trucks not far from Ben's place. Delicious smoke curled from the mobile restaurants, tempting them as they wandered to check out the menus. When Seth lingered in front of a barbeque spot, the owner sprang out, wanting to catch up with the guy who'd built his food truck.

Kelsey found an empty table and put her spicy gumbo and grits bowl down. Ben joined her with a plate of Peruvian wood-fired chicken and two German-style lagers. "I hope German beer goes with Cajun and Peruvian." He reached over her shoulder and set the beer in front of her plate.

"Very international." Kels tipped her head back to meet his smile. Her upturned face gave him the perfect opportunity to taste her sweet tempting lips.

"Delicious," he murmured against her mouth.

"You like spicy?" she whispered, accepting another kiss.

"I like Kelsey." When his tongue danced across her lower lip she hummed, and he felt the vibration in his groin. He moaned, so gone for this girl.

Ben spotted his sister studying them from afar. Natalie's eyes narrowed, and he waved her over. She joined them, digging into her food right away. Even though this morning's drama still lingered like a thin, gray cloud, Kelsey's mood was light. After everyone settled, she asked Seth questions about the vendors. "How many of these food truck chefs do you know?"

Seth pivoted in his seat and surveyed the entire parking lot. "I put together two of these trucks, but I've got builds scattered all over Portland. There was a time when I could assemble a commercial kitchen in my sleep. Did Natalie tell you we're thinking about converting her old place into a food vendor and putting it up for sale? It already has the food service window."

Kelsey tensed. "That's sad."

"Where would I stay when I visit the lake?" Ben protested with a laugh.

Natalie grinned. "We're toying with the idea of building a lakefront cabin."

"Would I still be welcome?" Ben knew he didn't have to ask.

"Of course." Seth nodded. "Would you like to lend a hand with the build?"

"Count me in."

Natalie's pointed attention skated from her plate to Kelsey. Her eyes shimmered with an intensity that Ben recognized. He scooted closer to Kels, wanting to protect her, wondering what was wrong. His sister took a drink of her wine and asked, "Kels, one thing has always bugged me . . ."

"Only one?" Kelsey laughed, but his sister's stiff smile didn't convince Ben.

"A few days after . . ." Awkward silence hung over the table.

"The accident." Kelsey finished Nate's thought and shook her head.

"Yes, the accident. Well, I found this note you'd left at the tiny lake house. I think it was from the night before."

Kelsey tensed and nodded slowly. "You know I can't remember much about a few days before or after."

"Right, right. But I just wondered . . . it looks like you crashed there to escape Parker's mob at your house."

"Sounds like something I'd do. But I'll probably never remember it." Kelsey pushed her plate away and stood. "I'll be right back," she said before snaking her way toward a line of port-a-potties.

Ben waited until Kelsey was out of sight. "Shit, Sis. What was with that interrogation?"

"Today was weird, with Kels taking off." Natalie shrugged. "I feel like she's ready to face some of this stuff, and you need to know her, *really know her*, before this thing between you and Kelsey gets serious."

Seth put his arm around his wife. "Honey, Ben's got this."

"It wasn't just the note," she blurted. "There were guy's socks stuffed under the couch, and a lot of the basics we stock were eaten. Kelsey wasn't alone. Ben, I just thought you should know." Clearly upset, Natalie pulled her lips between her teeth.

Ben's neck heated as he fought a wave of untargeted jealousy. "So, she had a friend over, no big deal." He shrugged and took a long slow breath. "That was *before . . .* She's *different* now."

***

Kelsey waited until she knew Ben was asleep in his room to turn on her phone. In the time it was off, she'd missed three of her usual calls—Kent, Sig, and her mom, and another text waited from Mark.

Please tell me where you are. I'm ready to buy a ticket the moment I hear from you.

She couldn't see him. Not yet. Without thinking, Kelsey typed furiously.

I can't have visitors. It's part of the treatment. The stress might cause a relapse. I'll call when I can see you.

The thought of seeing him, of enduring the disappointment on his face made her stomach turn. She wasn't ready. Just putting her feet in the swimming pool this morning had sent her into a panic. What would happen if she fell off a surfboard and tumbled into turbulent waves? Kelsey sighed and let go of her past, knowing that she'd never be his Mermaid again.

***

Mark sank onto the squeaky motel bed. A plane shook the building as it came in for a landing at the nearby airport.

"This doesn't make sense. No visitors?" Still, how would he know? He'd never recovered from anything worse than a broken arm.

"Fuck, I hate this," he mumbled. Three surfboards lined the wall, and head high waves waited for him at his small home on the beach in Kauai. If Kelsey needed time, he'd give it to her, at least for a little while. He packed his duffle and grabbed his gear, ready to catch the next island hopper. A few days on the waves would clear his muddled mind.

Kelsey was alive. And that was enough for now.

EIGHTEEN

One day passed and then another. When Mark didn't text, she figured he'd accepted her lie. Kelsey smothered her guilt with a heavy dose of justification. Mark was part of her past and wanted a woman who didn't exist any longer.

After spending all this time with Ben, she discovered he was a man who deserved her full attention. With endless patience, he watched out for her while still respecting her boundaries. And he seemed to prefer the tamer version of Kelsey she'd become. Once she found her footing in a regular life, at Venture or a random nine-to-five, she'd reassess. Until then, therapy and getting in the water had to come first.

That, and working in Nancy's garden.

When they ran out of weeds, Nancy began to teach her home canning. She'd done so well, they'd run out of jar lids during the last batch. Nancy dashed out and left her in charge in the kitchen while she ran to the store.

***

1970s rock blared in the alley separating his house from Nancy's. Ben knew where to find Kelsey and let himself in through the back door. She smiled when she heard him cross the threshold but couldn't turn away from her work. Using long metal tongs, Kelsey carefully fished glass jars filled with salsa verde from a hot canning bath.

Ben approached her slowly and slipped his hands over her hips. "This kitchen smells as spicy as you look," he said, giving her a gentle squeeze.

She'd put on red cotton shorts and a tank to cope with the steamy kitchen. Her hair was up and out of her way, trapped in a messy bun. Ben bent his head and took a taste of her salty skin at the nape of her neck.

"Stop, you'll give me a hickey!" She giggled and squirmed but didn't struggle too much.

"Mmm." He added teeth to the pressure. "I like the idea of leaving my mark on your neck."

"I'd like those bites better where no one can find them."

"Great idea. Where's Nancy?" he asked as his jaw nuzzled her top away from her shoulder.

"She ran to the store for more lids." Kelsey held her breath when his hands slipped around her waist and spread across her tummy.

For the past few days he'd given her time, keeping their nights somewhat chaste with light petting and kisses, but the way she writhed beneath his touch erased any lingering hesitation—Kels was ready for more.

"How long ago did she leave?" he asked against her slick skin.

"Ten minutes."

"Mm, so little time." Ben spun her away from the stove and caged her against the kitchen counter. Her hands drifted from his chest to his neck as Ben's grasp went from her waist to the plumpest part of her ass. He pulled her hips up and forward, putting Kels on her tiptoes, wonderfully off-balance and under his control.

"Oh, God," she whispered against his mouth, when the hard evidence of his desire pressed against her heat.

He thoroughly tasted her lips, then licked a path down the column of her supple neck, biting the spot where her shoulder took a gentle sway. Bending his knees, he traced a line across the swell of her breast.

The slam of Nancy's car door jolted their bodies apart. "Damn, I almost forgot we weren't at home," Ben moaned. "Tell me you can get away soon."

"I'll try," she promised with one more kiss.

***

Nancy had spotted the pair in her kitchen when she pulled past her house coming up the drive. A grin paired with a vivid memory—those days when her husband came home early while the kids were still in school. She knew that the kitchen counter was a great spot for an afternoon rendezvous. With a toss, she abandoned the canning lids she'd bought on the passenger side floor, leaving them there for another day. After waiting another moment in the car, she made plenty of noise, slamming her door before going inside.

Fortunately, Ben chose to dash out her front door as she made her way into the back. "They were out of lids and rings, Kelsey," she said trying not to laugh. Her friend's shirt was hanging at an angle nearly off her shoulder. "Should we call it a day?"

"Sure. I'll start cleaning up," Kelsey said on a turn toward the sink.

"That's okay." Nancy waved her off. "I think I saw Ben's car parked at your place. I've got this handled."

With an eager nod and a quick goodbye, Kels scooted next door. Nancy chuckled. There was nothing like the promise of hot sex to make a girl move that fast.

***

Ben didn't expect her so soon. He was upstairs changing from slacks to shorts when Kelsey burst into his room. A flurry of clothes fluttered to the floor in a blur.

Naked, and painfully erect, Ben paused to stare at the goddess he longed to explore, savor, and cherish. "Kelsey," he whispered hoping she wanted him half as much as he wanted her.

A blush spread over her ivory skin as she licked her lips, devouring him with her eyes. She stepped forward and outlined his chiseled chest and abdomen with trembling fingers. Each stroke left a trace of brilliant heat.

"Are you sure?" he asked as he wrapped his arms around her and painted a ribbon of desire down her back and over her ass.

A small nod answered Ben's question and he didn't hesitate. She stood perfectly still while he worked his way from her lips to his neck, over her breast, down her stomach, eventually falling to his knees to taste the wet evidence of her longing. Kelsey's fingers pulled his hair and her legs parted a fraction, as he wrapped his hands around the soft globes of her butt, holding her in place to plunge his tongue deeper.

"Mmm, right there," she moaned and pivoted forward to press against his marauding tongue. Gripping his shoulders, her body began to shake as her pleasure coiled. Delicious and wet, he lapped her arousal, and her thighs trembled. She inhaled, held her breath, holding precious oxygen tight. He sensed her urgency and quickened the pace, while slipping two fingers into her wet heat. She cried out when the detonation hit her body, powerful and explosive, releasing tension that had coiled for weeks. He rode out her craving, relishing her taste and the control he had over her pleasure.

Kelsey collapsed, giggling and satisfied, next to Ben on the floor. Their arms and legs tangled, and he took her face between his hands, kissing those giggles to desperate moans.

"On the bed," Ben commanded, bringing her with him as he stood. "Lie down on your stomach."

She crawled to the middle of his king-size bed and peeked over her shoulder when he didn't join her immediately. "Ben?"

"Enjoying the view. Good God, you're stunning," he growled. "Don't move." Over her prone form, his hands began a slow trek, massaging her feet and ankles. When he reached her calves, he parted her legs and settled his knees on the triangle of mattress between them. She moaned as his palms skated up the back of her thighs.

Kelsey thought her first orgasm would take the edge off. It did, until his teeth nibbled each soft cheek. His hands, lips, and tongue touched her everywhere—the sway of her back, the edge of her hip, and the line of her spine. But the one place she longed to feel him most he avoided ... until Kels begged. "I need you inside me. Please."

He didn't speak. Instead, he tore open a condom and her lips tilted into a smile. Ben reached for her hips and began to turn Kels over, but she shook her head, and brought her knees under her torso.

"So vulnerable and wet for me," he groaned as he climbed forward and aligned their thighs. He stroked her folds first with his fingers, then with the crown of his cock. Slick and hot, she savored each sensation then closed her eyes, anticipating the plunge that would connect their bodies for the very first time. Slow and sensual, he took his time and Kelsey moaned. Stretched tight, she pushed back against his hips, taking in his generous girth.

He pulled out completely before impaling her again. The pace of his plunges sped, and Kelsey changed the angle of her hips. He slid his hand around her hip to the apex of her sex.

The moment he made contact she whispered, "Right there."

His careful movements shifted to frenzied and heat coiled at the base of his spine. Kelsey slid her fingers over his, adding pressure as she bucked. Deep inside, she clamped around him as his hips pumped hard and deep. She exploded, crested, and her bliss expanded again, radiating a current of electric release in waves that pushed him harder, took everything from him and bound Ben to her in a fiery sustained release.

Satisfied, Ben fell forward and pinned Kelsey to the mattress with his weight. They panted, waiting for the low hum of ecstasy to subside.

"Don't move," Ben said against her neck before he pulled away. She didn't stir when he escaped to get rid of the condom. When Ben returned, he pivoted Kelsey toward him and began his quest again, starting with a taste of her delectable mouth.

***

Kelsey's finger stroked the ridges of Ben's stomach when his gnawing hunger rumbled. He knew she had to be starving, too. "We both need fuel, because I'm not done with you," he said then gave her a kiss.

She moaned against his mouth, before she stretched and moved.

Ben detoured in the bathroom then found her in the kitchen, already cooking. This was another change in her, and she seemed to like it as much as he did. She worked in bare feet, silently grating cheese. Beside her was a plate of left-over roasted chicken, already cut in strips. He watched her assemble quesadillas, and his mouth watered when she turned it over, golden on top, sizzling in the pan.

"This one's yours," she said sliding it onto a plate.

While she waited on her quesadilla, he devoured his, then scrambled her senses with a kiss. She ate while Ben pulled together his second quesadilla, and then Kels put the ingredients away. He slid the tortilla from the pan, but wasn't very tempted by the food, not with Kelsey a few feet from him rinsing dishes. He spun her around and slid his hands beneath her robe.

"Aren't you gonna eat the second one?" she asked, squirming under his touch.

"I don't know . . . you're so delicious," he mumbled against her neck.

She wiggled away, grabbed his plate, and used the edge of it to push him away. "You need fuel, and I don't want to wake up to a messy kitchen."

Ben shrugged. "Okay, I'll eat this first, then I'll eat you later."

The spatula in the sink was a handy weapon. She raised it with a grin, and he backed to the other side of the small kitchen and took a bite of his food. Kelsey secured the robe around her waist and turned back to cleaning.

Ben dipped a corner of his tortilla into a small bowl of salsa. "This fresh stuff is great."

"That's the salsa Nancy and I made yesterday. Nearly every ingredient is from her garden, even the fresh herbs."

"Did you have a garden at home?" he asked between bites.

"It wasn't really Mom's thing. Dad has some tomatoes, but he spends his free time fishing. We had fresh trout from the lake instead."

"Not a bad trade-off."

"What time is it?" Kels asked with a yawn.

"After one. Too bad you're tired. I'm not sure I'll be able to get to sleep." Ben grinned, lifting one eyebrow—teasing, hoping.

Kelsey's grin tipped playfully at the corners. "Really? I'm so exhausted." She stretched her hands over her head, exaggerating her yawn. The mischievous move teased her robe open, revealing a lot more skin. Ben tossed his plate into the sink with a clatter and the race was on. She bolted upstairs and squealed with delight when he caught her and carried her into his room.

***

Ben slept past the first alarm and was forty minutes late to work. The grumble from that guy in the office who always complained didn't faze him. He hadn't felt this fantastic. Ever.

Staring at his calendar, Ben wondered if he could get out of his next trip to North Carolina. This was a short project—only a week—but he didn't want to leave Kelsey, not now. He couldn't get out of it but settled for changing his Friday flight to Monday, trimming a few days from his usual routine. His friends at the North Carolina office would understand if he didn't want to hit the bars over the weekend and hang out. It wouldn't be long before she'd be able to take a break from The Center and join him on his business trips.

NINETEEN

Parker Knight grabbed her assistant by the shoulders and shook him. "This is amazing," she said. "Have you confirmed your research?"

"Yeah. I went the extra mile and drove out to some dumpy place on the coast and talked to the owner. She was a legit hippie. Anyway, she was shaken up when I mentioned what happened to Kelsey. This old woman owns some vacation spot, I think it was Driftwood Shores. She doesn't even own a computer and hadn't heard about the kayak footage. Can you believe that?"

Parker paced and listened, thinking so much better while her body moved. Her eyes flicked up, impatient for more details.

"I didn't even have to ask about Mark," her assistant continued while his head tracked her back-and-forth path. "This Faye woman blurted out Mark's name and wondered if the surfer knew what had happened to Kelsey. Looks like Mark Lance and Kelsey Fisher have a long history, and they are way more than friends. They meet out at the coast and surf together, sometimes for weeks at a time."

"Shit, this story keeps getting better and better. Great work. Now I just need to finesse this."

"I checked Mark's blog, and it looks like he's in Hawaii. Hmm, maybe they split up." Her assistant flipped through his notes. "That would explain why he stayed away while Kelsey was in the hospital."

Parker shook her head. "Mark's focused on surfing, and probably doesn't want to get tied down." She wouldn't admit the truth—that she'd tried to hook up with Mark and failed. His loss, asshole. Hell, she still admired his relentless drive, but knowing that Kelsey had got to the guy pissed her off. Her hands fisted, knuckles popping—she hated coming in second to anyone.

"Do you want me to give Mark Lance a call?" her assistant asked. "I'll dig a little and see if I can get his reaction to Kelsey's injuries." His eyes glimmered hungry for the chance.

Parker held up her hand. "No, no. I want to give this some thought. This is *too good*. I've been trying to find a way to feature his surfing business for years. He's intensely private, but this might be the tasty bait I need to lure him in."

***

With her elbow bent and her hand supporting her head, Kelsey watched from his bed as Ben packed his sleek suitcase. He paused, hesitating before he added another pair of pants.

"I'll be fine," Kelsey said, as she reclined on his pillow.

"But you can't drive. What if you need to buy something you can't carry home?"

"What? Like a watermelon? Seriously, Ben, Nancy's right next door."

"Does Natalie plan to visit?" he asked, as he stuffed a pair of dress shoes in the side compartment.

"Your sister will be here on Wednesday," she nodded and laughed, "*Dad*."

He tackled her, pinning her beneath him on the mattress. His suitcase tumbled to the floor, and Ben didn't seem to care. "I'll miss you," he said between kisses.

"Mmm-miss you, too." Her humming words tickled the spot where their lips connected. "You're gonna miss your flight."

"Good plan."

"Go!" She wrestled away from his exploring hands. "I still need to get ready before I catch the train to The Center. Do you have everything packed?"

"Yeah," he grumbled and zipped the bag shut. They kissed goodbye halfway down the stairs and again up against the front door. After she shoved him outside, Kels propped her shoulder against the doorframe and watched Ben toss his bag in the backseat. He ran back to the porch and stole another kiss before he left.

"Baby, be good," he said over his shoulder as he bounded back to his car.

Be good? She tipped her head against the frame of the open door and watched as he disappeared down the street. *Where had that come from?*

Fighting the empty echo of the house, she was about to turn up the music when her phone vibrated on the desk by her laptop. *Ben better not be texting while he's driving.*

The screen lit, and she spotted his name. *Mark.*

Please call me, Kelsey. I need to see you.

Not yet.

With shaking fingers, she swept the message away, suddenly relieved that Mark didn't know where to find her.

***

"Today, Coach. I'm getting in that pool and swimming laps today," Kelsey insisted.

"You got this Kels, I know you're ready," Travis agreed. "Get your suit on, I'll meet you in the pool."

Chlorine and moist air hit her as she pushed through the door separating the locker room and the pool. Travis stood waist-deep in the water at the shallow end, his solid torso and olive skin a warm, tangible lifeline.

Her bare feet slapped across the tiled floor, and she found herself standing at the top of the half-moon steps. She stared at the distorted cement beneath the rippling water and inhaled. Grasping the round rail, her hand slid down the perfect metal tube as she took three rapid steps without thinking about the consequences.

There were none.

Her fear evaporated in the water, melting away with the tears streaming down her face. Squeezing her eyes together, she forced the last salty tear out—it disappeared with the rest, into the chlorinated water.

Travis laughed. "That was easier than I expected."

Kelsey whooped in celebration and slapped the water with her open palm. "Race you to the other side," she challenged.

"You're on." Travis didn't need to wait on Kels. She sailed past him, her clean, confident strokes slicing through the water. Her physical therapist never had a chance.

Half an hour later, he had to drag her from the pool. "Save something for next time, Kels. Go home and celebrate."

"I can't believe I did it. I swam." She stood on the lowest concrete step, still panting hard from the workout. Her eyes perused different sections of the pool. The friends she'd made at The Center each sought their own victories—walking through shallow water to improve balance, kicking while supported by a noodle, or floating above the arm of a therapist.

"I never doubted you." Travis grinned on his way to the locker room. "See you tomorrow."

Her breathing slowed, but her entire body still trembled. She'd overcome her greatest challenge and had one final hurdle on the horizon. Once Travis got her behind the wheel of her car, she'd be ready to ease back into her old life. She wouldn't need his help much longer.

***

Kelsey sat outside The Center while the warm summer sun dried her hair. She pulled out her phone, and Kent answered her call on the second ring.

"What's up, Kels?" he asked, worry in his tone. She wondered how much time would pass before her friends stopped answering her calls that way.

"I need to celebrate. Are you busy?"

"Celebrate? I'm in." Kent chuckled, "What's the occasion?"

"I swam laps in the pool today." Happiness turned to laughter as her joy sprang free.

"That's awesome. How do you want to celebrate?"

"Doesn't matter. I just miss hanging out. Why don't you come into Portland and spend the night?"

"I'll talk to Seth, but I know it won't be a problem, so long as Ben's okay with it."

"He's in North Carolina for work," she said. "Want to stay a day or two?"

"Perfect, I'll see you in a couple of hours."

**

The text Ben read in his meeting was happy and short. Kelsey's victory over her fear of water distracted him from his colleague's PowerPoint.

Ben sent her a '*congrats*' message and promised to call her later. When her longer reply included her plans to spend the evening celebrating with Kent, he clenched his jaw, combating misplaced jealousy. He reminded himself, again, that Kent was more brother than friend.

**

On the train ride home, Kelsey read Ben's reply *twice*. **Have fun with Kent, but don't overdo it.**

"What the fuck does that mean?" she whispered and glared at the screen, though she didn't bother to reply. Anything she typed right now would be horribly wrong. Dealing with Ben would have to wait until she calmed down. She shut off her phone and refused to let him diminish her happiness. By the time she got off the train her joyful mood was back in place.

Kent didn't have a chance to knock before she pulled the front door open and flew into his arms. Jumping, Kelsey wrapped her legs around his hips, nearly toppling Kent over on the porch. "I did it! I swam. Underwater, too!" Her lips on his cheek surprised him, and Kent jerked away with a laugh. Kelsey didn't even let him come inside before she grabbed her backpack. "Let's get out of here and find a place to party."

"I'm all yours," he said jogging to his truck.

Even the ride felt like a celebration. She cranked up the music and directed him to a pub with a popular happy hour. After greasy appetizers, they shot some pool. When the sliders wore off, they headed downtown for a sugar feast.

Kent parked a couple of blocks away from Voo-Doo Donuts and let the delicious smell pull their feet in the right direction. He went for the maple and bacon, and she chose a Tang-topped donut with mango filling.

They joined a group of German tourists at a long table in the alley next to the donut shop. The tourists asked for recommendations about the best waterfalls in the gorge. Kels shared her secret spots and they thanked her, surprised by her depth of knowledge. It all came flooding back as the conversation flowed. She ached for the outdoors, the solitude and freedom she knew could only be found on a lonely trail. A hollow longing in her chest expanded, and Kels realized that a part of her was waiting for her in the mountains.

When the hit of sugar drained from her system, Kelsey began to fade. "Why don't we take a break?" Kent offered, sensing the change.

"Are you sure?"

"Yeah, we can go out again later if we catch a second wind."

In the warmth of his truck, her head drooped, snapped up, and drooped again. Kelsey lost the fight and slipped into a heavy sleep.

When a jolting stop popped her eyes open, she discreetly swept drool from the corner of her mouth with the back of her hand. "How long was I out?" she asked, now wide-awake.

"An hour-ish. I drove around a while," Kent answered with a shrug.

"Hey, I don't need you babysitting me," she snapped, feeling embarrassed and disoriented.

"I wasn't. You were tired, and I felt like driving."

"Bullshit."

"Where's this coming from?" He gave her a look, and she knew instantly he wasn't going to put up with her crap.

Kels wrapped her arms around her torso, ready to pout, and grumbled, "Let's go home."

Kent took a long breath and kept on driving. "Could we at least stop and grab pizza? I'm starved. We've only had sliders, beer, and donuts."

"Whatever." A noiseless, awkward mile stretched between them while Kelsey stared at the shimmering streetlights. Damn it, she didn't want to cry. Apart from a sniffle, the silence lingered, and Kent drove farther away from her neighborhood while stubbornly refusing to give into her tantrum.

Her shoulders relaxed and she swallowed hard. No matter how hard she tried, her best friend wasn't going to let her ruin her celebration. Right now, Kels couldn't have loved Kent more. He was perfect . . . stubborn, but perfect. "I'm sorry I snapped at you. I'm such a bitch." She shook her head, regretting the explosive outburst of napalm temper.

"That's okay." He smiled but didn't disagree with her self-assessment. Kels chuckled, happy that things were getting back to normal between them. She grinned when another unexpected bonus hit—even though he'd driven miles from home, she recognized where she was.

"I know a barbeque place that stays open late, it's not far from here."

Kent licked his lips. "Ribs?"

"The best. Spicy and sweet."

"My mouth is already watering. Point the way."

Kelsey aimed her arm like a compass, and he took a right at the light.

***

Shit, another call went directly to voicemail. Ben felt her chill across the three thousand miles that separated them. He looked at his last text again. It *was* a little bossy. Still, she could cut him some slack. He was only thinking of her. Weren't they a couple now? Didn't that entitle him to something? Concerned and curious, he pulled up the app and tracked her movements again. She was only a few miles from their place, probably out with Kent.

As he paced the concrete in front of his office, Ben nearly ran into his supervisor.

"Whoa, Ben. You're working late. Have you got a lot on your mind?"

"Sorry. I didn't see you." Ben chuckled—he'd never unloaded his personal life at work, and he wasn't about to start now.

"Not a problem. There's a few of us meeting at Lucky's for a drink. Want to join?"

Ben hesitated. Susan might be part of that crowd. He'd tried to avoid his ex since they broke up when he made is move to Portland. Hell, it really didn't matter if she was at their old haunt. Lucky's was big and loud, with plenty of space to avoid Susan. "Sure. I'll stop in for a beer."

***

Kent leaned against the counter and munched on a buttery slice of toast. The coffee pot hissed— the first cup almost ready. "What's the plan today?"

"It's going to be nearly ninety. We should drive up to Lost Lake. I want to swim."

Kent agreed and they packed up their gear—an old blanket, towels, and a cooler filled with snacks. After a two-hour drive Kelsey leapt from the car, ready to spread out the blanket on the wide day-use lawn. Everything looked picture-perfect—families sat at picnic tables, a guy was tossing a frisbee to his dog, and couples dotted the lake in rowboats. A row of yellow rental kayaks on the shore made Kelsey feel a little queasy. That would *not* be happening today. She slipped off her T-shirt and revealed her orange bikini, then dug into her bag for her SPF 70 sunscreen.

"Let me get your back," Kent offered. She knew she needed it. Her skin was so pale this year from weeks spent indoors focused on treatment and therapy.

"Don't you want any?" she asked as he flipped the cap shut.

"Maybe later, if we rent a boat." She grinned when he surrendered all the choices to her. He didn't seem to care if they swam, stayed on shore, rented boats or not.

The day passed like a lazy vacation. They wandered hiking trails, ate lunch at the General Store, and when Kels was ready, climbed into a bulky green canoe. The lake spread out into small channels, and they paddled away from the day-use area, leaving the laughter of children and barking dogs behind them. She swept the paddle through the water with expert ease. A fish splashed, an insect buzzed by her head, and far in the distance the shriek of an eagle carried through the air. The environment welcomed her. Portland was fine, but *this* was her natural habitat.

Kels lay her paddle in the bottom of the canoe and spun to face Kent from her spot on the narrow front seat.

"Thanks for today," she said. "I love it here. It's been years."

"I'd love to stay tonight, but the cabins are all booked, and we don't have a tent."

She laughed aloud. "You already checked?"

He nodded and shrugged. "Of course." Neither of them wanted to leave. "How's that alcove look for a swim?" he asked.

She twisted and shaded her eyes to get a better look. "I like it." Spinning back around, Kelsey drew her paddle through the water, slicing the canoe toward the graveled shore. They hauled the canoe onto the bank and tucked it next to a weathered snag.

"I'm going in," she said while stripping off her cut offs, down to her bikini bottoms.

"I'll be right behind you."

In moments Kelsey plunged into the icy water. Shocking cold almost drove her back to dry ground, but she gritted her teeth, worked through tiny remnants of fear, and swam farther into the crystalline lake.

While treading water, she turned to discover Kent watching. His sandy hair fluttered in the breeze, and his grin was wide. He was the same disheveled boy she'd loved like a brother since first grade. Splashing in, he joined her, and being Kent, he eventually challenged her to a race back to shore. A race he won, but not too easily.

Eyes closed, arms tucked behind their heads, they lay together on the bank, drying in the warmth of the sun.

"When did you and Ben *do the deed*?" he asked abruptly.

"Who says we did?"

Kent turned his head, leveled a stare, but didn't answer.

"Did Natalie tell you?" she asked.

"No, she didn't need to. Kels, I know your tells."

"Fine, asshole. Ben and I hit the sheets *recently*."

"Aren't you officially a couple now? I've been hanging out with you for more than twenty-four hours, and you haven't even texted the guy. Is he blowing you off?"

Kels sat up and wrapped her arms around her legs. She didn't want to share this stuff with him today, but they'd always been honest with each other about everything. That wasn't going to change. "No. He sent a bossy message. I'm pissed and taking a stand."

"There's nothing like the silent treatment to solve relationship problems." Kent huffed. "Come on Kels, this isn't high school, you've never pulled that manipulative shit."

She stood, needing distance, but Kent followed. Ignoring him for a moment, she picked a stone from the shore and hurled it into the lake. "I don't know what to say. And I'm afraid I'll make it worse if I choose the wrong words."

"What did Ben say that was so awful? Did he tell you to eat your veggies?" Kent teased, and in a flash, she spun and landed a punch on Kent's bicep.

He laughed and rubbed the spot. "Ouch. Damn it, you're getting your strength back. Travis must be doing something right."

Kelsey sighed, and decided she wanted Kent's opinion. She reached for her pack and pulled her phone from a side pocket. After turning it on, she swept past a long list of apologies and found the words that had pissed her off.

Kent took the phone she offered and read the message back to her. "Have fun with Kent, but don't overdo it." He chuckled. "That's it? Seriously, there has to be more."

His eyebrows hitched, he took a step away, and scrolled through a few more messages. Kelsey tried to snatch her phone while Kent scanned the litany of Ben's apologies. She lunged again, and he dodged. "Give it back. Give me my phone."

Spinning, light on his feet, he read all he could as he eluded, sidestepped, and laughed. "You were foolish enough to hand your phone over. I'm just trying to get the big picture."

She darted and almost retrieved the device, but his size, strength, and long reach won. Their wrestling brought up a different screen, and Kent found another lengthy list of texts.

"Who's this Mark guy?" he asked, trying to remember the men she favored before the accident. "Wait, is he that surfer?"

Her arms went limp and fell away from Kent. She turned from him, wandered off, and stared over the lake. "Please, just give me back my phone." Her whisper bounced, amplified by the glittering water.

"I'm sorry," he said close behind her. Kent slipped the phone into her hand, his other arm slid loose around her waist, easing her against his frame.

Her shrug put a few inches between them. "I don't know what I want. Everything's twisted together and happening too fast. Mark wants someone I'll never be again. And there's Ben. How can I make promises to Ben when I'm not sure who I will become? Every day I wake up a slightly different person."

"Give it time. Ben will understand."

"Will he? I'm living in his house. I owe him everything. But I can't mold myself into someone I don't recognize just to please him."

"He'd never ask you to do that," Kent insisted.

"I'm not so sure. He always wanted the white picket fence, kids, and probably a dog. Shit, the guy drives an Audi." Kelsey laughed and moved away from Kent to sit on a weathered log.

He followed and sank to the spot next to her. "There's nothing wrong with that . . . well, except the car." His grin made her feel a little bit better. "The white picket fence thing can't be all bad, it's what Seth and Natalie have," Kent pointed out.

Kelsey accepted the vein of truth and admitted, "I envy it—from a distance. But I can't picture myself trapped inside that kind of cage."

***

A buzzing sound woke Ben. He searched in the dark with one hand to locate his phone. "I'm sorry," she said immediately, and a wave of relief swept over him.

"Kels, is everything okay?" he asked, his words graveled by sleep.

"It's fine. I know it's really late, but I was waiting for Kent to leave before I called. Ben, I'm sorry for being . . . such . . . a bitch."

He chuckled and propped an arm under his head. "Don't think that, you weren't. Hey, I'm sorry. I know you don't need a babysitter."

"Really, Ben, I totally overreacted."

"Don't worry about it." He cleared his throat. "I haven't heard about your victory laps in the pool. Tell me everything."

Her voice brightened as Kelsey's joy spilled across the distance, rising an octave as she told him about swimming in the pool, the lake, even paddling in the canoe. He asked questions and shared her happiness. She told him that the cold water scared her at first, but not enough to push her back to shore. The canoe was great, but she wasn't ready for a kayak, not even those yellow plastic ones for rent at Lost Lake.

Ben leaned against a stack of pillows and listened to Kelsey. God, she was exciting—all sexy-independence and untethered strength.

"Can I meet you at the airport?" she asked when he yawned.

"Sure, but it's a long ride on the train."

"I don't care. Are you still scheduled for Friday afternoon?"

"Yeah," he said, putting her on speaker to text her the exact time.

"Good, I'll come over from The Center. Go to sleep. I just needed to say I'm sorry and hear your voice. Miss you."

"Miss you too, Kels."

She hung up first and he smiled, buzzed by her passion.

Too wired to sleep, Ben read for a while. His mind wandered from the words on the page to Kelsey, then to the night he'd spent out with his friends. At first, it was awkward seeing Susan again, but then it was okay.

Kelsey and Susan couldn't be more different, but it was nice talking to someone who knew him so well. It confirmed what he already knew—the heat he'd shared with Susan burned out long ago. His ex was firmly planted in the *good friend* category.

Ben clicked off the bedside lamp, slid back under the sheets, and his thoughts lingered on Kelsey. She would be getting ready for bed, brushing her teeth, taking off her clothes. Just thinking about her got him hard.

His hand drifted down to stroke his lengthening shaft. Each pull evoked a memory of Kelsey—her taste, her moans, the line of her leg, and her firm, supple ass. Lost in the height of his orgasm, he called out, but Ben didn't notice when the name *Susan* slipped from his lips.

TWENTY

Kelsey stared at her phone. She couldn't avoid Mark forever. Without overthinking it, she took a deep breath and punched in words.

I'm beginning to improve, but I can't see you right now.

Mark's text came before her screen darkened.

I saw Parker's article about your accident. Her blog seemed optimistic. Was that just positive spin?

He'd been digging. Not a shock—he'd already given her more time than she deserved.

Yes and no. It was Parker's take on things. I'm improving, but I'm not your mermaid anymore. Probably never will be.

She held her breath, and imagined Mark reading the truth. The sun didn't go out, and the earth didn't stopped spinning. She exhaled, wondering why she'd waited so long, it wasn't as terrifying as she'd expected.

Nothing will ever change who you are to me, Mermaid. Can't we at least talk? I need to hear your voice, if only to know that you're okay.

At first, she typed *No*.

But she wasn't ready to say a forever goodbye. She erased those two letters and replaced them with *Soon.*

***

Mark paced the white sandy beach behind his Kauai home. Something was off. And after an aggravating call from Parker Knight, he couldn't stay on the island any longer.

As he had always done in the past, he'd refused to give Parker any personal information, but the adventure photographer wasn't satisfied with his generic answers. He'd given her something—yes, he knew Kelsey, their paths had crossed professionally, and he wished her well in her recovery.

The lines he fed Parker couldn't have been farther from the truth. What he shared with Kelsey never felt professional. She was wild, untamed, and he hoped that hadn't changed. Wished her well? He wished so much more than that.

He'd wasted enough time and had to get back to the mainland to find out what was really going on. His fingers scrolled through his contacts. Maybe Natalie could help. He wanted to respect Kelsey's boundaries, but the hair on the back of his neck prickled as he touched Natalie's name on the screen. He knew he needed to make this call. The only other person he knew in Ashwood picked up on the third ring.

"Hello?" she said quickly.

"Natalie, is that you?"

"Yes, who is this?" she asked.

"It's Mark, you know, *Driftwood Shores Mark*."

"Oh, Mark! How are you? I thought you were surfing on some remote island or something like that," she said with her usual sunny voice.

"I was, but I'm in Hawaii now. The reason I called . . . well, I've tried to reach Kelsey. Hey, I'm really sorry, by the way, it must have been hell for you."

"It was scary, especially right after. It's not nearly so bad now."

Mark smiled. "Good to hear that. Kelsey and I have sent a couple of text messages. Can you tell me which hospital she's in? I'd like to send flowers or maybe visit once I get back to the mainland."

She hesitated. "Mark . . . she left the hospital weeks ago."

He let that sink in for a moment. "Is she home?" he asked. "Should I call her parents' place?"

"No. She's still working on physical therapy in Portland."

"In a recovery unit?"

"During the day, yes. But she's staying with my brother Ben, now. Do you remember him? You met him on that day at the beach, right after you met Kelsey. He has a place in Portland, close to Kelsey's therapy center."

"I remember him," Mark answered, wondering if Ben was the reason Kelsey had lied. "How is she?"

"It was difficult at first, but she's doing great. Almost back to her old self."

Mark nearly dropped the phone. Everything he'd expected to hear didn't include this. Kelsey wasn't hurting—fuck no, she'd moved on.

"Mark, are you there?" she asked carefully.

"I'm here. Hey thanks. I appreciate the update. Like I said, I was worried when I heard about the accident."

"Should I have her call you?" Natalie seemed a little too cheerful, her sunny disposition almost forced. An uncomfortable ache settled in his gut.

"No. You know me. I have a tendency to go off grid. I'll talk to her later."

After he said goodbye, Mark paced the beach. He cocked his arm ready to hurl his phone into the waves, but he couldn't release the one thing that still connected him to Kelsey. No, letting her go wouldn't be that easy.

In just a few clicks he'd selected two flights—an island hopper to Honolulu and a flight to the mainland. He chose San Francisco instead of Portland to buy extra time. He needed to think, and nothing helped him concentrate better than his sailboat. Time spent sailing up the coast was exactly what he wanted before he faced Kelsey and learned the truth. If his Mermaid was determined to end things, he wouldn't let her go without a fight.

***

Natalie's cup of coffee went cold as she stared over Osprey Lake.

"Who was on the phone?" Seth asked from behind her when he found her on their deck.

"Mark. That surfer. The guy I met on the Oregon coast. He heard about Kelsey's accident, but it's weird . . . I think Kelsey's lying to Mark. God, I hope she's not lying to Ben, too."

"Lying about what?"

"Not what, who. Mark. The guy thought Kelsey was still in the hospital." She shook her head.

Seth's hand squeezed her shoulder. "Maybe he only spotted Parker's first video."

"That would make sense, but he told me they've been texting. Why would he be worried if they're keeping in touch?"

"Has Kelsey talked about him since the accident?"

"No, I don't think so."

"Maybe he's just passing through and wants to stop in and visit." Seth bent and took her nearly empty coffee cup then turned toward the sliding glass doors. "Want a refill?"

She stood to follow. "No. We're already late as it is. Let's stop by Goldfinch instead of making breakfast."

For the entire drive into town, Natalie worried a little about Kelsey and even more about Ben.

***

Kelsey ducked her head into Travis' office before beginning her therapy circuit. "You wanted me to stop by?"

"Have a seat. How was your time off?" he asked.

"Amazing. We went up to Lost Lake, hiked a bit, swam, and get this, I paddled a canoe!"

"Well, that brings up what I planned to talk about." Travis rolled his chair away from his desk. "You're ready for more. It's time for you to start driving."

"Seriously. That's awesome, but I thought I couldn't get behind the wheel for another month."

"Your seizure wasn't part of a pattern. We'll get a waiver and get you back on the road. Listen, I'm not going to just hand over your keys, but I'm not concerned. Shoot, I'd let you drive my kids to soccer practice."

"Would it be okay if I use my own car?"

"Sure. Why don't we plan for next week?" Travis stood, and Kelsey shot out of her chair to wrap her arms around him.

"Thank you, so much," she said, before bouncing away.

"We're not done, yet. One more thing . . . You need to choose a return date for work. Part-time at first. Talk to your business partner and jot down a list of things you'd like to focus on before returning to Venture."

"Driving I'm excited about, but work?" Kelsey wrapped her arms around her middle. "I'm not prepared. I can't tell you how many times I had to carry an extra pack out when a guest turned an ankle or got blisters."

"Hey, you'll get there."

She wasn't so confident. The walls of The Center weren't anything like the wilderness. Those winding trails weren't labeled with friendly directions, and the harsh elements didn't give anyone second chances.

After her swim and a shower, she pulled out her phone ready to share the terrific news about driving with Ben. She bit her lip and stared at the screen. Chuckling to herself, she planned a playful surprise instead.

***

The train ride home seemed to take forever. After changing into shorts and a tank, Kelsey ran next door to find Nancy. "Where are you?"

"Behind the wall of corn!"

"This is insane," Kelsey said, making her way through the tight maze of squash, beans, and eggplant. "I've got great news, but you can't tell Ben because I want to surprise him. I'm going to be driving soon."

"That's terrific. You must be so thrilled." Nancy gave her a quick hug. "Wow, does that mean you'll be returning to Ashwood?"

Her buoyant mood deflated—she hadn't thought that far ahead. "I guess so. I've got a house and a job to get back to."

"And Ben?"

"We've got something great started, but we both knew this living arrangement was temporary. Driving won't change how I feel about him." She blushed. "We'll just move forward and start dealing with everyday stuff, like a regular couple."

Regular. Her stomach trembled—she was so close to finding out what that felt like again.

***

Friday morning Kelsey hopped on the train, but she headed toward Portland International instead of The Center. She'd asked Sig to meet her at a diner near the airport, and they had plenty of time to eat before Ben was due to land. An airliner roared overhead. Wheels down, it shook the atmosphere as it descended.

Kelsey pushed through the swinging glass door of the twenty-four-hour diner—the smell of onions, bacon, and coffee clung to the air. Her stomach growled as she slid into the slick red vinyl booth.

"You look terrific, kiddo. When are you coming back to work?" Sig had always rushed like a bull straight into business.

She smiled and loved that he wasn't careful with her. "Let me order something first, and then we can talk."

After scanning the menu, she ordered the special. When her chocolate shake arrived, she smiled—loving the tall glass and the second metal cup holding extra shake beneath a glistening layer of frost. Two fingers plucked a maraschino cherry from a mountain of whipped cream, and she popped it into her mouth.

"Sorry, not sharing. You'll have to order your own," she said while scooping some whipped cream with a long-handled spoon.

He laughed and shook his head. "I'm happy with iced tea. Glad to see your appetite hasn't suffered. Other than a need for a shake, why did you call this meeting?" Sig asked.

The sugar seeped into her bloodstream and she could think again. Kelsey leaned closer to the table, looking forward to a familiar battle. "Before the accident, we talked about bringing in another partner. We need help now, more than ever."

"Whoa, Kels. Until you come back, we shouldn't do anything drastic." She tried not to laugh—this big, tough guy had always hated change.

Kelsey took a deep breath, knowing Sig wouldn't want to face the facts. "Our clients want a challenge. I can't bring that, at least not right away, and *never* in a kayak."

His hand stretched over his bald head, then he blew out a slow breath and nodded. "Fine. Let's say you're right. Who do you have in mind?"

"Kent."

Sig's booming laughter turned a few heads. "I don't think so. Shit, I'm not running an escort service."

She scowled, her glare unwavering.

Sig leaned in, resting his weight on his forearms. "You think I'm kidding? I get calls from women who've been on his rafting trips trying to book another, but *only* if Kent Thomas is along. And it's not because he knows how to handle a paddle."

Kelsey laughed so loud the rest of the patrons in the diner turned to look.

Sig actually blushed—he was such a teddy bear. "You know I didn't mean it that way," he said.

Still chuckling, she swept tears from her eyes. "I know, but hey, it wouldn't be funny if it wasn't true. Let me talk to him. Kent's changed."

"Changed? I doubt it."

"Really. I promise, he's ready."

Sig's forehead furrowed, "Ready for what?"

"A life away from Ashwood."

"Why would he want that?"

"Because it's the right thing. He needs more."

He flattened his hands on the table. "Fine. Go ahead and talk to him. You are part owner, but I think we need a woman to help out with Venture Sister more than we need a major liability like Kent."

Kelsey nodded and grinned while sucking her thick shake through the large-bore straw. "Let me work on that, old man. I've got an idea, but it may take some fine-tuning."

"What are you up to, Kels?"

When Sig's eyebrow quirked, she gave him an innocent wide-eyed stare. "Who me? I'm not up to anything."

***

With Ben's flight delayed, Kelsey killed time in a bookshop near ticketing, thumbing through books about artisan glass, mushroom gathering, and lighthouses on the Oregon coast. Her eyes began to swim, and she bought a coffee and found a small table to watch travelers with rolling bags rush by.

The aroma of chili from a fast food spot next door took her mind back to the beach, and she recalled rich details of her trip with Mark, drifting from campground to campground. The joy and freedom of surfing flooded her senses with unusual clarity. A laugh echoed in the concourse, and she swore she heard him—even lifted her chin on a quick search, half-expecting to find him coming her way.

But it wasn't Mark, just a guy playing tag with a toddler. With a shake of her head, she brought up his surfing blog and sighed, relieved that he was still so far away. That wouldn't last forever, after essentially giving him up weeks ago, she didn't know if she wanted to go through that pain again. Saying goodbye face to face would simply hurt too much.

Yet, strangely, his presence closed in, and Kels had to remind herself that he couldn't possibly be in Portland. Moments later, her phone rang, and she dropped the device on the teal carpet. Scooping it quickly, she swept the screen.

"I'm on the ground," Ben blurted.

"Great! I'm at a coffee shop near ticketing, killing time."

"I know, just stay put and I'll come to you. Missed you, babe."

He knew? Kelsey shrugged off a comment that didn't make sense then added, "Missed you too."

***

The closer Ben got to home, the harder he pressed the accelerator and the Audi's engine roared. Kelsey took over the race and beat him in a sprint for the front door. Running upstairs, he grabbed her and towed her into the bathroom, leaving a trail of their shirts, jeans, and underwear along the way.

He turned on the shower. "I've been on a plane all day. Join me?"

"Mm-hmm." Kelsey nodded, stepped into the old tub, and pulled the curtain shut. It was snug but there was just enough room to explore every inch of his chiseled body. Her fingers traced the contours of his shoulders as his tongue invaded her mouth.

"I dreamed of this," Ben murmured against her lips. He bent to lick droplets of water from her breasts, drawing her nipple in for a taste. His teeth grazed gently across the tip before sucking away the sting.

Kelsey's touch drifted down his back, over the angled contours of his ass. Her hands traveled forward to glide up and down the hardened length of his shaft. His hips shifted, increasing the pace as she tightened her grip.

"Shit, Kels," he moaned, arms surrounding her, as his breath heated a spot on her neck.

When she moved a fraction away, they both looked down as her hand jacked his cock. The smooth plum at the end invited her, and Kelsey dropped to her knees to take a taste.

Her tongue slid out and circled the velvet skin, teasing along the slit, pushing slightly inside. His guttural groan brought a satisfied smile to her lips, and she opened to take him deep. In one long plunge, Kelsey took half his length, relaxing and swallowing. She wanted this to last and pulled away to tease his balls with the luxurious heat of her tongue's languid glide.

"Fuck, do that again," Ben groaned, holding her hair to slow her pace.

Kelsey angled her head and crisp hair tickled her nose as her lips and tongue danced across his contours. She shifted and took him deep again, sliding her fingers behind his balls, massaging as his anatomy tensed. Her lips tightened, and his hips took over, thrusting instinctively.

"I'm going to come," he warned. Kelsey increased the pressure, wanting to drink him in. His fingers tangled in her blond hair, and his thighs shook as masculine moans echoed off the tiles.

The explosive release painted the back of her throat with his seed. She swallowed, caressed, and devoured his length until his legs stopped trembling. Ben removed his grasp from her hair and leaned against the tiled wall, needing the support.

Kelsey eased away, licked the V at his hips, then grasped his hand as he helped her stand on the slippery surface.

"The water's getting cold," she said as she pressed against his chest for warmth. He turned off the cool water and found two towels. Ben covered her in one before wrapping the other around his waist.

Up on tiptoe, Kelsey kissed him quickly, flashed a sly grin, and said, "Welcome home."

Ben peeled away her towel. "Let's see if I can find another way to heat you up." He grasped her ass, lifting her around his hips.

"How about my room?" she asked, her voice shaking. "It's on the sunny side of the house and I'm freezing." Kels clung tight for the ride to her bed. By the time they got there, she could already feel the head of his jutting cock prodding her sex.

Laying her down, his gaze consumed every inch of her form. Sunlight bathed her with bright afternoon rays. Ben climbed over her and covered her chilled damp skin with his warmth.

"Mmm, that feels wonderful," she purred as his heat transferred. "I don't know why I'm so cold. Stay still while I warm up."

"Anything you want," Ben said against her lips. Every few seconds she quaked, still shivering from the effects of the cool shower. The trembling decreased as Ben's kisses heated. His warmth soaked in and her body relaxed. Eventually, desire took over and she writhed, moving her legs wide, seeking a cure for her urgent need.

His lips traced a path south, and Ben held his torso aloft, tasting and sucking the tip of each breast. His afternoon beard chafed against the sensitive skin, heightening the sensation. Each suck and nibble, more intense than the last, shot heat to her core.

She wriggled until her center aligned with his engorged cock. Unable to resist, he dipped in before Kelsey squirmed away. "Condom," she murmured and rolled to her side table, reaching for the drawer. Ben groaned.

After she ripped the condom open with her teeth, she sat up and sheathed Ben in moments. He watched her quick movements from his knees between her thighs. Kelsey took advantage of her new position and skated her tongue from one small, dark nipple to the next.

He let his hands wander. Two fingers trailed over her sex and slowly eased inside. "So wet, so fucking tight for me," he groaned. Shocked by the sheer pleasure of the invasion, Kelsey sucked hard on Ben's small nipple.

"I like that," he growled, and she tugged harder. When he curled his fingers inside her and pumped, she moaned against his chest and widened her legs, increasing his access.

"She likes it, too," he plunged his fingers deeper, adding the pressure of his thumb to her clit.

"Not yet . . . I need you inside," she begged, flopping back on the mattress.

Ben kept up the teasing and the potent pleasure levitated her hips.

"You're so beautiful, I have to see you come," he insisted. On his knees between her legs, his sheathed cock bobbed, ready for her heat. She wanted the owning invasion, but his thumb was doing things that scrambled her will.

"That's it, Kels," he said as his fingers felt the ripples on the leading edge of her orgasm. Cheeks flushed, eyes wide, Kelsey detonated, lost in the quakes that ransacked her frame. Before she descended, Ben bent over her and plunged hard and deep, setting off her second surprising wave. With greedy delight, Kelsey fastened her arms around his bicep, lifting her hips to take him. The heat, the slick, and the tight squeeze stripped Ben to his core.

Without warning, his reckless thrusts climbed toward a powerful orgasm. The force of the hunger traveled his spine, ripped through his body, and stole his control. He collapsed on Kelsey—quaking, sated, and spent.

"God, I missed you. I hate being apart. Next time, come to North Carolina with me."

She smiled, knowing that her life was going to get too busy to join him on business trips, but telling him now would break the languid, sexy spell that still hung over them.

As the sunset painted the white walls in her room a soft pink, she straddled Ben with her hips, kissed him, and made up for their time apart.

TWENTY-ONE

"Our kitchen looks like a farmers' market." Ben hadn't noticed anything except her until morning—not that she minded. He pulled her close and pressed a kiss to her temple.

She grinned, happy he was home. "Nancy's kitchen is worse. I've started taking veggies to The Center and sharing them with the staff. I even gave a sack to a girl I see almost every day on the train."

"If you want, I can drive you over one day next week. You could fit more in my car than on the train."

"I know it's Saturday, but could we run over today?" she asked, worried that the produce and all her hard work would spoil if she waited.

"Sure, what do you want to do after?" He looked ready for anything she thought up.

"Maybe go up to Ashwood?" she asked. "And have dinner at The Northside?"

"Why don't we spend the night? We could use the tiny house by the lake or stay at your place," Ben suggested.

Kelsey weighed her options—Natalie's tiny home had too many ghosts, and her house was still a mess, untouched since the accident. No, she wanted this weekend to be effortless.

"I may regret this, and you can say *no*—but how would you feel if we spent the night at one of the guest cabins at my parents' place? I haven't seen Mom and Dad in a while. Maybe we could join them for breakfast Sunday morning?" Kelsey worried her lip while waiting for his answer. They both knew breakfast with her parents was a big step.

Ben's chest swelled and he pulled her close. "I'd love that," he said, kissing her until she melted.

If he kept up that magic with his lips, they wouldn't leave at all. She moaned and inched his distracting body away. "I'll call Mom and Dad."

"And I'll get ahold of Natalie. They can meet up with us later." Ben took one more kiss, released her, and called his sister.

***

"I'll just be a minute." Kelsey grabbed bags of green beans, squash, lettuce, and cherry tomatoes from the rear seat of Ben's Audi and jogged across the lot. He stayed in the car, giving her time to talk with Travis and her other friends inside.

When she didn't come back right away, he turned off the engine and rolled down the windows to let the warm east wind blow through. Her phone buzzed, still attached to the charger in the center console. Ben answered, expecting a call from her parents about their plans for tonight.

"Hello?" Ben said quickly.

"I must have a wrong number," a guy answered.

"Uh, this is Kelsey's phone. Who's this?"

A short hesitation floated in space. "I guess you can tell Kelsey that Mark called..."

"I'll do that." The line went dead. Ben held her phone mid-air, stared at the screen and wished he hadn't picked up—but knew it was probably good that he did.

"Fuck! How long has this been going on?" His hand slammed against the steering wheel, beating away jealousy.

Teeth clenched, he stared at The Center's entrance and battled over what to do. If he confronted her with this, he'd get her unguarded reaction. But the timing sucked. *Goddamnit.* Kels had just taken such a significant step—an invitation to spend time with her parents. He took a deep breath and calmed his fury. Overreacting to Mark's badly-timed call would only ruin their plans.

Ben glanced across the lot again—she still hadn't come outside. In a few short clicks he deleted the call history from her phone. As he took control, he knew that talking about Mark right now would destroy their weekend before it even began.

The automatic doors slid open and Kelsey jogged back to his car, smiling. "Sorry that took so long," she said climbing in, "Travis has a new patient he wanted me to meet. It's awful. She was riding her bike home after class and someone hit her and kept driving. She's lucky a jogger found her in the ditch."

The jealous anger he still fought eased when he saw the concern on Kelsey's face. "Is she going to be okay?" he asked.

"I think so, depending on what her definition of okay is. You know, I wonder if I could take her on a hike sometime. Indoor physical therapy sometimes feels like a prison. I'll have to run that idea by Travis on Monday." Kelsey kneaded her lip and Ben hated himself for doubting her. She always seemed to be looking for ways to help her friends. Ben pressed the accelerator and exited the parking lot quickly, eager to leave his anger and guilt behind.

"That's a great idea, babe."

"It doesn't take much to change a bad outlook. That day you took me to the beach turned me around. I bet this girl just needs someone she can relate to. She seemed pretty depressed, and I totally get it—there were so many times I wondered if I'd get any part of my old life back."

"What do you still miss?" he asked, needing to know.

"The outdoors, wandering away from everything and losing myself in the mountains." Kelsey looked toward Mount Hood in the distance, then turned to him. "Could I talk you into a camping trip before summer ends?"

Ben nodded. "Sure, what did you have in mind?"

"Maybe the Olympics or the North Cascades? You know a real vacation, at least four or five days, just you and me." Kelsey's smile spread, reaching her shimmering eyes.

"We could go to the coast. I've always wanted to learn how to surf," Ben suggested carefully, trying to read her reaction.

"Really? I never got that impression." Her hands gripped her thighs. "I'm sorry, but I don't think I'm strong enough to take on any waves."

Her answer left Ben satisfied that Mark wasn't really an issue. He covered her hand with his. "This year we hike. Next summer we surf."

"Awesome." Kels settled in, turned up the music, and opened the sunroof. Summer sun flooded his Audi and he slipped on his Ray-bans. He couldn't be happier. All of Kelsey's long-term plans included him, and Ben wanted to keep it that way.

**

They pushed through the doors together and Kelsey gripped Ben's hand tighter. No one inside Northside Grill seemed satisfied with a quick glance of their *infamous* hometown girl. Her steps sped to the corner where her friends were gathered.

Kent made room just as Rick and Linnea pulled up a second table. The extra space welcomed Justin and Grant, who were still in uniform after an aid call. In no time, conversation and laughter stacked and toppled, competing for airtime.

Kelsey coaxed Kent to the dance floor, needing to pull him aside. "I've got news, and I need your help," she said close to his ear to be heard over the music.

"Anything for you, Kels." He gave her a friendly squeeze around her waist.

"Travis told me I'm ready to drive."

"Hey, that's great. When do you start?"

"Soon. And that's where you come in. I need to practice. Could you bring my car to The Center?"

"Sure, I could bring it this weekend."

"Not yet. Ben gets uptight when things move too quickly. I figure it will be easier to surprise him after I've got my wheels."

"Uptight? Shit, I thought he'd changed."

"He'll come around. And it's not like I'll be guiding for Venture anytime soon." Kelsey had another reason for asking Kent for this *little* favor. She kneaded her lip and tossed her idea out there, hoping he'd consider it. "You'll have to find *someone* to bring you back to Ashwood . . . I think you should ask Amanda."

His feet stopped moving as he laughed. "Yeah, right."

"I'm serious. I've only seen Amanda once since the accident, and I know she's avoiding me. Do this for me, please," Kelsey begged.

Kent shrugged. "Fine. I'll do it . . . for you."

"Thank you." She gave him a peck on the cheek. "Do you still have a key to my house?" He nodded and she continued, "There's an extra set of car keys in that skinny drawer in the kitchen. I don't know where my old set went . . ."

"Actually, it's at my place. Along with some other stuff."

When his expression tightened, she knew that he had everything—her keys, some gear, and what was left of her battered green kayak.

"When do you need your car?" he asked once he'd smoothed his reaction.

"Early next week. Is that okay? I know you've already missed a ton of work because of me."

"Not a problem." He shook his head. "Seth's cool with it."

"I'll buy lunch for you and, I hope, Amanda."

"Don't count on it. Parker's got her claws in deep and Amanda's avoiding everything and everyone in Ashwood."

The song ended and the pair dodged tables while snaking a path back to their clump of friends.

Ben reached out, and Kelsey couldn't resist bending in half to plant a kiss on his tempting lips before she took her seat.

***

The guest cabin at her parents' place was cozy, private, and chilly. Kelsey rushed from the bathroom to jump under the covers with Ben.

"I love it when you're cold." He wrapped a leg and arm around her to pull her close. "This place is great. Why did you ever bother with a house in town?"

"Privacy and distance. I like living close to everything."

"Do you want to stop at your house tomorrow?" he asked while using his leg to pull her on top of his body. Naked, she centered over his hips with a wiggle and sighed.

"Not this trip," she murmured against his lips. "No more talking . . . unless it's *dirty*."

He grinned and took her dirty-talk challenge. "Let me grab this sweet ass of yours and take you for a hard ride on my cock."

When he chuckled, she rewarded his efforts with a grind of her hips then leaned forward to give him a taste of her breasts.

After finding a condom, she moved above Ben and nested over his hips, nudging his length against her heat, yet she kept the crown from sinking in. He grasped her hips and pressed in slowly, the teasing climb was unhurried and exactly right. The cold air heightened her senses, and she kicked the blankets away.

Mesmerized by Ben's focus on her desires, she trusted him with her pleasure. Sometimes she felt overwhelmed by his intensity, but she was growing accustomed to the way he cherished her so completely—body, mind, and heart. Yet, she doubted Ben would willingly give her the space she needed, and knew she'd eventually have to compromise her freedom and meet him halfway.

She lost herself in his strength when Ben's hand tightened on her hips and he increased the power of each plunge. Her legs began to tremble, and he changed the angle slightly to bring her with him. Eyes focused, Kelsey watched him join her in glorious release. Satisfied, she bent to claim another kiss.

Ben pulled the cool blankets around them, and Kelsey cuddled tight. The temperature dropped and their bodies entwined, taking heat from each other.

***

Ben woke first and grabbed the first shower. He glanced out the window as he passed, expecting to see the lake, but fog obscured his view and cloaked the cabin in muffled gray. By the time he emerged from the bathroom, the cabin was toasty and warm.

In his T-shirt, Kelsey was out of bed, and she tossed another log into the wood stove. Ben watched her from the bathroom door, thankful for the heat. "Sorry, I didn't think to build a fire. This city kid looked around for a thermostat."

"I'm glad you didn't. I'm a pyromaniac." She stirred the fire with a metal poker and secured the stove's cast-iron door.

The fog broke, and Ben wandered outside while Kelsey showered. Ambling across the wide lawn, he stayed on paths close to the cabin. The lights at the Fisher house glowed—this visit felt important, meeting her family, being welcomed deeper into her life. But Ashwood reminded him of her roots—wild and untamed—and he didn't know if Portland would ever satisfy her.

After she dressed, they hurried hand-in-hand across the lawn. Kelsey pulled Ben onto the deck and burst inside. Her mom trapped Kelsey in a long embrace before Ben even shut the door. When Ben extended his arm to shake her father's hand, Dale hauled Ben in for a hug. He'd seen them often at the hospital, but far less since Kelsey had progressed to The Center.

The meal hit the table, and at the last second Kelsey dashed to the car to bring in jars of fresh salsa. They opened one to add extra spice to the eggs.

After breakfast, Dale pushed Mary and Kelsey out of the kitchen and Ben grabbed a towel to dry the big platters. Her dad took advantage of the moment alone with Ben. "Thank you for everything you've done for our Kelsey," Dale said, his gratitude catching in his throat.

"I would do *anything* to make sure your daughter's happy," Ben admitted quietly to himself and to her father. Dale sniffed back a tear, while unspoken solidarity passed between them with a nod.

Kelsey and all her energy burst into the kitchen. "The fog's lifted. Do you want to take out a canoe?"

"Absolutely," Ben agreed while drying the final dish. She took the big bowl from his outstretched hand and put it away. Ben thanked her parents for breakfast as he followed Kels outside.

***

Kelsey ignored a spike of anxiety when she hefted the long green canoe toward the lake. Paddle in hand and sleek life jacket zipped, she helped Ben slip the canoe from the pebbled shore. Glassy and dark, the surface of the lake looked steel gray in contrast to the silver mist burning away at the edges. A goose skimming the surface drew her eyes across the lake, where Natalie and Seth stood at the shore near their tiny home. Kelsey swept her paddle through the water, closing in on her friends.

"You're out early," Ben said as Seth held the canoe, keeping it steady as they climbed to shore.

"We stayed in the tiny home by the lake last night and tried to figure out where we want to build our cabin." Seth led Ben toward that spot and Natalie shook her head.

"I think Seth's looking for an ally." Nate said to Kelsey. "We can't agree on the plans for this place." When the guys started talking about the best location for the cabin, Natalie pulled Kelsey a little farther down the beach, increasing the distance until they could no longer hear the men. "So, I got a call from a friend of ours asking about you."

"Is Parker digging again?" Kelsey asked, controlling a blast of anger.

So far, Parker and her minions hadn't found her at Ben's place in Portland. And The Center was private property, with a layer of security built in. They'd bothered everyone around her, but never her directly, and for that, Kelsey was thankful.

Natalie hesitated, then whispered, "No . . . actually, it was Mark."

Kelsey's heart skipped a beat when she heard his name. "Mark? What? Why?"

Pulling her closer, Natalie's cool fingers wrapped around her forearm. "I think he's worried about you."

She twisted her arm away and asked, "Is he coming back?"

"He didn't say, but I don't think so. He said something about being off the grid."

The unexpected news was too much to take. Kelsey lost her battle with anxiety and hurried farther down the beach. Natalie followed—her voice raised with worry. "It will be fine, I'm sure he'll call back."

Panic took control, and Kelsey couldn't get away fast enough. She broke into a jog and rushed back to her canoe. The water splashed and soaked her pants from the knees down as she pushed the narrow craft onto the lake. Her lifejacket went on as her butt settled on the seat. Efficient paddle strokes sped her a few yards from shore. Natalie's cries bounced from the lake, "Kels, wait!" She needed to escape the sound and dug her paddle harder, increasing her speed.

"Stop!" Ben yelled as the distance between them expanded, but she never looked back, only paddled away.

Kelsey floated for over an hour, yet she avoided disappearing into the hidden alcoves. She intentionally stayed where her family could see her, not wanting to worry anyone. She simply needed to think. Fortunately, everyone had the good sense to leave her alone. A potent mixture of panic and anger ricocheted in her gut, but humiliation took over when she'd calmed enough to paddle back toward home.

Dad met her to help lift the canoe. "Are you okay?"

"I guess. I'm embarrassed that I overreacted, but glad that I took the time to calm down."

They stored the canoe in the boathouse and hung the lifejackets on the wall before heading in.

"Well, you've got a worried man pacing the floor back at the house."

"Crap. Natalie must have told him about Mark."

Her father's steps slowed, and he turned. "Mark? Has that surfer stopped by to see you?"

"No. I messed up. I dodged his calls, and he reached out to Natalie to see how I was doing."

"Avoided his calls? Why?"

Her voice tightened, and she couldn't talk. The lake looked inviting again, but she took a breath and blew it out. "I just wanted one person to remember who I used to be." Her chin dropped to her chest to conceal her tears.

"Come here, baby-girl." Dad opened his arms, and she accepted the space to let her father absorb some of her pain. "Maybe you need to give yourself a little more time to get your footing. Have you considered this thing with Ben might be too much too soon?"

She nodded, relieved that she wasn't the only one who felt that way. "I care about him and owe him so much." Kelsey closed her eyes and breathed in Dad's clean scent—feeling small, accepted, understood.

"I don't want to go in." Her whisper trembled, raw and exposed. After sniffing back the remaining tears, she pulled away from the safety of her daddy's arms. "I'm gonna pack up our stuff in the cabin. Then I'll come over and say goodbye to Mom. Could you try to stall Ben?"

"And Natalie and Seth."

"Seriously? They're all here." Kelsey laughed with her Dad.

He shrugged and tried to downplay her predicament. "I'll do what I can."

Ten minutes passed before Natalie showed up at the cabin to help her pack, saying she was sorry. Kelsey assured her there was no reason to apologize. They walked back together, arms around each other. Ben met them half-way between the cabin and the main house and took his duffle from his sister.

"Ready to go home?" he asked.

"Let me say goodbye to Mom first."

***

Ben filled the silence between Ashwood and Portland with Kelsey's favorite playlist. She seemed content, so he buried the few words he'd heard from Mark. There really wasn't any reason to tell her—it would only set Kelsey off.

TWENTY-TWO

The favor was a big one, but Kent would do anything for Kelsey, and he had his personal reasons too. Amanda's boycott of everything Ashwood had lasted long enough. Until Amanda faced Kelsey, she'd never realize that everyone had moved past her role in making that video.

"You want me to do what?" Amanda blurted.

"Kelsey needs her car in Portland, and I'll need a ride back."

"Can't you ask Rick?"

"Uh, Linnea hasn't been feeling that well," he lied. If anything, Linnea had more energy now that she was in the homestretch of her pregnancy.

"What about Justin?"

"He's got fire department shit." Another lie.

"You really can't find *anyone* in Ashwood to help?" Amanda's tone lowered. She definitely knew he was up to something, but he could tell he was wearing her down.

"Nope. You're it. My last hope."

"Fine, what do you need me to do?"

Kent grinned, hearing the smile in her voice. He explained his predicament and her role in the plan. He'd come to Hood River in Kelsey's SUV so Amanda could follow him to The Center. Now that Kelsey had been cleared to drive, she wanted to practice in her car, and she needed their help to surprise Ben with this new milestone.

On a giggle, Amanda promised to keep the plan quiet. God, he'd missed that musical sound and couldn't wait to see the grin that matched it.

***

Impatient, Kelsey paced the sidewalk in front of The Center. A familiar engine growled and her eyes shot to the parking lot entrance. When sunlight bounced off dented metal, her stomach jumped, and she stood on tiptoe to get a better view. She knew she should be happy to see her friends, but the love that swelled her chest right now was reserved for her silver Xterra. With a little rust coming through around the wheel wells, that beautiful, battered four-wheel drive looked like freedom.

Her happy feet skip-hopped across the pavement. She pulled the driver's side door open before Kent even had a chance to cut the engine. Kelsey held the door wide. "Thank you for this. You have no idea how excited I am. Move already! I need to get in."

"Impatient?"

She grabbed his arm and yanked. "I'm not kidding. Move, move, move."

Amanda stopped in the spot across from them but stayed in her car. Kent took his time as he turned off the engine and slowly set the parking brake. A teasing grin spread across his face as he jingled the keys in front of Kelsey. "Here's your baby."

"Give 'em." She snatched her keys from his fingers as his feet hit the pavement. Pushing past him, she fumbled into the driver's seat. The familiar smell set off rapid-fire memories. She closed her eyes to enjoy the mental slide-show—taking this rig to her first festival, digging it out of a sand dune, and camping in the back when a thunderstorm flooded her tent.

When her eyes opened, she found Amanda hanging back. Kels climbed out of her car without ever turning the engine over and reached for her absentee friend. "Thanks for helping me out. Damn, it's great to see you again." Her hug squashed any tension lingering between them.

"Aren't you going to take it for a spin?" Amanda asked when their torsos parted.

Kels took an over-the-shoulder glance at her beautiful SUV. "Not today. I've got to do a couple ride-alongs with my physical therapist first. But I'm glad you're both here. I need to talk to you. Together."

Kent glanced at Amanda on a shrug, unaware of Kelsey's plans.

Kelsey headed for Amanda's car, ready to climb in the backseat. "Let's get going, I'm starved. Lunch is my treat."

The local spot was nearly empty between the lunch and dinner hour. Kent led them to a booth near the window. After placing their orders, Kelsey waited for the usual news about Ashwood to pass before bringing up her idea about the future of Venture Sister. They nibbled the last of their fries as she tried to convince them.

"I brought this up with Kent before, but he didn't take me seriously. Amanda, I need you to help me change his mind."

"But isn't Venture Sister your baby?" she asked with a tinge of worry.

"Yeah. Which is why I want to know it's well taken care of," Kelsey insisted.

Kent frowned. "It's too soon . . ."

She held up her hand to quiet him. "I need to make some decisions about my half of the business, and Sig's been swamped since the accident."

"I'm so sorry," Amanda tried to apologize again.

Kelsey reached across the table and squeezed her hand. "Hey, none of that. I've moved on. I already talked to Sig about this. I'd like for you both to think about coming over to help run Venture. Obviously, it might be a while before you could buy in, no rush. You'll have—"

Kent cut her off, "Don't do this." The hurt in his eyes was all for her. Kelsey had already come to terms with everything she had to give up—kayaking, rock climbing, and mountain biking. But her best friend still refused to say goodbye to the version of Kelsey he'd once known.

"Listen. It's okay. I've talked to my doctors. Anything that has a high-risk of head injury is out—forever. The other stuff? Well, I'll have to see what my body will let me do."

Lowering his face into his hands, his fingers pulled his hair at the roots. "I gotta know one thing, Kels. Is Ben pressuring you into this?"

The question caught her off guard. Was Kent seeing something she was blind to? "No. Ben's got his priorities, and I've got Venture. I only want to make sure my business has what it needs to thrive."

Amanda leaned in. "Kelsey, why are you bringing me in on this?" Kent shifted his eyes up to hear her answer.

"Sig needs a woman for Venture Sister," she said, "and I know you've built some mad skills keeping up with Parker."

Amanda shrugged. "I've been forced to—it was either that or get left behind."

Kelsey's eyes flicked between Kent and Amanda. "When I look at the two of you, I see a set of skills Venture desperately needs. Could Sig and I hire someone else? Of course. Would I trust them like I do both of you? Absolutely not. Please, just think about it."

A smile tipped the corners of Amanda's mouth. "I've got school. And Parker's internship lasts through the end of the year."

"The Patagonia trip?" Kelsey asked when the memory of that conversation in her living room flashed in her mind.

"Do you still plan to go? I'd love for you to come."

Kelsey swallowed hard, letting go of another tempting dream. "I'll probably have to pass."

**

Ben couldn't ignore it. Kelsey was hiding something. Every day this week she'd stayed later at The Center and had met with Sig twice. The woman was preparing for something, yet when he asked about her future plans, she wouldn't give him any solid answers. His stomach tightened as he anticipated the moment when Kelsey left Portland with no real reason to return.

Needing time to think and advice from friends he trusted, Ben rebooked his flight and extended his upcoming business trip to North Carolina by a couple of extra days. He'd hoped to take her along this time, but after the unexpected call from Mark his perceptions had changed.

Getting on a plane and leaving her in Portland wasn't nearly as hard this time. He kept an eye on his tracking app and could tell she spent most of her nights at home and her days at The Center. Still, their calls weren't as frequent, and when they talked, Kelsey's voice had a strange excitement that reminded him of the woman he knew before the accident. It hurt, and he wondered how long she'd need him in her life.

Each evening when Ben met up with his friends at Lucky's in downtown Charlotte, he stayed out a little later. And when his phone buzzed with Kelsey's call in his pocket, he let it go to voicemail. Ben didn't want to blow off the woman sitting across from him to take Kelsey's call. He and Susan sat together every night, at their same quiet table near the back.

His ex knew about Kelsey and even wanted to meet her on her next business trip to the Portland office. Susan admired everything he'd done to help Kelsey after the accident. Patient as always, Susan listened, and her attention felt good. It was nice to have someone looking out for him for a change.

***

"Relax, you're doing great," Travis said from the passenger side. Even though sweat slicked her hands, after a third day driving Portland's city streets, she felt more confident. At a stoplight, she let go of the steering wheel and wiped her palms across her jeans.

"Do you want to take your car home today?"

Kelsey turned to Travis and grinned. "Yup. I've got this."

Her plans were in place and tonight would be perfect. Ben had been so distracted after returning from North Carolina, he'd barely noticed her mounting nerves. And he planned to work late again, but that was okay, she'd have extra time to prepare a special celebration dinner. She already had fresh vegetables from the garden and only needed to stop at the store for a bottle of wine and Romano cheese.

This morning she took extra care getting ready. She'd shaved her legs and straightened her sleek blond hair. She even had time to change the sheets on Ben's king-sized bed—and couldn't wait to mess up those fancy new sheets tonight. Without the Max train to slow her down, she had plenty of time before Ben came home from work.

Kelsey hid her car at Nancy's. She didn't want to risk Ben spotting her SUV when he got home tonight. With two sacks of groceries, she cut through the back gate from the alley, climbed the porch steps, and headed straight in through the kitchen door. Setting the bags and her leather backpack on the table, Kels spun to put the cheese in the refrigerator.

A strange sound spilling from upstairs alarmed her. She froze for a second, walked into the living room, and noticed Ben's car out front.

Crap, why was he home? She didn't want to spoil the surprise. Maybe he'd forgotten his laptop in his rush to get to work this morning. Kelsey tiptoed back toward the kitchen with a grin stretched across her face. She hoped he'd leave without ever spotting her downstairs.

Kelsey's smile widened when she heard his rolling laughter, but when a female's higher voice joined his chuckle she froze in place.

Irrational fear sought an answer. Maybe it wasn't Ben. Maybe someone was rifling through their stuff and they were being robbed. Please. Maybe. Anything made more sense than Ben with another woman.

She crept to the base of the stairs, wincing when the floors squeaked, and listened.

"That's it. So wet, so fucking tight." His rumbling voice echoed and wrapped around her, familiar words she'd heard just last night.

A breathy cry keened and added *his* name. Kelsey's heart stuttered, and nauseous pain spread from her stomach to her chest. Her plans for their future tumbled from her mind, and the weight of those broken promises held her feet in place. She couldn't move, couldn't breathe, yet her thundering heartbeat didn't mask the unmistakable sounds of pleasure echoing down the stairs.

Ben was fucking another woman on the fancy clean sheets she'd just put on their bed.

Dizzy, the colors in the living room muted. She staggered into the kitchen and grabbed her backpack and keys then found herself drawn to the safety of Nancy's green garden. Stepping outside, she realized that the colors looked different through a lens of hot, flowing tears.

Trembling this hard, driving had to wait, but the bench in the corner of Nancy's garden gave her shelter. She hid, waiting. Waiting for what? Nothing would draw her back inside. Time passed, she didn't know how much, but her eyes finally cleared. Kelsey watched a trail of small ants cross the garden path, following a chemical trail. She envied those ants—at least they had somewhere to go.

Footsteps caught her breath in her lungs, and she held it until a painful need for oxygen forced her to exhale.

"Oh, Lord. Kelsey, you startled me," Nancy said when she heard the strange gasp. She stepped across a knee-high row of lettuce. "What's wrong?"

Kelsey wiped the latest tears away with the back of her hand. "I'm hiding."

Nancy peeled away her gloves and wrapped a caring touch over Kelsey's shoulder. "Hiding from what?"

"Ben," she whispered.

"Did he hurt you?" Nancy asked carefully.

"No. He's . . . he's not alone. I came home early. To surprise him. But he's with another . . ."

Understanding spread across Nancy's face. "Oh, my God. Are you sure?"

"Very sure. I heard them, upstairs." Kelsey lowered her head. "Can I stay here for a while? Just until they leave. I can't go back in there to get my stuff. But I want to . . . I need to . . . go home."

"You can do anything you like, and I'll drive you anywhere you want to go."

Kelsey pushed her smile against taut muscles that held her sorrow in place. She took a breath and shared her good news with someone who cared. "I'm driving now. My car's parked out front. I wanted to surpri—" She began, but painful sobs wouldn't let her finish.

***

While driving home from work later than he'd originally planned, Ben knit justifications neatly in his mind. Their relationship still meant *everything* to him, but maybe he and Kelsey needed to take a step back. A little space would give her time to decide what she really wanted and what her future looked like with him.

She was already looking for the door, anyway. What happened this afternoon with Susan was half Kelsey's fault. No man could be expected to wait around while a woman played roulette with his future.

This thing today with Susan was random and unplanned—a sweet memory left over from their relationship. Landing in bed together bubbled from a place of unfinished longing, and filled a mutual, temporary need. It would never happen again, and Kelsey never needed to know.

The sweet temptation was gone, as Susan was already on a plane returning to North Carolina now that she'd wrapped up her business at the Portland branch. They both agreed to put this lingering attraction on the shelf until Kelsey finished her therapy. Asking Kelsey to move back to Ashwood now would only be cruel.

Susan understood, and her understanding meant so much. Trust was important to him and Ben couldn't trust Kelsey—not since this crap with Mark began. The old Kelsey was back—along with all the same traits that made him doubt her before the accident.

The sun had almost set when Ben pulled up to the curb. Strange, the house looked too dark. He unlocked the door, stuffed his guilt, and trudged upstairs, yet he couldn't make sense of things. Kelsey's bed was stripped and so was his. Their blankets, sheets, and pillows were piled in heaps on the floor.

Was Kelsey doing laundry? A smattering of Kelsey's clothes lay tossed across her bare mattress, the dresser drawers were open, and most were empty. Something was seriously wrong.

Taking the steps two at a time, he rushed downstairs to the living room then ran into the kitchen. Two bottles of wine—Kelsey's favorite—were in a bag on the table. A few other groceries lay scattered across the counter. Ben bolted next door and found Nancy sitting in her garden. She rose to her feet, seeming to expect him.

The look on his neighbor's face halted his forward momentum. "I'm looking for Kelsey."

Her eyes came to his, as she shook her head. "Ben, she's gone."

His brows furrowed, confused. Then Nancy filled in the single key detail. "Kelsey came home early this afternoon."

"Oh, God." Ben bent, supporting his shaking weight with his hands on his knees. "Did you take her home?"

"No, she drove. Travis cleared her to drive, and she came home early today to surprise you." Nancy's voice didn't hold a hint of sympathy.

Ben straightened. "I'm sorry."

Nancy backed a step away and sighed. "You need to tell that to Kelsey."

TWENTY-THREE

Sig dug through his top desk drawer and found her the spare key.

"Are you sure you want to stay here, kiddo? There's always room at the house for you."

Kelsey couldn't meet his gaze, and her hands trembled as her fingers wrapped around the key. He had to notice but must have realized she wasn't ready to talk. In a fog, she wandered down the hall and opened the small room she kept at Venture.

Sig's heavy steps echoed behind her, following to make sure she was okay. "It's all here, just like you left it."

A twin bed, smashed against the wall, was hidden beneath a cluttered accumulation of backpacks, paddles, ropes, and gear. He loitered, waiting to hear why she'd suddenly appeared, but Kels couldn't speak. Giving him a weak smile, she nodded then shut the door, having reserved just enough energy to sink in a ball onto that thin mattress.

She knew she had less than forty-eight hours before Sig would give Kent a call. And he didn't even give her that long. Kent appeared the next day. It was too soon to reveal the dirty details, and saying anything to Kent would only make matters worse. She knew he didn't buy her story about needing time to focus on Venture, but thankfully, he played along for now.

The following afternoon, Natalie found her, armed with accurate information.

"Not here." Kelsey grabbed Nate's hand and hauled her outside. The last thing she needed was for Sig to hear the truth and drive into Portland looking for Ben.

Out in the gravel parking lot, Natalie wrapped her hand around Kelsey's forearm, stopping her short, looking for an answer. "I called Ben to see if the four of us could go out this weekend. He told me you two broke up. What happened?"

"Just like he said . . ." Kelsey twisted from her grasp, backed away, and repeated words Ben should have said before she found him with another woman. "We broke up."

"Well, he also said it was his fault, and that you'd never forgive him."

A hard laugh leaped from her throat. "At least he's not stupid."

"Come on, tell me what happened," Natalie pleaded. "Did Mark call Ben again?"

Kelsey's gaze shot to her friend. "Again? What are you talking about? When did Mark call Ben?"

"The day you came up to Ashwood." Eyes wide, Natalie bit her lip. "Didn't Ben tell you?"

"This is bullshit! What is it with you and your brother keeping secrets?"

With an apologetic shrug, Natalie reached for Kelsey again. "What did my brother do?"

Her eyes fell away and she mumbled. "He's seeing someone else."

"What? Are you sure?"

Kelsey resurrected the memory, the woman's sultry sounds, Ben's sensual words, and her own vivid pain. "Yes. I'm sure."

"That doesn't sound like my brother. Did you find a text or something? Maybe you just misunderstood."

"It was a lot more than a text."

Natalie's face paled and her eyes brimmed with tears. "You might as well tell me. I'll find out all the details eventually."

"I drove home for the first time, a little early, and Ben just assumed I was still stuck to the train schedule. I planned to surprise him with a special dinner. He was . . . already at home . . . with some girl."

"No." Natalie's face fell. "Who?"

Kelsey's shoulder lifted a fraction. "They were upstairs," she whispered. "I didn't want to see what I could already hear."

"I'm so sorry. I never imagined my brother would do something like this. Maybe I should talk to—"

"No, please. I need to keep this quiet. Nobody else knows." Kelsey had layers of reasons for protecting her privacy—Kent, Sig, shit, even her Dad—she didn't want anyone interfering with her life. And Hood River was crawling with Parker's minions. So far, she'd been able to avoid them.

"Who knows about this?"

"You, me, Ben, and *the bitch*."

Natalie winced. "You didn't tell Kent?"

"Not yet."

"Seth will be—"

"Hey, I don't need anyone fighting my battles—not Kent, and especially not your husband."

"I don't know how long a sister can last taking sides against her brother, but I'm taking sides now. What Ben did was absolute shit." Natalie winced when the obscenity passed her lips.

Kelsey burst out laughing, enjoying the first hint of happiness she'd felt in days. "Nate, coming from you, that means a lot." She looked at the front door of Venture but didn't want to go back inside.

"I need tequila." Kelsey walked to her silver SUV.

"I'm in and I'm buying." Natalie climbed into the passenger seat and asked, "Should I text Amanda an invite?"

Kels laughed. "Why not. We might as well make it a party."

***

With a girl on each arm, Kelsey managed to guide both of her friends to Amanda's apartment. After helping her friends navigate the stairs, she got enough water into Natalie and Amanda to avoid a night of holding their hair while they puked.

Kelsey hadn't had much to drink, but she still paid a price for her night out. Someone from Parker's crew spotted her at the bar. An early morning phone call left no doubt when she overheard Amanda talking in her room. Propped against the door jamb, Kelsey listened, waiting for the call to end. "I know. This internship is a great opportunity. Of course, I understand. Not everyone gets a break like this."

Amanda's feet shuffled as she paced the carpet in her green fuzzy slippers. "I can't. That's Kelsey's personal life . . ."

"I get it. Yeah, our fans want closure." The bed creaked as Amanda sank to the mattress. "Yeah. I know. I'm part of the team."

A moment of silence stretched until Kelsey heard Amanda's phone clatter to the floor. "What a fucking bitch," Amanda whispered as Kels slipped around the corner to find a washed-out version of her friend. But her pale complexion wasn't due to the hangover.

"I guess you heard all that." Amanda tossed her body to the mattress, her legs dangling over the side.

Kels claimed the spot next to her, flopped backward, and stared at the glitter embedded into the popcorn ceiling. "I heard most of it. And I agree, Parker is a bitch."

"Sometimes I wish she'd never hired me, but damnit, I'm learning so much."

Kelsey considered her options for a long moment. "I'll give you some footage, if it will save your grade and keep your boss off your back."

"Not a chance, Kels."

"Think about it. At least if I'm in on the project, we can spin it our way."

Amanda kneaded her lip while thinking over Kelsey's offer. "I guess that might work."

Kels wanted to fix this, but she didn't mind asking for Amanda's help too. "Maybe you should join me on my first guiding trip when I get back in the field. You know, for an exclusive story."

"You'd do that for me even after all the shit I caused?"

"I'd like to have you along, with or without your camera, and if you enjoy it, I hope you'll consider my offer to help lead Venture Sister."

"After that phone call, I'd be a fool not to."

Kelsey's grin widened. "Parker might think she's the shit, but I've got a few connections too. And hey, I'm a local celebrity."

Their laughter woke up Natalie, and she rushed to the bathroom, still suffering the negative effects of the tequila shots. Nate emerged, mascara smudged, eyes red, her skin a putrid shade of green.

Kelsey led her back to the couch and covered her with a blanket. "Let me get you a cup of coffee."

"You're an angel," Natalie mumbled, and Kelsey had to laugh. Even with the memory loss, she knew she'd never been called that before.

***

Sticking it to Parker was tempting, but she talked it over with Amanda, and they crafted a short video instead. It revealed her plans to get back on the trail for Venture Sister, embellished with a few video segments already on social media. When Parker put her own audacious spin on the footage, Kelsey found herself under public scrutiny again. All the phones at Venture, including her cell, rang furiously.

With all the noise, she nearly missed the vibration in her pocket—a call from Mark.

Kelsey dove into her storage closet/bedroom at Venture and answered, "Hi." Her single word shook along with her hand.

"Kelsey. Thank God, I can't believe you picked up. It's great to hear your voice."

His voice sounded like heaven to her, too. "Yeah, about that . . . I've been avoiding you."

Mark chuckled, but she sensed his concern. "Kind of obvious. Do you want to tell me why?"

"Can you wait until I figure that one out myself?" Kelsey asked.

"Sure. No worries. Saw your latest video. You look great."

She laughed, actually giggled. *Where did that come from?* "Amanda and I put most of that together. I can't stand Parker, but she's got her claws into Amanda, so I thought I'd help out."

"Heard you were in Portland. I'm glad you're happy, Kels." Mark's gentle voice, as fluid as the surf, warmed a spot in her heart no one else could reach.

"I'm happy, but I moved on from Portland to Hood River. I'm staying at Venture."

"So, Ben . . . was he just?" He waited and let her fill in the blank.

"Ah, Ben. He was there for me when I needed help. And it was good, for a while. It's not good anymore."

"Hood River. Why aren't you in Ashwood?"

"Good question. I guess I'm avoiding home, too," she admitted, knowing she had to fix it. "Venture's busy. Sig's buried in admin and hired extra guides. Kent's even started to lend a hand. I can't wait to get back in the field."

"I'd be there now, if—"

"If I wasn't such a bitch?" She laughed and he huffed. "It's okay. I've always been difficult, and the accident only made me more . . . complicated." She hoped he understood, but how could he when she didn't fully get it herself. "Where are you now?" Kels asked.

"Sitting with my ass in the sand on a Northern California beach." Kelsey's sharp inhale made Mark chuckle. "I guess I surprised you."

Pacing her small room, she found her surfboard, and smoothed her hand over it, flirting with the idea of escape. "I miss the coast, the waves, I miss—" *I miss you,* she thought, but didn't say.

"I miss you, too," Mark cut in. "Kels, I know you've been avoiding me. Right now, I don't care why. But I'm giving you a heads up—I need to see you."

She jerked her hand away from her surfboard, fingers tingling, as if the object had formed a portal between them. Shaky steps carried her to the edge of her unmade bed. The metal frame squeaked as she sat. "I might be on a trail." She blinked, trying to remember Venture's calendar.

"I'll find you." Mark's words weren't a threat or a warning. His words were a promise.

She gave in to the inevitable. "Okay."

As comfortable silence stretched over the connection, she could almost see him gazing over the surf. Kelsey opened her mouth to speak but the words wouldn't come.

Mark cleared his throat. "I miss you, Mermaid. See you soon."

He ended the call, and Kelsey glanced around the room—one small window, bare walls, and a fluorescent light flickering overhead. She huffed and saw the space for what it was. "I'm living in a storage closet. This is bullshit."

Sig smiled and waved her out the door when Kels told him she was headed home.

***

It didn't take long before she was staring at her red front door from the safety of her SUV, half-amazed that it was still there waiting for her.

Inside, unexpected differences stood out. Everything was too clean, and Kelsey felt violated. Yet, she knew she should thank the intruder. If no one had come, rotting food would have stunk up the place.

The crap from that weekend was gone—no high-tech photography gear, no sleeping bags, no sneakers piled by her front door. Kelsey inspected her refrigerator, bathroom, and guest room. All were impeccably clean, like a staged home eager to welcome occupants.

Her bedroom door was closed. She grasped the cool knob and turned. The white paint on the frame stuck and Kelsey used her hip to give it a push. When she spotted her mess she sighed and said, "Thank you, Lord," to a deity she barely remembered, yet the words were sincere.

Other than a bed stripped down to the mattress, everything was untouched. Someone had left this room for last. If she'd waited even one more day, this place would look as sterile as the rest. Whoever it was—her mom, sister, or Natalie—she wanted to thank them for the kindness and put a stop to their progress.

Hesitating for a moment, Kelsey used her toe to examine a jumble of shoes. After kicking at the pile, she used the other foot to nudge her kayak gear—two spare helmets, a spray skirt, a rescue vest, and a tangled yellow throw rope with a metal carabiner on one end. As she examined the pile of equipment, she pictured what wasn't there. Her busted helmet was either in a landfill or incinerated, cast away with the emergency room garbage. After shaking away the thought, she bent and scooped up a handful of shoes, ready to toss them in her closet. Pulling the door open, she stared at the mostly empty space. "Where's my stuff?"

Damn it, a bunch of her clothes were still at Ben's. Her confidence hissed away like a flat tire. Unwilling to dwell on the small setback, Kelsey made a trip to the shed on the side of her house to store the kayak equipment. Hurrying back for another load, she came around the corner and shared a startled scream.

Her mother stood panting, holding a basket of dirty clothes on her hip, her hand slapped over her heart. "Kelsey Anne Fisher, you took ten years off my life!"

"Sorry, I didn't know you'd be here." She shrugged and apologized to the organizer of her house.

"Where's Ben?" her mother asked on a turn to search the house for signs of that man. "Why don't you two stay at the house tonight? It's so much nicer."

"Mom, it's just me. I appreciate the help, but I can handle it from here."

"What do you mean you can handle it from here?"

"My house, I've got it. I know you're trying to help, but I'd like to finish what you've started—when I'm ready."

Kelsey extended her hands and tried to pull the basket of dirty clothes from her mother's grasp. She looked over her mother's shoulder into the bedroom and noticed the partially made bed. An expensive new comforter lay folded neatly on the corner.

"Where's my old blankets and shit?" She won the short tug of war with her dirty clothes and put the basket on the floor.

"Your *shit*?" Her mom emphasized the curse word but winced. Kelsey's language had always bugged Mom. "It's in the landfill with the rest of the mess." Her mom used *the voice* that used to scare her, but the quality had lost its edge.

Kelsey took a step back. "The dump? What else did you toss? This is *my* stuff, Mom. My life. My shit."

Her mother's eyes flashed. "This place was destroyed by that horrible film crew. I didn't need a reminder of the way they cut our lives wide open. Those pigs left food and beer cans everywhere—for me to deal with."

She pushed past Kelsey and picked up her purse from the couch. "If it wasn't for me, your house would be crawling with rats."

Kelsey struggled to calm the crackling anger burning through her self-control. In a softer voice, she pleaded, "Please, Mom, just leave. I *need* to do this on my own."

"Fine, I'll go, after you tell me why Ben isn't here. He was one of the *good ones*, Kelsey. Did you push him out of your life just like you pushed your father and me away after you got what you needed?"

Kelsey's temper cracked like a whip. "I didn't push Ben away. That guy, the one you and everyone else thought was too damn good for me, brought a girl home and fucked her in the bed we shared."

Her mother winced first at the harsh words and then at the message. She hugged her purse tight against her body, trying to deal with her daughter's raw fury. "Oh, dear. I'm so sorry. I never thought he—"

"Could do something like that? Well, he did. And I left. And it gets better. That bastard didn't bother to apologize. Not a call. Not a text. Nothing."

Mary walked to the kitchen and sank into a chair.

Kelsey moved away from her mother and folded onto her couch. "Thanks for cleaning my house. I need to get settled. I'll come over for a visit . . . when I'm ready."

The dismissal brought her mother's eyes upward, clouded with tears and a silent apology. She toyed with the strap of her purse and looked at the ceiling, blinking back tears that won the battle and escaped down her cheek. "I'm so sorry, I didn't know. All of this is hard for me, too." She pulled a wrinkled tissue from her purse and dabbed her eyes. "Sweetheart, I want to help. I need to help. Please. Let me do something for you."

Kelsey pulled her knees to her chest, her heels on the cushion of her couch. She steadied herself and tried to find a way to soften the truth. "Mom, I can't let anyone help me, not right now. Don't you realize that everything I give up, I may *never* get back? I've lost too much of myself already."

Until her mother had tried to take over, Kelsey hadn't recognized Ben's overbearing control. He'd given her freedom within tight boundaries, like a wild animal in a cage. She'd paced the edges of the enclosure he'd created around her like a predator, safe but unsatisfied. Cared for, but discontent.

Her mom buried her face in her hands. Kelsey crossed the room and tried to soothe the sting of the truth. Bent at the waist, she hugged her mom's shoulders. "I'm sorry. I shouldn't have yelled. I hope someday you'll understand how much I need this. How much I need to figure out who I am on my own."

Mom nodded. "I'll try." She stood to claim the rest of her hug. "Did Ben really do that?" she whispered with an edge in her tone.

"Yeah. He really did."

"I'm not sure if I should tell your dad."

"Probably not." Their nervous laughter bounced off the linoleum floor. The receiving end of Dad's fury was not a place any man wanted to be.

TWENTY-FOUR

Fortunately, her mother didn't have time to hover, not when the chaos of the annual Fisher barbeque kicked into full swing.

The morning of the party began like every other year. Kent burst through the door for sunrise breakfast then went to work helping Kelsey. They strung volleyball nets and wiped down lawn chairs, then hauled the barbeque onto the lawn.

Kelsey loved this annual event more than Christmas. Everyone was welcome, and anyone who could walk, drive, or boat showed up. The potluck-picnic and games began at two and lasted well-past dark. Her dad pulled her into a heated horseshoes match, then later that afternoon, Kelsey joined a water-balloon war with her nephews. Letting them win was easier than last year—they were faster, and she wasn't as quick. The potluck picnic had twice as much food as everyone could eat, but when the crowd left, they filled their coolers with a sampling of leftovers.

Like every year since she was old enough to sleep outside, Kelsey and a few of her friends pitched a bunch of tents for a post-party sleepover. After the guests dwindled, Seth and Kent went to work pounding stakes before complete darkness set in.

The ringing of the hammer put a smile on Kelsey's face. She crossed the lawn with her sleeping bag under one arm and a thin hiking mattress under the other, ready to spend an evening getting a little drunk with her friends. The smell of pine mingled with campfire smoke—an addictive scent after months in the city. She ducked inside her tent, unfurled her sleeping bag, and sat on her butt on the slick nylon. The orange glow surrounded her with familiar light.

It felt perfect. She'd probably spent more nights in this cocoon than in a real bed. Conversations bled through the fabric walls—she wasn't alone, yet her false privacy seemed intimate. She didn't move until Kent called her name, forcing her to climb out of her orange cave.

When she straightened, he grinned and held a book of matches in his hand. "Do you want to do the honors?" he asked.

"Absolutely." Kent tossed the matches into the air, and she caught them on the downward arch, then bent in front of a small teepee of kindling and dry tinder. Grinning, Kels pulled a single match from the book and with a quick flick, ignited a sulfur flash. Her palm protected the fragile blaze until it caught a corner of torn paper. She crouched and blew life into the flame and the fire spread. Smoke lifted in a thin wisp, expanding as the pale wood blackened and snapped.

Satisfied with her work, Kelsey sat back on her heels and watched the dance of orange heat. When she lifted her eyes, she found Kent watching her instead of the flames. He extended his hand, and without a word, pulled her to her feet. She settled against his side and welcomed his arm around her shoulders, feeling almost guilty for how much she took from his strength. More than a brother or a best friend, she and Kent were bound. No matter how much time or space separated them, the connection never wavered.

"I'm hungry," Kelsey said, still trapped under his arm.

"Why am I not surprised? I brought some of your favorite provisions—hotdogs and s'mores."

Kelsey laughed. "I love you," she said with a hip bump. The move nudged him away, but he wouldn't let her go quite yet.

Pulling her in, he kissed her temple. "Love you, too." Releasing her an inch at a time, he left to pull food from the cooler. She was so thankful for him . . . for each person who moved in and out of the light spilling from the campfire.

Natalie took a seat next to her on a weather-smoothed log, worry plain on her face. "Don't hate me, but Ben is showing up soon."

"Here? Why?" Kelsey's head pivoted and searched the lawn for Ben. Expecting him to appear, her stomach sank with dread.

"He figured he could apologize to everyone tonight, after the party."

"Shit. Your brother has a death wish. Dad and Kent are still pissed." Her breath caught. "Damn it, I'm not ready to talk to him . . . not yet."

"I'm so sorry." Natalie's voice shook. "Seth and I both tried to stop him. The most we could do was ask him to wait until most of the guests cleared out. He's been at my tiny house on the lake all day, waiting."

"You're not serious." Imagining him so near made her queasy.

"I'm so embarrassed, Kels. I thought I knew him, but Ben seems to have picked up some of my father's awful habits."

Pulling her friend close, Kelsey whispered into Natalie's cloud of wavy red hair, "He's your brother, and I don't want you choosing sides. It will be okay." A familiar car pulled up near the house, and her head pivoted for a better look. Ben unfolded from the driver's side and shut the door. When he climbed the steps to face her parents first, she clenched her teeth. This wasn't good—Dad wasn't expecting this meeting.

Her stomach churned until Ben emerged less than fifteen minutes later. He crossed the lawn, rolling his shoulders, preparing for the awkward reunion. Blowing out a slow breath, Kelsey calmed herself, but hoped it was hard for him—he deserved the pain.

Kent spotted Ben when he moved from the deck. Anger propelled him from the campfire, and Kelsey jumped, hoping to stop him. "Wait . . . Kent, no!" But she couldn't move fast enough, her limbs felt as sluggish as the early days of her recovery. She covered her mouth when Ben held his position and Kent kept moving. Momentum launched his fist forward, but she knew he must have held back, because when fist connected with flesh, Ben was still on his feet. Dazed, Ben shook his head, wiped his lip, and widened his stance, bracing for another punishing jolt.

Kent's voice echoed over the lake. "Fight back, you miserable bastard. What the fuck are you doing here?"

Ben rubbed his jaw. "I'm here to apologize to Kelsey."

The voice that used to make her smile stole her breath, but she was finally able to move. She ran to Kent's side, and grabbed hold of his bicep to halt the short brawl. Shaking, heat rolled from his fiery rage. Ben studied her carefully, yet he didn't say a word.

She squeezed Kent's arm. "I'm okay. Please, give us a little space."

The muscles in his neck pulsed, but he nodded and moved away, yet not too far.

Facing Ben, Kelsey waited and watched a man she thought she knew, but apparently didn't. Ben's mouth opened to speak, though he hesitated, and closed his lips again.

She wanted this done and blurted, "Why?"

He swallowed hard then raked his hands through his trim hair, sending sections in different directions. "I'm a fool. I convinced myself that you were with—"

"With who? It was you and me. There was never anyone else."

His shoes stamped the turf. "I thought Mark was going to show up, and . . . and take you from me."

"Take me? No one *takes* me anywhere, you know that. If I go, it's my choice. And until you fucked up, I chose you."

Huffs of air shot from deep in his chest. "I know. God. I'm sorry. I never meant to hurt you."

Kelsey looked up at the emerging stars and tried to slow the tears that streamed in hot lines down her cheeks. She walked farther from the fire and the house, needing the dark's protection. Her shoulders sagged as she wrapped her arms around her middle to contain the hurt.

"I didn't want to do this today, but . . . damn it, you're here." Her feet planted, grounding what she knew she had to say. "What you did for me, giving me a place to stay, being there for me through my recovery, for that, I will always be grateful."

Ben moved a step closer, his eyes widening with a glimmer of hope.

Kelsey let her tears spill. "Ben, I was downstairs that afternoon. I heard you. Nothing you can say will erase the words you said to that woman . . . in our bed. No matter how much time passes, I will never forget it. Not ever."

Ben swallowed hard. "I was stupid. I'm so fucking sorry." He inched closer and reached to comfort her as if nothing had changed.

It took a moment before she moved back a step. "Don't touch me." Angry with herself for wanting his arms around her, she clenched her fists. "I'm not ever going back. All my stuff that's still at your place—give it to Natalie. I don't need any more of this shit."

"Kelsey." Ben stepped toward her, and she winced when he tainted her name with his lips.

She spun away but didn't go back to the fire. Deeper in the shadows, she accepted Kent's outstretched arm. They wandered together skirting the shore, moving farther into the dark.

Natalie met Ben and hugged him. Kels caught the murmur of their short conversation before he walked slowly to his car, started the engine, and disappeared beneath a canopy of evergreens. When his headlights faded, Kelsey found a spot again with her friends. The crackle of the fire soothed her more than any words ever could. The group huddled around the warmth, a smaller gathering than in previous years.

Rick and Linnea had gone home at dusk with Ricky. The toddler might have loved an outdoor sleepover with his daddy, but the ground was not the place for Linnea's pregnant body.

Amanda had texted Kent and sent her apology. She had to cancel because Parker needed last- minute edits on work she was shooting in Alaska.

Annie missed the daytime half of the party. After her shift ended at Mosquito Creek taproom, she wandered in for the bonfire. She sat close to the flames, talking with the guys on either side of her. Justin and Grant both showed up dressed in their fire department uniforms in case they had a call.

Kelsey poked the fire with a long stick, watching as a flame ate away the end.

"Another marshmallow?" Natalie asked, holding the bag high.

"I'm sugared-out. Could you pass me a beer instead?" Natalie pulled two from the cooler, popped both caps, and passed the IPA to Kels.

"Thanks." Kelsey took a long gulp and a deep breath. The fire snapped and a log shifted, sending sparks into the air like fireflies.

All heads turned when a flash of headlights danced from the road across the trees. "I hope Ben didn't come back," Kelsey said, low and quiet.

Grant leaned forward in his seat. "Not Ben, the headlights aren't the same."

"It could be Dillon coming over after closing the taproom," Annie offered.

"Or Maggie," Justin added, interest in his gaze.

They all heard a door slam. When the dome light timed out, Kels lost sight of the outline of a guy headed their direction. Her legs twitched, and Kelsey stood as Annie said, "That's not Dillon, not tall enough."

Kelsey broke into a colt like sprint. The guy stopped, opened his arms, and braced himself for impact as she launched to grasp him tight around his neck. He spun her around, feet off the ground and her laughter rang. When she stopped laughing Kels whispered against his neck, "You weren't kidding when you said you'd find me."

TWENTY-FIVE

"No, Mermaid, I wasn't." Mark trapped her against his chest to inhale her ginger shampoo. The scent made him a little light-headed, finally, he was home.

The winding road he took to find her had included a stop at Venture. Mark thought she might be guiding in the mountains, and figured he'd wait in Hood River until she returned. Sig had pointed him toward the Fisher place, letting him know that almost everyone the Fishers knew would be there and that they would happily welcome one more.

On his way to their lakefront home, Mark gassed up his Subaru in Ashwood and spotted Ben coming out of the minimart. The guy looked broken—at least ten years older than the time they'd met at the beach. Those first days at Driftwood Shores seemed like another lifetime—trying to teach Natalie how to surf and failing, showing the basics to Kelsey and watching her take to the surfboard as if it was an extension of her limbs. God, she was exciting. He knew nothing, not even her brush with death, could change that about his Mermaid.

"Hey, Ben, hi." Mark greeted Ben with a chin lift, wondering what role this guy still played in Kelsey's life.

Eyes narrowed, it took Ben a moment to place him. "Oh, Mark, it's you. Are you coming to see Kels?"

"Thought I would," Mark said, topping off his gas tank.

"Good. That's good." Ben nodded, glanced down the road in the general direction of the Fisher place, then mumbled to himself, "I should have had Kelsey call you back that day. Things might have turned out differently."

"What was that?" Mark asked, confused.

"Oh, nothing." Ben didn't bother to say goodbye. He just climbed into his car and pulled from the lot, headed toward

Portland. As the taillights disappeared, Mark realized he'd be staying in Ashwood for a while. He glanced down the highway and considered his options, then spotted a lit vacancy sign partially hidden beneath a tangle of pine branches. Drawn by the neon, he parked in front of a small building just off the highway. The office matched a cluster of A-frame cabins tucked beneath the trees.

Not knowing how his night would unfold, Mark reserved a place for one night. He didn't dare assume anything. Kelsey might take one look at him and send him away. But if she let him stay, he was determined to set a slower pace. This time, pursuing Kelsey would be different. He figured he had only one shot to get this right.

***

Secured in Mark's arms, Kelsey absorbed everything he offered and a layer of loneliness she'd been carrying since he left for the Maldives bled away.

From across the lawn Natalie's voice echoed over the crackle of the bonfire. "I want to get out of here."

"Leave? Why?" Seth asked his wife.

"You're seeing this, right? Ben knew there was still something between them. *He knew.* He saw this coming."

Kelsey pulled away from Mark and turned to find Kent confronting Natalie as she hurried toward her ride home. "That's out of line, Nate."

Seth stepped between his wife and Kent. "She's just standing by her brother."

Kent yelled, "Maybe it's time someone stood by Kelsey."

"Please, don't." Kelsey hated that she was driving her friends apart, but Natalie sped past her and begged Seth with a trembling voice to take her home.

Seth slipped past and apologized, "Sorry, Kels. Natalie needs to get home."

Their truck pulled away, and Kelsey shrank into Mark, not knowing what she should do. It seemed like no matter how carefully she tried to balance her precarious life, someone she cared about was always getting hurt.

***

"I'm sorry. I didn't know coming here today would lead to this," Mark apologized to everyone around the campfire. Kelsey didn't want him to regret coming and squeezed his hand.

Kent shook his head. "It's complicated. And most of what happened today has nothing to do with you. We'll figure it out—it just might take some work." Kent offered a beer to Mark, but he held up his hand, declining it, accepting a soda instead.

Everyone seemed infatuated by him and the life he led. He tried to downplay the glamour of travel and surfing tropical spots all over the globe. When Mark rose to toss another log onto the fire, Kelsey was tempted to steal him away, but watching him mix with her crowd was nice, too. She intended to enjoy his visit for as long as possible—then her stomach tightened, anticipating another inevitable goodbye.

Eventually, blaring tones from two different phones spurred Justin and Grant's movements. Justin glanced at the message. "Looks like another brush fire near the highway." Worried about her friends, Kelsey told them to be careful as they jogged toward their trucks.

With so few gathered around the fire, the conversation slowed. Annie yawned, told everyone goodnight, and slid into her tent alone. Kent lasted longer, talking while the moon traveled across the sky. Kent finally took the hint and left her alone with Mark in the auburn light of the campfire's glowing embers.

Mark stood and pulled Kelsey against his torso and teased a careful kiss. "I'll see you tomorrow," he said against her lips.

"Tomorrow?"

"I'm staying at one of those cabins in town."

"Why?"

He inched away a fraction but held her eyes. "I didn't know what I was walking into tonight."

"Are you sure?" She slanted her head toward her tent, hoping he'd change his mind.

"I'm sure. Can I see you tomorrow?" he asked and caressed her face with his thumbs.

Her grin expanded. "Absolutely."

"Cool, it's a date."

A date. She knew Mark didn't date. He swept in with the wind and left again just as quickly. Something shifted between them as he laced his hand in hers while she walked him to his car.

"Why don't you come back in the morning? You can have breakfast with the crowd and meet my parents."

"I'd like that." Mark nodded and took a final kiss before he sank into the driver's seat and drove away.

***

The sky brightened to a deep sea-urchin purple as Mark parked beneath a canopy of evergreens in front of his A-frame cabin. The sunrise barely lit the broken gravel path that led to his rented front door. Nearby, a light in the office flicked on and he doubled back to extend his reservation to the weekly rate. Satisfied with his decision, he set an alarm on his way to the bed in the loft and slept better than he had in weeks.

Right on time for breakfast, Mark knocked on the Fishers' door, He had hoped to see Kelsey, but was met by Dale's thorough inspection. The cool greeting caught Mark by surprise. Still, after everything Kelsey had been through, her dad had the right.

Kent's quick acceptance seemed to put Kelsey's parents at ease. Annie left almost as soon as he poured a cup of coffee. Breakfast wasn't too awkward—Dale and Mary seemed too exhausted from the party to ply him with questions. Kent hung around longer and helped with the clean-up, but said he was bound for Venture in Hood River. Before he left, Kelsey teased her friend, knowing he'd also be making a stop to see Amanda.

Escaping the house, Kelsey led Mark toward the lake, and they sank to a log instead of taking out a canoe. The water gently lapped the shore and infused the atmosphere with peace. Kelsey's head fell to his shoulder, and she said, "Mom and Dad like you."

"Really? They seemed a little quiet."

"That's actually a good thing. Mom's the principal at Ashwood High. Questions from her tend to feel like detention."

"And your dad?"

"Oh, he's observant. Watches, waits . . ." she chuckled, "then strikes."

"Great. What, is he a cop?"

"Worse. A judge."

Mark's laugh echoed across the lake and back. Kelsey leaned into him and hid her face from his inspection, masking tears brought on by a wave of emotion. She was different—vulnerable, but also more guarded. Even though he wanted to protect her, he fought his natural instincts and gave her some emotional space, following as she led him on a quick tour of her parents' property. While they walked, he gently steered their steps toward his Subaru. He trapped her against the metal, warmed by the sun. She melted as his lips met hers, softening while accepting his patient touch. When their kiss parted Kelsey asked, "Are you headed for the coast?"

"Not yet. I've reserved a cabin in town for at least a week."

"What?"

"I've missed you, Kelsey. A few hours aren't nearly enough."

"But you should just stay at my place," she offered, clearly confused.

"Tempting, but no, at least not right away." He grasped her hips and pulled her toward him by the loops of her jeans. "How about dinner tonight . . . say around six?"

Nodding, she grinned, happiness flashing in her aqua eyes. "The Northside?" she mumbled as his lips made contact. He hummed an agreement against her kiss, and she licked the tickled vibration playfully. "Do you want me to meet you there?"

"No. I'll pick you up."

"I'll be at home . . . I'll text you my address."

"Don't bother. I know exactly where you live. When I set out from the coast, I left nothing to chance."

***

After a short nap and a quick shower, Kelsey stood in front of her closet and stared at her meager selections. The stuff hanging there seemed too young or too casual for how sexy she felt today. Unfortunately, half of her clothes were still lying in a crumpled heap on Ben's floor. She dialed her sister and stared at the hopeless choices with her phone to her ear.

Elizabeth answered in two rings. "Hi Kels."

"Hey, sis. Are you home?"

"Yeah, why?"

"I have a date, and I need to borrow something to wear."

"Ooh a date . . . and I'm guessing your things are still trapped at Ben's."

"Yeah. I'm not in any hurry to get them back, either."

"Who's the new meat?"

Kelsey laughed. "Classy, Beth." Her subdued sister had always lived out her wild side through her younger sibling. "Actually, he's not new. I've known him for a while. Mark. He's the guy who taught me to surf."

"Oh, my God! He's here . . . in Ashwood?"

"Yeah. Can we talk about this while I'm staring at your clothes? Mine are making me sad."

"Get your ass over here."

***

Her sister's house was too quiet. "Where are the boys?" Kels asked, disappointed that her nephews weren't bouncing around her legs.

"Mom has them. She took them to see that ninja cartoon at the theater in Hood River."

"The one I took them to see last week?" Her brows scrunched, confused.

"The very one. It's your fault, you know."

Kelsey shrugged. "My fault, why?"

"The costumes. They had to see it again. This time wearing the ninja costumes you bought them."

"That's awesome."

"Mom seemed to think so, too." Elizabeth coaxed her into the kitchen. "Should I make margaritas to celebrate your new beau?"

"You can have one, and I'll take a sip. If I finish one of your concoctions, I'll never make it home." She'd had her sister's margaritas before. The memory of that hangover left a permanent impression—even after a coma. "Can I take a peek in your closet while you run your blender?"

"Pick anything. I'll meet you there in a sec."

She loitered in her sister's bedroom, trying to ignore the feeling that she was spying on her sibling's personal life. Her husband's rugged work-clothes hung in one corner of the walk-in closet, and his steel-toed boots lay heaped on the floor. The scream of the blender stopped, and Elizabeth appeared carrying two top-heavy glasses in her hands.

"I promise this isn't strong. I know you have to drive." Kelsey thanked her, tasted the delicious frozen drink, and set it down. Beth had a much different definition of a strong margarita.

"Where are you going out tonight?" her sister asked, pulling a few skirts forward.

"Just The Northside." Kelsey shimmied out of her jeans.

Her sister hummed. "So, this outfit is about the guy and not the place. Maybe I'll drag the family out and meet him tonight, too."

"You should. He's great and I've probably kept him to myself long enough." While sliding into a snug skirt she told her sister how they'd met—when she was visiting Natalie while she lived on the Oregon coast.

Elizabeth's wide-eyed stare stopped her words.

"What?" Kelsey asked as she looked at her reflection in the full-length mirror. Something was off, but she couldn't place the problem.

"Don't take this wrong, but your brain trauma destroyed your fashion sense . . . well, what little fashion sense you had." They laughed hard and her sister spun her back to the mirror. "The top half looks like a job interview. The skirt is somewhat okay, but the shoes you slipped on, scream *fuck me now.*"

"Really?" Kelsey bit her lip. A month ago, her sister's comments could have brought on a mess of frustrated tears, but today she giggled at her reflection. "I'm glad I came over. This might be one of those brain glitches I'm gonna be dealing with forever."

"No worries. Snap a pic whenever you need help, and I'll be your fashionista."

Elisabeth whirled into action. "Keep the shoes, loose the jacket and the skirt is a maybe." Four changes later, they'd narrowed the options. Kelsey went for the skirt instead of skinny jeans and paired those with the *fuck me now* heels. Mark might remember what she looked like in a bikini, but he'd never watched her work a body-hugging skirt and strappy sandals.

TWENTY-SIX

Mark stared at Kelsey's front door, palms sweating. Dating was uncomfortable territory. He'd slipped in and out of uncommitted relationships, but after meeting Kels, he wanted more. This hiatus from his relentless chase of the perfect wave felt right because she was the only woman he'd ever wanted to pause his routine to pursue.

He rubbed his hands on his jeans, shook them out, and raised his fist to the door as she opened it.

"Mark, how long were you planning to stand there?" she asked with a sly grin.

The vision in the doorway jarred the Earth's rotation. Kelsey's eyes, more green than blue today, danced playfully, and a teasing grin decorated her sun-kissed face. Her pale hair hung long and loose and silky, begging to be messed up. She wore a snug, white top that showed an inch of lean stomach with a short suede skirt, and her legs stretched to the sexiest strappy sandals he'd ever seen.

"Ready?" Mark croaked from his spot on her front porch.

"Just let me grab my jacket in case it gets cold tonight."

"Too smokin' hot to get cold," he mumbled.

"What was that?" she chuckled and blushed.

"Kelsey, you look beautiful." When her color went from pink to crimson, he realized he needed to confess that truth more often.

Leaning in, she kissed his cheek. "Thanks, you look beautiful, too."

Stunned again by her smile, his knees locked while she pulled the door shut and turned toward his car. Mark followed the sway of her hips, mesmerized by the gentle hug of her skirt over her lush curves. Parking so close to her front door had been a mistake. He'd follow that ass for miles as long as she kept walking.

After he parked, he was tempted to lag a few paces behind and follow her inside Northside Grill. Because damn, that view still had his mind spinning. Having his arm wrapped around her turned out better than he imagined. Envy was spectacular witnessed from the other side.

She waved at plenty of friends and led him to a table in a darker corner of the bar.

Spinning to meet his gaze, she asked, "Is this okay?"

"Excellent." He leaned in for a quick kiss, needing a taste before she sat down at the opposite end of the small table.

Iris didn't take long to bring them tall glasses of water and menus. "Nice to see you again, Kelsey."

"Good to see you, too. This is my friend Mark. He's going to be hanging around Ashwood for a while."

"Hope you enjoy your visit. Have you decided on drinks?" she asked, while her friendly gaze inspected him carefully.

"Wine?" Kelsey asked.

"I've got a nice cabernet from Maryhill," Iris offered.

Kelsey looked at Mark and he nodded, pleased that they wouldn't be splitting a pitcher of beer.

Kelsey fidgeted with the hem of her skirt until the first sip of velvety, red liquid passed her lips. Fortunately, with her back to the dining area, she couldn't see the long glances aimed their direction. Mark counted the observers, wondering if he'd have trouble passing Ashwood's inspection. He didn't mind the scrutiny. In fact, he liked that her friends looked out for her.

The close attention reflected Kelsey's worth. She meant everything. And he wanted more from this relationship than their pattern of random hook-ups on the coast. Hearing about her accident from Brayden had almost killed him. Now that Ben seemed to be out of her life, he couldn't let her slip away again. He wanted this vibrant, independent woman to need him as much as he'd always needed her.

After her first glass of wine, he coaxed the details about the days surrounding the accident from Kelsey. Some she remembered, other details she'd pieced together from what family and friends had told her during her recovery.

By the time dinner arrived, Mark teased enough from Kelsey to satisfy his curiosity for now. Threading through it all, he saw a pattern. She'd pushed away her family and accepted help from Ben and Kent.

Ben abused her trust when he tried to shape Kelsey into someone she would never be. The guy was an idiot—nothing could improve Kelsey's rare spirit. Ben might never comprehend the scarcity of the gem he'd lost, and Mark swore to never make that mistake—he'd never underestimate her worth.

Halfway through their meal, Kent wandered over. "Do you want to get in on the next round of pool?" he asked.

Kelsey looked down at her short skirt. "Better not."

Her friend leaned back and peeked under the table, noticing her outfit for the first time. "Damn, Kels. No wonder half of the bar's been staring at you tonight. And here I thought they were wondering about the new guy in your life." Mark chuckled but saw in an instant that Kelsey didn't appreciate Kent's teasing.

Forcing a laugh, she shrugged it off. "I like to have a reason to get dressed up."

With a nod to his impatient friends at the pool table, Kent squeezed Kelsey's shoulder and said, "You two have fun."

As Kent walked away, Kelsey spun in her seat and scanned her small hometown crowd. By the time she turned back, her smile was gone. "I didn't realize we had an audience."

"We can get out of here if you want," Mark offered.

Kelsey looked at their half-finished meals. "Are you sure?"

"Yeah. Just a sec." He went to the bar and came back with takeout containers. Iris brought a cork and the bill. After Mark took care of the tab, they moved the party to the cabin he'd rented a few miles down the road. As he pulled in front of the A-frame, Mark was thankful he'd sprung for one that had a hot tub on a private deck.

They finished dinner inside, eating from the takeout containers at a small round table near the flickering light from a gas-powered fireplace. While Mark explored the cupboards for something to hold their wine, Kelsey peeked out the window toward the deck. She spotted the hot tub and grinned. "Could we finish that bottle outside?"

He nodded and changed in the upstairs loft while Kelsey disappeared in the small bathroom. Mark was thankful when she appeared on the deck still clothed in her bra and panties. Before the night progressed from simmer to white-hot, he wanted to talk about a few things.

He settled in the hot tub first, watching as she slowly approached. Her skin grew pale as she stared at the tumbling water. "Could we shut off the jets?" she asked. He looked at the turbulent surface through her worried eyes and couldn't kill the jets fast enough.

"Thanks. That reminded me of . . ." She laughed off the moment and her smile eased his concern.

"Never apologize, Mermaid." Mark supported her hand as she stepped in, then reached around her to pour wine into the mugs he'd found in the kitchen.

She took the cup, swallowed a sip, and said, "This is so much better." Up to her neck in the warm water, she heaved a contented sigh.

The heat, the scent of cedar trees, and the woman across from him combined to create a world of perfection that Mark never anticipated when this night began.

Her foot slid over the top of his playfully. "I'm glad you're here," she said.

The innocent touch sent a jolt of awareness through his entire body. "It's the only place I want to be." Mark fought the temptation in front of him until he had a chance to explain why he'd come to Ashwood.

"I know we've already talked a lot tonight—maybe too much—but there's something you have to know." He leaned forward, kissed her, and pulled her to sit on his lap. "I'll never forget the panic I felt when I heard about your accident. I didn't know if you were alive . . . or . . . or gone."

"I'm here." A caress from her sweet lips soothed the remnants of his lingering fear.

He pulled away and studied her in the low light. "That moment made things clear for me."

"This sounds serious."

"Yeah, it is. I'm serious about you, Kels. Our old pattern was easy and comfortable, but I want—"

"More?" she asked.

"Yeah."

"I'd like that too, but—"

"No *but*. Kelsey, please give us a chance."

She covered his lips with her fingertips. "Hear me out. I feel the same. I think I always have. Even though you weren't here during my recovery, you were a big part of my motivation to get back what I'd lost."

"That's good, right?"

"It is. But you haven't witnessed me when I'm tired and frustrated. I'm trying to control this *new and improved* version of me, but I'm afraid it's permanent. And what if I can't handle the waves? Some things will never be the same."

"It's *you* I want, not what you can do."

She nodded, yet he could see she didn't believe him. This stunning woman was so much more than her physical accomplishments. Mark could try to fight her misconceptions, but he knew Kelsey had to discover the enchanting woman she still was all on her own.

"I guess time will tell," she continued, "Which brings up another obstacle. Time. We're never in the same place long enough to see if we work."

"Are you willing to travel with me . . . even a few times a year?" He wanted her with him and would give up trips if it meant more time with Kels.

"Sounds super tempting." Her voice softened, and she nodded. "So long as we can work around my therapy schedule, I'm ready to make time *for you*."

Venture had consumed her before, and Mark hadn't interfered. If she needed that focus again, he'd gladly give it to her. But for now, she was carving out space for him, and he'd accept it. With the next crushing kiss, he claimed what she offered and gave her everything in return. The woman he'd nearly lost worked her way under his skin and into his heart.

Steam curled from the water's surface into the cool night air, cloaking the pair in a smokescreen of desire. The arch of her back begged Mark to slide the strap of her bra from her shoulder. His hands cupped her soft ass, and he lifted her to straddle him and sucked on the tender tip of her breast. The heat of the water matched the temperature of his lips, and he coaxed her body closer. Kelsey relaxed into the sensation of his tongue caressing her sensitive flesh. Her fingers laced through his hair, encouraging Mark to take more.

Her touch slid from his hair, down his shoulders, and traced the firm muscles roping his biceps, holding on, waiting. Chasing her need, Mark's hand slid down her back, over the swell of her hip, and beneath her panties. The scrap of fabric yielded, and he followed the seam of her ass to find her hot center. She lifted slightly, welcoming the intimate touch.

Kelsey moaned when her core was breached and shifted, taking more. She arched her torso into his lips, and he pulled at her nipple with his teeth. Her softest flesh rippled against his fingers and he groaned.

"I need more. Please," she begged.

Mark moved from the hot tub first. As she followed him to the deck, he asked, "Upstairs?" The loft's king-sized bed would be the perfect spot to trap Kelsey for days, if she let him.

With a nod, she dashed inside and up the winding staircase. They tumbled, limbs tangling, onto the soft mattress. Her eyes darkened as she moved over Mark and straddled his hips. Blond hair fell around them, mingling a warm musky scent and her familiar ginger shampoo.

Teasing and grinding over his shaft, she tried his patience, but Mark let her explore. Her fingertips danced over the contours of his shoulders, chest, and abs. She watched him as she teased his small, dark nipples across the sensitive skin at the center of her palm. He gasped and she shivered, enjoying the tactile bliss.

Mark's cock jumped, seeking her center. "I have to have you Kels, if you're ready." A nod was the only encouragement he needed. With a quick shift of his hips, he switched from the bottom to the top. The adjustment planted his length against her soft, wet juncture. A small wiggle of her hips eased the girth a fraction inside.

"Do we need a condom?" he asked, more than ready to commit to an exclusive relationship.

"I'm on the pill . . . and . . . well . . ." She stopped not wanting to say anything, but when she looked away, he knew that she'd been tested the moment she realized Ben had cheated.

Kelsey bit her lip waiting. Mark kissed her worry away before teasing her again, skin to skin. He took his time, savoring the way she writhed beneath him—her soft places beckoning his hard. When his attention had her moaning again, Mark slowly plunged inside.

Simultaneous sensations overwhelmed him—her welcoming tongue, the give of her breasts, the sway of her stomach rising and falling against his rigid abs, but nothing compared to the gentle way her center hugged his rock-hard cock.

Pulling out, he leisurely entered her again and her body welcomed his entire length. Kelsey hitched her heels higher, circling her hips with a tentative grind. Her breathing sped as her sensitive flesh opened and rubbed against his groin.

"Please," she begged, and he knew she needed more.

Mark planted his hands above her shoulders, and she grasped his bicep with a sexy grin. One powerful thrust filled her with his length. With each outward tug and inward glide, the velocity increased until there was nothing gentle about his claim. Kelsey's breath and body held, both equally tight.

"Fuck." He pulled out and speared again. Deeper, harder, they connected everywhere. Supported by trembling limbs, he sped the pace until his balls slapped her wet, soft skin with each powerful thrust.

"Come for me." Mark's feral tone and savage thrusts tore her orgasm free. He exploded as she tightened around his shaft, and he caged her in his arms, claiming everything from the connection. More than physical, his soul reached out and blended with hers, meshing in ways he never knew possible. Their breathing slowed, pacing as one, and Mark realized that Kelsey was the only woman he'd ever love.

TWENTY-SEVEN

Kelsey insisted on going to Venture Sister in Hood River alone and wouldn't be back for hours. Even though her place was great, the walls seemed to shrink around him. Mark grabbed his computer and drove to Northside Grill. The low hum of conversation in the bar suited him better than the dead quiet in her home. Iris brought him a water and a menu and asked what else he'd like to drink.

"Iced tea?" he asked.

"Sugar or lemon?"

"Just sugar, the real stuff."

"You got it." She came back with tea, and as he ordered a burger and fries, he loaded his glass with two packets of sugar and stirred.

"I thought I heard a slight drawl," Iris said letting her accent bleed through. He glanced up and she grinned. "The sweet tea gave you away."

"Where are you from?" Mark asked with a smile.

"Kansas," Iris admitted with a chuckle.

"Hey, so am I . . . born and raised."

Iris took a seat across from him for a moment. "What brought you to Washington?" she asked.

"Wanted something different, so I started out in California. I went to school near the coast and got a degree in computer science. Surfing became my passion, thanks to a roommate who eventually flunked out and nearly took me with him. I recognized a need and wrote a surfing app. Now I live off that and a few other projects."

Iris grinned, and he knew she saw past his easy shrug. He didn't like to talk about his success or the wealth that seemed to fall into his lap as he did what he loved most.

"How about you?"

A flicker of apprehension creased the corners of her eyes, then she smiled. "Well, after a storm took the house I grew up in, my family sold what was left of the farm. I used my share of the sale to buy this place."

Mark looked around, admiring the bar's easy appeal. "It's the heartbeat of Ashwood."

A wide grin erased the last traces of stress from her face. "Thanks . . . I love it. Hey, I don't want to keep you from your work. I'll keep the tea coming and get your order in."

As she wandered back toward the bar, a guy came out of the kitchen, wiping his hands on a towel. Tattoos covered the arms he wrapped around Iris. She smiled, stretched up on tiptoe and planted a kiss. Their natural connection launched his thoughts to Kelsey, and he wondered if surfing and a life in Ashwood could mesh.

***

Kelsey savored a final morning of sleeping in late with Mark next to her in bed. Exhausted by working full days at Venture, she refused to move and sighed, loving the tangle of legs in warm sheets with her hand splayed across Mark's muscled chest. Sliding her eyes open, she gazed at a still-sleeping man who had the power to drive her to addiction—an addiction to happiness.

Her world seemed so complete, now that he'd settled in her cottage in the woods that she regretted the hike looming in her future, and the temporary separation that came with it. It was strange, but nice, needing him this much.

A warm east wind whistled past her opened window. The vine maples, already red and gold, released a few dry leaves. It wouldn't be very long before the first fall storm stripped the limbs bare. He stirred, pulled her in, and kissed that spot that made her sigh. "Good morning, Mermaid."

"Yes, it is." She tilted her head, giving him better access to her sensitive skin.

"Why don't you let me drop you off in Hood River? It's on my way to the beach." He asked again, while his lips moved to another spot on her neck. "I'd love to meet you at the end of the trail to celebrate."

"No. I'll drive straight to the coast after this hike and join you there." The longing in his eyes tempted her to blow off the hike and go to the beach with him instead.

"Are you ready to get back on a board?" he asked with a no-pressure smile.

"I won't know until I try," she said with a burst of confidence.

"If you change your mind, I'll come back to Ashwood or Hood River . . . whatever works for you." Neither wanted to lose the progress they'd made in what was turning into a comfortable relationship. Last night, while their bodies shared a hot goodbye, he'd confessed that he'd never felt this alive. Kelsey had never felt this loved but wasn't ready to exchange those cherished words. It was still too soon.

After a shower, Kelsey stood at her gold-flecked formica kitchen counter slicing peaches to put on top of her granola. Mark snuck in behind her and she took her time, savoring the warmth of his lips against her neck. Morning light slanted through the window, and Mark's hands drifted across her hips, inching her closer. She was mid swallow, enjoying a slice of sweet peach. "Here, try it." she said, sliding a bite between his lips.

He devoured the fruit, turned her body to his, and claimed a taste of her sticky lips. She shared another slice, this time using her mouth. Slippery, delicious liquid dribbled down their chins.

Mark licked away the juice, stared into her eyes, and confessed, "Beauty this stunning should be forbidden." He stripped off her shirt and bra, then painted her breasts with peach-flavored kisses. Alternating her pleasure, he moved from one ruched tip to the other and feasted. When she was panting, he picked up another slice of fruit and fed it to her.

Kelsey moaned when he kneaded her breasts, pinching and deepening her insistent need.

"Mmm," Kelsey squirmed against his cock. "Will you let me swallow you up?"

His grin angled sinfully. "Sugar, do you even have to ask?" He nodded. "I'd like a taste of you, too."

Kelsey pulled him to the bedroom, leaving a trail of clothes. "Why don't we appreciate each other at the same time?"

He growled and chased her to the bed.

Naked, hard, and inviting, Mark reclined and let her lead the way. Her sweet ambrosia glistened against his mouth as she hovered over him on her knees. Grasped tight, his calloused touch positioned her exactly where he wanted. Moaning against her folds, his lips and tongue went about their wicked work.

Urged by the pearl of cum leaking from the tip of his cock, she swallowed him deep and covered the distance to the base of his shaft with her hand. Her fist and lips worked him in tandem, as his hips lifted to chase a hastening pace.

With her senses scrambled by the blitz at her core, Kelsey barely held on for the wild ride. Hips grinding, mouths devouring, she reached the sharp edge of her precipice and thought she couldn't take another moment. With a growl, Mark plunged two fingers inside and she detonated, but he didn't halt his feast. Sensitive and ready, her orgasm crested and fired a second time.

Dazed with pleasure, Kelsey bucked and fisted his shaft, swallowing his liquid heat while his hips continued to pump. The sound bouncing around the room began with echoed cries of ecstasy and ended with panted versions of each other's names. Still gasping, her legs and arms trembled, and she collapsed beside Mark, their limbs entwined, hot breath huffing near each other's hips.

Kelsey's pleasure ebbed, and she savored each pulsing second. Her heartbeat evened out, and she sensed Mark's movement as he moved to spoon her, but she didn't want to open her eyes. After a long, satisfying moment, he whispered against her neck, "I'm gonna miss you, Mermaid. Actually, I wish I could go along."

Her heart tightened in a good way when she heard a hint of worry in his voice. "Uh-uh, no men on this trip. Amanda's going and I'll be fine." Kelsey had personally selected each person for this hike—a symbolic moment to celebrate her return to the wilderness and Venture Sister.

Yet, she shared his concern. Like Mark, she wouldn't relax until they met again on the coast. He stroked her hip, not laying on any pressure or trying to change her mind. They both knew this was a literal mountain she had to climb.

***

Before he left Ashwood for the coast, Mark made a final stop. Natalie might not be ready to hear him out, but the misunderstanding about the calls and text messages with Ben was keeping Kelsey from moving forward. And another idea kept bouncing around in his head, one that began not long after he'd met Natalie at Driftwood Shores.

After parking in front of Whitewater Homes, Mark made his way to the office. Staring intently at her computer, Natalie didn't notice as he passed her window. He tapped on the glass. Startled, she looked up and didn't have time to mask her frown.

"Can I come in?" he asked, already partway in the door.

"I guess." Keeping him at a distance, she pointed to the seat on the other side of the desk.

Mark sat and dove right in. "Kelsey misses you."

Shocked by his abrupt message, Natalie blinked hard. "Well, I miss her too, but that doesn't mean I can put everything in a tidy little box and forget about it."

"Everything being?" he asked carefully, seeing the hurt in Natalie's eyes.

She inhaled slowly through her nose, her lips tight against her teeth. "Ben barely had a chance to explain himself, to apologize, and then you magically appeared. Am I supposed to believe that was just a coincidence?"

Mark fought the inclination to combat her harsh tone with angry words of his own. "Believe what you like. Other than a few vague text messages, I had zero contact with Kels before Ben messed up."

"But you called me."

"I was only trying to find Kelsey because she wouldn't talk to me."

"And Ben told me you called her phone."

"Ben picked up. Kelsey never would have, but it didn't stop me from trying."

"Why did you have to push? If you'd left things alone, Ben and Kels might still be together."

Mark thought carefully and tried to keep his words from making everything worse. "Nate, I'm sorry you're stuck in the middle, but I'm not sorry about how things worked out."

"No kidding." She glared, but her lips trembled.

"Look, Ben's a great guy—for someone else. Not for Kelsey."

Eyes aimed at the ceiling, she blinked her tears away. "I realize that now . . . but this really sucks." Natalie sighed and slowly brought her eyes to his. "Mark, I miss her so much, maybe it's time for me to let this go. I need to apologize. Is Kels still in Ashwood?"

"She just left for Hood River."

Natalie huffed and blurted, "Crappity-crap."

Mark suppressed a laugh. He'd never once heard Natalie swear, probably never would. "I do have a favor to ask," he said, and she gave him a slight grin as she swept away a tear from the corner of her eyes.

"Will it make Kelsey happy?"

"I think so." When her smile finally reached her eyes he said, "Kelsey told me you planned to sell your tiny home."

"I do. Why? Do you want to open a coffee shop?"

"No. I just need something bigger."

"For you and Kels?"

Mark nodded and hoped she'd sell it to him but didn't assume. "I need a new place. The old home was already too small, so I sold it to a friend."

"That tiny home's not as mobile. You'll need a bigger truck with a fifth-wheel hitch." Natalie thought for a moment. "You know, I won't need my 350 if I sell that home. Do you want to buy both?"

Mark grinned. This was going to be easier than he thought.

She stood and headed for the door. "Come take a look. The miles are low and it's a diesel. My grandpa used it to pull his boat to and from the marina about twice a year before I inherited it."

"If you're really willing to let both go, I'm sure we can agree on a price."

He liked what he saw and took the truck for a drive. Once he'd settled on a dollar amount, Mark went over potential changes to the home with Seth. The minor remodel wouldn't take too long—modifying the storage to hold surfboards, replacing the commercial-grade appliances, and expanding the closet, making it large enough to fit all of Kelsey's gear. Mark asked if he could wait on the truck until Seth completed the job, and everyone agreed.

With Kelsey out of town for a week, it wouldn't be difficult to keep the whole plan a secret. After a hug from Natalie and a handshake from Seth, Mark drove to the coast alone. He only wished

Kelsey was already with him—he wanted his future with his Mermaid to start right away.

TWENTY-EIGHT

Amanda and Kelsey bent over the map, studying the route circling Mount Hood. Kels traced the contour lines with her fingers, concerned about the elevation. Amanda checked her weather app again and said, "The weather's holding."

They both knew a mid-September trip was a risk, but so far, other than the persistent east wind, the conditions looked good.

Tired of planning, Kelsey stretched her arms over her head. "Smoke blowing in from fires to the east may be an issue. I've had my eye on the reports and it's nearly contained." Her legs twitched, ready for the hike.

"Nothing to worry about, unless someone ignores the burn ban," Amanda agreed, but Kelsey shook off the concern, unwilling to waste energy on the unforeseeable future.

After Sig picked up the last hiker at Portland airport, the entire team planned to meet for dinner in Hood River. Once everyone signed the paperwork and waivers, the feeling of privacy would fade. Amanda would go to work with her camera, but Kelsey trusted her friend to edit everything honestly. What happened to the footage after Parker got her hands on the film was out of her control.

Amanda packed the maps, then lifted her head and met Kelsey's eyes. "Thanks for giving me access to your life. You know . . . after everything . . ."

Kelsey waved her hand and tried to dismiss the fragmented memories that were still returning in broken pieces. "That accident wasn't anyone's fault—not even the kid who dropped his kayak on my head."

"But if I'd listened to you, your life wouldn't have gone viral."

"How could you have known? If it had rained that day . . . if you listened to me . . . if those kids weren't on the river . . . if, if, if. We all need to move past it. You, me, even Kent."

"Thanks, Kels, for letting me be part of your comeback."

Comeback. The term made Kelsey cringe. Coming back meant a return to what she once was, and some things would never be the same.

She liked the idea of a metamorphosis better. Going into the coma as one person, emerging as another. The same, yet different, unbound by previous expectations, free to become someone new.

***

A golden-pink sky spread out as the sun rose in the east. Kelsey savored the crisp morning air, knowing the day would heat. She helped Amanda hoist her thirty-five-pound pack to her shoulders while Amanda adjusted the straps and tested the weight. The beast was heavier than usual, loaded with gear that would usually be split between a couple of photographers. But Amanda endured the extra weight to keep Parker's minions away. Kelsey appreciated the sacrifice and encouraged Amanda to capture this story honestly—she wouldn't want it any other way.

Moments after sunrise, eight other women climbed from Venture's vans, claiming gear, staggering under heavy packs. Kelsey greeted each member of the hand-picked group with an encouraging smile. They all looked fresh and excited, each one eager to take their first blister-free steps.

A face in the distance drew her eye. "Fuck me," Kelsey groaned.

Amanda swiveled toward the sight that had captured Kelsey's attention. "Oh. My. God."

Parker's gleaming, toothy smile looked hungry enough to gnaw every morsel of pleasure from the trip. The rest of the women didn't recognize the unexpected newcomer at first, but they all grumbled when Kelsey stepped between her team and the intruder, and said, "Parker, what a surprise."

"You know I'm here *for you*." The photographer searched for weaknesses and Kelsey's stomach tightened. "Can you believe I gave up caving in New Mexico for your little jaunt?" Parker's insincere smile laced the alpine air with tension.

For a moment, Kels considered banning the intruder but went the other way. "Fantastic. I'm so relieved you made time to come along." If she sent her away, Parker would only stalk her group from a distance, and being hunted seemed worse than having this predator in their midst.

Before leaving the lot at Timberline, Kelsey gave them all one final chance to use a toilet that flushed.

As she waited, she sent Mark a text, not knowing when she'd have a strong signal again. ***Leaving soon. I've got a surprise—Parker showed at the trailhead and invited herself along. Could be a very long week.***

She smiled when her phone vibrated with his call.

"Hey, Mermaid. I wanted to hear your voice before you set out."

"Mmm. That's nice."

"Sorry about the invader . . ."

"She's predictable. Like a shark with blood in the water."

Mark chuckled. "No shark talk. I'm surfing today."

"Oops." Kelsey joined his laughter and immediately felt a little better.

"What's your plan?" he asked.

"Ignore her and let her do her thing. It shouldn't be that bad—all these ladies have my back."

"Not surprised. They love you." The L-word hung between them, in a comfortable, foreseeable way. "Are you still heading for the coast after the trip around Mount Hood? The weather's stellar."

A short laugh tossed her head back. "Can I come now?"

"I'm here, Mermaid."

She wanted to talk and longed to feel his touch, but her band of friends were headed in her direction. "I hate to go, but—"

"Take it all in. Listen to the mountains, they have something for you." She turned toward Mount Hood as he said exactly what she needed to hear. A part of what she'd lost was out there, waiting for her on the trail.

**

Parker loitered while the women worked in pairs and made final adjustments to their packs. Kelsey was about to help the photographer, when Amanda noticed that her mentor was the odd woman out.

"Let me help," Amanda hurried to her boss to adjust Parker's light load.

"Don't worry about me. I can manage . . . Hey, don't miss this shot." Parker plucked Amanda's camera from her pack. "Never mind, I'll get it." She clicked as the journey began.

As much as it bugged her, Kelsey admired Parker's ability to see a moment before it actually happened. She'd caught the beginning of the journey—fresh faces, clean clothes, and bright smiles at the start of a long trek. In a moment, the camera was back in Amanda's hands. Kelsey noticed her friend's determination—she wouldn't make that rookie mistake again.

The group covered the first three miles at a steady clip. At mile five, they gathered at a reliable water source and devoured lunch. Amanda took a few shots as Kelsey tended hot spots that threatened to become blisters.

Two men taking on the northern end of the PCT joined them while they ate. Dirty and leathery from a season spent on the Pacific Crest Trail, they became an attraction. Parker hung back, disappearing to document the interaction from an invisible distance.

Making good time, they stopped that afternoon long before sunset. After dinner, Kelsey checked in with each group before heading into her tent. Spread over three spots in a sparse alpine forest, she wandered between the mini-camps to talk. Kels smiled uncomfortably as each woman thanked her for including them in this moment.

Amanda hung back until her friend finished her rounds. "Is everyone good?" she asked.

"Yeah. No blisters yet." Kelsey shrugged, knowing that problems worse than blisters always cropped up.

***

After a rocky river crossing the next morning, they merged with the trail to Ramona falls. This scenic section was congested with hikers speaking German and Japanese, all working their way to a one-hundred-foot veil of water cascading over black basalt. The cool, damp air trapped woody decay, and tasted a little like moss. Kelsey inhaled, feeling the moisture on her lips and in her lungs. The tumbling water spoke to her—she smiled when none of the watery-words brought fear.

"Ready?" Amanda asked. Kelsey turned and found her group assembled in a tight knot, their feet shuffling, anxious to move on. Had the water lulled her so much that she'd lost track of time? She shook her head, asked Amanda to take the lead, and took a mile to find herself again.

The narrow trail climbed, emerging from dense trees into fierce sunlight. Kelsey drank extra water and munched on a granola bar to fight a headache brought on by the elevation change. Once the pain passed, she inhaled the sweet scent of a mountain meadow, and grinned when a chipmunk ran ahead of her down the path. Burned years ago, husks of blackened trees stood out against the bright vegetation. As if on cue, fresh smoke from distant fires tainted the alpine air.

That evening, they followed a wide trail to a popular lake and set up camp for the night. The smoke streaked the sky with a stunning coral sunset but obscured the views of distant peaks. Escaping the dirty air, they hunkered in their tents early, hoping for a change in wind direction.

The smoke layered in thick by morning, leaving an ashen layer of grey on their brightly colored tents. To avoid the terrible air quality, Kelsey opted to try a lower route beneath a denser canopy of trees. The day was cut short when a minor asthma attack hit one of her team.

"I'm sorry to slow us down," she said at camp.

Kelsey took her aside. "Never apologize for listening to your body. I'm feeling it, too."

"Thanks, Kels," she said, "I knew you'd understand."

The click of a shutter brought Kelsey's eyes around. The lens had captured it all, and she couldn't ignore the intrusion, not when it impacted someone's safety.

With a sweep of her hand, she drew Parker away. "Give her space," she warned.

"Not a chance, Kels. This is the stuff I've been waiting for. I have hard drives full of scenic mountain shots and I don't need more. I'm here for this—the struggle, the recovery, or the failure."

"You hope I fail?" Kelsey asked, teeth clenched, barely containing her fury.

Parker huffed. "Hell no, I'm only an observer. I'd never interfere with anyone's attempt to conquer nature. Law of the jungle, survival of the fittest, call it whatever the hell you want, but enduring the struggle beats a pink sunset every damn day."

Kels opened her mouth to argue, but Parker cut her off. "Don't lay your guilt on me. You and me . . . we used to be the same. Hell, someday I hope you find your edge again. But while you're searching, I want to document the shit out of your struggle."

Nausea boiled. Kelsey's heart slammed against her chest and fury stole her speech. Finally, she blurted, "Fuck you." She turned away and escaped Parker on narrow trails flanking their campsite, yet she couldn't run away from the brutal truth. Her body and mind were permanently altered, and the struggle would never end. Kels didn't emerge from the dark until most of the hikers had climbed into their tents for the night.

"Are you okay?" Amanda asked when Kelsey returned.

"Yeah, I'm fine." The sympathy captured in the lamplight on Amanda's face turned her stomach, but she had to eat something, or she'd be worthless on the trail. She picked up her mess kit and headed toward the pot propped on top of the camp stove.

"I saved you some stew," Amanda said. "And there's cornbread wrapped in foil."

"Thanks."

"Want to take a look at the maps?" Amanda asked as Kelsey scooped the lukewarm meal into her mouth.

"Yeah." After another bite, her mind focused on the journey again. "I checked the weather. The wind's shifting and will push the smoke to the east."

Using rocks to secure the edges of the map, the pair plotted a route back to the original trail. From their lower elevation, the hike would take Kelsey on paths she hadn't visited in years.

***

The sun rose in clear blue skies, and a salty taste seemed to hang in the air as a change of weather pushed in from the coast. Rested, the team hiked with as much energy as they had on day one. Kelsey took the lead, followed by four of her clients, Parker planted herself in the center, and Amanda pulled up the rear. In a flat section, Kelsey slowed her pace, and Amanda caught up, meeting her at the front.

As they loitered in the sun, Amanda downed a long swallow from her canteen. "What's up?" she asked.

"Why don't we take a break?" Kelsey hoisted her pack from her shoulders, looking for a spot to put it down.

Amanda glanced down the wide, welcoming path. A few yards ahead, a narrow fork peeled to the right and left. "Why here? There's a water source in about a mile."

"Of course, that makes more sense. I've got a rock in my shoe. Why don't you go ahead and take the lead?" Kelsey stepped out of the way to let everyone move on. She lagged a bit, following to the spot where Amanda chose for lunch. Kelsey ate her meal apart from the group, until her friend joined her and handed her a protein bar.

Passing the snack over, Amanda asked, "Are you going to tell me what's going on? Or do I have to just play along with a grin on my face?"

"That obvious?" Kels, pinched her lips between her teeth.

"Not very, not yet."

Kelsey scanned the area, looking for one particular set of prying eyes. "I'm lost."

Amanda's mouth popped open. "We're on the trail we planned to take. You chose the route."

"I did, but I don't recognize anything. And when I checked the map again, all the lines look like spaghetti. I hoped it was the change in altitude, but we both know that's not the problem. Now that we're on unfamiliar trails, I can't match what I'm seeing with a mental image in my head."

"How can I help?" Amanda asked.

"Take the lead, at least until I recognize where I'm going."

"Anything else?"

Kelsey looked around before she leaned in a little closer. "Yeah, don't tell Parker."

Amanda nodded and folded the map, putting it in her pack instead of Kelsey's. A faint shutter clicked and captured the moment.

***

The sets rolling in across the Pacific should have held Mark's interest, but he couldn't shake this feeling—something was wrong. He needed to get to Kelsey. Mark took a chance and looked up Venture's number, hoping Sig could reveal something that would ease his concern.

Learning the trip had been extended by a day due to poor air quality settled his mind for a time. Perhaps that was the cause for his restlessness. This unexplainable tie to Kelsey had always been there, but it had been faint. Since he'd returned the connection had deepened. His heart skipped a beat when he realized it was love that had strengthened the undeniable bond.

***

Familiar landmarks dropped mental images into place, and Kelsey relaxed as Mount Hood's snow-covered peak came into view. Amanda hung back to give Kelsey the lead position once again.

"Better?" Amanda asked quietly.

"Much better, thanks." Grinning, Amanda jogged ahead with her camera in hand. She crouched, the shutter on rapid-fire as each woman hiked the trail with Mount Hood framing the shot. Snippets of animated conversation passed among the group, joyful anticipation of their last evening in camp.

After dark, they hunkered together around a couple of camping lanterns, the conditions too dry for a fire. Kelsey's eyes slid from person to person, knowing what she had to do.

The camera lens was no longer a distraction, and Kelsey gave up her last thread of privacy to reveal the truth. A lull in the cheerful conversation urged her on. "I want to thank all of you for sharing this experience with me. I didn't realize when I chose this route around Mount Hood that the journey would mean so much to me."

She inhaled a staggered breath. "I've tried to hide it from all of you, but that would be living a lie. I was lost on the trail today, and Amanda took over until I recognized the path again. This will be my final trip with Venture Sisters . . . at least for a while."

A chorus of murmured *oh, no* coaxed a chuckle from Kelsey.

"Hey, I didn't say I was falling off the Earth. I'll still take on these mountains, and when I'm ready, you can join me on a different quest."

Kelsey stood, stepped past the lanterns, and pulled Amanda into a hug. "Thank you. I love you," she whispered close to her ear.

"Love you, too." Her friend held on a little longer, sharing a connection that began in Ashwood and extended beyond. One by one, each woman stood, hugged Kelsey and thanked her for her honesty and this journey.

Parker waited on the edge and was the last to approach. "Amanda may have wondered why I stuck her with all the equipment. I needed room for the wine I've been carrying the entire trip. Will you all join me in a toast?"

"Hell yes." Kelsey laughed, as the mood shifted from serious to celebration.

Parker brought out a large canteen filled with delicious red wine. They passed and poured the cabernet into tin cups. "I was tempted to share this on the first day, because, damn, it was heavy."

"I'm glad you waited." Kelsey nodded and lifted her cup. "To things we've lost along the way and what we'll find on the journey home."

***

At first light, Mark turned his back to the ocean and pulled his keys from the pocket of his faded jeans. Unease eroded his calm, and he had to get to Kelsey. If he hurried, he might catch her at Timberline. After a four-hour drive, Mark parked next to the Venture Van in the lot on Mount Hood.

The stone entrance at Timberline Lodge led Mark to a lofted beamed lobby. He spotted Sig sitting on a leather couch near the fireplace, his head tipped while studying the screen of his phone. "Sig?" he said, and Kelsey's business partner looked up.

"Hey, Mark, what are you doing here?" Sig grinned and gave him a knowing look.

Mark's shrug admitted how gone he was for Kelsey. "I couldn't shake the feeling that something was wrong."

"Gotta trust your gut. But as far as I know, it's all good. Why don't you hang out with me and wait for their call? They'll have service near the ski area."

"Sure, but do you want to grab a beer?"

Sig stood. "Sounds great. Let me pick up the tab while we talk."

A mural of Babe the Blue Ox peered over their shoulders as they each chose a perch at the long bar. Sig dove in, talking business without hesitation. "I'm worried, Mark. It seems like Kelsey's only committed to Venture Sister halfway. I had hoped that bringing Kent on board would pull her back in."

"But it didn't?"

"No. And she's worked up this idea that she's dead weight—that she somehow has less to offer."

Mark leaned forward on his elbows and shook his head. "Shit, I was worried about that."

"And nothing could be farther from the truth. I've known Kels for a long time, watched her grow up on the river. She thinks The

Little White took something irreplaceable from her, but that injury only changed her strengths. It slowed her down enough to take notice and actually opened up a window of understanding." Sig pulled his calloused hand over his face. "Before, she pushed people hard enough to discover their potential . . . which was great. But now she's beginning to understand that everyone deserves the opportunity to get out there and see what nature can teach them, regardless of their physical gifts."

Hand wrapped around his pint, Mark nodded. "Venture needs her now more than ever."

"Absolutely. And the choice is hers. She could take Venture out to the coast or help us tailor different journeys for guests with specific physical needs . . . like outdoor therapy."

A smile spread across Mark's face. "That would be amazing. Have you brought this up to Kels?"

"I've tried. But like I said, she seems to be looking for the nearest exit. It's been a struggle to convince her she still has something to offer."

Mark nodded. "I'll try to help." He didn't want to determine her future. He only knew he wanted to be part of it, no matter what she decided to do.

They ordered a second beer, gulped the first bit in silence, both lost in thought. A buzz on Sig's phone brought them back and they both abandoned half-full pints when Kelsey sent a text.

***

Her team sped up the pace. Parker and Amanda jogged ahead, taking knee-stances to frame finish line shots. Kelsey slowed and savored her final yards. Eventually, Amanda stowed her camera and joined her. "Are you okay?"

"Yeah. I'm good. I wish I could disappear for a while. Long goodbyes aren't my thing, and Sig doesn't know what's coming," Kelsey said.

"You're not leaving Venture today, are you?"

"I don't intend to, no. I just don't have a solid answer for Sig and the other guides." Kelsey turned to stare at the mountain. The massive volcanic peak still hid so many secrets, mysteries too profound to decipher in one journey.

Amanda's laugh spun Kelsey toward the lodge. "Looks like your wish to disappear just came true. I don't think you're going back to Venture today, because that man of yours has no intention of letting you out of his sights."

Loitering next to Sig, Mark looked out of place in board shorts, flip-flops, and a bright T-shirt. Drawn to his smile, her pace quickened, leaving Amanda behind.

Mark shot into a jog, and her pack hit the dirt moments before Kelsey found herself lifted into a spinning hug.

"Why are you here?" she asked. "Not that I'm complaining."

"Couldn't wait, Mermaid. Had to know you were okay." A kiss covered her sun-chapped lips, and when Mark pulled back, he used his thumbs to wipe away a few tears that were leaving tracks on her skin. She refused to ruin the moment by turning toward the click of Parker's camera.

"I stink." Kelsey tried to squirm from his arms while she laughed.

He only held on tighter. "You smell great, but I'd be happy to peel these clothes off and wash away the dust in a shower."

"You don't have to twist my arm. Can the beach wait? I just want to go home."

"Sounds perfect." Mark hung her backpack on one shoulder and followed her to the parking lot.

"Could you toss my gear into your Subaru? I need to talk to Sig." Kelsey planned to ride with Mark, not caring if her SUV sat at

Venture for a few days. What she needed to discuss with her business partner would have to wait.

She'd given it a lot of thought all morning, and she knew that staying with Venture wasn't going to work. Her skills were compromised and could someday put her clients at risk—a risk she wasn't willing to take.

Staying on as a figurehead at Venture wasn't for her. She figured it was better to bow out and find another way to make a living. There was that new pot shop in town, or maybe Linnea could use a little help at Mosquito Creek taproom.

Sig grabbed his Venture ball cap from the driver's seat and pulled it on his head.

"Gotta protect that dome, old man," she teased as she walked up to the Venture van.

His grin crinkled the corner of his eyes. "Hey, has my wife been talking to you?" He smiled and she laughed. "Hearing nothing but praises about the trip, kiddo. Your comeback was a success." Sig tossed an arm over her shoulder.

"Uh, yeah, it wasn't perfect, but we can talk about that next week. I wanted to let you know that my rig will be parked in the lot for a few days. Mark and I are headed back to Ashwood."

"Great plan. Take a few days off, but not too long. I can't wait to put you back on the schedule."

Sig's grin was too joyful to ruin—the truth could wait. Kelsey nodded and leaned in to give him a quick hug. "See you next week."

Sig held her a little longer than his usual squeeze. "I've missed you, Kels." His voice caught, and the sound brought hot tears to her eyes.

"Missed you, too." Kelsey turned away before her face got messy. As she rounded the tail of the Venture van, her feet stuck to the pavement.

Parker Knight was leaning against Mark's car, her head tilted up while she talked. If she'd been closer, Kelsey figured she'd be able to see the photographer bat her eyelashes. The back and forth between them seemed too familiar—*they knew each other*. No fucking way was this the first time they'd crossed paths.

Was Mark into that bitch? Was her trust-meter broken and she'd missed the signs? Jealous anger tightened her gut until Mark's expression mutated from pleasant to *really pissed*. The visual contest ended with Parker turning away. And when Parker completed that turn, their eyes connected. Kelsey closed in but couldn't catch the photographer. The woman spun toward her car, climbed in, and drove away.

The first few miles passed in unusual silence. Kelsey didn't want to pry, figuring if Mark wanted to talk, she'd listen. She'd never been the meddling possessive type and that wasn't going to change now.

Mark shrugged, took a long breath, and forced out quiet words. "Parker's tried to feature me on her blog before. And I've managed to avoid her. Today, in the parking lot, she was digging for info about you . . . about us."

"I'm not surprised. Nobody in my family was off-limits after the accident, not even my great-aunt Elsa."

His jaw tightened and he glanced her direction. "I don't know how she connected the dots, but she's been bothering Faye."

Kelsey gasped, fearing the damage Parker's spotlight could do to a place she thought was untouchable. The oasis would be ruined if it was thrust into the public eye. And Faye wouldn't know what hit her—she didn't even own a computer. A nonexistent internet footprint preserved Driftwood Shores, but with a few keystrokes, the quiet refuge on the beach would be gone.

"Don't worry about it yet. Parker will be busy editing the footage from your trip for a while . . . we still have time."

TWENTY-NINE

The steaming shower slid dirt from her body, and the heat relaxed her muscles, but the stress left by Parker Knight lingered. Mark's attentive hands caressed every inch of her skin with her favorite vanilla sugar soap, and he washed and conditioned her long blond hair. Ignoring his jutting hard on, he wrapped Kelsey's hair and torso in separate towels and slung another around his waist.

"Lay on your bed, face down," he said, grabbing her lotion from the nightstand.

Kelsey's breath held when she heard Mark's towel fall to the floor. She listened as he squirted lotion into his hands and sighed when his touch began with her trail-battered feet. His strong, calloused fingers eased the fatigue of her calves and thighs, soothed that tight spot that ached in her lower back, and gently caressed her bruised shoulders.

She giggled. "So, how long are we going to ignore that steel rod that keeps bumping my ass?"

"Noticed that?"

"Uh, yeah. It's a little obvious."

"Little?" He chuckled and settled his length against her crack.

She moaned, "Sorry, I meant gigantically obvious."

"Better." Mark hummed, while nestling kisses against her neck.

Anticipation coiled when he eased her thighs apart with his knees. His breath hit her shoulder and his chest settled along her back, then every nerve in her body rejoiced when his cock began a long slow slide, stretching her core, invading her heat. Kelsey hissed and tipped her hips, seeking his entire length, savoring the fullness of deep penetration.

"Perfect," he whispered near her ear. Moving with extra care, wanting to soothe as much as excite, Mark's gradual push and pull created a relaxing warmth all its own. She sighed and absorbed the comforting friction on her back and butt, nestling into the rasp of his whiskers against her neck.

Tilting her head, she encouraged his kisses, and he nibbled and sucked as his pace increased. Shifting to his knees, she moaned in protest when his cock left her body, but it didn't last long. He lifted her hips and turned her over with a quick flip.

Eyes on her, Mark stared with unusual intensity. As much as she wanted to feel that fullness again, she fought the urge to squirm, because his gaze was too urgent, too penetrating. He reached out and gently brushed a few strands of wet hair away from her face, then left his palm against her cheek. Mark's thumb traced her jaw, then her lips. "I love you," he confessed.

She froze. Unexpected fear broke to the surface and memories of misplaced affection for Ben stole her joy. Kelsey had wanted those words from Mark, but now that he'd uttered them, she couldn't share his precious gift.

Mark inhaled a staggered breath, and his eyes softened. "I told you I love you because you deserve the truth, not because I need to hear anything in return. Get used to hearing, *I love you, Mermaid.*"

A small nod tipped her head and she swallowed hard. Mark eased his torso over hers while his lips communicated the depth of his affection. Wrapping her arms around him, she urged his weight against her body. Mark entered her again in one smooth slide. The easy cadence of his hips matched the sweet caresses that danced across her mouth. She lost herself to the weight, taste, and heat of him.

Mark took control of her surrender, cherishing the moment when she sighed and accepted everything from him. He didn't ask for anything in return—only deepened the plunge. As her hips elevated, her breathing escalated and her hands slid from his shoulders to grasp the hard plane of his butt. Tingling began low in her belly and blossoming heat radiated out. Her breath hitched and her hips rose, chasing the beat of his groin against her sweat-drenched thighs.

"That's it, Mermaid," he whispered against her ear before nipping at her neck just below her earlobe. Mark's body tensed as her slick center swelled around his cock, linking her pleasure with his.

Kelsey's legs trembled moments before her climax took over. Her incoherent cries scrambled Mark's control and his hips slammed powerfully into her core. He growled as his seed spilled, releasing mind-altering bliss. He'd surrendered every part of himself to Kelsey, and she'd let herself accept his unconditional love.

**

Kelsey snuggled into Mark's chest and ignored the rattle of her phone on the dresser. She glanced at red numbers on her clock and smashed her eyes shut. Sleeping in a bed again was too precious to give up at three in the morning. The call quit and she mumbled, "Must have been a wrong number."

The insistent buzz resumed, seeming louder now that she was wide awake. Mark reached across her body and grasped the device. "It's Kent . . . maybe you should take it."

"This better be good," she groaned into the phone.

"Are you back?" The growl of his truck's engine bleeding over the call sped her pulse.

"Yes. What's wrong?"

"I'm on my way to the hospital. Linnea's having contractions. Rick asked me to meet them, take Ricky home, and tuck the little guy back into bed."

Kels kicked off the covers. "Where's Rick's mom?"

"Out of town. No one expected the baby this soon."

"She's not due, what . . . for another month?"

"Yeah. Rick's worried. Shit, Kels. Can you help me out? I've never changed a diaper or even fed a kid. What if Ricky starts crying?" Kelsey bit her lip and suppressed a chuckle. The guy navigated unforgiving rapids with intuitive ease, but the thought of changing a diaper terrified him. Her eyes followed Mark as he shrugged into his jeans then dashed into the bathroom to brush his teeth.

When her man disappeared, her attention skated back to Kent, and she was relieved to be the one helping for a change. "It'll be okay. Why don't you just stay at the hospital and I'll be there as soon as I can to take the baby. The little guy doesn't know me very well, but if I'm lucky, the car ride will put him to sleep. That way, you can stick around at the hospital in case Linnea and Rick need anything."

"Thanks. Are you good to drive to the hospital on your own?"

"Mark's here." Kels rolled her eyes, tempted to tell Kent to quit worrying. But Mark drove the thought from her mind, coming back into the room looking messy and mouth-watering wearing only faded jeans. *Damn.* "We'll be there as soon as we can."

Ten minutes later they stepped outside, the air smelled crisp and she could see her breath. She sank into the seat, and Mark revved the engine. He pushed a few buttons on the dash and she sighed. "Oh my God, heated seats."

"I aim to please," he said backing out.

They were the only vehicle using the winding road down Mount Adam's foothills. Mark's heavy foot pressed the accelerator and they came to a stop next to Kent's rig twenty minutes later. Kelsey's shoulders relaxed when Kent emerged from the sliding doors with the baby in his arms. She hadn't been in a hospital since the accident and wasn't looking forward to that antiseptic odor.

"How's Linnea?" she asked.

"They've got her hooked up to monitors and an IV. She seems fine, but Rick's a mess."

"I'm glad you're here for him." Kelsey gave Kent a hug and took the baby. After a quick transfer of the car seat, they left the brightly lit parking lot with Ricky strapped inside Mark's Subaru. It took less than a mile for the toddler's whimpers to progress to heartbreaking wails filled with, "Daddy, Daddy, Daddy."

Feathering the brake, Mark rolled to a stop in front of Rick and Linnea's cabin, but didn't utter a word. He killed the bright headlights and used hand signals to let Kelsey know that he'd get Ricky from his seat. She dashed to the front door and waited while Mark carefully scooped the baby into his arms, trying to keep the toddler from wailing like he'd done for most of the ride home.

A faint glow coming from the baby's room shed enough light to lay Ricky in his crib. When Mark eased the toddler down, the baby fussed for a moment, tucked his knees under his body, and settled after he found his thumb. They tiptoed into the hall, easing the door closed with a held breath.

Mark pulled Kelsey to the couch and collapsed. "You have baby experience," she said.

"Friends in San Diego have two kids, both still in diapers. I sometimes stay at their place near the beach while we work and surf."

"Kids and surfing? How do they find time to hit the waves?"

"It's a balance, and she set a rule—the babies have to walk before getting on a board."

Kelsey covered her mouth, stifling her laugh. "I better be quiet, or I'll wake the baby." She giggled again, succumbing to the layers of physical and mental exhaustion that had her feeling a little high. A yawn engulfed her laughter and Mark shifted, pulling her tight against his torso. Her hand rested on the rise and fall of his chest while he drifted to sleep. When the fire in the wood stove settled and crackled, Mark's arms tightened around her.

"Love you," he murmured. Kels hummed, accepted the words, and closed her eyes, realizing that a path forward with Mark didn't have to be hemmed in by a white picket fence, one country, or even one continent. She could have any future she wanted and spend it with a man she loved deeply.

***

"Wake up, Kelsey." She squinted and tried to make sense of her surroundings. *Why is he standing over me?* Rick stepped away, giving her time and room to get her bearings. A smile from the kitchen steadied her thundering pulse. *Mark.*

"Coffee?" he asked, lifting the cup from the counter.

"Please." She stretched and remembered why she was here. "How's Linnea?"

Rick took a seat in a worn recliner, and Ricky scrambled into his lap. "She's good. I'll go pick her up as soon as Mom arrives. Wade's not going to be happy—the docs want her off her feet until the baby comes."

She reached up, accepted her coffee from Mark, and took a sip. "Mosquito Creek Taproom won't know what to do without her," Mark said while claiming the spot next to Kelsey on the couch.

"Wade can deal." Rick looked tired and a little irritated. "And he can hire more staff."

Ricky scooted from his daddy's lap and brought Kelsey a fire truck. Sliding her butt to the floor, she pulled the fire truck back and let it go with a quick zip toward the kitchen. The toddler squealed and raced after it, then brought the toy back to his daddy. As Rick gave his adopted son a kiss, Kelsey couldn't believe how much had changed or how perfect this all seemed. Life in Ashwood might be different then running Venture, but it could be satisfying.

Mosquito Creek taproom definitely needed more help, and a local job would weave her into the fabric of her small hometown. Still, she couldn't even imagine what a regular job would feel like. She'd been guiding on rivers or trails since she was seventeen.

A crunch of gravel from a car pulling up outside brought her to her feet.

"Thanks for helping out," Rick said as she headed for the door. "We've missed you."

"Happy I could help." Needing another hit of baby smell, she doubled back and pressed a kiss into the toddler's curly hair. Content, she passed Rick's mom with a hello on the way to Mark's Subaru.

"Are you as hungry as I am?" Mark asked as she settled into the leather seats.

"Starving. Northside?" She peeked in the mirror under the visor. "Lord, I look like crap." Hands flying, she braided her long blond hair and managed the mess.

Mark found his beanie stuck in the pocket behind her seat and pulled it on. "Good to go," he said with a chuckle, then pressed the accelerator harder when his stomach rumbled.

Iris waved hello when they took a seat at the Grill. As they scanned the breakfast menu, the screen behind the bar filled with a familiar, unwelcome face. *Parker Knight.* Kelsey jumped to her feet, bolted behind the bar, and cranked the volume, grimacing at news intended to set off another media bomb.

Parker had spliced snippets of conversation from the Mount Hood hike with footage from nearby forest fires. The fabrication painted a picture of Kelsey Fisher as a guide who recklessly led Venture Sister's clients into the path of a raging inferno. A rehearsed voice punctuated the most alarming footage—images of Kelsey walking off her fury near camp in the dark. "Disoriented by her recent injuries, she became hopelessly lost. This well-known guide wasn't fit to lead anyone into the wilderness."

"That bitch." Kelsey stormed from Northside Grill.

Mark followed her out and yelled as she dove into the driver's seat. "Kels, wait!"

"Give me your keys, I need to grab a shower before I head to Venture. I've rained another shit-storm of publicity on Sig, but this time it may destroy the entire guiding business."

Mark's even tone tried to calm her down. "There's nothing behind it, Parker's flat-out lying."

She gritted her teeth and held out her hand, demanding the keys with her narrowed gaze. "It doesn't matter." He circled the vehicle, fell into the passenger seat, and gave her the keys. Kelsey started the car and raised her voice over the revving engine. "Lies become the truth, once enough people get hold of them. I have to find a way to shut this down."

Kelsey drove home in silence, her head aching as she tried to run through every scenario. One thing became clear—she needed to do this alone. If Mark showed up and media was there, he'd be hit by collateral damage. She wasn't willing to let that happen.

Skidding to a stop, she jumped from the car, and ran inside, heading straight for the shower. Mark met her in her room and was pulling on clean clothes, but she couldn't look at him. She kept her eyes on her feet as she tied her shoes. "I need to go to Hood River alone."

"Not happening, Kels."

Shoulders square, she stood and faced him. "You don't get to call the shots. It's about time I took responsibility for my own messes. Maybe you and I need to take a break until I can sort this shit out." The harsh words stung but destroying Mark's future would hurt even worse.

Mark covered her hands with his, holding her in place. "Don't do this, don't push me away. Please, let me be there for you."

His touch was tempting, but everyone close to her kept getting hit by an ever-widening shotgun blast of publicity. She wouldn't let it happen to Mark and forced his fingers away.

After taking a deep breath, Kelsey chose words that would hurt enough to get him to leave. "You're trying to change me. I never *needed* anyone, not until the accident. And that didn't work out too well. I want to be on my own again, to go back to the way we were before you left for the Maldives. Please, leave, before one of us gets hurt."

Mark met her fury with patient strength. "You're free to run for now, Mermaid. But I'll find you. There's nothing you can do to make me stop loving you."

She'd hurt him. The anguish in his face nearly stopped her from walking out the door. And as she sped away, his image in her rearview mirror—shoulders slumped, arms limp at his side—reflected his pain.

Tears streamed down her face as her foot pressed the accelerator. Kelsey drove ten miles before she realized her hands weren't wrapped around her own steering wheel. Her Xterra was still parked at Venture. *Shit.*

Her palms pounded the wheel until it stung. "God damn it. I wanted a clean break, and I ended up stealing his fucking car."

***

Mark packed a few things in his backpack and began the long walk into town. Kelsey needed time to think, and he knew invading her life and making demands would only push her away.

Her driveway led to a narrow road, completely free of cars. The rumble of logging trucks increased as he approached the main highway. The first few yards he plodded along in silence until a compact four-wheel drive rolled to a stop behind him. Mark turned and found Kelsey's mom smiling. She opened her window with a swift electric whir.

"Car trouble?" she asked.

Mark shook his head, and Mary read the worry on his face. "Oh . . . Kelsey trouble," she said. "Why don't you get in?"

He circled to the passenger side and buckled before she pulled onto the highway. "You don't have to tell me what happened . . . unless you want to."

Mark hated to bring her more bad news. "Parker released another video . . . and it isn't good. You and Dale should brace yourself for another—"

Mary held her hand in the air. "We know. Some station out of Portland already called. I don't even listen to them anymore."

"Good plan." Mark raked his hands through his hair. "Kelsey wanted to handle this latest storm on her own."

"And she pushed you away to do it?" When Mark nodded, Mary sighed. "Are you leaving?" she asked.

"Not permanently. I'm just giving her space to sort some things out."

"Thank you for sticking by Kelsey. I know it isn't easy."

"She's worth it. I love her."

The quick confession turned Mary's gaze away from the road for a moment, and her tilted smile gave him hope. Mark wanted to share his intentions with those who loved Kelsey as much as he did. "I don't intend to push her, but I want a future with Kelsey . . . if she'll have me."

Mary nodded and glanced at him again. "You've only been around Kelsey for a few weeks. I don't want either of you to get hurt."

"There's more than a few weeks between us. We've built something over the past couple of years, and it's solid. I intend to love Kelsey . . . forever."

Mary swept a tear from her eye. "That's so sweet. I should have known she was waiting for you."

"Waiting?"

"When Kelsey came out of her coma, she said some things that puzzled everyone. I finally had to Google it." Sighing, she swallowed back emotion. "Kelsey's first words were *Sunrise session. Pure glass.*"

Mark huffed a chuckle. "She was remembering surfing."

"Surfing? I don't think so." Mary shook her head. "She was remembering *you.*"

A hard sob caught in his throat, and he couldn't breathe. Since learning about the accident, Mark had so many regrets, the greatest one—not being there for Kelsey when she needed him most—still hurt like a deep, purple bruise. Somehow, this revelation soothed that pain. Maybe she'd found him in that dreamy-place, and had borrowed his strength for a while, until she could find her way back to him and everyone else who loved her.

Tears pooled in Mary's eyes, but she didn't bother to sweep the evidence of her emotions away. "Thank you for choosing to stay. Kelsey needs you . . . more than you know." Mary slowed at the edge of town, sniffled, and said, "Mark, I just realized that I don't know where you're headed."

"Oh, right. Could you drop me at Whitewater?"

"Of course." When she pulled into the gravel lot she asked, "Will we be seeing you soon?" Hope glistened in her eyes.

"Absolutely." Mark gave Mary a quick hug before he climbed from her car. "Thanks for the ride."

***

The visit at Whitewater was short. Buying a new home should have been a reason for Mark to celebrate, but it wasn't. He'd never intended to make the move to the coast alone.

Natalie signed over the title to her truck, and Seth followed Mark to the tiny home to answer questions. After Seth pointed out a few features, the conversation circled back to Kelsey. Mark revealed the latest news about Parker and the reason he was leaving Ashwood alone.

Natalie winced. "My apology is way overdue. When will she be home?"

A shrug lifted Mark's shoulders. "Your guess is as good as mine. It shouldn't be too long, but when you talk to her, could you keep this tiny home purchase a secret? I haven't figured out how I want to handle the big reveal." When he first thought about buying the home, he had hoped Kelsey would be thrilled. But after this morning, he wasn't so sure. Mark shuffled, eager for the feel of sand beneath his feet.

"We'll keep it quiet." Seth dangled a cluster of keys from his fingers and jangled them in the air. "Are you ready?" A nod was all it took. When Seth pitched the keys underhand, Mark caught them on the downward arch.

After he climbed into the truck, he revved the engine, checked the mirrors, and headed for Driftwood Shores. Alone.

THIRTY

Five satellite news vans crowded Venture's gravel lot, and Kelsey groaned, fighting the urge to drive until she hit the California border. She skidded to the rear entrance and rushed inside. A cacophony of phones rang, and desperate faces shot her direction. An apology sprang from her lips on her race to Sig's office.

"Thank God you're here," he barked. "We've got to deal with the piranhas outside, so they'll go away."

"We need a plan." Kelsey's phone buzzed, and her screen filled with the name of a person who might be able to help. "Hey, Amanda."

She calmed enough to listen. "Not a chance. You can't do that. You'll lose credits and your job."

Sig ignored his ringing phone and stared in Kelsey's direction. "Fine, I'll consider it, but why don't you come over to Venture and let Sig and I take a look."

After she ended the call, Kels hissed out a deep breath. "Amanda's got footage on a thumb drive that will expose the truth."

Sig leaned his elbows on his desk. "She'll be fine—we've got a spot waiting for her here."

"I know, but this thing with Parker . . . it's Amanda's dream job. If she does this, her future in photojournalism is screwed. I want her at Venture, but I won't do it at the expense of her career."

Sig tilted back in his chair, straining the limits of gravity. "How long until Amanda gets here?"

"A half-hour, tops."

"Damnit, that doesn't leave us much time." Sig had always been able to read her mind. They both knew the sacrifice Amanda offered was way too much. That day in May on The Little White took and took and took—Kelsey wouldn't let the river claim Amanda too.

She gathered the team from Venture, and they filed out in solidarity behind her as she settled in place in front of the cameras to share her version of the truth. A random quote she'd learned in high school popped into her head, and she began, "A lie can travel halfway around the world while the truth is putting on shoes."

She explained what actually happened on the trail and asked the reporters to leave her staff and her clients alone. As she answered their questions, she knew it didn't really matter what she said, because the damage was already done. Parker's social media inferno had too much fuel to extinguish the fire with the truth.

Sig stepped forward when the reporters' questions shifted from intelligent to ridiculous. "Last question," he said, ending the impromptu news conference.

She pointed over a sea of heads to a tall woman in the back. "What will you do next?"

Kelsey struggled to suppress her groan before she gave an answer. "When I figure that out, you'll be the first to know." She exchanged a smirk with the reporter and turned back toward Venture's doors.

Sig grasped her shoulder and followed her inside. "Let's get out of here."

After the parking lot cleared, the Venture team met at a sports pub. Kent walked in and bought a round of drinks for his new second family. "I can't believe I had to learn about today on the local news." He took a spot next to Amanda, and she tipped her head in a quick hello.

Kelsey apologized, "Sorry. It all happened too fast."

Amanda leaned into him. "I was left out of the loop too—I even had some killer footage that would have brought Parker Knight to her knees."

"I don't think it was necessary," Kent offered. "It looks like the other women who went on the trip are coming out and backing up the truth."

Kelsey shrugged. "Not that it matters. It's already old news."

They stuck around at the bar, waiting for the news at six. The Portland station led with footage filmed in Hood River in front of Venture. The crowd whooped and hollered when their girl filled the screen. Pitting one version of the trip on Mount Hood against the other, Kelsey endured a few more minutes of fame—fame she hoped would be her last.

Kent's laughter brightened Kelsey's mood, but not enough to keep her from looking toward the door. Today's ordeal was over, but what she'd done to Mark left her feeling raw. Kelsey wanted to get home and apologize to the man she'd abandoned in her driveway. Her backpack hit her shoulder as she stood. "I'm heading out."

"You sure?" Sig's brows furrowed with worry, and he glanced at her empty glass.

"I switched to tea hours ago," she said with a reassuring smile. The caffeine kept her buzzing during the drive home, but when she walked through her door, her shoulders slumped.

Mark's blue backpack was gone, but some of his things were still scattered around her place—hiking boots, a puffy coat, and the book he was reading. Kelsey held onto hope that he'd run into town and would walk through her front door at any moment. Yet, without a car, she couldn't figure out how he'd left. It was almost as if Mark had vanished. Curiosity sped her fingers and she tapped out a text to ask where he'd gone, but her pride kept her from hitting send. After dark, he sent a short message saying he'd caught a ride to the coast. Not surprising—she'd put him through hell today. An apology might bring him back, but to what and to who? Until this cloud of uncertainty lifted, Mark was better off without her.

She heated chicken noodle soup and ate alone. Turned on music, but her home still seemed eerily quiet without Mark singing along. Missing him desperately, and too numb to think, Kelsey walked through the house and flicked off all the lights. Laying on top of her blankets, fully clothed, her head hit the pillow on a bed that felt way too big without Mark.

***

Covered with sweat, Kelsey woke with a jolt and tried to control her panic. She searched for Mark, but he wasn't there. She could almost hear him say, *go back to sleep, Mermaid, it was just a dream.*

Fully awake, the dream was fresh and disturbing. It wasn't the inky oppressive water that terrified her tonight—those nightmares happened often, and she'd already learned to cope. A distressing image lingered at the edge of her mind, in the space where reality and dreams connected. The arms that had pulled her to safety from the dark churning water weren't Kent's. This time, those rescuing hands belonged to Ben. And in her dream, he had caged her, held her too tight, swearing to never let go.

Something connected to Ben still lingered, troubling and unresolved. Kelsey couldn't shake an overwhelming feeling that she'd depended on him too much to fix her, when all along she'd needed to rebuild what was broken on her own.

***

Sleep didn't return until sunrise, and her day was shot to hell. Kelsey slept late and was brewing her second pot of coffee when a car pulled up outside. A peek through the window found Natalie on her front porch holding Rice Krispy Treats, in the same nine-by-thirteen pan.

She eased the door open. "Are those for me?" Kelsey asked, fighting a smile.

"Yeah." Natalie extended the peace offering.

"Extra butter and marshmallows?"

"Just the way you like them."

"Awesome. I didn't know what I was having for breakfast. Get in here." Kelsey hauled her in. "Want some coffee?"

"Sure." Natalie glanced at the clock. Even though it was half-past eleven, Kelsey didn't bother to explain why she was ready for breakfast at this late hour—those nightmares weren't worth reliving.

After pouring cream in both coffee cups she said, "I've missed you."

That was all it took—Natalie wrapped her in a hug, trapping the small paper carton of cream between them. "I've missed you, too. I'm so sorry. There's no excuse for the foolish way I acted. And I can't help it—I'll go to my grave worshiping my stupid big brother."

"It's okay. I never wanted you to pick sides." Kelsey sighed as their hug faded.

Nate took her time making a slow inspection. "What's wrong?" she asked.

"I chased Mark away."

"Well, drag him back."

"I can't, at least not yet." Kelsey hung her head. "I'm a mess, and I think a small part of me isn't over Ben."

Not expecting that, Natalie's eyebrows lifted, but Kelsey shook her head. "I still *really, really* hate him, but now, I'm falling in love with Mark, or maybe I never stopped loving him. And I'm all confused. What am I supposed to do?" Kelsey bit her lip and waited for Natalie's answer.

"Go sit down."

Wracked with worry, Kelsey obeyed and plopped on the couch with her coffee.

Natalie found a knife and sliced a mammoth Rice Krispy Treat, a full quarter of the pan. She put it on a dinner plate and said, "This will have to hold us until it's five-o'clock somewhere, cause I got nothing for you. Hopefully sugar now and alcohol later will actually help."

Kelsey laughed. "Shit, I missed you." she said, as her fingers tore off a corner of her favorite, sticky treat.

THIRTY-ONE

With Venture on hold and Mark gone, Kelsey looked forward to seeing her friends at The Center three days each week. At least the routine helped to fill her time. When Travis pulled up a chair, Kelsey glanced from the computer monitor.

"How's it going?" he asked.

"Great. I think your team is running out of things for me to do," she joked and grinned. Kelsey stopped chuckling when he didn't join her laughter.

Travis nodded. "Do you have time to stop by my office before you take off today?"

"No problem."

When she sat across from him later, they talked about the progress she'd made and her options for the future. The meeting was short, exciting, and a little scary. But the warm goodbye put Kelsey at ease. Travis gave her a hug and told her to set up an appointment six months out.

Before she left, he asked Kelsey if she'd be willing to meet with younger patients when the need arose. She liked the idea and encouraged him to give her a call.

From the parking lot she turned back and gazed at The Center's well-groomed exterior, Kelsey realized she would miss the place that she once thought was a prison. Conflicting emotions—joy, loneliness, and pride—fought for space as she took a few steps and dug in her pack to locate her keys.

At least she was headed for her own rig again. A few days after the disturbing dream, she'd talked to Mark briefly and offered to meet him in Portland to deliver his Subaru. But he said he didn't need it, at least not until she was ready to stay with him at the beach for a while. The call had gone quiet as Mark waited for her answer, but she'd asked him for more time because she wasn't ready to face him, not yet.

She dug deeper into her backpack, trying to find her keys. Not paying attention, Kelsey ran into a wall of solid man.

"I'm so sorry," she said, "I wasn't looking where—" As she looked up, her eyes connected with Ben, but he looked different. He'd grown a beard and it looked good, more Northwest, less Southern charm.

"Why are you here?" she asked, taking two paces back.

"I saw that crap with Parker on the news and wanted to make sure you were okay."

"You didn't need to bother, I'm just fine." She tried to sidestep around him, but Ben blocked her path.

"Please, Kels. Can we get coffee? I'd like to talk."

"What's the point?" Her eyes narrowed, finding this ambush irritating.

"Can we at least take a walk?" he begged, glancing down the sidewalk. She turned her eyes away from Ben and scanned the trees surrounding The Center. With fall approaching, the leaves were just beginning to turn.

Kelsey had wanted to say goodbye to the place in her own way and would rather be alone, but he'd supported her while she was here and helped when she needed an escape. Maybe she owed him. Shrugging off her frustration, she took a few steps down the shaded path and he followed.

He reached out and grasped her arm, slowing her quick pace. For a moment, his hand slid into hers and their fingers laced. Kelsey would have flinched if there had still been a spark, but his touch had lost its power. Flexing her fingers, she eased her hand away.

Ben began the conversation with safe territory. "Nancy asked about you."

"How is she?"

"Good. Her kids came for a visit. And she found a shelter that welcomed the extra food from her garden."

"I'm glad."

"She sent some salsa. I've got three jars in the backseat," he added.

Kelsey stepped away, her eyes narrowing. "How did she know you were meeting me?"

Ben swallowed hard. "I must have told her that I wanted to get in touch."

"In touch," Kelsey mumbled to herself, "what a stupid phrase. It never occurred to me how personal and distant that sounds at the same time." Laughing, she shook her head. "Whatever."

Already regretting this walk, she turned the corner that rounded the back of the building, rushed her steps, and wished he would go away. Kelsey inhaled the faint smell of chlorine coming from the exhaust fans near the indoor pool. The smell brought back vivid memories of childhood vacations.

"Kels, you have to know how sorry I am," Ben said, struggling to talk and keep up.

She wanted to dwell on the happy childhood memory but turned to face him and deal with this, with him. "Yes. I know."

In the autumn sun, his trim beard looked red. If she had passed him in a crowd, she might not recognize him at all. As he watched her, his green eyes sparkled but lacked warmth. Had she missed that detail, too? What she'd felt for Ben was gone. It was a thin and fragile thread compared to the ropy bands that tethered her soul to Mark.

"Ben, how did you know I'd be here today?" she asked.

Looking at the sidewalk, he shook his head. "I had to see you, Kels. Natalie wouldn't tell me when you were coming to Portland . . . there was no other way."

"No other way? What are you talking about?"

His shoulders curled inward. "When you moved in, I was worried you'd get lost in Portland, or on the train, and I wouldn't be able to find you. I put a tracker on your phone."

"You *what*?"

"I had to, Kels. I couldn't work knowing you were out here, trying to navigate the city on your own."

Kelsey yanked her phone from her purse and held it away from her body as if it were about to explode. "Take it off," she seethed.

His eyes met hers, wide with panic. "What? I didn't mean any harm."

"Take the fucking app off my phone."

Mouth gaping, he reached out, but at the last moment she snatched the phone back.

"Forget it. Why should I trust you?" Kelsey pitched the phone to the ground and smashed the screen with her heel, savoring the crunch of plastic and glass under her shoe.

"God, Kelsey, you didn't need to do that." Ben scraped a trembling hand over his face.

"You stay away from me." She snatched the carcass of her phone from the ground and sprinted away, never looking back. Swift feet carried her around the corner of the building and to her car. A stop at a strip mall erased any remaining worry. With help from the girl behind the counter, she switched carriers and got a new number, sent a text to her sister Elizabeth, Sig, and Kent, and asked them to pass her new number along.

***

Music blasted in Mark's new tiny home. Seth had installed a fantastic sound system, but even when the walls shook, the bass couldn't chase away tingling fear. Worry overtook him, and when he called, he discovered that Kelsey's number was disconnected. She'd shut him out. *Damn it*, he'd pushed her too far.

Mark brought up the YouTube clip from Venture and watched it for the hundredth time. When that last reporter asked Kelsey what she planned to do next, Mark held his breath, hoping her words would be different—that this time she would say she was heading for the coast. But her words hadn't changed. *"When I figure that out, you'll be the first to know."*

The camera had caught the truth, and he felt the sting as if Kelsey was talking directly to him—their future together wasn't certain. Mark stared at the bare walls of his tiny home and groaned. He'd be damned if he had to live in this place alone.

***

Kelsey pulled into Whitewater Homes, ready to call in a favor. Natalie had once offered the tiny home if she needed to get away for a while. She wanted to, *needed to* take it to the coast and hopefully cross paths with Mark . . . if he was still there.

The office was empty, and Kelsey wandered farther into the shop to find the light on over Natalie's darkroom door. Fortunately, Kelsey only had to wait a few minutes before her friend finished developing a roll of negatives.

"Kels, I'm so glad you're here. Ben called yesterday—he was worried about you. Does that make any sense at all?"

"Yeah. It makes sense, and everything's fine." Kelsey didn't want to taint Ben's image in Natalie's eyes and quickly changed the subject. "Do you want to grab lunch?"

"Sorry, I already ate. I could go for some coffee, and you can see what we've got to eat in the break room."

Kels shrugged, not all that hungry. "That works for me."

Seth spotted them and followed Kels and Natalie. "How are you handling this new round of news coverage?" he asked.

"No biggie. This will burn itself out. I do feel bad that Amanda's still trapped in Parker's internship."

"Growing up with three older brothers, my baby sister is tougher than she looks." Seth said as Natalie rummaged in the break room refrigerator.

"Never doubted that." Kelsey agreed.

Humming to herself, Natalie seemed pleased when she found a bag of grapes, washed them, and put them in a bowl on the center of the table. Kels popped a grape in her mouth, and let the sweet fruit distract her for a moment. "Thanks, these are great. Though I actually have another reason for stopping by."

Seth and Natalie glanced at each other but didn't say a word.

"About Parker's footage from the hike, it does have a vein of truth. I'm having trouble with maps and navigation. It may work itself out over time or it might not."

Seth nodded and Natalie frowned, clearly disturbed by her honest reveal.

"Sig wants to expand Venture to the coast or offer trips for people with specific needs, but I need time to think it over," Kels said. "I was wondering if I could rent the tiny home for a while. You know, spend some time at Faye's place on the coast and figure out my future."

"That's a great idea, but . . ." Natalie leaned forward and squeezed Kelsey's arm, "maybe we can help you figure out something else, because my old place already sold."

Kelsey withered and glanced between her friends. "When did you sell it?" Disappointed, she couldn't say anything more—not without revealing how much she'd loved that tiny home.

Seth tapped the table, taking extra time before he answered. "It sold a couple of weeks ago. A guy stopped by, in a hurry to buy a bigger place and he made a great offer—"

Natalie nodded. "One we couldn't pass up."

"So, it's really gone?" Tied to her past, and the place she first met Mark, the tiny home meant so much to her. Kelsey closed her eyes, mentally said goodbye, and mourned a small, personal loss.

Natalie bit her lip. "Yeah, we didn't know you were interested. Sorry, Kels."

"It's fine. Maybe this is better. I'll have a chance to plan something . . . perfect." Her defeated words didn't convince anyone.

"Why don't we start planning your new home today? How about over pizza, our treat?" Natalie offered.

Kelsey stood, anxious to be on her way. "Pizza? No, I'm not hungry. I need to take off." Escaping Natalie's quick hug, she hurried out the door, and evaded the tears that were already brimming her eyes.

***

Mark answered the call from Ashwood on the first ring, "Seth, is everything okay? Did something happen to Kelsey?"

"It's all good. Listen. I thought you'd like to know, Kels stopped in today. She was asking to buy your tiny house and was disappointed it had sold. She had planned to take it to the coast, and it kind of felt like she might still be headed that way."

"Did you tell her I bought it?"

"Nope. That's on you."

"Cool. I appreciate the heads up." Mark's heart rate jumped, propelled by a jolt of eager hope.

"Good luck," Seth added before he said goodbye.

***

Seth's call propelled Mark's feet to his truck. He drove into town without a specific plan and with no idea when Kelsey might show at the coast. Still, he sensed a change, and needed to be ready to send

Kelsey an undeniable message—That their love was permanent—A love that couldn't be undone.

A flower shop in town was his first stop. He gazed at the case, but roses were too ordinary for his girl. Next, he drove to a surf shop, but a new board was too impersonal, and he didn't know if she'd ever want to surf again.

Across the street from the surf shop the window of a jewelry store sparkled in the afternoon sun. He dashed across the road and stared through the window, paced a wide circle across the sidewalk, and glanced through the window again. Palms sweating and shoulders squared, he worked up the courage to go inside.

The door chimed as he entered. "Can I help you?" a woman asked.

Mark's voice and hands trembled. "An engagement ring. It has to be perfect." She smiled, and he met her at a wide glass case. As she pulled ring after ring from the display, a wave of disappointment swept over him. Kelsey's ring wasn't here.

When his shoulders slumped, she said, "Our main location has a much larger selection."

"Where's that?"

"Newport. Give me a moment, and I'll call ahead. The owner would be happy to stay open late if he knew you were on your way."

Mark shook his head. "No, I'll go tomorrow." That would give him time to see if Faye could come along. For a decision of this magnitude, he wanted someone who knew Kelsey well to give him a second opinion.

***

It was after eleven. Sleeping late was becoming a bad habit. Curled in a ball, Kelsey wondered if a smaller bed would feel less lonely. Her entire life echoed like an unfurnished room. She missed the sound absorbing presence of Mark cluttering her life. When he said he'd give her space, she hadn't counted on this much.

Pivoting to sit on her bed, she let her feet dangle over the side. "Move your ass," she said but didn't.

If Natalie's home hadn't sold, she'd be at the coast instead of staring at her bedroom walls. It would take months for Seth to build her another. *Months.* Could she sit here that long?

If she went to the coast with only a tent, she'd probably run headlong into the first storms of fall. And that would suck. But if Mark was with her, those storms would be an adventure.

His blog was silent. He could be anywhere. And he didn't know her new number, but pride stopped her from making a call.

"This is bullshit." Kels hated wallowing. She'd bought gear to handle wind and rain. Maybe Mark was still at Driftwood Shores or if he wasn't, their paths might cross the next time he wandered through.

She packed quickly and thoroughly, making one more pass through her house before she left. The garbage was out, and she'd emptied her refrigerator. The heat was set at fifty, and the front blinds were down. At the last moment, she left Mark's keys on her coffee table, where he'd find them if he happened to return. Pulling the door closed, she locked the deadbolt and made her way to her SUV.

As she started the engine, she gazed at her front door, and put her life in Ashwood on permanent pause. This place never changed much anyway.

Forty miles closer to the coast, her phone rang. Kent. Damn it, she didn't want to hear a voice that might turn her around. Her thumb silenced the device, and she blew out a slow breath. She'd call her best friend from the safety of the coast.

***

Faye hummed along with the music and her silver bracelets jangled as she burst with bits of random conversation. Mark stopped at a vegan place Faye loved and bought her a late lunch before they headed to the jewelry store. The salesperson had their most unique rings waiting, arranged beautifully in the case.

He saw *the one* immediately and pointed it out. Trying to picture it on Kelsey's beautiful hand, he slipped the ring on his pinkie.

"It's perfect," Faye said on a sigh. The sculpted platinum ring caught the light. Sapphires and diamonds wove with the precious metal in a design that mimicked the sea. It seemed to be designed for only one woman—Kelsey.

"I'll take it," he said. "And a chain."

"A chain?"

"One that will fit around my neck. I'll wear it on a chain until she says yes."

"Platinum, like the ring?" the jeweler asked with a hopeful smile.

"Sure, that would be great."

Mark pulled out his card and handed it to the jeweler. After Faye glanced at the price, she turned to study him, and he grinned. With a chuckle, the owner of Driftwood Shores took a spot on the list of friends who realized that his beach bum vibe was way off.

"Thanks for helping me today," he said as they waited.

"Happy to be part of your journey. I was glad to witness the start."

An interesting twinkle in her eye made him look twice. "Huh, I guess you were there from almost the first moment I met Kelsey."

The jeweler returned with two lavish boxes. Mark opened the first and lay the chain on the glass counter. Next, he snapped open the small box and revealed her ring. He stared at the diamonds and sapphires flashing against the white fabric and considered the wisdom of his plan. Sure of himself, he nodded and slipped the ring onto the chain then eased it over his head. After tucking the ring under his shirt, he pocketed the small velvet box.

"Ready?" Faye asked.

"As I'll ever be." Against his chest, the ring felt right, but Mark knew this was a risk. He was trusting his gut because Kelsey wasn't a white picket fence kind of girl.

***

On a stop for fuel, Kelsey glanced at a group text that included a picture. *Congrats, Linnea and Rick.* Wrapped in a pink blanket, their baby girl filled the screen. Kelsey smiled, scrolled to the next photo, and sent a loving message that would have to do for now. She'd mail a gift tomorrow—a starfish mobile or cuddly plush orca from the toy store on the coast would be perfect. If she turned back to Ashwood now, she may not find the courage to leave.

Before she left the mini-mart, temptation won a battle, and she checked Mark's app and blog again. The latest surf conditions were updated, but nothing revealed his exact location on planet Earth. She felt like he was close, but that might mean anywhere on the west coast. Reaching out tempted her, but pride won out again. As she tossed her phone on the passenger seat, Kelsey laughed. At least this time she had a legit excuse, she couldn't remember his number, anyway.

THIRTY-TWO

She'd won her race with the sun and arrived at the coast before it set. The sight of the weathered Driftwood Shores sign settled her world—this perfect place hadn't changed since her accident. Waves crashed in the distance, blocked from view by the rolling sand dunes. Tiny homes and a few modest RVs dotted Faye's community. Nestled in the tall sawgrass, the high spot where she planned to pitch her tent waited for her arrival.

She parked next to the clubhouse, hoping to see her friend, but the owner of Driftwood Shores wasn't around. A wave of disappointment swept over Kelsey. Still, why should she expect Faye's greeting? The free-spirited woman must have a life beyond this place.

Arms loaded with her belongings, Kelsey scaled the dunes, panting salty air as she climbed. Grains of sand topped her hiking boots, snuck into her socks, and gritted around her toes. She sank to the log at her campsite and peeled away her boots and socks, rolled up her jeans, and shivered.

From her perch above the community, Kels scanned the homes and recognized some, but fewer than she'd hoped—some residents moved with the seasons. Squinting, her eyes locked on a home she knew far better than the rest.

"Fuck me," she said staring at Natalie's perfect little house, the one she'd intended to buy. "You've gotta be shitting me."

Her feet propelled her toward the home. A large glass window replaced the spot where her friend had served coffee. The lights were off, and the place appeared empty, almost sterile. Kelsey crept closer and peeked inside. No plants, no knick-knacks, no fancy Italian espresso machine—all of Natalie's happy touches were gone. It looked abandoned.

White-hot envy took hold, longing for something that was out of reach. "Thieving rat bastards," she muttered, head hung, as she trudged in bare feet back to her uninviting tent.

Propelled by the wind, she walked past her campsite and aimed for the sea. Brisk gusts lifted dry sand and stung her ankles with abrasive grains. The wind pounded the waves, and she was lured by the sound. Ignoring a light drizzle, she broke into a run. Her legs pumped, burning until she met the cold, churning foam.

Kelsey splashed into the fifty-five-degree water until her jeans were soaked thigh deep. Braced against the push of the surf, the rolling waves splashed higher, soaking her shirt and spraying water as high as the ends of her long pale hair. Like an old friend, the powerful crashing waves welcomed her return. Winning a battle with a thin layer of clouds, the setting sun broke through and bathed her shivering skin in relative warmth.

Giggles shifted to laughter, and then to tears. Kelsey gave all her pain and loss to the sea until the numbing cold chased her back toward dry land. Scanning the low dunes on the horizon, she searched for Mark's silhouette against the chalky sky, but he wasn't there.

After a hot shower, Kelsey slipped into warm sweatpants and a bulky sweater. She made Top Ramen to heat up. A familiar meow begged for her attention, and Bramble twisted around her calves.

"Hey, kitty, I've missed you." Kelsey fished a noodle from her paper cup and dangled a particularly long one for the orange cat. He sniffed the offering, twitched his tail, and disappeared into the manzanita. "Really? It's not that bad." Flinging the noodle by the end, she tossed it into the dying fire.

With nothing in particular to do, she crawled into her tent and neatly arranged her belongings in the same position as at home.

Sleep overtook her interest in a book, and she slept hard until showers pattering against the tent woke her. Snuggling in, she turned over on her thin mattress and listened to the rain until she fell back to sleep.

***

Mark rolled into Driftwood Shores. Low clouds grayed the skies, and he knew without checking his weather app that a storm wasn't too far off the coast. Rain speckled the windshield, and his fingers drifted to the heavy platinum ring resting on his chest.

"Is that Kelsey's SUV?" Faye asked.

"Where?"

"Next to the clubhouse."

"It is. Damn, I wonder if she spotted the tiny home," Mark worried.

"I'm sure she did." Faye squeezed his hand. "Not that it would make much difference. The place looks abandoned."

"Hadn't thought of that." Mark seized new hope that he'd still have a chance to surprise her. On that clear spot high on the dunes, her tent looked black against the wheat-colored grass, but it was there, and Kelsey waited for him inside.

"I'll chill extra bottles of champagne and pop them when you're ready to celebrate," Faye said before they went in different directions.

"And if she says no?"

"Not possible." Faye's steady gaze wouldn't let Mark protest. "Bring Kelsey by. I miss that girl." As she wandered away, Faye's denim skirt skimmed the long grass and darkened as it soaked up the wet. Mark spun and looked between his home and Kelsey's tent. The weight of the ring around his neck felt too heavy. Tonight wasn't the right moment to ask any questions, he just had to see her. He stopped by his house and stowed the ring in one of the many hiding spots Seth had built into the place.

Even though the sun had gone down, it was still relatively early. He climbed the sand to Kelsey's camp, expecting to find her snug in her tent, hiding from the rain. The faint zip of the tent stirred her. "It's me, Mermaid." Mark whispered. "Didn't mean to scare you, I thought you might still be awake."

"I am now." Her laughter erupted in a nervous burst.

He crawled in, bringing cool air with him. Mark shucked off his jacket first, then needing to feel her warmth, he peeled away his clothes.

She eased her sleeping bag open, welcoming him as she always had in the past. "You found me." Her quaking words revealed how desperately she wanted him there.

Mark settled against her sleep-warmed skin. "Don't you know I can't help but find you? You're my magnetic north."

She sighed and took his arm, easing it around her middle. "I missed how good you feel." He took her words as acceptance and hoped Kelsey had also made room for him in her life.

Ginger-scented hair ignited his quest with a light kiss at her temple. Kelsey relaxed, and Mark savored the taste of her skin. As heat filled the space around them, she kicked off the sleeping bag, freeing their legs.

Mark eased over her long, lean form as her fingers traced the line of his jaw. She studied his features in the dark with only her touch. "I'm sorry I pushed you away," she said on a whisper.

"Did you work everything out?" he asked, not wanting or needing her apology.

"Almost."

"I'll give you all the time and space you need." His hand slipped behind her neck, pulling her lips to his.

"Guess what I spotted today?" she said as she relaxed against him.

"Mmm?" he hummed against her sweet mouth.

"Someone bought Natalie's tiny home. It's here."

"At Driftwood Shores?" he asked.

"Yeah."

He could hear the sadness in her voice and nearly told her he'd bought the home with her in mind.

Kelsey sighed. "I'm thinking of having Seth build me one of my own."

"Until he finishes it, why don't you stay with me?" he offered, hoping.

She didn't ask where, just accepted with a nod. "I'd like that."

Only a thin layer of cotton tank-top separated them. Mark rolled to the ground beneath her and she lifted her arms over her head as he eased it up and off. After he tossed the fabric aside, he took her face in both hands and thoroughly explored her mouth. Soft to hard, she writhed above him, as he mapped the line of her spine with his fingertips. Kelsey arched and twisted when his touch found that sensitive spot just above her butt.

He knew every inch of her body. His fingers knew where to press. His lips knew the exact spot to taste. His tongue knew the precise place to draw a delicious line. Spreading her thighs apart, she lifted her hips a fraction and settled, giving everything to Mark in a long, slow glide. His groan accepted the slick pleasure.

The fingers of one powerful hand threaded in her hair as his other palmed her hip. He lifted her hips and let them settle, assisting her steady cadence. As she bent to kiss him, her pale golden hair escaped his grasp and trickled over her shoulder. He caressed the soft waves, then used both hands to take a stronger hold of her ass.

Holding nothing back, Mark explored lower, inch by glorious inch, igniting points of pleasure where his hard cock slid in, slid out. Moving his knees upward, he separated her legs farther, touching her intimately as she writhed.

"Oh, God," she said before her moans became incoherent, and he dove again. He explored her everywhere and slithered a ribbon of desire to her clit, pressing and circling with his thumb until she murmured his name.

The edge of her orgasm quivered around him, and she sped her frantic ride. Feral need took hold, and he wanted to claim her body and soul. Mark spun her body below his, and Kelsey sensed the shift in the hunger that drove him on. Her hands slid to cup his face and accepted his urgent need to plunge harder into her sex-swollen entrance.

"Please," she begged, wanting all of him. Mark eased his girth from her body and surged forward again. She met each impale with a lift of her hips, angled to add pressure where she needed it most. Her body grasped his cock as he charged and drew back, eager for release.

"That's it," he growled quietly as she gave him everything. "Let go, Mermaid."

With a cry, she found an overwhelming release. Absorbing the hungry impact, she called his name and Mark crested with her. He pinned her tight against the hard ground, claiming her pliant body, savoring every ounce of his orgasm with insatiable greed. Still hungry for her salty taste, his kiss meandered down her throat to linger on her over-sensitive breasts. As her breathing slowed, Mark threaded his fingers through her hair and met her lips again.

She drank in the sensation of this man covering her, relishing the weight. Her hands stroked the ropy muscles of his back while Mark's attention lingered with lazy attention. He sucked her throat until she giggled and squirmed.

"That tickles, and you're kinda heavy," she huffed, unable to take a full breath.

Mark wished he'd coaxed her into a proper bed, in his new tiny home only yards away. Rolling to his side, he drew Kelsey across his chest and grabbed the extra blanket to trap their combined heat against the September chill.

When he slid his palm to her stomach, she laced her fingers over his and brought his hand higher, covering her heart. "You always manage to find me," she whispered, content.

"And I promise I always will. I love you, Kelsey."

She kissed him sweetly, then pulled away. "Mark, I love you, too."

He wanted to rejoice, to turn on a light and gaze at the woman he loved. But what she gave him in the dark was more. She lifted over him and tears fell from her eyes, adding salt to another tender kiss.

"Make love to me again," she asked. His thumbs smoothed away her tears as their bodies met in another, even sweeter collide.

THIRTY-THREE

She woke alone. Last night's rain moved west, and the sun heated the interior of her tent. Kelsey pulled on yesterday's clothes before she moved outside marveling at the unusually warm fall morning. When she couldn't find any sign of Mark, she wondered if last night was just an enchanted dream.

From her perch on the dunes, she scanned the horizon and found three surfers paddling out. She studied them for several minutes, wondering if one of the wetsuit-clad men was Mark. Each in succession caught a promising wave, and she shook her head. Not Mark. No one rode the waves with his effortless finesse.

***

Mark spotted Kelsey from the window of his tiny home. She stood at the apex of the dunes, then stretched her arms overhead. Twisting at the waist, she eased kinks from last night's reunion. From her elevated perch, she scoured the community before turning from her search to study the tempting surf.

Yesterday's choppy mess had improved overnight, but the fantastic conditions might not last. A distant storm churning in the Pacific produced clean shoulder-high breaks. The timing was too perfect, as if nature was begging her to take on a long-awaited challenge.

While she was distracted, Mark poured coffee into paper cups and grabbed a brown paper bag holding muffins delivered by Faye early this morning. Two waxed boards already waited for them near Kelsey's camp. Mark wore his wetsuit folded at the waist. On his upper half, his T-shirt hid a diamond and sapphire ring that dangled from a platinum chain around his neck. Nervous excitement wasn't mixing well with his coffee, but he brought along his cup to share breakfast with Kels.

***

She heard Mark humming before she saw him coming her way. Her smile spread, recognizing the song he had lodged in his head. Already clad in black neoprene, the wetsuit revealed the contours of his chiseled physique. He flashed that familiar smile, the same one that caught her breath when they had first met two years ago.

"Where did you get coffee?" Kelsey asked, anticipating the caffeine.

"Stopped in to see Faye, and she also sent muffins."

He handed over the smooth paper cup and Kels popped the lid to sip the steaming drink. "Mmm, thank you."

"Someone beat us to dawn patrol," Mark said sinking to the log, while digging into the bag for one of the muffins.

"I saw that. Sorry, I guess I slept too late for a sunrise session." Kelsey jolted, spilling some of her coffee as tangled recollections and dreamy images flashed through her mind. She shook her head and blinked at the horizon.

"Babe, are you okay?" Mark dropped his muffin to the sand and put his arm around her waist to steady her.

She tipped her head from side to side. "Yeah. I'm good. Sometimes my memories feel like dreams." Blinking again, she couldn't shake the impossible mental image of Mark with her at the hospital right when she woke.

Pulled close, his sweet kiss on her temple was soothing. Kelsey spotted his muffin in the sand, dug hers from the bag, split it, and handed him half.

"You sure?" he asked.

"Of course, silly." She smiled and he reflected it with a chuckle. The warmth of him hit her, and she was touched by the way his grin wrinkled the corners of his eyes. His effortless love reached out and wrapped her up like a comfortable leather coat—snug, yet roomy in all the right places.

"I love you." She repeated the words she'd said in the dark last night. A blush raced over her skin as she admitted these deep emotions in the light of day.

Mark used his free hand to draw her close for a coffee-flavored kiss and murmured, "I love you, too. What did you just remember?" he asked.

"Surfing, last spring. You and me, a campfire in Florence, or maybe it was here . . . then I remembered something from the hospital. But it doesn't make sense, like I said, sometimes, it's like waking up and trying to recall a dream." Determined to move on from the past, she stood, reached for his hand, and pulled him from the log, "Enough with the memories. I want to see if I remember how to surf."

Mark nodded and grinned. "The boards are ready. Is your wetsuit in your car?"

She nodded, sprinted toward her SUV, then called over her shoulder, "I won't be long."

***

The ring seemed to pulse against his chest when Kelsey appeared in her black wetsuit. Excitement stretched her grin, and her aqua eyes danced as she closed in to claim a kiss. "Let's do this," she said, after their lips separated.

From the top of the dunes, they counted six surfers paddling out, three looking young enough to be locals ditching school. Kelsey headed for the waves with her surfboard under her arm. Mark hung back, surprised when she didn't hesitate before taking a plunge. Eager to meet the challenge, she hopped on and began her paddle.

He wanted this for her, but didn't get in the way, content to watch from a distance while she reclaimed the waves.

Her duck dive wasn't smooth, but she made it beyond the break. Unaccustomed to the long paddle, she straddled her surfboard, shook out her arms, then wheeled around and watched the group take prime position. When Mark met her beyond the swells, she took a deep breath and admitted, "I'm nervous."

He nodded, nervous for her too. "That's okay." Their hands made contact, and he pulled her close for a quick kiss.

Whistles from the teens put a smile between them. Mark pulled back and looked into her aqua eyes. "Someday the right woman will mean more to them than this break." He kissed her again. "I love you, Mermaid."

"I love you, too." She blushed and lifted her brows. "Let's see if I can still do this. And if I can't, there are sexy ways to get shaky and tired," she teased.

"I'm willing to head back anytime," he said with intent.

Kelsey pushed his board away, ready to take on the challenge of the waves. Timing her launch, he watched as she lay down on the board. Two of the kids snagged the first wave, and then she spotted her shot. Plunging her hands, a burst of adrenaline gave her too much speed, and she nearly outran the swell. Tucked, then standing, her board lifted, and she found a glide, laughing when her body took over.

Mark watched with satisfaction as Kelsey let the surfboard run, sailing over the surface, relaxing with effortless speed. The wave died, and she waved to him from the shallow water, smiling before heading toward the wide channel to paddle back.

A heavy set cleared the younger surfers and Mark found his first wave of the day, then another. With each successive wave, the gang of surfers discovered that he was something more than the average old guy. The afternoon wore on, and the sets strengthened, moving the boys to ask the legendary surfer for advice.

Even though Kels had taken it easy, she told him her arms were getting noodly. But she encouraged him to take advantage of the mounting waves while she watched from shore. On the beach, she rolled down the top half of her wetsuit and let the sun warm her skin. Covered in her tiny turquoise bikini, she grinned his way and waved. He groaned, knowing he wouldn't be able to resist his beautiful Mermaid much longer.

After being tossed into the churning foam, two guys in the group of six called it a day. The swells chopped and a kid wiped out, but without thinking he paddled directly into Mark's chosen line.

Sensing the danger, Mark bailed into the white turbulent froth.

When he popped to the surface, he saw Kelsey scrambling toward him. Disoriented, Mark gave her a quick thumbs-up, because he didn't want her to worry. They closed in on each other and she reached out. "You're not okay."

Her fingers traced a gash where the cold had numbed a blunt force split on his shoulder. After he unleashed his surfboard from his ankle, Kelsey grabbed his board and he followed her to a log for a quick inspection. She shifted behind him, crouched over his shoulder for a closer look. And before he could stop her, she released the zipper on his wetsuit.

"Let me take a look at this cut," she said, as she peeled away the black thermal layer.

Mark froze as her fingers explored. Focused on his wound and perched at his back, she hadn't noticed the thick chain around his neck or the ring hiding in his grasp.

Her gentle touch smoothed over his skin. "Looks like the water made the blood spread. It's not as bad as I thought." She crawled around, kneeling in front of Mark then smiled up at him. "I think you'll live."

He went silent and his mouth popped open.

"Did your board hit your head?" she asked. Concern narrowed her eyes, then her gaze drifted down when Mark released a glittering object from his fingers.

He had planned to be so smooth—to go down on one knee and surprise her with a big reveal. His fingers touched her chin and tipped her face to meet his gaze.

"Do you love me, Mermaid?" he asked.

"Yes," she whispered in return.

"And you know I love you."

She nodded, but before he could ask *the question,* she launched forward, wrapped her arms around his neck, and covered his lips with hers. The moment she tilted away from his kiss, Kelsey said, "Yes."

"You'll marry me?" he asked with a silly grin.

When she nodded again, his lips devoured hers in a desperate crush. Releasing her from his embrace, he yelled, "She said yes!"

Mark's fingers shook as he pulled the chain from his neck, and the clasp barely gave up the ring. When he slid the platinum band over her finger, he knew he'd never been this happy.

"I love this ring, and I love you," she said as she held out her hand and inspected the glittering diamonds and sapphires in the sun.

Mark trapped her face in his hands and drew her in for another kiss. Wanting more, her body climbed his. "Um, could we go back to my tent?" she murmured, barely coming up for air.

"Do you have to ask?" Standing together, he trapped her in his embrace. "Mermaid, I have one more surprise."

She kissed him again then said against his lips, "After finding that ring around your neck, I may be immune to surprises."

"I won't try to top it." He lifted his board under his arm and waited for Kelsey to hoist hers.

"Where are we going?" she asked as they passed her camp.

"Wait for it . . ." he laughed and picked up the pace. Anticipation pulled them like a magnet toward the tiny home.

"You didn't . . ." she said, giggling.

"Oh, yes I did." They broke into a jog and dropped the surfboards outside. Blocking her path, Mark flung open the door, scooped her into his arms and carried her up the steps. She wrapped her arm around his neck for the ride over the threshold.

He paused inside and spun her around. "I haven't really moved in, because I wanted it to be our first home together."

"Thank you—for finding me, for being my everything, for loving me unconditionally."

Once her feet found the floor, Mark wasted no time peeling her from the neoprene skin and she worked quickly on his. Tumbling into the tiny shower, the small space provided him just enough room to tease her senses. He placed her palms against the wall, smoothed shower gel over her skin and ignited every nerve, except the place she wanted him the most.

Her body trembled as he orchestrated her pleasure with delicate precision. Their breath mingled and his tongue danced, coaxing extra bliss from the frantic crush against her panting mouth. Mark cupped her ass and trapped her against the shower wall with his weight. A single thrust pushed him deep inside. He growled as her silky entrance gave under his desperate assault.

Driven by intent, he lunged. Arms tight around his shoulders, her thighs gripped as her orgasm drew close. Tangled together, he increased the pace, hoping he could last.

She captured his mouth in a moaning kiss. His hands, his tongue, his invasion possessed her as she cried out her release. Heat filled her as he followed Kelsey in a blinding cascade of bliss. Mark's movement slowed and his grip eased, then her feet sought the floor. Kelsey's arms went slack, and she shivered.

In his few belongings, Mark found a towel and wrapped his Mermaid in the soft cotton. Her spent legs trembled as she climbed into the sparsely furnished loft.

"Where's all your stuff?" she asked as she made her way up the stairs. Mark tore his eyes away from the sway of her curves to form a coherent answer.

"Some is tucked away in the storage compartment below the home, and the rest is at my place on the beach in Kauai."

Kelsey fell to the bed and her mouth dropped open. "Kauai. Why didn't you tell me?"

Mark shrugged. "You never asked."

"I knew your app did well, but you seemed to be—"

"A beach bum. Maybe I am, I never felt connected to one place because I'm only home when I'm with you."

Kelsey pulled him onto the bed. "Home. I like the sound of that. But you have a place in Hawaii . . . maybe you're out of my league."

Mark fought a wave of panic. "This doesn't change anything. It's still just me, the guy who's completely, hopelessly in love with his Mermaid."

"I was teasing . . . and even if I have to swim, I'm going there soon."

Trapping her hands above her head, he pinned her to the mattress. "We could leave this afternoon if you want to take the sailboat." He laughed and watched her eyes go wide. "Apparently, you aren't completely immune to surprises."

He smothered her laughter with kisses and showed her how much he loved her again.

Kelsey insisted they keep the news of their engagement to themselves for a few days.

The following week, they filmed a reveal and sent the video to family and friends. This private message didn't go viral. Grasping a large stick together, they scraped three words in the sand . . . *SHE SAID YES.*

***

November rains let up, and the wind wasn't too strong. Kelsey paced the Driftwood Shores parking lot while Mark took care of last-minute arrangements on the beach.

The first van pulled in, and she waved while Kent took the access road directly onto the sand. A second vehicle followed, and she jogged behind, hurrying to keep up.

Kent stopped, jumped from the Venture van, and hauled her into a hug. "You ready?" he asked.

"As I'll ever be."

Amanda exited the passenger seat but didn't come to greet her right away. She hurried to the back to unload two all-terrain wheelchairs.

Sig and Travis emerged laughing like old friends. She never dreamed that her injury could lead to this. Over the past month, Venture had worked with The Center, merging skills to give guests with brain injuries something different. Kelsey loved these excursions more than any back-country trip she'd ever led.

Mark's hand landed on her hip. His rubber boots squeaked, and he handed her a shovel. Today's adventure was a clam dig and getting dirty lay ahead.

"Ready, Mermaid?" Mark asked as the wind whipped his hair and his smile creased the corners of his eyes. Leaning in, he stole a kiss.

Kelsey twirled the engagement ring on her finger. "I'm ready for anything, as long as I'm with you."

*****

Thank you for reading.

I love to hear feedback from my readers. If you enjoyed this book, please consider leaving a review. Even a few words are valued more than you know.

All of Kinney's books are full length, standalone novels.

Here is the list if you would like to read them in order.

In Ashwood series in order[1]

Inheriting Trouble

Trouble Brewing

Chasing Trouble

Addicted to Trouble

Let's keep in touch -

Check out my website - kinneyscott.com[2]

Kinney Scott Author[3] on Facebook

Bookbub[4]

Pinterest[5]

Instagram[6]

---

1. *https://www.amazon.com/Kinney-Scott/e/B074NY1W6C*

2. http://kinneyscott.com/

3. https://www.facebook.com/Kinney-Scott-Author-127170094583662/

4. https://www.bookbub.com/authors/kinney-scott

5. https://www.pinterest.com/kskinneyscott/

6. https://www.instagram.com/kinney.scott.author

Did you love *Trouble Undone*? Then you should read *Addicted To Trouble*[7] by Kinney Scott!

Passion and politics feed more than one vice in *Addicted to Trouble*.

Iris loves Northside Grill as much as an old friend, but if her customers keep leaving for her hometown rival, she may be forced to sell. Her best option? To run for a vacant seat on the City Council and use the position to instigate change.

Her hot-as-hell opponent has the same idea, and Lincoln craves competition.

When Iris challenges him in the local political race, he's intrigued.

---

7. https://books2read.com/u/4Xaz81

8. https://books2read.com/u/4Xaz81

A woman as fine as Iris shouldn't trust a man like him, but Lincoln can't resist twisting his interest into a provocative game. Will his high-stakes gamble pay off? Maybe a few rides on his Harley will tip the odds in his favor, because Lincoln definitely isn't a sure bet.

Read more at https://kinneyscott.com.

Also by Kinney Scott

In Ashwood
Inheriting Trouble
Trouble Brewing
Chasing Trouble
Addicted To Trouble
Trouble Undone

Watch for more at https://kinneyscott.com.

About the Author

Kinney Scott writes contemporary romance from her home near Puget Sound on the rainy side of Washington State. Her steamy heroes and complex heroines feel most at home in the rugged and uniquely romantic environments of the Pacific Northwest. When she has a moment away from her computer, Kinney escapes to her garden or spends a few hours hiking trails near her home.

Want to know more? Visit Kinney at https://kinneyscott.com

Read more at https://kinneyscott.com.